FROM HEAVEN TO EARTH THEY CAME

BOOK 1

GODDESS FROM THE LOST PLANET

A Sci-Fi Adventure of Gods and Aliens

BY NEAL ROBERTS

DEDICATION

To Myra, Adam, Julie, Gigi, Justin, Aviva, Jonah, Lily, Uncle Jack, Aunt Michelle and the Rest of My Wonderful Family

ACKNOWLEDGMENTS

I'd like to extend my heartfelt thanks to my treasured wife Myra and to Uncle Jack for all their help and advice, to the award-winning mystery writer Pamela Burford, to Nick Stamos (1SG, US Army, Retired) for his knowledgeable and patient advice on handheld firearms (especially for selecting Catharine's nine-millimeter Glock 46), to Dr. Jeffrey Laitman of the Icahn School of Medicine at Mount Sinai for taking time out of his busy schedule to provide the author with his well-grounded advice concerning the characteristics of humankind's nearest living earthly cousins, the chimpanzees and bonobos, and to my dear friend, John Wassenbergh, for sharing his industry-based knowledge about the customary correlation between the wholesale and retail prices of top-shelf liquor.

Any mistakes are solely my own.

To my editor, Martin Jones, I extend my sincerest thanks. To my publicist Samantha Williams of Aurora Publicity, for her extraordinary indulgence and her Herculean efforts in helping to move the author from historical fiction to science fiction.

PROLOGUE

"AN ANGEL OF the Lord has summoned the Prophet Elijah to ascend into heaven as a living man," said Elisha to his friend.

The friend nodded. "I heard that the angel told him when and where he must appear to be taken up by the whirlwind."

Many years before, Elisha had been summoned to Yahweh's service by Elijah himself. Elisha had been tilling the soil with a team of oxen when Elijah threw his mantle around Elisha's shoulders.

Since that day, Elisha had been a steadfast follower of the aged prophet. Now he stared into the burning desert contemplating what he must do, for the day appointed for Elijah's departure had come. But how could he allow old Elijah, who'd performed so many miracles and risked his life so often in the service of Yahweh, to leave their little encampment and plod off into the desert alone? *What if the old man were set upon by animals or thieves and unable to complete his journey to heaven?* The thought was simply too painful to bear.

"As I did the day he found me," Elisha pronounced, "I shall go with him."

His friend raised an eyebrow. "Oh? So, the Lord Yahweh has sent an angel from heaven to tell his prophet to come alone, and the great *Elisha* countermands the Lord's order? I doubt you'll receive much thanks from the prophet, who's dedicated his whole life to the service of Yahweh." He shrugged flippantly. "But perhaps he'll toss you a remembrance as he flies up to heaven."

II Kings 2 (Gently Abridged)

AND IT CAME to pass, when the Lord would take up Elijah into heaven by a whirlwind, that Elisha went with Elijah from Gilgal.

And Elijah said unto him, "Elisha, tarry here, I pray thee, for the Lord hath sent me all the way to Jericho."

And Elisha said, "As the Lord liveth, and as thy soul liveth, I will *not* leave thee."

So together they came to Jericho and the River Jordan.

And Elijah took his mantle and wrapped it together and smote the waters, and the waters parted so that the two went over on dry ground.

When they had gone over, Elijah said unto Elisha, "Ask what I may do for thee, before I be taken away."

And Elisha said, "I pray thee, let a double portion of thy spirit be upon me."

And it came to pass, as they still went on and talked that—Behold!—there appeared a chariot of fire, and horses of fire, and parted them both asunder.

And Elijah went up by a whirlwind into heaven.

And Elisha saw it, and he cried, "My father, my father, the chariot of Israel, and the horsemen thereof!"

And Elisha saw him no more, and took hold of his own clothes and rent them in two. He also took up the mantle that had fallen from Elijah. And as Elisha stood by the bank of the Jordan, he took the mantle and smote the waters.

And they parted.

CHAPTER 1

WHEN DAVID'S MOBILE phone rang on that rainy November morning, he expected to awaken to an ordinary day—certainly not to the day when mankind's creators would begin their return to Earth.

Before answering the phone, he glanced at the undisturbed pillow next to him and was dismayed to recall yet again that his wife Sharon was gone for all time. His heart sank as he picked up the phone.

"Hello?" he said dismally.

"Well, hello!" said the chipper voice of his oldest friend Shawn. "Is that your *courtroom* mumble, counselor?" Static crackled on the line, but it was good to hear Shawn's old familiar voice.

With feigned formality David said, "Who is this, please, and where are you calling from?" Shawn worked for the U.S. State Department and was known to call at will from any point on Earth. Though he was sometimes forbidden to say precisely where he was, just now he was openly stationed in the Middle East.

"It's Shawn, as if you didn't know, calling from beautiful downtown Jerusalem. Good afternoon. Are you in a rush to get somewhere?"

"I'm always busy," said David. "It's morning here, by the way. What's up?"

"Well," said Shawn, "I thought I'd share with you a photo of the Old City I just took from my hotel room."

"Seriously?" moaned David. "You call me this early to announce you're sending a photo I could just as well look at after I get up?" Though this seemed foolish on Shawn's part, David knew that Shawn loved to play the fool—but only to make a point. "What's so special about the view from your hotel? Are you staying at the one overlooking the Temple Mount?"

"Bingo," said Shawn. "I'm looking at the Foundation Rock right now."

This was a little confusing. "The—the mosque on the Temple Mount is called the *Dome* of the Rock or Al-Aqsa, Shawn. Perhaps you'd recognize it from the big gold dome on top."

Shawn snorted derisively. "You don't say?"

David could recall the view from that very hotel, which he'd visited years before. "You can't *see* the Foundation Rock from the hotel, Shawn; it's inside the mosque."

Shawn's voice suddenly became serious and he exhaled loudly. "So it was," he said, and repeated softly, "so it was."

David wiped his eyes with his fingers. "You're taking your sweet time to get to the point, Shawn. I have a class to teach."

"You're on a smartphone, right?" asked Shawn.

"Yes."

"Check out the photo, dude," said Shawn. "I thought it might be interesting to someone like you, who posted a few articles on that old guy's blog."

David had submitted a few extensive posts to a website moderated by the Sumerologist Abraham Azeri, the granddaddy of all *ancient alien* blogs.

The phone vibrated in David's hand, signaling the arrival of an email. "Okay, hang on a sec," said David, fumbling with the phone. He loaded the email app, where the incoming photo topped the list. He tapped the email and enlarged the photo using two fingers.

The photo depicted the platform of the Temple Mount lit by a setting sun. To his surprise, the vast stone platform was vacant and flat, as though it had been lovingly swept clean. Just as Shawn had suggested, near the center sat ... a big rock.

"Did you send me a photo of a scale model, smartass?" David demanded with annoyance.

"No. What you see there is the real deal, I'm afraid," replied Shawn wistfully.

"Okay, I give up. Where's the mosque?" asked David.

"Right question!" replied Shawn. *"Where's the mosque?"*

David sat up in alarm. The mosque—despite its considerable age and beauty—had ever been a point of contention between Muslims and Jews. The Muslims built it centuries ago to commemorate the night Mohammed was taken there on a winged horse by the Archangel Gabriel, transported up to heaven from the Temple Mount, then returned to Earth the following morning.

The Jews, for their part, regarded the mosque as a deliberate impediment to the construction of a third Temple on the holy site, the first (the Temple of Solomon) having been destroyed by the Babylonians 586 years before the birth of Jesus, and the second, destroyed by the Romans seventy years after Jesus' birth.

David furrowed his brow. "Was the mosque *blown up?*"

"You tell me," replied Shawn. "Does it *look* like somebody blew it up?"

David studied the platform in the photo, which eerily showed not the least sign of demolition. No visible damage to the platform or surrounding structures. No scorching of stone. No sign of fire. Not a thing out of place. *Except that the mosque is gone.* "No sign of explosion," said David. "When did the mosque … disappear, if that's the right word?"

Shawn replied, "That's the *only* English word anyone here can come up with: *disappear*. Of course, *vanish* might serve. Here's all I know: This morning, I'm in the New City. I walk back to the hotel for a late lunch, and the mosque is there, where it's always been. But, while I'm in the hotel restaurant, there's a loud, low … buzz … a vibration—whatever—and for just a few seconds there's a *really* bright glow outside that lights up the whole restaurant like a bolt of lightning. This is all taking place in broad daylight, mind you, but the glow is so bright it seems to pass right through the walls. Then it stops suddenly like somebody turned off a switch. Everybody runs to the window overlooking the Temple Mount, and …" Shawn's voice trailed off.

"No mosque," muttered David, as if in a dream. "The Arabs will take this as an act of war. You *know* they'll blame the Israelis, right?"

"Who *else* could have pulled it off?" said Shawn.

"What do you mean?" protested David. "That's ridiculous. Even the Izzies can't make a mosque … disappear … in a few seconds."

Shawn sighed. "I don't know about that. The Izzies seem to live about twenty years in the future. Every few months they come out with some new … *thing* that's going to change the world."

"That's mostly hype," said David. "If they'd wanted the mosque gone, they could have blown it up long ago—without need of any new technology."

"Ah," said Shawn in sage tones, "but—back then—could they have made it *disappear?*"

"A mosque doesn't just vaporize," said David, flustered. "It must be *somewhere.*"

A click on the line was followed by silence. After a full minute of waiting, David was considering whether to hang up when there was a sharp crackle on the line and he could once again hear Shawn's breathing.

"Sorry, David," said Shawn. "Got another call. Well, it looks like you're right again, dude. The mosque *is* somewhere."

"Where?"

Shawn sighed. "You wouldn't believe me if I told you … and then I'd have to kill you."

David rolled his eyes. "How dramatic … and original."

"Turn on Fox News," said Shawn in his wrapping-up-the-call voice. "One of their trucks with a satellite dish just parked up against the Mount. Gotta go, bye."

Click.

David turned on Fox News, muting the sound. Sure enough, video was being relayed from a handheld camera traversing the Temple Mount with rushed and jerky movements, as though the cameraman was desperate to find a mosque that he suspected was hiding from him.

David looked longingly at the pillow beside his, and thought of the deceased Sharon once again. Something big is happening. Something *very* big and *very* dangerous. And it would surely have been a comfort to have her around.

⟶◦〰◦⟵

An HOUR LATER, David emerged from the subway at the edge of campus and began the short walk to the law school. Across the quad—by the Linguistics Building—several FBI vehicles idled silently with their red roof lights spinning, a combination of auditory stealth and visual commotion that always struck him as peculiar. It seemed to say: Something serious is going on here, but not *so* serious as to warrant the disturbance of anyone not directly involved.

While an occasional drug raid seemed unavoidable on every urban campus, such raids generally took place near the student dormitories, not the academic buildings. He shrugged.

It occurred to him in passing that the Linguistics Department also housed the much smaller Assyriology Center, which served as the academic home to one of his more important clients, the Egyptian expatriate Fareed Sinar. What Fareed brought to the Center was a lifelong (if esoteric) interest in ancient cuneiform, the first known form of writing, which sprang up spontaneously in Mesopotamia about six thousand years ago. Fareed was a swarthy, balding, middle-aged fellow with a paunch—a born academician who relished the quiet of his study and *abhorred* the limelight. He also sprang from a very wealthy family with extensive oil holdings throughout the Middle East.

As David entered the law school, the phone vibrated in his jacket pocket. With a scarce two minutes remaining before the start of class, he didn't bother to check the phone. It was probably Shawn, he thought, wishing to share some update of the morning's events in Jerusalem, about which David could do nothing anyway. Even if it were a client, he'd be unable to resolve anything of importance in the two available minutes. Instead of answering, he tried to concentrate on the topic of this morning's class.

The vibrating stopped. He reminded himself to switch on the phone's *do not disturb* feature before class began.

"Good morning!" he said to the class, garnering a collective reply that bore only a slight resemblance to the word *morning*. He plunked his copy of the casebook onto the lectern. Just as he was about to remove his jacket and hang it on the back of a convenient chair, his phone vibrated again.

He rolled his eyes in exasperation, but his curiosity got the best of him, and he glanced at the screen, which flashed the name *Fareed Sinar*.

Fareed? He expected this had something to do with the FBI vehicles parked across the quad.

"Professor?" said a student in the first row.

David shook his head gravely and pointed to the phone. "Sorry, I have to take this. It'll be just a moment." He put the phone to his ear. "Hello, Fareed?" he said, with a hint of worry.

"David!" said a desperate-sounding Fareed. "Thanks to God you're there. David, the FBI is *arresting* me!"

This was a surprise, as Fareed had never shown the least interest in doing anything remotely unlawful. "On what charge?" David asked.

Fareed said nothing for a moment, but David could hear an FBI agent on the other end of the phone trying to explain to Fareed that he was *not* being arrested.

"Fareed," said David. "I can't help you right now. I have to teach a class. I'm not a criminal lawyer, anyway. Call my office and ask for Sandra. She's—"

There was a commotion on Fareed's end, during which the phone dropped to the floor. Evidently, it was picked up by someone else, as Fareed's pleading tones could now be heard in the distance.

"This is Agent Duffy," said the new voice in the foreground. It was a New York gumshoe's voice if he ever heard one. "Is this Mister, Professor ... David?"

"Yes, Agent Duffy, this *is* Mister Professor David. However, I'm about to begin class—"

"Where?" asked Agent Duffy.

"At the law school, of course."

"Where's that?" asked the agent, clicking his pen to write.

"Across the quad from where you are," said David.

"Room number?" asked Agent Duffy.

"I don't know the room number," replied David curtly. "I have to go right now."

"But he won't come without you!" said the agent just as David hung up.

David's heart was weighed down by the certainty that whatever was happening simply *would not* await the end of class.

He looked up and found all eyes expectantly upon him, the students' interest having evidently been piqued by his stern demeanor and what little they'd overheard of the conversation.

He glanced up at the big frosted windows facing the quad, through which he could see silent red police lights speeding towards the lecture hall. Almost immediately, they screeched to a stop outside, and car doors swung open.

A couple of burly young students, probably halfbacks in college football, rose from their chairs. One asked loudly, "Should we bar the door, professor?" A half-dozen more male students rose to the ready.

David shook his head glumly. "No," he said with a sigh. "Welcome to legal practice. Please keep your seats and remain calm. And, remember, you're now in the business of seeking *peaceful* resolution to conflicts."

The halfbacks reluctantly resumed their seats, but leaned forward at the ready.

An agent wearing a black jacket with yellow FBI lettering came in through the open door of the classroom, leading three more agents. The lead agent walked right up to David, flipped open his pad, put his pen to it, and said loudly, "And you are?"

David glared at the agent. "Who wants to know?" he demanded.

The class erupted in laughter and applause.

The agent looked at the class as though surprised to see anyone out there. "I'm Agent Duffy. FBI. Who are you?"

David shook his head incredulously. "I thought we established that a moment ago. I'm 'Mister Professor David.' Have you forgotten already? Well, that's understandable. I told you back when you were across the quad."

The agent flipped his pad closed. "You need to come with me."

"Not so fast, Agent Duffy," said David observing the class's horror that their professor might be escorted away in handcuffs. "Am I under arrest?"

The agent shook his head almost imperceptibly. "But you'll have to come with me anyway."

David moved close enough to the agent to mutter privately. "Could you find it in yourself, Agent Duffy, to assure the members of this *law school* class that their professor is *not* being arrested?"

The agent answered by turning to the class and making a general announcement. "Professor … David is not under arrest. His country needs him." He turned to David and asked quietly, "How wuzzat?"

David nodded his approval and turned to the class. "I'll do a podcast of this class as soon as possible and email you a link. For next time, please read through Unit 3 of the syllabus. Class dismissed."

As the students gathered up their papers and coffee, David turned to Agent Duffy and pointed his chin toward the door.

"Lay on, Macduff," said David, certain his literary referent would go unappreciated.

The agents who accompanied Duffy into the lecture hall were first to return to their cars. As David was escorted toward the exit, Duffy's face assumed a dubious expression. "When *is* your next class scheduled for, professor?"

"A week from right now. It's a two-hour session, so my absence imposes something of a burden on the class. Why do you ask?"

"It's just that I'm not … sure you'll be back by then."

David halted and Duffy turned back to him.

"You're not sure I'll be back?" asked David. "Where the devil am I going?"

Duffy's eyes darted around, obviously to assure himself that his reply would be unheard. He leaned into David and said under his breath. "I'll tell you, but you have to promise not to tell anyone."

David nodded skeptically, and waited to find out his destination.

"The Pentagon."

David shrugged. "There's a shuttle from D.C. Getting back here shouldn't be a problem." Just as he resumed walking, he stopped suddenly. "But you already *know* that. So what you *mean* to say is that I'm going to D.C. *first*."

Duffy nodded guiltily.

David prodded him. "Where to, after that?"

Duffy shrugged. "I have no idea, and that's the truth. Maybe straight back here." He looked around dubiously. "Maybe." He pointed at the car waiting directly out the door. "Look, professor, we gotta go. I don't want to embarrass you, but we both *gotta* move our butts and get in that car."

David looked out the window, and could make out Fareed's profile in the back seat; he was alone back there, anxiously staring out the window. David shrugged. "Then let's go."

As they stepped out, an agent opened the back door and David got in.

Fareed's relief upon seeing him was extraordinary. David shook his hand reassuringly. "A rough morning, my friend," said David, "but things will turn out just fine, I'm sure."

"What are they arresting me for?" whispered Fareed.

Whispering seemed pointless, as there was no barrier between the front and back seats. "You're *not* under arrest," said David.

"Then … can I go? Makbule will be worried sick!"

Duffy glanced expectantly at David.

"I expect," said David, "that Makbule will understand that they want to speak with you about your academic expertise." As none of the agents reacted, he assumed he'd said the right thing … or one *possible* right thing, anyway.

But Fareed looked at him as though he were mad and asked in exasperation, "They want to interview me for a new position?" He shook his head. "I'm happy where I am."

David glanced warily at Duffy, and said to Fareed, "Have you had the news on this morning?"

Fareed shook his head. "No. I was in the basement by the time the sun came up. Why? What's happened?"

"Well, apparently, the Al-Aqsa Mosque has … disappeared from the Temple Mount." He cringed at the vagueness of his own report.

Fareed turned to him in wonderment. "That's terrible!" he said. "But I know nothing about it. Do they suspect *me?*"

Duffy turned around in his seat. "Professor Sinar, no one suspects you of doing anything wrong. Your country … *this* country … needs you to answer some questions about your knowledge of that part of the world."

Fareed rolled his eyes. "I know nothing about that part of the world any longer," he complained. "I've been here for twenty years."

"That's not so, Fareed," said David equably. "No one alive knows more than you do about what happened there … six thousand years ago."

At first, Fareed's jaw dropped in confusion, but then he shrugged. "If it will help, let them ask me about that."

Duffy looked at David, and nodded approval.

David asked himself silently: *But what the devil am I doing here?*

⁂

THE DRONING ENGINES on the small military jet were soporific, and David soon dropped off to sleep. His dream was simple, but no less soothing for its simplicity.

His dear departed Sharon was asleep in the seat next to him, her chest gently rising and falling with each unlabored breath. He admired both the thick auburn hair that fell down past her shoulders and the beautiful face he'd hoped to watch over breakfast every morning as she matured.

But her face on this occasion seemed *changed* in some undefinable way. Not only was it more achingly beautiful than he'd ever seen it in real life, but it was somehow … *different*—as though it was being not so much *seen* as *shown*. Though he'd often dreamt of Sharon since her passing, this was the first time he'd ever detected a subtle *change* in her face, and he found it strangely invasive, as though it had originated somewhere outside his own heart and memory.

After what seemed no more than a few minutes' shuteye (but must have been at least an hour), he felt a gentle tap on his shoulder.

"Professor?" came a woman's voice from the waking world, its tone gentle, but adult and confident. This was no teenage flight attendant.

David opened one eye, which lighted first on a navy-colored skirted suit. He wondered if its unusually vibrant hue denoted some service or rank he didn't recognize. Before replying, he glanced into a pair of sparkling green eyes set in an extraordinarily pretty face outlined by shoulder-length blonde hair, pert but professional.

Clearly appreciating the attention, the woman smiled at him coyly. She was on the tall side, maybe five-eight, perhaps five years younger than he, which would make her about thirty-five. "We'll be landing in a few minutes," she said. "There'll be an agency car waiting for you." She pointed her chin at Fareed, who was strapped into the adjacent chair. "Perhaps you should wake up the professor," she suggested, then smiled apologetically. "I mean the *other* professor, of course."

David smiled dreamily. "In a moment," he said, and sat up. "First, whom have I the pleasure of meeting?"

"Whether it's a pleasure, I'm sure I don't know," she said. "But I'm Catharine Weldon. And you are … Professor … David?"

"That I am," he said.

She laughed. "Do you have a last name?"

"I do indeed," he replied with a smile.

"Care to tell me what it is?" she asked.

He smirked. "I'd bet dollars to donuts you already know, Ms. … Weldon." The nice thing about using the *Ms.* form of address was that it didn't require one to know the woman's marital status. All the same, he glanced down at her finger, which was ringless.

She smirked. "I was just being polite, Professor *Schubert*."

"Feel free to be impolite to me whenever you're so inclined," he said.

She regarded him skeptically and pointed to the simple gold band on his ring finger. "I doubt *Missus* Schubert would take kindly to my rudeness."

Her words hit him like a punch in the gut, shattering the peace that had lingered from his dream of Sharon, replacing it with the waking memory of her labored breathing during those last cruel days and of the oxygen tent that, like some unwelcome sentry, had warded him away from her … when all he wanted to do was hold her in his arms.

Then that old familiar emptiness returned, and he could feel his face fall.

Ms. Weldon seemed alarmed. "Oh, I'm sorry, professor. Did I—?"

As always, he forced the blackness back long enough to offer reassurance. "I'm … a widower," he said, his voice sounding a bit strangled. He held up his ring finger with chagrin. "I haven't been able to take this thing off just yet."

"Oh, forgive me," she said empathetically. "I'd no idea."

He shook his head reassuringly. "You *couldn't* know," he said, then added, "In case you're wondering what kind of damaged goods I am, it's been two years."

The pilot's voice came over the public address system. "We're five minutes out of Joint Base Andrews. Please sit down and strap in."

Ms. Weldon touched his shoulder lightly. "We'll continue this later, if you're up to it," she said, and returned to her seat where an open laptop waited.

CHAPTER 2

DAVID LOOKED OUT the window of the stretch limo as it climbed the long driveway to a stately private home overlooking Chesapeake Bay.

"So, *this* is the Pentagon," he jibed. The house was elegant and inviting, but it certainly was *not* the Pentagon. "I always thought the Pentagon would be … *bigger*, somehow—" he said, prompting a dirty look from Agent Duffy "—and that it would have, you know, *five* sides." Duffy didn't turn around this time, just shook his head. "*And* that it would be in Washington, D.C.," added David, never wont to cease needling prematurely.

The house was a venerable example of upper-class American residential architecture, circa 1890, with symmetrical wings flanking a large central structure. Each section was fronted by countless windows sporting functioning shutters designed, no doubt, to protect the panes and the home's interior from any tropical hurricane that might wend its way up the coast.

Red and gold leaves sparsely dotted the many deciduous trees on the estate, while there was no sign of any leaves that had wafted to the ground. No doubt they'd been raked away by the family's ancestral gardeners. The central exterior stairs, apparently granite, were flanked by ornately carved concrete balusters topped with a nautical-looking brass handrail maintained at a high polish.

As the limo approached the house, an appealing, casually dressed older woman emerged through the front door. Her right hand firmly grasped the handrail as she descended to the driveway.

Light-grey gravel crunched noisily under the limo's tires as it pulled up to the house. To David, everything about this place said *old money*, which was more than a bit foreboding to many Jews, such as he.

The limo came to a halt, and FBI agents immediately sprang out and opened the doors.

Agent Duffy stepped out, his steps crunching along the gravel as he approached the lady of the house. He bowed to her deferentially.

"Mister Duffy," she said with a smile, "your friends arrived about a half-hour ago. They're already with the admiral in the second-floor parlor. He's expecting you." She approached the limo's open doors, raised her hand to shield her eyes from the glare, and peered in at David and Fareed. "Are you two dark-haired fellows the Middle East experts?" she asked.

Fareed stared shyly down at his hands, so David answered for them both. "My friend Fareed is the only expert here, Missus—"

"Simmons!" she said with a laugh. "My, my! Mister Duffy *has* kept you in the dark, hasn't he?"

"He *has*, ma'am," said David jocularly as he stepped out of the limo and drew up to his full six feet, then helped Fareed out of the limo. "He even confiscated our mobile phones back in New York, if you can imagine."

Missus Simmons brought her hands up to her cheeks in feigned shock. "The horror! The horror!" she said, and David couldn't help but admire her homage to Joseph Conrad.

So, *Admiral Simmons* was the one they'd been brought here to meet. David had never known Simmons's precise status, but he'd heard that the admiral had maintained a close relationship with several recent Presidents while they were in office, and after. There were a couple of other things David knew: Simmons was regarded as the *de facto* head of the U.S. Navy, and his wife seemed like a very nice lady.

Duffy, for his part, seemed a little annoyed that a personal welcome by the lady of the house had been squandered on a pair of transient passers-through such as Fareed and David.

Duffy quickly escorted them through the house, which wasn't nearly as stuffy as David had expected. Passing the dining room, he noticed two servants at work. The decorations were of a dignity to be expected of a venerable house of the period. Oil paintings of Simmons ancestors hung on the walls and, atop a few dark wooden pedestals, sat detailed models of late nineteenth-century sailing vessels. While the woodwork throughout the house was kept well-oiled in keeping with formalities, the place had a homey look that David took to immediately.

They climbed the stairs to the second story. As with every old staircase David had ever climbed, a few stairs creaked loudly underfoot. Duffy stopped outside the closed door of the second-floor parlor, and knocked.

"Come in," said the commanding voice of an aging admiral.

Duffy cracked open the door only slightly, so as to conceal the room's occupants from the newcomers' view, and stuck his head in.

"Morning, admiral," said Duffy. "We brought you the Middle East scholar you asked for, and—" he glanced back at David in search of a word.

"His *lawyer*," David quietly suggested.

Duffy stuck his head back through the doorway. "His lawyer."

"Fine," said the admiral jovially. "Bring them in. Then feel free to rejoin your agents downstairs and reap your reward in the family dining room. Missus Simmons has a bagel spread waiting."

Duffy nodded respectfully to the admiral, turned on his heel, and closed the door behind him on the way out.

Bagels? The very word gave David hope that he might not be the first Jew ever admitted to the house.

The parlor, like the rest of the house, beautifully suggested the "old navy," with plenty of dark wood paneling and a massive wooden conference table fashioned from the timbers of some retired naval vessel. Though the vessel's name appeared in black on an elegantly engraved brass plaque, the plaque was inset at the far end of the tabletop, rendering it illegible to David.

The admiral stood with his arms at his sides, studying the newcomers' faces. He wore no necktie, and was the only one in the room not attired in business dress or a navy uniform, resembling rather a country gentleman outfitted for a long autumn walk. His clothes were all greens and browns, as though he'd dressed from an L.L. Bean catalog. *No,* David corrected himself. The admiral was more likely sporting the bespoke originals to which the catalog referred in designing its mass-produced versions.

Before David and Fareed arrived, there had already been five in the room in addition to the admiral. All but the admiral were now seated; the mood was serious, though not alarmingly so. The admiral waved Fareed and David to a couple of vacant chairs, and they sat.

Directly across the table, David was surprised to see Catharine Weldon once again. Since she hadn't boarded the limo after the plane landed, he'd thought she'd moved on to other business, but realized now that she'd been heading to the same destination, albeit by navy chopper. That brought to mind a couple of possibilities about this meeting: Either there were items of business under discussion having nothing to do with the Jerusalem incident, or the admiral wished to discuss both the Jerusalem incident and (in advance of their arrival) Fareed and David.

David nodded to Ms. Weldon, and she smiled pleasantly in return, but there was something unnerving about her focus. Rather than looking into his eyes, she seemed to be studying his whole face, even his posture.

The admiral cleared his throat. "Before we begin," he said, turning to Fareed, "Professor Sinar, though I don't mean to interject religion into this discussion, if you're Muslim, permit me to express my condolences for the disappearance of the Al-Aqsa Mosque."

Fareed nodded his appreciation for the sentiment.

David could see that, despite the admiral's gruff reputation, he knew how to conduct himself diplomatically.

"Now," said the admiral, "what can you tell us of events in Jerusalem this morning?"

Fareed sat in wonderment at the breadth of the question, and glanced at his traveling companion. When David merely shrugged, Fareed said, "I don't know what you mean, admiral. My field of study is limited to the first known method of writing, namely, cuneiform, which as you may know was carved with a stylus onto clay tablets. Although such writing (indeed, writing itself) originated in the Middle East, by no means does that make me an expert in the *modern* Middle East."

David was, as ever, as impressed by Fareed's eloquence as by his upper-class English accent, picked up through years of tutoring at home and education at Oxford.

The admiral nodded grimly and Fareed apologized at once.

"I'm most sorry, admiral," said Fareed, "that you've evidently been misinformed as to the limited scope of my learning, and I regret that your valuable time may have been wasted while I was being escorted to your lovely home. Of course, if anyone had *asked* me—"

The admiral smiled. "I'm afraid *asking* is not Duffy's way," he said. "He can be rather ... peremptory. Tell me, professor: Do any of your clay tablets shed light on the disappearance of the Al-Aqsa Mosque?"

Fareed thought for a moment and shook his head. "The mosque was originally constructed in the eighth century of the Common Era." He smiled with chagrin. "That is to say—after the birth of Jesus."

"So, what does that mean?" asked one of the guests in service-dress blues.

Fareed gave him a patronizing smirk. "The mosque was built about *three thousand years* after my period of primary study."

David glanced at Catharine Weldon to see her reaction to this exchange, and was surprised to find her still focused on *him*, rather than on Fareed or the questioner. He began to wonder what her role might be in this affair.

The admiral posed another question. "Do your clay tablets make any mention of Jerusalem?"

Fareed shrugged. "For most of its long life, I'm afraid Jerusalem was a fairly insignificant bywater. For one thing, it lacked a water source within its walls, and so was unusually prone to siege by foreign invaders."

The admiral nodded. "All an attacker needed to do was besiege the town and block off its only source of fresh water. After that, the town would have to surrender or die of thirst."

Fareed smiled, as though pleased to see that at least one of these bureaucrats was not utterly lacking in practical knowledge.

Not for the first time, David wondered whether Fareed had read the books published by Abraham Azeri, the cuneiform scholar who, like the Bible, claimed that Jerusalem held a place of practical significance in the ancient world.

David glanced at Ms. Weldon again and, *damn* if she wasn't still tracking his every movement. This was becoming embarrassing. It was as though she regarded him as the only person in the room who mattered, when nothing could have been further from the truth. He looked to see if the admiral was aware of what she was doing, but his expression was sphinx-like, no doubt a great advantage for one in his profession.

David silently confronted Ms. Weldon, looking her straight in the eye and arching an eyebrow, as though to say, *I see what you're doing.* She reacted by pretending not to notice. Cheeky.

The admiral continued questioning Fareed. "Professor Sinar, you said that the mosque on the temple platform was built in the eighth century. Do I have that right?"

Fareed nodded. "There *was* a small temporary structure there before that," he conceded, "but nothing one might call a 'mosque.'"

The admiral continued. "When was the stone platform built on the Temple Mount? By that, I mean the huge platform on which the mosque was eventually built."

"When was the *platform* built?" Fareed echoed. "I don't know. Why? Is that of some importance?"

"Perhaps you could tell us," suggested the admiral, "why the Temple Mount is so sacred to Muslims."

Fareed nodded. "The Koran teaches that the Prophet Mohammed was brought there from Mecca one evening by the Archangel Gabriel, and that the two of them visited heaven together for one night and returned the following morning."

"*When* would that have happened?"

Fareed looked at the admiral askance. "*When?*" The admiral nodded. "Well, the Prophet lived from 570 to 632 of the Common Era. Presumably this would have happened when he was a grown man, so sometime between 583 and 632, I'd imagine. Is that of some significance to your problem today?"

Once again, the admiral ignored the question and posed another of his own. "Was the stone platform already on Mount Moriah when Mohammed was brought there by the archangel?"

Fareed seemed lost in thought for a moment, then snapped his fingers. "It *must* have been there already, as the Hebrew Temple had already been built on the Temple Mount, then destroyed and rebuilt, and destroyed again. But the platform remained … and remains to this day."

The admiral nodded. "So the platform was there when Jesus was born?"

Fareed nodded with somber assurance. "And when He died."

By this point, it was clear to David that the admiral was asking only questions to which he already knew the answer. He seemed to be testing the depth of Fareed's knowledge. *But why?* he wondered. He stole another glance at Ms. Weldon, who continued her study of his face. When the admiral wasn't looking, David cast her an expression of exasperation.

"So," said the admiral, "*who* built the platform?"

Fareed shrugged and ventured a guess. "King Solomon, perhaps?"

But David, whose understanding of the subject was based on the best of authority, knew that his friend's conjecture was wrong. He looked down to his hands to conceal his disagreement.

The admiral slapped his thighs and rose, as though he'd had a productive morning. "Gentlemen and lady, my stomach is grumbling. I propose we join Duffy and his fellow agents in a sandwich and a cup of coffee. Professor Sinar, won't you join us? Missus Simmons made sure to have suitable *halal* food items, should you choose to remain within those dietary strictures." He winked at David. "Of course, we have kosher items, as well, Professor Schubert. But, why don't you remain here with Ms. Weldon a moment? You two can come down and join us when you've finished."

David was surprised. *Finished? With what?*

Fareed looked to him. "Should *I* go with them?"

"Admiral," said David, "have I your assurance that nothing Professor Sinar says will be used against him in a court of law?"

The admiral chuckled benignly. "Absolutely, Professor Schubert. He's not being charged with any crimes. That's not what this is about."

David, satisfied by that response, whispered to Fareed, "Go with them, but don't say a thing you wouldn't want published in the *New York Times* tomorrow morning."

Fareed nodded and left with the others. The admiral, who was last to go, smiled wryly as he pulled the door shut after him, leaving David alone with Ms. Weldon, who continued her study of his face.

Neither wished to be the first to speak.

When David could bear the silence no longer, he said, "If you don't stop staring at me like that, I'll head back to New York right now."

"But it's what I do for a living," she said with a wry smile.

"*Stare at people?*" he asked incredulously.

She nodded.

"You know," he said, "if a *guy* does that, he gets sued for sexual harassment."

Her eyebrows rose. "I'm sorry. Are you feeling sexually harassed?"

"Harassed? *Yes*," he said. "Sexually? *No*. Why do you keep looking at me that way?"

"My specialty is non-verbal communication," she replied. "You know, *kinetics*."

He looked at her askance. "So, you're reading my body language?"

She smiled in a patronizing way that irked him. "After a fashion."

"And what have you learned from your ... reading?"

She frowned. "My *reading?* You make me sound like a fortune teller. I said I read non-verbal cues, not chicken entrails." She put her pen down and slid back in her chair, obviously deciding how much to tell him. "I can tell you're a little embarrassed by your friend's reticence—"

"*Client's*," he amended.

She accepted his emendation. "—your *client's* reticence. And also at his paucity of relevant knowledge."

"Why should *I* feel embarrassed?" said David. "The admiral didn't ask *me* to recommend a Sumerologist. More fundamentally, perhaps you can answer this: Why am I here? Fareed patently doesn't need a lawyer. He's being consulted about his field of academic study."

She pursed her lips. "Oh, I don't know if I should say this. But— what the hell?" She looked him straight in the eye. "He was bait to get *you* here."

"*Me?*" said David, raising his voice. "What the devil do *I* know about the disappearance of a mosque in Jerusalem? Has everyone gone mad? Besides, why would you need bait? Did anyone *consider* calling me on the phone? I would have come, although only after I'd finished teaching class."

She shook her head skeptically. "You wouldn't have come *at all*. You would have insisted that you know nothing about any disappearing mosque." She calmly opened a manila folder on the desk and put her glasses on to read (which he had to admit he found sexy). "Ah, here it is," she said. "Have you published on a sci-fi blog under the name Richard Elm?"

His mouth hung open.

"About six years ago?" she specified. "A ten-thousand word article about the platform on the Temple Mount in Jerusalem?"

He regarded her suspiciously. "What else do you know about me? You were investigating me on your laptop on the plane, *weren't* you?" He threw his hands up. "And here I thought you might be a 'friendly.' And so I play the fool!"

She looked at him skeptically. "Why the indignation?" She indicated the open file. "This is all public knowledge."

"Not the author's true name! That was between me and the publisher." He folded his arms suspiciously. "What else *did* you know about me when we met on the plane?" His eyes opened wide with the realization that, as she knew his surname, she could have used it to find out his marital status. His face reddened. "You *knew* I was widowered, didn't you? Why, you *phony*—"

She looked at him aghast. "I would *never*—"

"I was brought here under false pretenses!" he said. "Besides, what knowledge do I have that your precious agency couldn't have gleaned from reading the same books I've read?"

Now it was her turn to go red-faced. "The admiral read half your article, and found it a clear and concise explanation of some very esoteric material. He thinks you're a natural teacher. You ought to be *flattered*." She turned her head in a huff. "For my part, I'm sorry I tried to foster a personal rapport with you." She straightened her collar and turned up her nose. "Perhaps we should keep this relationship totally professional."

"Perhaps we *should*," he said with equal panache, but in his heart he knew that would never happen. She was intelligent, interesting, and beautiful. And he could see that she admired him. Before his harsh words could fester, he said, "I'm sorry I suggested you would do such a thing. That was … hasty. It's just that I've never actually missed a class I was teaching before, and the law school frowns on that. Virtually no excuse will do."

His apology seemed to be having some effect. She softened. "I suppose trickery was not the only way to obtain your assistance," she conceded. "It wasn't *my* idea, anyway. It was—" she leaned forward and whispered "—the old man's." She hastened to add, "But don't call him that. He hates it."

Out in the hall, the staircase creaked loudly.

"He's coming," she warned.

It took an unexpectedly long time for the footsteps to reach the parlor door. When no one entered and there was no immediate knock, David rose and opened the door. The admiral stood in the doorway holding a weighty tray with a nicely prepared bagel spread. David was delighted to see that there was Nova Scotia lox.

Ms. Weldon hurried around the table to clear a place for the tray. The admiral put it down on the newly cleared spot and rubbed his hands as he smiled knowingly at David and Ms. Weldon.

"I heard excited voices up here in the salon," he said, "and thought I'd bring a peace offering. The two of you must be starved. Dig in."

David put a plain bagel on a red plastic plate and brought it back to his seat, together with a black coffee. Taking a first bite of the bagel (which was excellent), he could feel the tension melt away.

The admiral sat down with a coffee, as Ms. Weldon carefully selected two cookies to go with hers.

"So, David," began the admiral, "you think the Temple Mount was built long before the First Temple?"

"There can't be much doubt of that, admiral," replied David. "At least if you believe in the essential historicity of the Old Testament."

The admiral nodded for him to continue.

David was happy to oblige. "According to the Second Book of Samuel, King David was told by Yahweh that a temple would be built in Jerusalem to permanently house the Ark of the Covenant containing the tablets on which the Ten Commandments were inscribed. David obediently traveled to Jerusalem. There wasn't much there at the time, except a gigantic stone platform on Mount Moriah that was being used as a thresher's floor by a Jebusite named Araunah."

"Wait!" said the admiral. "You mean the platform was already there before King David went to Jerusalem?"

David nodded. "That's what the Bible teaches."

"What's a Jebusite?" asked Ms. Weldon. "And a thresher's floor?"

"A Jebusite was a local non-Hebrew," said David, "someone we might today call a Palestinian Arab. And a thresher's floor is a hard (preferably stone) floor where a thresher would separate grain from chaff using a flail, which is just a stick attached to a heavier stick by means of a short rope. The thresher would lay the stalks on the floor, then swing the stick so hard that the heavier stick would smack the grain loose from the chaff. Then they'd dispose of the chaff and gather up the grain for use."

"So," said the admiral. "*Araunah* built the thresher's floor?"

David hid his amusement at the suggestion and shook his head. "No, admiral. Whoever built the Temple Mount must have had the skills and equipment necessary to cut large stones quite precisely from a nearby quarry, transport them to Mount Moriah, and lower them perfectly into place at the base of the western wall."

The admiral shrugged. "I suppose the process would have presented some logistical issues at the time, but it doesn't seem to have been impossible."

David sipped his coffee. "I haven't gotten to the impossible part yet. You see, among these stones were *megaliths*, each weighing *six hundred tons*. Araunah would have lacked the technology to perfectly cut such a megalith to match the space it was designed to occupy on the Temple Mount. The cutting would have had to be *so* precise that, once any two stones were brought together, a sheet of ordinary paper would be too thick to insert between them." He smiled. "You see, there's no mortar so close to the base of the wall."

"None?" asked the admiral.

"None," David confirmed.

The admiral, having no doubt had plenty of experience with the machinery used to load heavy items onto ships, seemed to be performing some mental calculations. He cocked his head and asked, "*Are there* such megaliths in the western wall?"

As David was in the midst of sipping coffee, he replied by holding up three fingers.

"There are *three?*" asked the admiral incredulously.

David nodded. "They call the three megaliths a *trilithon*. And they can be found near the *base* of the wall," said David. "As any archaeologist will tell you, the deeper you dig, the further back you've gone in time."

The admiral's expression was one of incredulity. "So these megaliths were put in place at—or before—the beginning of recorded time? But— even today—*we'd* have enormous trouble cutting and moving stones of such size."

David nodded. "All we know (or think we know) is that the stones were laid well before Yahweh told King David that a Temple would be built on the platform. Any suggestion that such massive stones were put there to support a *thresher's* floor is ridiculous. The floor of a common barn would have served the thresher's purposes well enough. It seems rather that the gigantic platform had been erected for a completely *different* purpose, and that, by the time of Araunah, people had simply forgotten its original purpose (if indeed they ever knew). Since no one was using it, they put it to use as a thresher's floor."

"So what was the platform's original purpose?" asked Ms. Weldon.

David looked at the two inquiring people and struggled for a way to say something that was sure to sound outlandish. "Bear in mind, I wasn't there at the time," he ventured. "All I can do is repeat what I've read."

The admiral scowled, as though expecting a heavy blow, but nodded for David to continue.

David looked anywhere but at his inquisitors. "It was built as a control center for the spaceships of … the gods." He cringed as the words came out.

"The—?" began the admiral skeptically, but his words were cut off by the clamorous buzz of an old-fashioned landline phone with a flashing light. He picked up the handset, and his look of annoyance was quickly replaced by one of concern. He hung up and stared at David contemplatively. "Professor, you had a conversation this morning with Shawn McCauley of the State Department?"

David sat erect and scowled. "You bugged my phone? I'm a *lawyer*, admiral. How can you *possibly* justify that?"

Evidently exasperated by the implication that he'd been engaging in unlawful surveillance of a U.S. citizen, the admiral shook his head indulgently. "The NSA wasn't tracking your calls. They were tracking *his*. He works for Uncle Sam, and he's signed the same NSA privacy waiver as the rest of us."

"The National Security Administration?" replied an astonished David. "Why would they bug Shawn? I've known him since childhood. He's a true-blue patriot."

"What did the two of you talk about this morning?" asked the admiral.

David's mind swirled with the possibility that Shawn's call might have compromised national security. "He was in Jerusalem when the mosque disappeared. He told me to turn on cable news, which I did.

What difference does that make? By the time he told me, the *whole world* knew about the missing mosque. Is telling news to a friend a security risk nowadays?"

"Of course not," replied the admiral. "What else did he tell you?"

David calmed down and dug into his memory. "The call was interrupted for a minute. Then Shawn came back on the line and told me the mosque had been ... *found*." He shrugged. "Oh, but he didn't say where. Then he hung up." He let his annoyance show once more. "Why are you interested in a private call?"

The admiral shook his head gravely and muttered, "The mosque has been found in Mecca. But *Shawn's* missing."

CHAPTER 3

DAVID WAITED ON the tarmac with the admiral and Catharine Weldon while a military aircraft was prepared for boarding. In the afternoon sunshine, it occurred to him that this might be the same aircraft that brought him to Andrews but, upon reflection, he realized that this one was a good deal more compact. Though it carried a fair amount of cargo that was still being loaded, it was only slightly bigger than a private passenger jet.

Ms. Weldon said, "I take it Professor Sinar wasn't too disappointed to be heading back to New York with Agent Duffy?"

"No," said David with a sigh. "He was okay with it. He's well aware that he wouldn't be of any use to the admiral without his precious cuneiform tablets. Anyway, he feels more comfortable in a museum basement than an airplane, and Duffy will help him upload his findings to the admiral's plane."

"It'll take Fareed nearly as long to get back to New York as it will for us to get to Paris," she remarked.

David looked to her mournfully. "At least he gets to go home. *I*, on the other hand, don't even have a change of clothes."

She smiled knowingly. "No, but you have an expense account at some pretty swanky Paris clothiers."

He raised an eyebrow. "Oh? And when did that happen?"

"I set it up online while you were saying goodbye to Fareed. Courtesy of your Uncle Sam."

"Well," said David with a laugh, "Uncle Sam's not here, so I'll extend my thanks to *you*." He winked at her, which made her laugh. "Please call me David … or Dave."

"Catharine," she said, as though introducing herself for the first time.

The cargo bay door closed, and the admiral darted past them on his way to the aircraft. A moment later, a mobile stairway was wheeled over to the passenger doorway and locked in. As soon as the door opened, the admiral bounded up the stairs and disappeared into the cabin.

David turned toward Catharine. "Pretty spry for an old fellow, isn't he? Sure he's retired?"

She smirked. "Well, he's still doing the same things he did before retiring. But GSA says he's retired, so he must be."

"GSA?" he inquired.

"Government Services Administration. They keep track of everything about Government employment."

⟶∘⟩⟨∘⟵

THE PASSENGER CABIN was outfitted as an airborne conference room, with a central table big enough to comfortably accommodate ten. Much of the cabin was lined with bunks folded up into the walls, discreetly out of the way.

A doorway behind the cockpit slid open, and a young male flight attendant emerged. Spotting the admiral, he jumped to attention and saluted.

The admiral snickered and asked him, "First time on an admiral's plane?"

"Yes, *sir*, admiral," came the reply.

"Well, you can dispense with the salute," said the admiral. "Under the regs, you're a person at work."

"Yes, sir," said the attendant, dropping his salute and trying to look relaxed. "Can I get the admiral anything?"

"No. Wait! Can you bring down the projection screen?"

"Sure thing, admiral." The attendant disappeared for a moment and a six-foot-wide screen lowered from the ceiling at one end of the table.

"Cath," said the admiral, "can you send what's on your laptop to this screen, so we can all see?"

The attendant reappeared smartly, obviously having overheard the question. "*Can do*, admiral," he said as he unfurled a cable, plugged one end into the laptop, and the other into a port built into the wall.

Catharine fired up the laptop, and its handshake melody emerged from the cabin's high-quality public address system, universally known as the PA.

"Good afternoon, admiral," came the pilot's voice with a thick West Texas accent, reminiscent of flight controllers at NASA's Houston Control.

The admiral smiled, obviously recognizing the pilot's voice. "Afternoon, John. How are you this fine day?"

"*Well,* admiral," said the pilot. "It'll be nighttime pretty soon, especially once we're aloft. We're lookin' at good weather the whole way, with the sun up our ass and a nice tail breeze." There was a momentary silence, and the voice returned. "Admiral, we're being cleared for takeoff and about to head out to the runway, so if you'd be kind enough to tell those civilian types to sit down and buckle up, this proud navy pilot would sure appreciate it."

"The lady's navy, John, but I'll be pleased to tell them," said the admiral, winking at David and Catharine, who were already buckled in. "Meanwhile, keep your eye out for bogeys."

At first, this remark rolled right off David, as it just seemed a continuation of the casual banter between the admiral and his pilot. But after a momentary silence from the cockpit, the pilot's voice came on again. "Was that a feeble attempt at humor, admiral?"

It occurred to David that, although this trip was supposed to be a jaunt over the Pond, the man in the pilot's seat was a U.S. Navy fighter pilot … for whom caution was *always* the order of the day, and whose voice was clearly that of a flyer who'd seen his share of bogeys. *Real* bogeys.

The admiral half-smiled. "Only partly joking, John. Eyes wide."

David and Catharine looked at one another, a little jittery.

"Admiral," said the pilot's disembodied voice. "I've got a snotty young rulebook co-pilot up here. Wants me to ask you for a clue what kinda bogey to expect."

"Tell him I haven't the vaguest idea, John."

"Yes, admiral," said the pilot cautiously. "Eyes wide, sir, as you said."

They began zooming down the runway and in what seemed less than a minute they were aloft and up in the clouds.

Catharine pulled up a video streaming service on her laptop, and they were soon watching videos in which the Sumerologist Azeri, who'd died five years earlier, spoke at length about his extensive findings on ancient aliens.

After a half-hour's viewing, the admiral held his hand up. Catharine put the show on hold with a click of the mouse.

The admiral said, "David, Azeri was talking about markers for two flight corridors that the ancient gods—the Anak—"

"Anunnaki, sir," said David.

"—that the *Anunnaki* used for landing on Earth. He said one set of markers was destroyed, and replaced by a second. What destroyed the markers for the first flight corridor?"

"The flood, admiral," said David.

"*Which* flood?"

"The Great Flood, sir. *Noah's* flood. As the admiral might imagine, it covered nearly the whole Middle East with billions of tons of mud that took many years to dry out."

"*Noah's* Flood," said the admiral skeptically. "That really happened?"

"About thirteen thousand years ago, sir."

"Thirteen thou—Now how the *hell* would the Sumerians know that? Wait, *did* the Sumerians know about Noah?"

"The Sumerians attributed *all* their knowledge to the Anunnaki, sir. Their tablets say, 'All we know, we were taught by the Anunnaki.' And the *Sumerian* version of the Flood story is the oldest. It tells what *each* of the Anunnaki did in respect of the Flood. The story was changed by the Hebrews many years later to reflect only one God—which makes the narrative pretty awkward. Instead of having *two* main gods, one who couldn't stand humanity and another who loved us, the Hebrews were only allowed one, so the Hebrew scribes tell the story with God changing his mind about destroying mankind, talking to Himself in the first-person plural, and acting in inconsistent ways."

"How so?" asked the admiral.

"Well, in the Sumerian narrative, Enlil, the top god (who couldn't stand us) learned that a natural event was about to occur that would result in the granddaddy of all tsunamis—"

The admiral cocked his head. "What could cause such a huge tsunami?"

"The cuneiform writings say that Enlil had learned that there was an oncoming catastrophe and decided that humanity should not be forewarned of it. As the Flood happened at the end of the latest ice age, Azeri speculates that there was a precariously balanced Antarctic ice shelf (nearly as wide as the whole continent) that was about to fall into the ocean and create the Mother of All Waves. As I'm sure you know, a tsunami is more than just a wave."

The admiral nodded. "A tsunami can actually raise sea level for a time. But how could Enlil know when the ice shelf would fall?"

David admired the admiral's skepticism. "Well, the Anunnaki's home planet was about to make a close approach, which was known to shake things up pretty badly on Earth. I guess they learned about the ice shelf pretty much the way we would. Eyes in the skies."

"Their home planet was Nibiru?" asked the admiral.

"Yes, sir. Anyway, Enlil learned about the impending disaster, and he welcomed the prospect that it would drown all the pesky earthlings. On the other hand, Enlil's half-brother *Enki*—who'd had a big hand in transforming us from early hominids into *homo sapiens*—loved us. Enlil overruled his brother Enki, and extracted a promise from *all* the gods not to tell the earthlings about the coming disaster. As Enki couldn't bring himself to allow his new race of beings to be wiped out, he had one of his servants bring Noah to his temple and place him on the other side of a screen so he could 'overhear' Enki spill the beans about the coming flood. Enki told 'the screen' that Noah needed to save his immediate family, and also gave him strict instructions on how to design and build the necessary boat, as well as how to becalm the earthlings who were unaware they were about to drown. When the Hebrews incorporated the tale into the Bible, they had God doing all these things, which doesn't make much sense."

"Noah?" asked Catharine, who seemed rapt with the tale. "Is that what the Anunnaki called him?"

David shook his head. "The Sumerians' Noah was known by several names: Ziusudra, Utnapishtim … Atrahasis. I forget which of those was his birth name and which were honorifics. And the size and shape of Noah's boat was completely different in the Sumerian and Biblical versions."

"And what does *Anunnaki* mean?" asked the admiral.

"In Hebrew, it means, 'those who from heaven to Earth came.' In Genesis, they're referred to as 'Nephilim.' Among them were royals descended from *Anu*, King of Nibiru."

"And Jerusalem was the control center for the landing corridor established *after* the Flood?" asked the admiral.

"That's what Azeri says," said David.

The admiral posited a hypothesis. "Assuming, as crazy as it sounds, that the Anunnaki moved the mosque so that they could land on a platform they'd built more than six thousand years ago and that they'd want to land in *additional* locations, what would be the *next* platform they'd be tempted to clear?"

"Numerous sites could fit that bill, admiral," said David, "some in Mexico, some in Peru … some in southern Italy."

"Okay. Assume they'd want to land other ships at a *big* landing site in the flight corridor controlled from the Temple Mount."

"Well, there's one remaining *big* site," said David hesitantly, "but—

no, that would be impossible."

"Let *me* decide what's impossible, David," said the admiral. He sighed. "And right now nothing much falls into that category."

"Well," said David, "this *big* site would require an even greater feat of magic—pardon me, *engineering*—than they used to clear the Temple Mount."

The admiral nodded curiously.

David hesitated to speak his mind, as he felt certain the admiral would place too much stock in what he was about to say. "It's the gigantic platform under the equally gargantuan Temple of Jupiter at Baalbek in modern-day Lebanon."

"Wasn't Jupiter a *Roman* god?" asked the admiral. "I thought the Sumerians worshiped older gods."

"They did but, like King David, the Romans knew how to bring an old platform into service of their own gods. The Temple of Jupiter is quite an achievement in design and engineering."

"Is the Baalbek platform as big as the platform in Jerusalem?"

"*Much* bigger," said David. "And it has its *own* trilithon … but each of the Baalbek megaliths doesn't weigh a mere *six* hundred tons like the ones under the Temple Mount. At Baalbek, each stone in the trilithon weighs about *eleven* hundred tons—and even the Romans couldn't cut and move stones that big and that heavy."

"But evidently the *Anunnaki* could," said the admiral. "Architecturally, a trilithon is like an Anunnaki fingerprint, isn't it?"

David shrugged. "Suppose so."

The PA sounded a beeping alarm that was instantly silenced, followed by the pilot's unflappable voice.

"Admiral …. we've got company. *Fast* company. More than one, by the looks of 'em."

"What's their range?" asked the admiral.

"They're about twenty miles behind us," said the pilot, "coming straight at us."

"How many?"

"Looks like two, sir. They're about a thousand feet apart, both matching our altitude."

"How long till they overtake us?" The admiral looked worried, and that got David very worried indeed.

"Hold on a sec, sir," said the pilot, "… checking their airspeed." Then, barely audibly, he said, "Yikes."

"What is it, John? Don't keep me in suspense back here."

"They just halved their distance to us, sir, in … twenty-two seconds. At this rate, admiral, they'll be here on a count o' ten."

"Better maintain course, altitude, and airspeed, John," said the admiral.

"Concur, sir. We can't outrun 'em. We'll just have to hope they're not hostile."

The admiral looked to David. "What do *you* think? Are they hostile?"

David swallowed, using what little spit he could muster. "If they're who we think they are and they wanted us dead, we'd already *be* dead. Best guess is that they don't think of themselves as hostile. But they'll sure want to know if *we* are."

"John," the admiral said, "take no hostile or evasive action. Can you get a visual on them and throw it up on the screen here?"

"It's not full dark yet, admiral, and they're coming out of the sun," replied the pilot. "I'll polarize the lens to cut down glare, and throw 'em up on your screen, but they'll just look like cutouts until they get alongside us—if that's what they have in mind."

A hazy picture appeared on the screen, and Catharine lowered the cabin lights slightly. Coming on fast from a bright background were what appeared to be two identical cigar-shaped craft.

The pilot came on. "If they're gonna pass by, sir, better not blink, 'cause you'll miss 'em."

Full of dread, David slowly shook his head. "I don't think they're just gonna pass us by."

The admiral replied, "I don't either. Leastways not till they're damned good and ready."

He'd barely gotten the words out when the plane was flanked by two metallic cylinders, their cigar shape suggestive of attack submarines. Each was about twice the length of the navy plane, with bright green lights revolving around their circumference, their speed and altitude so precisely matched to the plane's that they might as well have been a boarding party. They were most certainly *not* passing by, but holding in tight formation.

"Holy Mother o' God!" the admiral muttered as his eyes darted from the port windows to starboard and back again.

The casual pilot's unflappable voice came on again. "Friends o' yours, admiral? You might want to ask 'em to move off a few yards, 'cause if they get any closer they're gonna scratch the paint."

Even immobilized by fear, David took some comfort from the captain's humor and steady tone. But then, a louver opened on the near side of each of the flanking cylinders revealing what looked to be a laser rifle.

Much to David's shock, Catharine grabbed him and dropped to the floor, being careful to place him beside her. She looked at him wide-eyed with terror.

"You okay?" she asked.

He nodded, but was too terrified to speak.

The admiral remained in his seat, as though he had a box seat to Armageddon and had no intention of missing a damned thing.

A low humming started, seeming to come from nowhere, bringing to David's mind the way Shawn described the disappearance of the mosque—a humming and a bright light—and his stomach turned at the prospect that they might be transported somewhere ghastly.

But instead, a second later another unexpected thing happened. A red beam like a vertical film appeared at the rear of the cabin and began slowly moving forward. To David, it appeared to be *scanning* every-thing. As it moved steadily forward, everything it touched emitted a dull red glow; the *edges* of everything—of every item of furniture and every loose paper on the conference table—glowed brightly, as though it might burst into flames at any second.

The beam moved inexorably forward until it passed over (or through) the admiral, who lit up like some life-size Christmas tree ornament.

The bottom of the beam seemed to pass only a few inches over Da-vid's head, appearing as thin as a razor from his vantage point on the floor. David and Catharine seemed to be the only things missed by the beam.

David's momentary sense of relief at being overlooked was shattered as the red beam passed forward of the passenger cabin, and he realized it was going to pierce the cockpit and blind the pilot and co-pilot, if only momentarily. The prospect of being a passenger in a plane flown by a blind pilot terrified him. He shuddered.

"Goddam you, son of a bitch!" said the formerly calm pilot. "I can't see a goddam thing."

The admiral, who'd momentarily sat immobile, ran toward the cock-pit. "Well, *I* can still see, and I'm certified to fly this plane."

But before the admiral could reach the cockpit door, the pilot's voice came back on. "It's okay, admiral. I can see fine now. Let's just hope they don't shine that damn light through the cockpit again."

It took a moment for David to realize that the cabin lights were no longer *low* as Catharine had left them. They were now *off*, so that the only things illuminating the cabin were the running lights on the flying cylinders. That thought remained with David only a split second before the whole plane shuddered under him.

The engines had shut down. He just knew it.

There was a deathly silence in the cabin, overcome only by the rushing of air around the fuselage—a sound never meant to be heard in a noisy jet aircraft like this.

The nose began to pitch slightly, but the saucers remained in perfect formation with the plane. The pilot's once-again professional voice came on.

"Uh, admiral—" There must have been some confusion in the cockpit, because there was a moment's crosstalk. Then the PA went silent for a moment.

"Admiral," said the pilot at last, "we have a complete flameout here. Don't know what's causin' it, but the usual reignition protocol isn't cuttin' it. Fortunately, we've still got plenty of altitude. *Unfortunately*, the altitude won't do us much good if we can't re-light the engines ... so I'm sendin' our trusty flight attendant back there with some parachutes—"

On the word *parachutes*, David's eyes turned up in his head and he felt as though he'd swallowed his heart. The only way to parachute out of a plane in a nosedive was by means of an ejection seat. And there were none aboard—with the possible exception of the pilot's and co-pilot's seats.

Even if they'd each had an ejection seat, the prospect of leaving a distressed airplane over the North Atlantic at night would still have lacked a certain appeal.

The flight attendant entered the passenger cabin encumbered by numerous parachute packs that he immediately began distributing.

"Each of you is gonna strap on one of these the way I'm gonna show ya," he said.

David was so horrified by the prospect of jumping from the airplane that he just stood there in shock with his mouth wide open, his pack dangling from his hand. Which pretty much reflected Catharine's condition.

At that moment, the alien cylinders broke out of formation and instantly disappeared from view. The cabin lights came back up. The airframe shuddered again as the engines restarted and the plane leveled off.

"Got engines and instruments back," said the pilot. "Everything's nominal. We're gonna be okay."

Flight attendant and passengers together collapsed with relief, their untied parachute packs dangling loosely from arms and shoulders.

"That was a *perfect* operation on the part of the cylinders," said the admiral grudgingly.

The attendant suggested a possible flaw. "Maybe they didn't mean to cut our engines, sir ... but they did it anyway."

Despite his relief, the admiral scowled. "You don't recognize intimidation when you see it. Do you, son?"

"Well, sir, *I'm* not feelin' intimidated," said the flight attendant. "Scared to death, but not intimidated."

The admiral nodded. "It wasn't directed at you, son. It was directed at *me*."

David chimed in. "And whoever that was, got a damned good look at every piece of paper in this cabin. And also Catharine's computer, I suppose."

Catharine shook her head. "My computer's *gone*," she said mournfully.

David's eyebrows shot up. "Destroyed?"

She shook her head. "It's *gone*. They filched it with their filthy ray gun."

And so they had. There was now no computer on the conference table where Catharine's had sat not five minutes earlier.

The admiral looked to Catharine with concern. "Did you have classified material on there?"

At first, she shrugged and opened her eyes wide, as though it was a distinct possibility. Then she exhaled with relief. "No, usually I would have, but that laptop was brand new. All I put on there were some programs and a copy of Professor Schubert's article from that weblog." When David's face sank in dismay, she added comfortingly, "Fortunately, that's not classified."

"No," said David with a sigh, "not classified. It's a little worrisome for me, however, that the only thing those *creatures from another world* will find on your computer is a copy of *my* frickin' article."

The admiral laughed with relief. "David, they probably knew about it anyway."

David shrugged. "Maybe, sir. But they *definitely* know about it now. Besides, they surely know who *you* are, admiral." Now it was the admiral's face that fell. "That is, unless they're sending a two-saucer escort for every plane crossing the Atlantic."

The admiral nodded, deep in thought. "And if they've done that, we're going to have the biggest panic on our hands in the history of the world."

"Signals traffic, admiral," said the pilot, "from FBI Agent … Duffy. It's a short video."

"Put it on the screen, would you, Johnny?"

"Comin' up now," replied the pilot.

There on the screen was a disheveled-looking Agent Duffy, with no jacket, his tie askew. "Admiral, NSA told me not to send any data from the professor to your plane because you may have been tracked by a couple of … unknowns." He smiled with chagrin. "I hope that works out okay. Anyway, I wanted to tell you the news while you're still up there. It's already on the networks. What happened to that mosque in Jerusalem … just happened to the Temple of Jupiter in Lebanon—"

The admiral scowled at David.

"—and the only thing left is the platform. Anyway, we've encrypted Professor Sinar's message and sent it to you care of Central Intelligence in Paris. So it'll be there when you arrive. Godspeed, sir. Signing off."

The admiral rubbed his eyes. "Hell, this is breaking so fast, I should probably turn around and go back to Washington. The President will want to see me."

"Okay by me," said David. "I'd like to go home."

The admiral shook his head incredulously. "You correctly called the next platform that would be cleared by these bastards, and you think you're going *home?*" He shook his head. "With what appears to be happening, I'm not sure any of us are going home … *ever.*"

The pilot chimed in over the PA: "Admiral, you got any more fly-by buddies between here and Paris? I'm only askin' 'cause I got no extra skivvies in the cockpit."

"It's okay, John," said the admiral. "I'm pretty sure they made their point. I don't expect 'em again on this flight." He rubbed his eyes. Lowering his voice, he said to David and Catharine, "Can you imagine if they have *nukes?*"

David felt so sorry for the old fellow that he broke the bad news even more quietly. "They *have* nukes, sir. And they've had them for at least four thousand years. In fact, they've used them against each other on their home planet … and here on Earth."

"On Earth? When was *this?*" asked the admiral.

"Two thousand twenty-four years before the birth of Jesus, sir."

"*Where?*" demanded the admiral petulantly, plainly annoyed that he had to take all this outlandishness seriously. "Did it leave a trace?"

"The weapons were used on the Anunnaki's main landing pad, which was located on the Sinai Peninsula, sir," said David. "The same series of explosions destroyed Sodom and Gomorrah. Those in the Sinai left a *huge* crater. You can see it from up here if you do a flyover. The white sands are still scorched into black glass for miles around."

The admiral looked dismayed. "It's the first day of school."

CHAPTER 4

Five hours later, deep inside CIA headquarters in Paris, the three Americans awaited playback of the message from Fareed that had been recorded at CIA headquarters in New York.

David must have slumped in his chair, because the admiral quipped, "Long day, professor?"

David sat up despite the difficulty he was experiencing in keeping his eyes open. "Well, sir. Today didn't turn out precisely as expected. I feel like I've been awake for a year."

Catharine added, "Same here, sir. We don't seem to have your stamina."

The admiral smirked. "You two thought we were going into the drink. That'll take a lot out of you."

David was surprised. "*You* didn't think so, admiral?"

The admiral shook his head. "No. I can tell an intimidation job when I see one. And nobody bothers to intimidate you if they're planning on killing you … at least right away."

A female voice came over the two-way PA. "Admiral Simmons?"

"Here," he replied.

"Admiral," said the voice, "I'm shutting off the microphone in your conference room, so your message remains private. If you need me, just pick up the handset and hit zero."

A large flat screen lit up, and the image of David's friend Fareed Sinar appeared.

"Now?" asked Fareed of someone offscreen who evidently encouraged him to proceed. "Okay," said Fareed, turning to the camera. "Admiral Simmons, you asked me to research several questions. First, you asked me to advise you whether the Anunnaki were physical beings, as distinguished from stone idols or disembodied spirits. Until now, the evidence had appeared somewhat equivocal to me, but I have come 'round to the view expressed by the Sumerologist Azeri that they were physical beings, perhaps somewhat taller than the human beings of their day, but largely subject to the same vanities and passions.

"I came across a message written by Hammurabi to a functionary who'd been sent to retrieve several goddesses and priestesses threatened by the politico-religious upheavals of the day. Hammurabi's note said"—Fareed picked up a scrap of paper and held it to his eyes—"'Thou shalt cause the goddesses to journey in a processional boat as in a shrine, that they may come to Babylon. The temple-women shall accompany them. For food of the goddesses thou shalt load pure cream and cereals unto the boat; sheep and provisions thou shalt put on board for the sustenance of the temple-women enough for the journey to reach Babylon.'"

Fareed looked at the camera. "It strains credulity to posit that Hammurabi was ensuring adequate provisions for women made of stone, or having no corporeal presence. Moreover, one might infer that the goddesses ate foods different from those eaten by their human servants. Although I suppose special foods might simply have served as a symbol of high status, it is at least possible that these ... *goddesses* ... were women of a different species, thus having different dietary needs.

"Further support of the argument for the Anunnaki's physicality is legion, admiral. The written records (including the Book of Genesis) show that Anunnaki males had sexual relations with human females, resulting in numerous live births. Anunnaki males also had sexual relations with *Anunnaki* females—and some of those females were their close relatives. In fact, each royal male Anunnaki was encouraged to breed with a half-sister, that is, a woman of the same father but a different mother. *Why would they do so?* That leads me to your second question.

"As you will recall, you asked whether the most powerful Anunnaki who visited Earth were royalty on their native planet. It appears quite clear that they were. Two princes, sons of the same father but different mothers, were put in charge of the Earth. Their names were Enlil and Enki. Their common father was King Anu who, for the most part, remained on their home planet—although there are records of Anu's physically coming to Earth on a few ceremonial occasions, when he stayed only briefly. Sumerian records specify the extensive preparations made for his arrival, and identify the places where he spent the night.

"Enki, the first of the two brothers to come to Earth, was born of an Anunnaki mother of a lesser bloodline, whereas Enlil was born of Anu's official consort, a half-sister. Consequently, as Enlil's royal blood was more highly concentrated than Enki's, Enlil was awarded higher status. Enlil was put in charge of overall administration of the Earth, while

Enki, who was clearly the more scientifically curious and capable of the two (by many orders of magnitude), was placed in charge of the physical layout of the Mesopotamian settlement and the business of mining gold.

"Your third question was whether the Anunnaki were immortal. As far as I can tell, although to their contemporary human beings they might have *seemed* immortal, they do not live forever. They were known to die by accident or violence and, although they appeared to be highly resistant to illness and old age, eventually they succumbed. Compared to humans, the Anunnaki appeared to age only very gradually and lived for many thousands of Earth's years. Some of the Anunnaki alive when man was created could still be alive today.

"Your fourth and final question was simply: *What do the Anunnaki now want from Earth?* At first, it seemed that might be a simple question to address, as Enki was originally sent here to obtain the gold necessary to maintain the atmosphere on their home planet, thus enabling life to continue. At first, Enki tried to sift gold from the waters of the Persian Gulf, which didn't work. So he set up gold mines at several places in Africa which, for thousands of years, were worked by Anunnaki of lower status.

"When the miners finally balked at the prospect of working indefinitely under such conditions, Enki experimented with genetically transforming a late hominid, perhaps Cro-Magnon, into an intelligent mining slave. Enki and his half-sister Ninharsag engrafted Anunnaki DNA onto the hominid's. After much trial and error, they finally developed a working model, which Enki dubbed *the adam*. As you can read in Genesis, the earliest references in the Hebrew Bible to the first homo sapiens were as *the* adam (The Anunnaki—and eventually Semitic homo sapiens—referred to Earth as *adama*, so *adam* literally means *earthling*).

"Assuming that Enki sent all the mined gold to his home planet (and assuming the amount was sufficient to preserve life there), I have been unable to identify a specific motivation for the Anunnaki to return to Earth, except—and this is pure conjecture on my part—they may simply enjoy being worshiped."

Fareed wavered nervously, but quickly recovered the courage to conjecture aloud. "Another reason they may wish to return to Earth is that, in 1945, we developed a weapon so terrible that they might wish to … *remove* it from our control to prevent us from posing a danger to *them*, since our respective planets inexorably approach each other every thirty-six hundred years or so."

Fareed's countenance relaxed again, and he said, "If you see my good friend David, please apologize on my behalf for having dismissed all this Anunnaki business for so long without adequate investigation on my part. Goodbye for now. Please do not hesitate to call on me if you should need me again. And please be sure to thank your lovely wife for her warm hospitality upon my visit to your home."

The screen went blank and the room lights came up.

The admiral rubbed his eyes, and it was clear that fatigue had finally caught up with him. "Fareed thinks they want our nukes," he declared. "What do you two think?"

David shrugged. "I don't know if they want to take away our nukes, but I expect they'll neutralize them before setting foot on this planet again."

Catharine spoke up. "This is all conjecture. We have no idea *what* they want. And there's one thing they may want that Fareed didn't mention." She regarded the two men gravely. "They may want this planet returned to its pristine condition for their own use. At one time they liked it here, and after all, they *did* allow us to be wiped out once—all but Noah's family."

"I wonder," said the admiral. "When was the most recent time that Anu visited Earth?"

"I know what Azeri said about it," said David.

The admiral nodded encouragement.

"Sorry to answer a question with a question," said David, "but what is the current year of the Jewish calendar?"

Catharine said, "5794."

When both the admiral and David regarded her with wonderment, she blushed and said, "I'm half Jewish."

The admiral was evidently as surprised as David.

"Go figure!" shrugged the admiral, in his best impersonation of a New York Jew, which was more accurate (and much less offensive) than others David had seen. He returned his attention to David. "Why's the Jewish year important for our purposes?"

"Because," said David, "the Hebrew calendar—to this very day—has remained the *Sumerian* calendar. In honor of the great King Anu, the Sumerians designated the day of his state visit as Day One."

The admiral was incredulous. "You mean to say Anu's latest visit was nearly fifty-eight hundred years ago?"

David nodded, his eyebrows raised.

"Well, I'll be," said the admiral. "And Anu would have come roughly at the time of Nibiru's *closest point of approach,* as we'd say in the navy. Correct?"

David could see where the admiral was heading with this logic, but there was a fallacy in his thinking. "Maybe," said David, "but he's more likely to have come slightly *ahead* of Nibiru's closest point of approach," said David. "If he came to Earth at *precisely* the closest point of approach, he would have been under pressure to limit his stay, because, if he tarried here too long, he'd be left playing catchup with his home planet."

Catharine picked up on David's thinking. "But, if Anu arrived on Earth *prior* to Nibiru's closest point of approach, he could stay a while and then return to Nibiru at the closest point of approach." She picked up a pencil and started to write some figures on a scratch pad. "On the other hand," she said as she continued writing, "David, you said Anu stayed for only a few days."

The admiral smiled. "True. So he probably came only slightly before closest point of approach. That would give him an excuse, if he needed one, to go home sooner." He turned curiously to Catharine. "What are you adding up there?"

Catharine took a moment to finish her calculation before replying. "If you'll follow my reasoning here: First, we need to use a single reckoning. Just for the sake of convenience, let's use the Gregorian Calendar we use every day. To calculate the year of Anu's arrival on *our* calendar, we have to take the present Jewish year of 5794 and subtract the number of years since the birth of Jesus, conveniently provided by our present year of 2034. That means that Anu was last on Earth in 3760 B.C. If Nibiru shows up every 3,600 years or so, then Nibiru would have appeared again about 3,600 years from Anu's visit, which would be approximately the Year 160 B.C. After that appearance, the *next* time Nibiru would appear would be 3,600 years later, which would be the Year 3440 A.D." She put the pencil behind her ear, folded her arms, and looked up at the admiral.

"They're 1,400 years early," said the admiral. "Nibiru is on its *way* here, but nowhere near its point of closest approach. What do we learn from *that?*"

Catharine removed the pencil from behind her ear, brushed back a stray blonde lock of hair, began doodling absentmindedly on the pad, and said, "It could mean they've improved the technology they use to travel over extremely long distances." She pursed her lips and shrugged. "No surprise there. They probably improve their technology all the time, same as we do."

David scowled. "Azeri conjectured, however, that Nibiru actually arrived nearly five hundred years early on its latest pass, because all the Anunnaki appear to have quietly departed Earth in about 650 B.C., which was probably Nibiru's closest point of approach."

Catharine looked up from her figures. "Even if we correct for that five-hundred year difference by timing Nibiru's previous closest point of approach at 650 B.C., if they were to show up today, they'd still be about 900 years early."

The admiral shook his head. "Not exactly. If Azeri was right, and Nibiru's periodicity had been abbreviated by about 500 years by the time of its latest approach then, presumably, its *next* orbit would have been of the same abbreviated length. So, we'd have to subtract that 500 years from the time of its *next* approach, which would make an arrival today only about *400* years early. And that's assuming Nibiru's orbital period hasn't been *further* abbreviated. David, what might have abbreviated Nibiru's orbital period? I thought those things were pretty much unalterable."

David shrugged. "Yes, *but*—Nibiru is not native to our solar system. As the Sumerians would say, Nibiru is an *invader*, having been captured into solar orbit by the gravitational pull of the gas giants, Jupiter, Saturn, and so on. Because Nibiru is a johnny-come-lately to our solar system, its orbit is unlike those of the other planets in important ways. First, Nibiru revolves around the sun in a *retrograde* direction, that is to say, the direction *opposite* that of the other planets. Second, although the home-grown planets all revolve on a single plane (known as the *ecliptic*), Nibiru revolves on an off-kilter plane, approaching the sun from south of the sun's (and Earth's) equator.

"Those peculiarities in Nibiru's orbit *multiply* the likelihood that Nibiru's orbit will be significantly modified by another planet's gravity. It also multiplies the possibility that Nibiru will collide with another planet, which supposedly happened in the primordial past." He looked at Catharine, who'd begun drawing what looked like classic science-fiction aliens, with round heads and giant round eyes. He looked to the admiral. "Even with all those calculations and adjustments, it appears that the Anunnaki are planning a lengthy—possibly indefinite—stay on Earth."

The admiral nodded and yawned. "You two should head to the hotel. I'm going to rest a few hours on one of the bunks here at headquarters. I've left instructions at CIA and Department of State to locate David's friend Shawn. If they can't find him, I'll have them report twice daily on their search."

"Admiral," said David. "I know I'm not cleared for this but, if the Anunnaki have … hostile intentions, do we have any way to resist them other than … the unthinkable?"

The admiral smirked. "You'll be cleared to know soon, and you'll have to sign some documents. Meanwhile, I'll be trying to find out what capabilities we have against them."

"You don't know?" asked David.

The admiral shrugged. "I didn't know that I'd *need* to."

⟶∘〰∘⟵

DAVID AND CATHARINE shared a cab to their first-class hotel. As they arrived, morning was breaking in the east, lighting up the sky with many colors. Fortunately, traffic was still sparse and the street quiet.

"Stick with me," said Catharine as they entered the lobby. "I'll check us both into the suite."

David raised an eyebrow. "You and I are sharing a suite?"

She snickered. "Keep your shirt on, buster. You and I *are* sharing a suite … *with the admiral*." She regarded him skeptically. "No names."

"*What?*" he asked, befuddled.

"We're registered in the name of Uncle Sam. We don't register under individual names, real or otherwise. You and the admiral are *monsieur*. I'm *mademoiselle. Et c'est tout!*" She walked off to the concierge's office, leaving him in the beautifully appointed lobby with his pick of chairs.

David chose an upholstered beauty by the fireplace just outside the concierge's office and drowsily watched the day brighten while over-hearing Catharine's conversation. Though David was reasonably proficient in French, he was amazed at Catharine's fluency—and her *savoir faire*. In a comic role reversal, she ushered the concierge through the check-in process in what seemed no more than a minute, and returned to the lobby alone.

She said with a tired smile, "Our bags … pardon … *my* bags have already been brought up to the suite." She began walking down the hall, and he followed her to the elevator in silence. They got in, and the doors closed. She fished a business card out of her pocket and handed it to him. "You have an appointment at *Petit et Fils* clothiers at two in the afternoon," she said, "which is, sad to say, eight hours from now. They're around the block. If you haven't changed the time on your watch, you should do so before lying down … and set your alarm for noon."

When the elevator door opened, there were three ways one could go. Without so much as looking at the signs, Catharine confidently turned right.

He smirked. "Evidently, you've been here before, *mademoiselle*."

She smiled. "A few times, *monsieur*. There's been a hotel on this site owned by the same family for more than two hundred years. The admiral likes the place because it's old-line. I like it because it's famous for not disturbing guests, especially if they're signed in as Uncle Sam." She used her mobile phone as a key and noticed him looking at her inquiringly. She pointed reassuringly at the breast pocket where he might be expected to keep his phone. "I've sent you a digital key by text message. It's one of those tic-tac-toe designs. The doors to the individual rooms don't have keys, but they can be deadbolted from the inside."

"I'm sure Agent Duffy will make good use of your text message."

"Pardon me?" she said wearily.

"He still has my phone," said David, just as wearily. "Remember?"

She nodded, remembering, pulled a keycard out of her purse, and handed it to him. "Use this for now," she said.

The suite consisted of a small common area and three private rooms. Catharine shut the suite door behind them and claimed the center room for herself. Before entering it, she turned around and pointed toward the room to David's right. "That's yours," she said and gave him a wry smile. "Are you going to invite me in for a glass of wine?"

He recognized the invitation as being a little too coy and less than sincere. *She's attempting to find out what kind of man I am.* He smirked. "That depends. Would you find it insulting for a gentleman to begin snoring while still opening the bottle?" He arched an eyebrow and cast her an oily grin. "Yes," he joked, "I'm *that* kind of suave."

She laughed. "You *snore?*"

"Only when I'm this tired."

"Is it bad?"

"Let's just say … you may want to change hotels."

She giggled, and turned toward the door to her room. Just before entering, she turned back and winked saucily. "Maybe sometime when you're not so tired," she said and shut her door.

He plodded to his room and barely hung up his coat, suit, and tie before flopping on the bed asleep.

AS ORDINARILY HAPPENED when David was overtired, his first dreams were uneventful and unmemorable.

But then his mind became troubled by what seemed an intrusive resumption of the dream he'd been having on the plane to Andrews. Except that now it was set in the bedroom he'd shared with Sharon.

Sharon smiled at him and rose from her chair. It was good to see her moving about so easily—with no mask affixed to her mouth, no equipment hanging from her arm, no intravenous pack suspended from a pole being wheeled beside her.

Instead, she wore a black sheer nightgown that showed the prominent swell of her breasts. And she was brazenly enjoying his gaze, which was a little disturbing because she'd never done that in life. Not that she hadn't loved being admired; no one's exempt from that vanity. But now she jiggled her breasts ever so playfully and snickered smugly at his rapt enjoyment.

She took a step backward, slowly and seductively pushing each strap off her shoulders, and her nightgown fell to the floor, exposing the irresistible curves of her body.

But something was wrong. Her breasts were larger than they'd been in life. He looked up at her face, which was … perfect … so perfect. He ached to kiss those voluptuous lips. They were swollen, far more than he remembered them, and her lipstick was a darker shade than he remembered her wearing. She leaned forward to kiss him, but before she could reach him, it occurred to him that this … might *not* be Sharon.

A jolt shot through his body as though he were strapped to an electric chair, and he woke in a sweat. It took him a moment to realize that he'd been awakened by the overloud ringing of his room phone.

For some reason, he expected it might be Shawn calling, and he instinctively reached for it.

"Hello?" he said, still quite groggy.

"*Monsieur?*" said a male voice in a perfect Parisian accent, reminding him where he was. It was assuredly not Shawn.

Oh, that's right, he thought. *I'm "monsieur." They don't use our names here.*

"Yes?" he said. The clock on the wall said it was ten o'clock in the morning. He'd been asleep only five or six hours. So much for the hotel's reputation for not disturbing guests. "What is it?"

The voice seemed a bit hesitant. "Ah, *monsieur.* You are not quite awake. I apologize. Please, if you will go back to sleep."

"No, that's … quite alright," said David, moistening his lips and trying to sound rested. "Why did you ring?"

"It's Doctor Zia, *monsieur*," said the voice. "The good doctor has requested the pleasure of your company in a half-hour in a private dining room here on the street level, if that is convenient for you."

"Doctor *Zia?*" asked David. "Who's that?"

"Ah. He is a fine older gentleman, *monsieur*. Doctor Zia's family members have stayed with us when they come to Paris for the greater part of … oh, *deux siècles* … two centuries. He assured me that he has business with you. He said that you are a law professor from New York." When David said nothing, the voice on the phone hesitated. "Perhaps not, *monsieur*. Perhaps it is, as they say, a mistaken identity. Shall I decline on your behalf?"

"No," said David. "Just because I don't remember him doesn't mean I've never met him. To whom am I speaking just now?"

"*Moi, monsieur?* I am Jacques de la Fontaine, sir. I am the fellow who spoke with the lady you arrived with early this morning."

"It's your family that owns this fine hotel?" asked David.

"*Mais oui, monsieur*," came the proud reply. "I am at your service."

"Do you know this … Doctor …?" The name escaped him.

"Zia, *monsieur*," said Jacques. "Yes, I know him. My father knew *his* father. My grandfather knew *his* grandfather, and so on. I believe he works in the field of … finance, if I say that right, *monsieur*. I don't know much about his travels, but he is … how do you say? … a *fixture* at our hotel. A very pleasant and learned dining companion. Of this you may be certain."

"You vouch for his good faith?" asked David.

"*Absolument!*" said Jacques. "Without a moment hesitation, *monsieur*."

"Then please accept his invitation on my behalf. I'll—"

"There is just one more thing, monsieur," interrupted Jacques. "Doctor Zia has asked that you tell no one that you meet with him. Is this satisfactory?"

David was considering changing his mind. Who was this old fellow to forbid him from telling his companions whom he's meeting? But something deep inside told him he should meet this Doctor Zia. *For heaven's sake,* he told himself, *you're an adult. Act like one.*

"It's quite satisfactory, Jacques," said David. "Thank you for waking me."

Before hopping into the shower, David called Jacques and asked him to send to *Petit et Fils* right away for a new set of underwear, socks, and a shirt of the proper dimensions.

"Yes, monsieur. Shall I charge it to Uncle Sam?"

Charge it to Uncle Sam?

"That's a terrific idea," David said, and hung up.

He could get used to this treatment. Though he'd been sorely tempted to double the order, he recalled that he'd be at the clothier in person shortly.

After a quick shave and shower, there was a knock at the suite door. David answered it in a hotel bathrobe he'd found in his closet. There was no sign of Catharine, so she was either already gone or still asleep in her room.

The bellboy handed David the bagful of fine clothing and David signed for a good tip. He dressed quickly and checked the mirror. After one minor adjustment to the back of his collar, he was surprised to find himself quite presentable. He grabbed his wallet and keys and went down to the lobby. As he left, he realized that, despite all his rushing around, he was a quarter-hour late.

As soon as David stepped off the elevator, Jacques appeared and escorted his guest to a private dining room.

"I expect that Doctor Zia may be short of time," said Jacques, "but it will be well for you to meet him." He swung open a set of double doors with a dramatic flourish and a bow. "Doctor Zia," Jacques said deferentially, "I believe you are expecting this gentleman." He cordially waved David into the room and discreetly closed the doors as he backed out.

Despite David's curiosity about the man he'd come to meet, his first impression was of the dining room itself. Though nearly vacant, it was at least twenty times the size of his bedroom and could have housed several banquet tables. Instead, nestled into one corner was a single square table, perhaps twice the length and width of a common card table, which only made the room seem more capacious. A tasteful vase holding an array of fresh-cut flowers served as the table's centerpiece.

At the table's far end, facing the door, sat a gentleman whom David took to be a fit eighty-year-old—thin, well proportioned, and two or three inches taller than David. The man's haircut was a bit old-fashioned. His hair and beard (both of which were well-groomed and distinguished-looking) were neatly brushed and, remarkably, still boasted a bit of the original blond. His eyes were powder blue, lending him a kind of radiance. His face, fair and smooth, appeared to be well tended, though

David thought he could detect the weathered skin of a Scandinavian who'd spent much of his youth outdoors, perhaps under difficult circumstances. His left temple bore the long, faint scar of an ancient wound.

Without any sign of stiffness, the gentleman rose and invited David to take the seat perpendicular to his own.

"Sorry I'm late," said David.

"Not at all, not at all," said Doctor Zia, "although I regret that I am now even shorter on time. I see you've noticed my scar." When David was about to deny noticing any such thing, Zia said, "Oh, tush. It's nothing, Professor Schubert. This scar is from a wound suffered long ago, and what little discomfiture it causes me at this late date is purely social. But the truth is, as it's not too disfiguring, it gives me something to brag to the ladies about." There was something vaguely Middle Eastern in the accent, though, like Fareed's English, the good doctor's was well-schooled and technically perfect.

David smirked knowingly. "If you don't mind, Doctor Zia, may I ask how you suffered that wound?"

Zia responded rotely, as though he'd answered the question too many times to give it any novel thought. "Once, long ago, I was in a boat that capsized."

"Rough waters?" asked David.

Zia laughed softly. "Yes, *uniquely* so."

"As I now know you came through such hazard," said David sympathetically, "I feel even more fortunate to have the opportunity to meet you."

"Well," said Doctor Zia, waving away the injury, "the vessel righted itself almost immediately. I was the only unfortunate to suffer any real injury on that occasion. Though we remained afloat for a long time after the incident, fortunately my wife, may she rest in peace, tended me day and night until the danger passed."

"Oh, I'm sorry to hear of her passing," said David. "Was it recent?"

Zia's countenance became very faraway, and he paused a long time with no sign of self-consciousness.

David took the opportunity to size up his companion's appearance. Doctor Zia's suit was obviously handmade of the finest quality, and showed not the least sign of wear, yet it seemed ... *old*, somehow; it was unstylishly dark and unusually heavy, bringing to David's mind the clothes he helped his parents remove from his grandfather's closet a few days after his passing. David's father had explained that, when his grandfather had bought those clothes, buildings (and even homes) were badly underheated, as fuel was expensive and in short supply.

Finally, Doctor Zia returned to the present with a soft expression. "My wife passed long ago, Professor Schubert, and very far from here. But it's still kind of you to ask."

David bowed his head respectfully. "I'm sure she was quite a special woman."

This remark cheered the old man. "If only you knew the half of it. Tell me, professor, what do you think of this business of the mosque disappearing from the Temple Mount? It's all anyone's talking about."

David sighed. "Well, being a Hebrew myself, given that the mosque has reappeared in perfect condition at a Muslim holy site, I can't honestly pretend that it troubles me that it's been moved. I certainly hope it doesn't start a *war*, however. That's the last thing the world needs right now."

"I see we have much in common," said Zia thoughtfully. "The avoidance of war is a goal of mine, as well. Perhaps you and I may have the opportunity to work together to that end." Before David could reply, there was a knock at the door and Jacques thrust his head in.

"Doctor Zia," said Jacques, "the … event you wished to see is about to commence." He pointed to a large-screen television suspended by a brace bolted to the ceiling. "Allow me to turn the power on for you."

Doctor Zia looked to David apologetically. "I'm sorry for the interruption, professor," he said, "but I've been waiting for some time to see this and I may not have another chance to see a television today."

Jacques carried a remote control into the room, powered up the television, changed the channel to an American news station, and turned the sound up just enough to be heard. He bowed to Zia curtly and placed the remote control on the table at the doctor's right hand. David turned his chair to watch along with Zia.

A waiter appeared at the door, and Jacques waved him in and left. While Zia and David watched the television screen, the waiter set about serving a modest, but tasty, breakfast of oatmeal porridge and fresh fruit, in which the two indulged without delay.

The newsreader looked concerned as he spoke. "The video appearing on your screen right now was taken about eight hours ago by a U.S. Government-operated telescope in geosynchronous orbit several miles above the Earth."

The screen showed a black sky with a few points of light, but nothing seemed to move—or even change. After a few dull seconds, the announcer said in a subdued voice, "The telescope is set on a moderate resolution. It's aimed in the general direction of the planet Mars or, more specifically, one of the moons of Mars, known as *Phobos*. In about ten seconds, the spacecraft—or whatever they are—will enter your field of view from the upper-left corner of your screen."

As promised, six green dots in close formation came into view and grew slowly larger. After about thirty seconds' silence, when it became clear that these were identical spacecraft of some kind, the announcer said, "At this early phase, the consensus of the space community is that the appearance of these craft may somehow be related to the recent loss of contact with a Russian probe that had been approaching Phobos. The Russian probe is still failing to respond and is feared lost. Fortunately, there were no cosmonauts aboard."

David caught Zia looking curiously at him.

Zia shrugged. "Who ever would have thought we would live to see such things? Beings from another world." He sighed.

"Indeed," said David as he munched on a brioche, "so many strange things happening nowadays. 'People from another world'? A strange appellation. Shouldn't we at least have a name for the creatures in those spacecraft?"

Doctor Zia shrugged. "What might *you* call them?"

David watched Zia's face for his response. "I don't know," said David. "Perhaps … *Igigi?*"

Zia's eyes flashed in recognition, and he nodded to David with new-found respect, as David evidently knew that the *Igigi* were lesser Anunnaki who long ago maintained a base on Mars and spent much of their time orbiting Earth, keeping an eye on terrestrial activity and reporting to the Anunnaki on Earth by radio and other electronic means.

More importantly, now David knew that *Doctor Zia* knew. He wondered: *Is Zia just a curious fellow like me who happens to be fascinated by ancient-alien theories? Or does he have some connection with the Anunnaki? How did he learn that this news was about to be reported? Did he hear a teaser on the news? Or did he have his own inside sources? And who the devil is this old guy?*

"Pardon me, Doctor Zia," said David. "I don't believe you've mentioned how you and I met before, and I confess to having no such recollection."

At that moment, Zia's cell phone began to buzz. He looked at the screen with chagrin. "I'm afraid I'm going to have to take this call, professor, and then leave immediately. You and I have never met before.

I know of you by reputation alone. Incidentally, I am of the Hebrew line, as well … in a way … and I expect you and I are blood relatives. We may be able to assist each other." Zia answered the phone with a subdued *hello* and began listening intently to the caller.

David glanced at a wall clock, and was surprised to see he had only minutes to get to the clothier. Though he had a thousand questions for Doctor Zia, he could see by the old fellow's level of concentration on his call that he wouldn't have a chance to pose them now, let alone get satisfactory answers.

He rose and silently bowed his thanks to Doctor Zia.

Seeing that David was leaving, Doctor Zia held up one finger to delay his departure a moment, deftly reached into his breast pocket, and handed David a beautifully engraved business card identifying the bearer as *A.H. Zia, M.D., Ph.D.* There was a mobile phone number but no address. In the top right-hand corner was a finely rendered golden Mercury's staff, known as a *caduceus:* two snakes wrapped around a winged rod. Though David knew of the universal mistake by which the caduceus was believed to be the ancient symbol of medicine, he assumed the old man knew that and was simply following convention.

David made a show of accepting the card as something of great value, smiled at the old man, and left.

CHAPTER 5

IN THE WELL-APPOINTED fitting room of *Petit et Fils*, David stood for a complete fitting such as he'd never experienced before, having till now bought all his suits off the rack. His every dimension was measured— even a few that seemed to have no possible relation to the cut of his clothes.

Suspended from the ceiling in a corner of the room was a wide-screen television fixed on a Parisian news channel. Though the sound was turned all the way down, the expression on the faces of the news readers and the occasional cutaway to prerecorded video clearly showed that the world at large remained preoccupied with the usual fare: fires, murders, and pompous pronouncements from leaders of government and industry—no wall-to-wall coverage of disappearing mosques or Roman temples, no creatures from space, no video streamed from U.S. satellite telescopes. David found it amazing that cable news had evidently moved on from such things in the mere hour since he left the hotel. So much for the modern attention span.

An older fellow with a tailor's tape deftly measured the number of centimeters on David's person from one point to another, pronouncing each number aloud, while a younger fellow, holding a pad whose every page bore the outline of a man, repeated the number and neatly recorded it at the appropriate place on the outline.

The older fellow finished with a smile, draping his tape measure about his neck, the ends dangling over the front of his open vest. "Would *monsieur* wish to choose his favored cloth?" he asked.

"Thank you, *Monsieur* Petit," replied David. "That *would* be the logical next step." He quickly donned the clothing he'd worn into the shop.

Petit snapped his fingers, and the young fellow, apparently the *fils* of the company name, smartly gathered up four bolts of woolen cloth and carried them out to the shop's public room. The shop phone rang and the younger man went to answer it. Petit lay the bolts out before David, turned up the display lights, and invited him to feel the weight and hand of each cloth.

The son hung up the phone, hesitantly approached his father, and whispered something too softly for David to hear.

Petit nodded discreetly and turned to David. "Is *monsieur* meeting someone here at the shop this afternoon, perhaps?"

David smiled and said, "Yes, in fact."

Petit looked up at David with a serious expression. "Please look at my face, *monsieur*. If you would discreetly glance over my shoulder and tell me, perhaps, if you know those two gentlemen standing on the sidewalk? My son tells me they have been outside for some time and have taken an interest in observing *monsieur*."

Petit was evidently accustomed to working for people who checked into the local hotel as *Uncle Sam*, and took their business seriously.

The two men outside were young and thin with dark curly hair. They sported identical squarish beards that seemed to hearken back to the 1870s, and looked vaguely Middle Eastern. They wore identical, nondescript warmup suits.

David said discreetly, "I've never seen them before."

"*Ach*," said Petit. "So, I expect *monsieur* is meeting *madame*? The pretty blonde lady?"

David nodded hesitantly, as the clothier's use of *madame* in place of *mademoiselle* seemed to imply that he believed Catharine to be David's wife.

"Very well," said Petit, then turned and told his son in French to call *madame* and tell her to enter the shop through the rear. He turned back to David. "Perhaps *monsieur* has time to choose the cloth?"

David felt the four cloths, each so far superior to anything he'd ever worn that he hadn't the slightest notion which to choose. Though every fabric was either blue or grey, each differed subtly from the others in undefinable ways.

David smiled. "*Monsieur* Petit?"

Petit wagged his finger and clucked in characteristic Gallic manner. "Please, *monsieur*, I call myself Alphonse. Please that you would do the same."

David feigned confusion. "You want me to call myself Alphonse?"

It took a moment for Petit to catch on, but when he did, he laughed aloud and patted David on the shoulder. "*Pardonnez-moi, monsieur*. My English is not so good."

"Well," conceded David, "it's better than my French." He looked at the bolts. "You have far greater knowledge of your trade than I, Alphonse. Was it you who selected these fabrics?"

"*Mais, bien sûr!*" Petit assured him staunchly.

"Then make me a suit of each cloth and, while you're at it, choose an appropriate shirt, necktie, shoes, and accessories for each. As for the accessories: Please choose nothing so expensive that my uncle will be upset with me."

"Excellent, *monsieur*," said Petit with deep admiration, as though unaccustomed to being given *carte blanche* by any but his most impressive clients. "They will be ready for a fitting tomorrow morning."

Petit's son appeared from the back of the shop, caught his father's eye, and nodded curtly.

Petit turned to David. "Perhaps *monsieur* would accompany my son to the rear of the store, where *votre femme* awaits."

There it was again, Catharine being characterized as David's wife.

The young man escorted David to a small antechamber where Catharine sat, wearing a form-fitting skirted suit. She beamed at him and stood up. Not for the first time he remarked to himself how very attractive she was.

While the young fellow was turning to go, Catharine approached David and said, "Oh, darling! How I've missed you!" And before David could reply, she kissed him on the lips.

To David's own amazement, he closed his eyes, took her in his arms, and kissed her with more passion than he'd thought was left in him.

The young man discreetly turned about and shut the door behind him with a click.

In mid-smooch, David opened his eyes to find that Catharine's were open as well, regarding him with a mix of emotions, a bit of pleasure, some level of surprise—and just a touch of horror, as though she'd unleashed an animal of unknown ferocity, in response to which he released her from his embrace.

She drew away slowly, and assiduously avoided eye contact while pretending to adjust her clothing. "I spotted those two goons outside," she explained, "and called to ask Petit to let me in through the back door, but—in keeping with their custom—they won't do that for any but a member of the customer's family. Hence, our *marriage*."

"And now what?" asked David indignantly. "We're divorced?" Without awaiting an answer, he said, "Well, Kate, it was fun while it lasted. And—never you worry—I'll see to it you'll never want."

"I haven't decided about the divorce," she said wryly, "so watch yourself."

He loved the playfulness in her eyes.

"How do you know they're goons?" he asked.

"*What?*" she asked.

"Those two bearded guys out front. How do you know they're goons?"

"Well," she said, "it's a habit of mine to assume the worst about people who steal from me."

David was alarmed. "Have they hurt you? Are you okay?"

"I'm fine," she shrugged. "They didn't rob me, but one of them *is* carrying my laptop from the plane." When David didn't understand right away, she reminded him. "The one that disappeared when that ray gun zapped through the cabin."

"Are you sure he has *your* laptop?" he asked skeptically.

Catharine put her hands on her hips and glowered at him.

"Well," he said apologetically, "laptops *do* look alike from a distance."

She dug through her little handheld purse and pulled out an unused sticker about the size of a postage stamp showing an American flag waving in the breeze under an azure sky. "You see this?"

He nodded.

"This sticker is issued by the U.S. Navy," she said. "Naval personnel can put it on their laptops anywhere they want. Everybody puts it in the center of the lid. I'm the only one who doesn't. I use it to block a port that hasn't been in common use since the early days of laptops."

"Why?"

"So I can tell at a glance that it's *mine*," she said indignantly and tossed his own words back at him. "Laptops *do* look alike from a distance, y'know."

"And the guy outside has a laptop identical to yours—with the sticker blocking the same port?"

She smiled condescendingly.

"That's pretty persuasive," he admitted, "but still—"

Catharine turned on her heel and took a step toward the door.

"*Hold it!*" he said. "Where are you going?"

"I'm going to ask that goon where he got the computer," she said.

"And what if he … takes you hostage?" demanded David.

Catharine reached under her jacket and drew out a nine-millimeter Glock 46. "I don't think that'll happen," she said, returning it to the holster.

"But what if it does?" David asked. "What'll I tell the admiral?"

"Oh, so now *you're* answering to the admiral?" Her hands returned to her hips. "You seem to forget who's navy here, and who's not."

"I'm sorry, dahling," he said, lowering his eyes bashfully, "but ever since the wedding I've felt"—he looked at her doe-eyed—"*ever* so protective of you."

Catharine regarded him skeptically, but before she could reply, there was a clandestine knock on the other side of the exterior door, and her eyes went wide. She removed the gun from its holster and offered it by the handle to David.

His eyebrows shot up. "If you intend to hand me that, your next words had better be 'hide this,' because I wouldn't know what else to do with it."

She took back the gun impatiently. "Here," she said, shoving her purse at him. "Maybe you'll do better with this."

"Really?" he said skeptically, taking the bag in a huff. "*That* purse with *this* suit?"

Catharine rolled her eyes and went to the back door. Avoiding the bar that would trip the automatic alarm, she pushed open the door. Though there was a fair amount of shouting going on across the street, the man just outside, by appearance an Orthodox Jew, was quiet and alone.

"Won't you come in for a chat?" she said, pulling him inside by his lapel and brandishing the Glock.

The man's eyes were frozen on the gun. "You won't need that," he nervously replied. "I'm a friend." His accent was strictly North London.

Catharine let the door shut behind him. "What's your name?" she asked.

"Yakov," he replied.

"Who sent you?" she demanded.

Yakov looked to David. "Doctor Zia," he said.

"*Who?*" Catharine demanded, wagging her gun.

So much for Doctor Zia's request that David refrain from telling anyone they'd met. "It's all right, Catharine," David assured her, "I met Doctor Zia this morning at the hotel. A nice old fellow. He introduced himself, and we shared some breakfast."

"Well, when the devil were you planning on telling *me?*" she demanded.

"When *could* I have told you?" David huffed. "You just got here! I know very little about him," he admitted, and addressed the orthodox fellow. "What did Doctor Zia tell you to do?"

"First, who are *you?*" the fellow asked David.

"I'm Professor David Schubert."

Yakov regarded him a bit suspiciously and said, "The doctor told us to chase away those two galoots in warmup suits."

"Have you managed that?" asked Catharine.

The fellow nodded. "My blokes were already in the process of doin' that. You might 'ave 'eard the shouting."

"Thank you for that," said David. "Is that all?"

"No," said Yakov, pointing his chin at David. "He told me to tell *you* two things."

"And those are?" asked David.

"First, stay away from those galoots out front."

"Done, thanks to you," said David. "What else?" The fellow glanced nervously at Catharine and her handgun, and looked pleadingly back to David, who took pity on him. "Did he want you to tell me something *privately?*" asked David.

Yakov nodded.

Catharine stamped her foot, and the fellow's eyes went wide.

David scowled at her and reassured Yakov. "The lady is entirely trustworthy, I assure you. You can tell us both."

Yakov pressed his back against the door and looked at David. "Doctor Zia said, 'Don't make love to her.'" The poor fellow cringed as though expecting Catharine to blow his head off.

David, who had no gun trained on him, could afford to be more level-headed. "Don't make love to *whom?*" he asked. He pointed to Catharine. "To *her?*"

The cowering fellow looked as though surprised by the question. "He just said *the girl of your dreams.*"

"All right," said David. "Peggy Sue from Garfield High is safe for now. You've delivered your message. Now, how are you going to get us out of here?"

"If you come with me through this door, there are some blokes outside who'll 'elp me escort you to the American Embassy so you won't be seen by those galoots."

David turned to Catharine. "See, Ms. Smartypants? They're not goons; they're *galoots.* Now, as I see no path forward other than to follow this fellow and his friends, I suggest we take him up on his offer."

Catharine wasn't quite convinced. She gave the fellow a dirty look, and thrust the point of her handgun at him. "How do you know this

Yakov guy's not one of the *goons?*"

Yakov glowered back at Catharine, evidently more confident now that he'd persuaded David of his good faith. "*Galoots,*" he uttered defiantly.

David broke the tense silence. "Oh, come on, dear," said David. "Just look at him. His beard's not square. He's an Orthodox Jew who doesn't pray to any god but Yahweh." He pointed to the man's gabardine. "And he wouldn't be caught dead in a warmup suit."

She gave it a moment's thought and said to the fellow, "All right, let's go. But the first sign of anything unexpected and you're history."

⊸∘⋙∘⊷

THE FIRST HALF of their escorted trip to the embassy was uneventful. Catharine and David walked on the inner half of the sidewalk while a half-dozen burly (but not particularly athletic-looking) men walked between them and all other traffic.

As they walked through a well-heeled district of three- and four-story commercial buildings, it occurred to David that, although all the men wore skull caps, they seemed of quite different kinds.

David beckoned Yakov with a crooked finger as they continued their brisk walk.

"Yes, David?" said Yakov, his eyes darting about cautiously.

"Are all these men … like you?" asked David.

This got Catharine's attention and garnered a look of confusion from Yakov.

"How do you mean?" Yakov asked.

"Are they all … Orthodox *Jews?*"

Yakov laughed to himself. "All except Ibrahim and Suleiman."

David's eyebrow's shot up. "They're"—his voice dropped to a whisper—"*Muslims?*"

Yakov smiled and whispered his reply. "Yes, and—what's more—you don't have to whisper. They *know* they're Muslims."

"But this is Paris," said David. "And the mosque has disappeared."

Yakov regarded him skeptically.

"You're supposed to be at each other's throats," said David.

"Ibrahim!" said Yakov aloud. "Apparently, we're supposed to be at each other's throats!"

A short fellow up ahead in a small, colorfully woven skullcap turned back. "Not while we have a common enemy. Come back tomorrow," he said with a laugh, "when we get your friends to where they're—"

Suddenly, the air above them was filled with a low hum so loud it hurt David's ears. Ibrahim ran off into the street.

Yakov glanced up quickly, and shoved David and Catharine into the recessed entryway of a jewelry store surrounded by display windows.

"Stay here!" Yakov shouted over the din. "Don't come out! They're looking for you!" He pointed wildly at the ceiling. "They can't see you under here!"

David and Catharine exchanged a shocked glance and watched events from the shelter of the recessed doorway.

Ibrahim and Yakov drew repeating firearms from under their coats, took careful aim at something in the sky, and began firing in short bursts.

Though David could hear the impact of some of the bullets above, he couldn't see their target.

"Go for the glass!" shouted Yakov.

David turned to Catharine. "Do you have a compact?"

"A *what?*" she asked. "Oh, a mirror?" She opened the little purse and pulled out a makeup kit.

David was about to grab it when Catharine realized what he was about to do with it. "Wait!" she shouted, pulling off her belt. She deftly wrapped it around a slot in the open compact case. "This will give you safer distance," she said, handing the assembled device to him.

While firing continued in the street, David knelt down and thrust the compact out onto the uncovered sidewalk. He jiggered it about until it gave him the view he was seeking.

Just above the store was a cigar-shaped aircraft identical to those that had flanked the admiral's jet over the Atlantic Ocean. It was slender enough to fit between the buildings on opposite sides of the street, so that it *could* land on the street if that was the intention—except for the hail of bullets it was now enduring from a half-dozen tenacious Jews and Muslims.

David hadn't gazed at the reflection of the craft for more than a few seconds when a blinding light from above fried the compact, and the mirror shattered. David instinctively tossed it away and retreated into the jeweler's doorway.

"Thanks," he said returning to Catharine. "That little extension you gave me came in handy," he said, then added with chagrin, "I owe you a compact … and a belt."

Catharine brushed a few shards off David's hair. "Who's up above us?" she demanded. "Is it them?"

He nodded. "It's the admiral's fly-by buddies from over the Atlantic."

Suddenly, a new sound was added to the cacophony: the beating of helicopter blades.

"*Arrêtez!*" came a megaphoned voice. "Stop at once," it said in French that echoed off the street and surrounding buildings. "You must follow this helicopter to the nearest landing field."

Evidently perceiving no sign of cooperation, the voice on the megaphone said, "Please signal that you will follow us to the nearest airstrip," it said, "or we will have no choice but to open fire on you!"

Suddenly, the chopper blades began to decelerate and whine loudly. An alarm dinged above.

David looked at Catharine, eyes wide. "Did the bastards shoot at the chopper?"

Catharine looked around desperately. "Worse! Can't you hear it? They shut down its engine." Her face was filled with horror. "It's coming down!"

Instinctively, David turned his back to the street and pushed Catharine as far as he could into the deep doorway, shielding her with his body and bracing for the worst.

In a series of loud chunks, chopper blades smacked into the facade of a building across the street. The doorway was filled with the sound of falling bricks, and rotor blades slicing into blacktop before flying off the rotor mast and spraying gravel and shrapnel everywhere. A moment later the chopper hit the street, smacking hard into the asphalt.

The fuel tank exploded, prompting the jewelry windows around them to implode, with shards shooting through the air and landing in great heaps. A hell of alarms sounded.

It felt as though David's back had caught fire. Instinctively reaching his hand around to his back, he realized that he hadn't caught fire, and that the heat was radiating from the explosion in the middle of the street.

Catharine looked up at him, shaken.

Then *screaming* could be heard from the street. Not the screaming of women and children who'd witnessed something terrifying. It was much worse: the screaming of a grown man being crushed and roasted alive. David turned and saw that Ibrahim was pinned under one of the destroyed helicopter's landing skids. Copious fuel had sprayed all over him and his torso was aflame, quickly burning to a char.

He was dying an unbearable death.

"Hand me that pistol of yours, would you?" said David.

"No, you're untrained," said Catharine. "And what can you do besides put him out of his misery?" She hesitated. "That's not what you're planning on, is it?"

The screams were tearing David's insides out. "No," he said, "I'd like to take a shot at that flying cigar."

Just then Yakov ran into the doorway with his rifle hanging from his shoulder. He briskly brushed the glass off David and Catharine and shouted over the din of the alarms. "You have to go *right now!*" he commanded. "Go to the next corner, make a right and then the next right after that. Flash your official ID and run past the embassy gate. With any luck, the marine won't shoot you. You gotta get underground as fast as possible. The spaceship has gone away"—he looked up apprehensively—"but who knows for how long?"

"Did you shoot it down?" asked David eagerly.

Yakov sighed, crestfallen. "No. We didn't even slow it down. It just flew away, but there's no telling how soon it will be back, so get going!"

"What about Ibrahim?" asked Catharine, though she could see the man had stopped screaming—in fact, had stopped moving.

"He's wasted," said Yakov with tears in his eyes. "Don't you understand?" he shouted. "If you're caught, then he died for *nothing!* Go! Go at once, and don't look back."

Catharine removed her high heels, but seemed reluctant to move. Yakov, seeing that David and Catharine were shellshocked, positioned himself behind them and shoved them out of the doorway. "Go!" he yelled after them.

And they ran. They ran as fast as they could. And they didn't look back. They couldn't help looking *up* a few times, but there was no sign of the spaceship.

En route, Catharine managed to extricate her navy identification papers from her purse. Reaching the embassy, she waved the papers at the marine on duty, who took them and sniffed the air suspiciously, evidently detecting the stink of unspent helicopter fuel.

"Who *are* you two?" he demanded. "Were you in that explosion we just heard?"

"I'm Catharine Weldon, Lieutenant Commander, U.S. Navy. I'm Admiral Simmons's aide. This gentleman is Professor Schubert—"

"I'm Marine Sergeant Anthony Hellum," said the marine.

Catharine quickly shook his hand. "The admiral expects to see us both *immediately*, Sergeant Hellum."

"Call me Tony."

"The admiral's at CIA Paris headquarters, Tony."

The marine shook his head. "No, he's not," he said. "He's here. Or at least, very close to here. And you can only reach him through this embassy."

All this evidently seemed mysterious to Catharine, and she let her impatience show. "Look, we weren't just *at* that explosion; we were the *object* of the attack. I don't mean to pull rank, but we're being hunted right now by some very *powerful* … people, and we need to get below ground right away."

Hellum nodded gravely and picked up the phone. "Stevens, I have to escort two visitors to the tank," he said. "You stand this post. Anybody tries to get through without papers, put a hole in 'im." He turned to Catharine. "Right this way," he said, and swiftly escorted the two guests into the building and through a locker room leading to an unmarked, heavy steel door, which he opened with an old-fashioned metal key. He led them down a grey-painted staircase that, to all appearances, seemed a passage that a janitor might use to gain access to a slop sink or a fuse box—except that it went down quite a ways.

Seven stories, in fact.

CHAPTER 6

As David, Catharine, and Sergeant Hellum dismounted the stairs at the bottom level, Hellum unlocked another steel door and swung it open onto what looked like the terminus of the U.S. Capitol Subway System linking the Capitol to Senate office buildings. Except the Capitol Subway was located in Washington and always seemed crowded with Senate personnel—while this system was in Paris, and there was not another living soul to be seen. The lights had been austerely dimmed to save energy.

Hellum's footsteps echoed through the cavernous space as he locked the deadbolt on the stairway door behind them and turned to them with a grin. "All aboard the Walt Disney World Railroad. I'll be your engineer and conductor." When that got no reaction, he added, "I'll take you to the old man right away."

Catharine turned to him sharply. "Better not let the admiral hear you call him that," she said.

Hellum nodded smugly and motioned them to their seats in the vacant car. He followed them in, switched on the motor and lights, and steered the car clear of the terminus.

"Please pardon my informality, lieutenant commander," said the marine, "but the admiral *told* me to refer to him that way."

Catharine's eyebrows shot up. "Seriously?" she asked.

"Yes, ma'am," said the beaming marine. "He acknowledged it as a sign of—*what'd he call it?*—'familiar respect'—or 'respectful familiarity.' I forget which."

Catharine shrugged at David. "Live and learn," she said. "Sorry, marine. I don't seem to have much of a sense of humor this afternoon."

"Did you take casualties at that explosion?" asked the marine.

Catharine nodded grimly. "One dead."

"Well, that explains your mood," said Hellum empathetically.

"First time I set eyes on the fellow," said Catharine, "he's wearing Muslim gear and takes a big risk by helping us. Five minutes later, he's crushed by a fallen police chopper and burned alive when it explodes on impact."

The marine nodded silently. As the car whirred down the track. he waited a respectful moment before speaking. "Lieutenant commander," he said, "I've seen action myself. Lost some good people. My condolences. Damned shame." He looked at her curiously. "Those people who were after you, did they shoot down the chopper?"

Catharine shook her head. "Not exactly," she said.

"So … if you don't mind my asking, how did he get crushed by a falling chopper?"

Catharine looked to David, obviously unsure how much to reveal. Eventually, she replied, "They had some gizmo that shut down the engine." She turned to the marine. "But that's confidential, marine. Stays between us."

To break the solemnity, David remarked. "My God, this is the longest private subway I've ever seen. Are we still in Paris?"

"Yes, sir," replied Hellum, pointing to the upcoming station. "That's your destination. Let me pull this car off the main track, and I'll take you both right to the admiral."

When they stopped, Catharine and David left the subway car and were escorted by the marine through what seemed a maze of sealed doors, each of which opened with a keycard and was shut tight after they passed through.

Finally, Hellum stopped before a steel door and turned to them. "This is the last one before the admiral."

On their right was a Dutch door with its top half open, revealing a twenty-by-twenty-foot dimly lit room filled with all manner of electronics efficiently arranged, pilot lights aglow everywhere. If it were outdoors, it might have been called a radio shack. There were large and small computers, desktops and laptops, video recorders, what looked like several sizable transmitter/receivers. And a topless plastic milk crate containing a haphazard pile of mobile phones of various types.

A weary clerk appeared at the door wearing a button saying *HARRY* in block letters.

The marine turned to Catharine and David. "Lieutenant commander. Professor," he said with a respectful nod, "Harry here would like to know if either of you currently possesses a mobile phone or other electronic device that can record or transmit information."

Catharine reached into an inner pocket of her jacket and pulled out her mobile phone. Reluctantly, she handed it over. "Please clearly mark this as mine, Harry. I don't want to—"

The clerk smiled, accepted the phone, and handed her a half-ticket bearing a serial number. The other half of the ticket, bearing the same number, had a gummed side. The clerk stuck it to the back of the phone before placing it in the milk crate alongside numerous near-identical phones.

Catharine's shoulders fell and she sighed. Though such treatment might be the best she could expect, she still found it far from satisfactory.

"And you, sir?" said Harry the clerk.

"I have none," David replied.

Harry looked at him skeptically. "Pardon me, sir, but it's very unusual for a gentleman such as yourself to be without a mobile phone."

David turned to him. "If you'd like to know, Harry, my mobile phone was taken from me under false pretenses by an agent of the Federal Bureau of Investigation in New York. The agent's name is Duffy." He pointed to a wallphone in Harry's room. "Perhaps you might call him."

The clerk, mistakenly thinking he was being reproached, blurted out, "No, sir. That won't be necessary. I was just—"

"Not necessary for *you*," said David affably, "but it would be most helpful to *me,* Harry. You see, I've been without a phone for a couple of days now, and it's left me—"

Summarily interrupting David's plea for help, Sergeant Hellum opened the steel door with his keycard, grasped David firmly by the shoulder, and led him through.

"Well, *that* was rude," muttered David.

<hr>

THE ADMIRAL AWAITED them in a study so cozy it might have been relocated from his home. Everything about it shouted, "Chesapeake Bay." Yet, here it was in Paris, four thousand miles away, strategically placed at the end of a subterranean tunnel at least a mile long.

Behind the desk sat the admiral, his hands solemnly folded on the blotter. "Front desk told me you were coming a few minutes ago, so I checked the television to see what you two crazy kids might have been up to. Please tell me you didn't knock down that police chopper."

Catharine chose the visitors' chair next to David's and shook her head solemnly. "No, sir," she said. "We never fired a shot."

"Well, then, who did?"

David could see that Catharine was struggling with a way to begin, so he did it for her. "I was busy at the Petit clothiers, admiral, and Catharine saw a couple of unsavory characters skulking around on the sidewalk. One of them appeared to be carrying her laptop, the one that disappeared from the admiral's jet. Catharine came to the back door to fetch me, where an altercation had already broken out between the two bad guys and a united group of Orthodox Jews and Muslims. One of the Orthodox Jews knocked on the back door and offered to escort us to the U.S. Embassy. As they'd just chased away the bad guys, we didn't see much choice but to accept the escort."

The admiral nodded for him to continue.

David took a deep breath. "They brought us to within a few blocks of the embassy, when one of those *things* appeared above the building."

"*Things?*" asked the admiral impatiently.

"One of those *flying cigars*—like the ones that flanked the admiral's jet over the Atlantic. Those things remind me of the Confederate ironclad *Virginia*."

The admiral rubbed his brow and waited.

"Anyway," David continued, "our ... escorts evidently regarded the flying cigar as hostile. They shoved Catharine and me into the shelter of a jeweler's recessed entryway. Then they opened fire on the cigar. Evidently, the Paris police take a dislike to unscheduled intruders invading their airspace, 'cause they quickly dispatched a chopper with a megaphone to demand that the ... cigar follow them to a local landing strip. Instead of complying, the cigar evidently stalled the chopper's engine. Chopper came down hard. Landed on one of the men, name of *Ibrahim*."

"It stalled the chopper's engine?" said the admiral skeptically. "How did it manage *that?*"

David had always harbored what he thought of as an *inner wiseass*, with whom he often had to contend when speaking with those in authority. His inner wiseass was itching to step out of line just now. "They didn't show us how, admiral. If I had to guess, it was probably the same way they stalled the engines on your jet."

The admiral raised an eyebrow. "While I appreciate your working for me ... do you think I have time to deal with your wisecracks, son?"

Catharine seemed alarmed and sat up straight, keeping her eyes firmly affixed to the floor. Evidently, she'd rarely seen the old man irritated before.

David shifted uneasily in his chair. "Sorry, admiral. I just watched a man being crushed and burned to death. That's ... new to me." He loosened the knot of his tie. "I have no idea how they stalled the chopper's engine. And, meaning no disrespect, admiral, I don't work for you."

The admiral snapped his fingers. "Oh, that reminds me …" he said, sitting up as though David's remark had shaken loose some neglected item of business. He pressed a button on the intercom and spoke into it, never taking his eyes off David. "Harry, would you bring me that paper for Professor Schubert to sign?"

David frowned. "Admiral, I still have no idea why you'd need *me*. I expect you have a half-dozen specialists already reading Azeri's work—"

"More like a dozen," said the admiral casually, taking a sip of coffee from the mug on his desk.

The heavy door opened, and Harry entered with a clipboard holding a single two-sided sheet of paper. David's name had been neatly handwritten under a signature line at the bottom of each side, with spaces left for his initials and the date. Reviewing the first couple of sentences, David turned to the admiral.

"This is a commonplace secrecy agreement," he observed. "It starts out like any number of non-disclosure agreements I've reviewed—or prepared—in my legal practice."

Catharine chimed in. "Except in this one you're acknowledging that a breach could put you at the target end of a firing squad."

David read the remainder of the document. At last he turned to the admiral. "It's okay, except for two things. First, my signing this doesn't mean I'm working *for* you. Second, I need to know why you want me to continue working *with* you."

The admiral shrugged. "Can't say until you sign it." He leaned toward David and spoke in a fatherly manner that David found unexpectedly persuasive. "C'mon, son. Time to man up. This is *Uncle Sam* asking for your help."

In a huff, David signed both sides of the document and handed it to the admiral. "You do know there *is* no Uncle Sam, right?"

Catharine smirked. "You better *hope* there is, David, or you've got quite a clothier's bill to pay."

David smiled. "Okay, admiral, now it's time for you to keep your side of the bargain by telling me: Why *me?*"

The admiral put the paper on his blotter and sat back with a skeptical expression. "You really haven't figured that out yet?"

David ran through his mental databanks, shook his head, and shrugged.

The admiral looked to Catharine to explain.

She said, "You spoke with Azeri on the phone, didn't you?"

"Yes," replied David.

"How many times?" asked Catharine.

David shrugged. "Oh, maybe … six times … over a period of a couple years."

She shook her head. "Seventeen times. At least four of those for more than an hour. Do you remember much about your conversations?"

"Well," said David, realizing that they'd checked his old phone records (which he would have thought impossible), "Azeri talked with me about the same topics he would have openly discussed with any book club: the Anunnaki, their landing sites, their wars, and so on. But I don't remember anything *secret*, if that's what you mean."

The admiral leaned forward. "Shortly before Azeri passed, did he mention to you what he was working on?" There was a strange expression in the admiral's eyes, such as David had seen in the past when a questioner posed a question he already knew the answer to.

After thinking long and hard, David shook his head. "I have no idea what you two could be talking about."

Catharine removed a piece of paper from her purse. "In the last article you posted on Azeri's blog, you said this: 'Although I'm not at liberty to write about it now, Mister Azeri is working on a complex idea he'll be disclosing in coming weeks. So, stay tuned.' You remember writing that?"

David was drawing a blank. Then an inkling returned to him. "You know, I *do* remember him telling me to insert that language. It wasn't in my original manuscript."

The admiral scowled. "Why would he want you to insert it?"

David exhaled loudly. "Well, he was always coming out with another book. How many did he ultimately publish, a dozen? He wanted to keep his audience engaged, so he'd drop hints from time to time. I remember him asking me to put that in."

"You didn't know what 'complex idea' Azeri was talking about?" asked the admiral.

David shook his head. "I can't say even *that* for certain. Our discussions were wide-ranging. I suppose he may have mentioned what he was working on, but I wouldn't have regarded it as some Earth-shaking discovery. You have to understand: At that time this whole Anunnaki thing was just a brain exercise. It shed light on some interesting aspects of the Old Testament that had always been a mystery to me, but my interest was mostly religious and … anthropological in a way."

"Because it had no application to the real world," suggested Catharine. "Purely academic."

The admiral was dead serious. "Well, it's not academic any more, is it?" He regarded David skeptically. "Did you take any notes of your conversations with Azeri?"

David shook his head. "None. I rely on my auditory memory for general concepts. And I'm pretty sure he never identified what he had in mind. Well," he sighed, "now that you know how little I have to offer, are you going to send me home?"

The admiral looked to Catharine as if the question was unexpectedly foolish, and allowed her to answer.

"David, this language was contained in a published article," she said. "The admiral and I are not the only ones who expect you know what Azeri was working on when he died."

David smacked himself in the head. "Oh, that's right! My article was the only thing on your laptop—the one filched by the cigar people. Wait … don't *you* believe me when I say I don't know?"

The admiral shook his head dourly. "Our Psy-Ops people tell us that *nothing* is truly forgotten. They'll have a battery of tests for you to take."

"But those tests can't work if I *never* knew, right?" asked David. "Seems like a waste of time."

"You wouldn't want to go home anyway," said the admiral. "What do you think *they'll* do to you if they catch up with you?"

Catharine added, "Their scanner rays have either been through your apartment or soon will be."

David shook his head in horror. "They'll give me the same tests *you* would."

Catharine nodded in agreement. "But they may not care what condition you're in when they're done. On the other hand, we *do* care."

"Heartwarming," said David sardonically.

"Got any *better* suggestions for finding out what Azeri was working on when he died?" asked the admiral.

"Absolutely," replied David. "Get ahold of *Azeri's* notes. He was an *assiduous* note-taker." He looked down. "On the other hand, why would *he* be taking notes of a conversation with someone as inconsequential as … yours truly?"

"Doesn't matter if he took notes of your conversations," said Catharine. "If he was working on something, it would surely be reflected in his personal notes. Problem is … our people have tried to *find* his notes, but they've come up dry."

"What do you mean?" asked David incredulously.

"It means," said the admiral, "that Azeri's publisher insists he has *nothing* that wasn't eventually published. And our people can't find Azeri's widow or any of his heirs. So, we're out of luck." He turned to David with interest. "That is, unless *you* know some way to track them down."

David, being careful not to betray his thinking, realized that he *might* in fact have a way. A narrow hope, perhaps, but it was *something*. "A definite *maybe*," he said.

As Harry barged in to retrieve the signed secrecy agreement, his mobile phone buzzed and he frowned at the screen. "Admiral, this is emergency traffic. I have to take it."

The admiral waved Harry away, who returned to his radio shack, closing the heavy door behind him.

A moment later, there was a buzz on the intercom.

"Speak, Harry," said the admiral.

"Sir," said Harry, "there's a call coming into the lieutenant commander's phone."

Catharine sat up in annoyance at the invasion of her privacy, but the admiral put on the visual brakes, mouthing, *That's his job!*

"Who's it from?" asked the admiral.

"I don't know, admiral," said Harry reluctantly. "The originating number on her screen is changing at least twice a second. It's being continuously scrambled."

For some reason, Shawn leapt to David's mind. *Shawn?* he mouthed.

The admiral silently conceded that David could be right; it could very well be Shawn. Just in case David *was* right in his guess, the admiral made a note in his file that David knew who was on the phone before picking it up.

"Won't the caller be expecting *my* voice?" asked Catharine.

"Maybe," the admiral muttered, "but it could be a hack. The caller may not know whose phone his call is being channeled to."

"Time for an executive decision," said Catharine.

The admiral nodded uncertainly. "Put the call on the horn, Harry," he said, and signaled for David to speak.

At first, David braced himself for the unexpected, then forced himself to relax.

"*Dude!*" said David in a stupid stoner voice.

"*Professor* Dude!" replied Shawn in the same stoner voice, albeit a nervous version. His voice seemed to come from everywhere at once. "McCauley Monster here."

"State your business, Monster," said David. "Hey, how come I haven't heard from you since you told me the mosque had changed zip codes?"

With David's mention of the mosque, there was a noticeable change in Shawn's voice; he now sounded like a grownup, friendly but serious.

"Been tied up," said Shawn. "You?"

A jolt of alarm ran up David's spine. *Tied up* was a code phrase they'd used as adolescents.

David began, "Funny you should ask, Monster—"

There was a momentary pause. "Dave," said Shawn, "am I on a squawk-box?"

David looked to the admiral who seemed deep in thought, and offered no suggestion.

"Yeah, Shawn."

"Can you pick up the handset?"

The admiral shook his head decisively.

"Can't do it, dude. I'd have to find my robe, which is a little out of reach right now." *About four thousand miles out of reach.*

"Tied one on last night, I s'pose?" asked Shawn.

"Yeah, but there's nobody in the apartment except for the customary blonde. And she's asleep in my room. I'm on the couch in the TV room. But to answer your question: I was out at a club last night, and you'll never guess who I ran into."

There was a long silence, during which David imagined that his apartment in New York was—at this very moment—being scanned by the same rays that had pierced the admiral's plane.

"You *got* me, bro'," said Shawn, at last.

"Remember *Valerie?*"

"Valerie?" asked Shawn blankly.

"Yeah, remember Valerie, the brunette? The one you fooled around with at summer camp?"

There was another silence, after which Shawn snapped his fingers and asked, "You mean the one with the great *legs?*"

"That's her, Shawn. She asked for ya, you devil you."

"Oh, yeah. Valerie was the leggy one, alright. If you see her again, say *hey* for me, will ya?"

"Sure thing!" said David. "Hey, where *are* you buddy? Last I heard, you were in Jerusalem."

"Not at liberty to say, dude."

"Oh," said David morosely. "Well, you know where I am, which I guess is what you called to find out."

"Oh … yeah," said Shawn absentmindedly. "Anyway, Dave. Gotta go, now. You be well," he said sadly. "Love ya, buddy."

"Right back at ya, Monster," said David, equally dismally.

Harry ended the call from the communications room.

David dropped his face into his trembling hands, and it was all he could do not to weep. When he gathered his thoughts, the admiral and Catharine were gazing at him in astonishment.

After a respectful moment, the admiral asked, "Care to explain?"

David nodded. "Shawn is being held against his will. His captors were listening in. That rot about being tied up was pre-established code for *I'm under physical restraint.*"

Catharine asked, "Is that the only thing it could mean?"

David grabbed a tissue from a box on the admiral's desk and wiped his eyes. "When we were fourteen, we agreed that *I'm tied up* was about the stupidest thing one could say in place of the mundane *I'm busy.* So, we agreed we'd only use it literally."

Catharine wasn't satisfied. "Couldn't it be used to mean *anything else?*"

David smirked. "At fourteen, I guess it could also have been used to mean, *I can't talk 'cause my folks are listening.* Hardly seems to apply now, though."

"Had you ever used it before to mean *I'm under physical restraint?*" asked the admiral.

"No," admitted David, "but when Shawn took the State Department job and we both knew he'd be traveling to some dangerous places, he reminded me that, from then on, we must use the phrase *only* in its literal sense, precisely so one of us could tell the other he was under restraint."

"But can you be certain that was Shawn on the phone?" asked Catharine.

"Absolutely," confirmed David.

"What was all that about Shawn's girlfriend Valerie from summer camp?" she demanded. "Who's Valerie?"

David shook his head emphatically. "There's no Valerie," he scoffed. "There never was, and Shawn never went to summer camp." He sighed. "*I* never went to summer camp nor wanted to go. Shawn *wanted* to go, but his folks refused to send him. After he nagged them for years, when he was fourteen (and old enough to be hired as a counselor) they finally relented, and agreed to send him for just one summer.

"Two days before he was scheduled to go, he was diagnosed with pneumonia, so the summer camp idea got flushed. Later that summer, when his pneumonia was no longer contagious, he and I camped out in an eight-by-eight canvas tent in his backyard—a sorry substitute for summer camp. I asked him why he'd been so bent on going to summer camp, and he told me that a mutual acquaintance had met a beautiful girl at camp the previous summer. They'd been"—he glanced discreetly at Catharine, who was listening intently—"*intimate*. The relationship had blossomed into a full-blown romance, and the two wrote each other all winter, conspiring to get together again the following summer."

"So why the mention of Valerie?" Catharine demanded. "Did *you* have a girlfriend named Valerie?"

David was amused at the hint of … *jealousy* in her question.

"No. As I told you, there *was* no Valerie. But the *idea* of Valerie comes from that same conversation, which, as you can imagine, went on for hours. Naturally, we got to talking about girls and, *uh*, their physical attributes. I don't know how the subject of *leg men* arose, but he and I agreed that we didn't know any *leg men*, that any guy who really *was* a leg man was probably a reprobate, and that the very concept was probably invented to placate a girl demanding to know what a guy's preference was. We agreed that saying you were a leg man would probably be deemed least offensive by a member of the fairer sex—if we're still allowed to refer to women in such terms."

"Why wouldn't a real guy be a leg man, as you call it?" asked Catharine.

David smirked. "Because adolescent boys have legs of their own. It's what girls have that boys *don't* that are the constant source of fascination. I assume that requires no elaboration."

While Catharine turned five shades of red, David continued. "I told him that if he'd gone to camp that summer, he probably would have met some stuck-up girl named Valerie with great legs. We had a good laugh, because no regular guy wants a stuck-up girl or gives a hoot about legs. From then on, Valerie was Shawn's mythical girl who got away."

"On her great legs," added Catharine dourly.

David finished. "You can see from that phone conversation that whoever was on the other end of the call remembered that Valerie had been Shawn's imaginary girlfriend with great legs. No one but Shawn would have known that."

The admiral nodded. "So it *was* Shawn, and he's under restraint."

The intercom hissed, and Harry's excited voice said, "Voice traffic from marine security at the embassy entrance, admiral. I think you'll want to hear this."

"Put it through, Harry," said the admiral at once.

What followed was the voice of Tony, the marine who escorted David and Catharine to the admiral. "Harry! Tell the lieutenant commander one of her cigar buddies is slowly approaching the embassy. He's about a thousand yards west as the crow flies, steady altitude, maybe … three hundred feet off the ground. He's sending down a continuous red beam that seems to be … scanning for something."

The admiral stood up in alarm. "Harry, can you throw my voice to Tony and give me his video feed?"

"I'll tell him to put on his helmet, sir. It's got a mic and a camera. Then you'll see what he's seeing." There was a moment's silence, and Harry came back on. "Got you queued up, admiral. Shall I patch you together?"

"Somethin' I want you to do first, Harry," said the admiral, kneading his brow. "Kill the power to every electronic device you've got in your shack, except the intercom I'm talking to you on and Tony's feed. Can you do that?"

Harry sighed a long one. "Admiral, some of this equipment is highly complex. It'll take hours to reboot it. Sure you want me to do that?"

"If I'm right," said the admiral, "anything you don't shut down now will be toast in a few minutes anyway. Shut it all down. But keep listening in on this intercom."

"Permission to remove battery backups, sir?" asked Harry.

"If that's what it takes to shut a device down, permission granted. Do it *now,* Harry. Got that?"

"Got it, sir. You're going *live* with Tony out front in three … two … one."

The video monitor in the admiral's study flashed on. The frame was nearly filled with one of those cigar things against a blue sky.

"Tony, this is Admiral Simmons. Do you copy?"

"Loud and clear, sir," said the marine. "Orders, sir?"

Chapter 7

"Do *NOT* FIRE on that thing!" ordered the admiral. "Make sure no one else does, either. You can't nail him, but you *will* piss him off. I can't detect his movement, Tony. Is he still heading your way?"

"Yes, admiral, but he doesn't seem to be in any hurry. Seems more interested in thoroughness than speed."

The camera angle changed to show a nearby building being scanned by the cigar.

The marine's voice returned. "Oh, *shit!* … Hold on, sir." The camera angle shifted to the cigar, then a patch of vacant sky. "Sir, there are … I count *four* Tiger helicopter gunships approaching. Altitude about a thousand feet. Distance about a half-mile, and they're chewin' that up fast. At least one of 'em … no, *two* … appear to be armed with Meteor air-to-air missiles, sir."

At last the choppers clearly appeared on the video feed.

"*Meteors?*" shouted the admiral. "They're expecting that bastard to sit still while they blow him out of the sky?"

"I just work here, sir," said the bewildered marine.

"Can you wave off the choppers?" asked the admiral excitedly.

"I doubt they'll take visual instruction from a Marine Security Guard, sir. They know our job's limited to making sure that embassy records don't fall into the wrong hands. But can *you* wave 'em off, sir? 'Cause there's gonna be one helluva bloody shitshow real soon if you can't."

"Not in time," said the admiral. "Besides, what would I tell them? We know nothing about the adversary's capabilities or intentions."

"From where I stand, sir, that cigar is looking pretty hostile," said the marine. "By the way, admiral, do you happen to know what the cigar guy has in mind for this embassy?"

The admiral sighed. "Like you," he said, measuring his words carefully, "I just work here. But my guess—based on experience—is that he's here to copy every record in this embassy."

"Well, that kinda changes things for me, doesn't it, sir? I've got to implement breach protocol."

The admiral's eyes flashed. "What does that entail, marine? *Wait a second.* Harry, you there?"

"Here, sir," said Harry dejectedly. "Just shuttin' down all my toys."

"You'll get over it. Meanwhile, is the signal on this intercom encrypted?"

"Of course, admiral."

"Good. Tony, how do you begin your breach protocol?"

"Well, sir, first we take care of non-military personnel. If we can safely disperse them into the surrounding area, we do that. If not, we move them into the safe room. As for data, we shield everything we can."

"Shield with … what?"

"We throw a switch," said the marine. "That lowers all the file cabinets and physical papers on street level into the floor and under a couple inches of lead."

"And how do you shield the data on levels below the street?" asked the admiral.

"Sir?"

"There are a bunch of levels below the street, right?" said the admiral. "How do you shield the data on the lower levels?"

"Admiral, they're also protected by the lead shielding in the street-level floor."

"And if that doesn't do it?"

"Well, sir, if that doesn't do it, marines shut down all flame-fighting systems and go to work with small incendiary grenades on every floor on the way down."

"Makes sense," mused the admiral.

"But—" said the marine.

"What's the catch?"

"Protocol requires the extraction of general officers *before* we burn the data, sir. That means you."

"Shit," muttered the admiral.

"Well," the marine conceded, "we can toast the lieutenant commander if you like, sir, and her civilian friend. That much is up to you."

David and Catharine looked at each other with chagrin.

"What if the general officer refuses to go?" asked the admiral.

"In that case—" the marine's voice became adamant "—we can't burn it. You gotta get out, sir." The video image joggled slightly. "Cigar's coming this way with the Tigers right behind. *Damn!* This is about to get exciting, sir. I think the lead Tiger is preparing to attack. What's their weapons sequence at close range in a populated area, sir?"

The admiral shrugged. "Well, they're NATO, so, cannon first, I'd imagine. You got anybody out there with you?"

"Just one more leatherneck. What the f—? Admiral, the Tiger's cannon is spinning, but no rounds are firing. Looks like they're just floppin' out whole, and fallin' to the ground."

"Better order your fellow marine inside the embassy," said the admiral. "And you come inside, too. If those dud rounds are coming out hot, they could cook off on impact with the pavement."

"Jesus, *yessir*," muttered the marine. "*Stevens!*" he shouted, waving to his fellow marine. "Take cover in the embassy, prepare personnel for the real thing, then go down one flight and wait for me. I'll be in. Gimme a minute."

Tony's camera showed Stevens dodging into the embassy entrance, then shifted skyward, where the dark grey cigar loomed slowly into position over the embassy, its surface featureless, its purpose enigmatic.

Suddenly, tiny glints fell from the cannon of the lead chopper, soon followed by a faint metallic tinkling on the audio feed as the unspent rounds struck the pavement. Fortunately, none discharged.

Tony sprinted into the embassy through the front doors. "What the hell is *that?*" he shouted as he entered, turning his helmet-cam toward a commotion inside.

Embassy personnel were gathered around a table watching helplessly as several stacks of paper were being methodically scanned by a red beam from above. The edge of each stack glowed brightly as its secrets were penetrated.

The helmet-cam looked up for the source of the ray; it seemed to originate at the ceiling. "It must be coming from the cigar, sir."

"We've seen that scanner beam before, Tony," said the admiral. "Just keep watching it for the time being. I want to see where it goes next."

The marine protested. "I should already be torching this place, sir."

"Is there highly secret information in those stacks?" the admiral demanded.

"Not *those* stacks, sir, but—"

"Then, stand by," said the admiral. "I'm temporarily countermanding your standing orders."

"Better stay healthy, admiral," said the marine. "I'll need your testimony at my court martial."

The admiral ignored the remark. "Just tell me the moment the ray moves away from those stacks. And tell me immediately if any more rays pierce the ceiling."

"Yes, sir," said Tony. "The ray's … changing, sir. It's still centered on the stacks of paper, but it's widening out. Seems to be looking through a half-dozen filing cabinets at the same time. *Uh-oh*. Changed again. It appears to be piercing the lead shield in the floor. How the *hell* does it do that? Hold on, admiral." The marine pressed a button on the side of his helmet. "Stevens, you on Level Minus One?"

"That's protocol, sir," said Stevens's voice through a tinny speaker in Tony's helmet. "Wow! I've got a red ray coming right through the ceiling. Geez, it's moving all over real fast. Wait! Now it's trying to penetrate the phone system."

"Shit!" shouted the admiral, looking sternly at Catharine and David. "I thought they *followed* you two here."

"You mean, they *didn't?*" asked Catharine.

The admiral shook his head. "No. I think they traced Shawn's phone call through David's phone and into yours, Catharine. It'll take them no time to locate your phone in Harry's nook. They could get a fix on us through the phone system and take us out in a few seconds. *Harry, you still there?*"

"Here, sir," muttered Harry. "All batteries removed. What the devil?"

"What is it, Harry?"

An incredulous Harry replied, "The lieutenant commander's phone just switched on."

"I *told* you to remove the battery," said the admiral.

"The battery's on the other side of the *room*, admiral. There's no conductive power source. This must be induc—" Harry suddenly began howling in pain.

"*What is it?*" shouted the admiral, but he could sit still no longer. He leapt out of his chair, ran to the heavy steel door, and opened it with his keycard. David and Catharine followed right behind.

On the other side of the Dutch door, Harry writhed, wrestling with Catharine's mobile phone as though it were a wolverine trying to rip his arm off. His eyes were filled with pain and terror as he pleadingly reached out his hand with the phone in it. The phone had literally *melted* into the skin of his inner forearm. The color drained from his face, his eyes turned up in his head, and he collapsed to the floor.

"We've gotta get him out of here!" said Catharine.

"Not with that thing in his arm," said David. "They can use it to track us."

David grabbed what looked like a graphite forceps from Harry's table, grappled the pincers around the phone, and tugged the phone off Harry's forearm, which made a sickening sucking sound as it came loose. Momentarily stunned by his own cold-bloodedness, David stood there for a moment gaping incredulously at the mobile phone and Harry's burned forearm. Unable to decide whether to vomit or pass out, he did neither.

There was surprisingly little blood oozing out of Harry's forearm. The skin seemed to have *melted* together, as though cauterized. The phone dropped to the floor, and continued to emit its menacing glow until Catharine put her stiletto heel through it and its lights went out for good.

"Might as well toss your phone-check ticket," remarked David as he took a clean handkerchief from his pocket and tied it around Harry's forearm snugly enough to keep it in place, but not so tightly as to cut off circulation.

Just as the crisis seemed to pass, a red ray pierced the ceiling of Harry's shack and began methodically scanning the room.

"They've found us!" shouted David. "We've gotta get out of here!"

"And right now!" added the admiral. "You two walk Harry out between you, and follow me."

Fortunately, Harry had recovered enough of his senses to bear most of his own weight. Still, Catharine and David had to struggle to support him from either side.

The admiral hit an elevator button concealed in the wall. The camouflage was so skillful that, until that moment, David would have sworn the button didn't exist. An elevator door, concealed equally well, promptly slid open and the admiral stepped into a small car obviously designed to carry no more than three.

Evidently, it was about to carry *four*, as the admiral beckoned them all in and pushed the only directional button in the car, which David was surprised to see showed an arrow pointed *sideways*. As the door began to close, the admiral pressed the Talk button mounted over the arrow and shouted.

"Tony, do you read me?"

"Loud and clear, sir," responded the marine with a great clamor behind him, which he didn't bother to explain. Evidently, he knew from the old man's tone that he was expected to *listen*, and listen he did.

"General officer departing!" replied the admiral. "We're taking the foremost tram, so don't count on it for evac. Read me?"

"Five by five. Orders, sir?"

"Secure personnel until rescue, and—"

"And?"

"Burn the records. *Burn 'em all!* Don't let those bastards see one more goddam thing. And Godspeed, marine. *Out.*"

The "elevator" door closed and the car moved rightward like a rifle shot, nearly knocking David over. "Whoa!" he said, disoriented by the unexpected trajectory. Fortunately, the admiral and Catharine were accustomed to the sideward motion, else they all would have ended up in a heap on the floor.

In a half minute, the car automatically slowed down, the door slid open with a bang, and David found himself back on the deserted subway platform.

The admiral slid open a door to what appeared to be the same subway car they'd arrived in, and switched on the motor and lights.

"Buckle up!" said the admiral.

With some effort, David buckled the seatbelt around the still-swooning Harry while Catharine helped him remain upright in his seat.

Catharine and David buckled themselves in while the admiral operated the steering mechanism. In a moment the car was in motion, traveling quickly in the same direction as when they came in. Which meant they were moving *away* from the embassy's street entrance.

The admiral must have seen David's confusion. "We're going to the end of the line," he said and turned to Catharine. "Lieutenant commander, draw one if you got one."

Catharine deftly reached under her jacket, drew out the Glock, switched off the safety, checked the chamber, and slapped it shut. "Ready, admiral," she said.

The car had been making good time for about a half-minute when there was a deafening boom in the distance behind them that echoed off the tunnel walls and momentarily shoved the car forward so hard it felt like it might jump the rails.

David discreetly glanced at the admiral and Catharine; neither flinched or otherwise acknowledged the explosion.

Up ahead, daylight seeped in around the edges of the exterior riot doors. Evidently, they were nearing the end of the tunnel.

Harry had passed out again. His head lolled about.

"When we reach the terminus," said the admiral, "we three will get out and leave Harry strapped in for the time being. He'll be safe enough till I come back for him. Once we shove open the riot doors, we'll be outdoors in plain view. Catharine, conceal your sidearm before we go outside."

She glanced questioningly back at the admiral.

The admiral nodded. "I don't like it either, but if they're waiting for us, they'll likely be able to overpower us anyway. Our best protection is to avoid being recognized. Stealth is the order of the day. We can't allow our weapons to be seen from above; they'll mark us as combatants. You two are just a nice married couple strolling with Dad along the Seine to a waiting pleasure craft—at least that's what I want us to look like."

"Yes, admiral," said Catharine and David at the same time.

The admiral nodded with satisfaction at their quick assent. "Follow me onto the craft. I'll introduce you to the river pilot, and he'll take the two of you below deck."

"Afraid my French is a bit rusty," admitted David.

The admiral suppressed a smile. "His is worse."

David looked at him, puzzled.

"He's English," said Catharine, "though, truth be told, his English isn't all that good, either."

The end of the rail line was only about twenty feet from the end of the tunnel. The car pulled up to the terminus with a bump and they leapt out, weapons secured once again.

They shoved open the riot doors and found themselves walking along a concrete promenade directly beside the Seine. David had lost his bearings completely, but this *had* to be the Seine; it was the only river of its size in Paris, and the tram hadn't crossed any others.

Tied alongside was a small fiberglass touring boat with a canvas roof suspended on aluminum poles that covered much of the deck. The canvas flapped lazily in the autumn breeze.

By the gangplank stood a fit-looking man of about forty, holding a book whose title began with the word *Perisher*. Though the man was clearly pleased to catch sight of the admiral, he was looking past (and over) them, evidently fascinated by something in the sky back the way they came.

"Don't look back," muttered the admiral quietly as they left the cover of the tunnel, "until we're under cover of the canvas."

The man stepped forward, smiled at the admiral as he approached, and shook his hand.

"William," said the admiral, stepping onto the deck, "it's good to see you. Let's get under the canvas before we talk. By the way, do you have a cell phone?"

"I do, admiral."

"Shut it down *cold*, please," said the admiral, "and don't turn it on till I say you can. Damn things have got us into enough trouble for one day."

"Yes, sir," said William, stepping under the canvas, removing his phone from its holster and shutting it off. "Am I mistaken, sir, or did you just narrowly escape a small air battle?"

"I expect we did, William."

"And a belching fire?"

At last, the admiral, Catharine, and David turned and gazed toward the sky above the embassy entrance well over a mile away. It was choked with flame and black smoke. No choppers or other aircraft flew there just now, but one could hear the sirens of several emergency vehicles heading in that direction.

The admiral sighed.

"I wonder how our marines are doing," muttered David.

The admiral nodded gloomily. "At this point, all we can do for them is pray," he said. "Okay, you two. I have to assume we're off the grid and out of sight. Here's the story going forward. David, you suggested you might know how to reach Azeri's heirs. Correct?"

David found it jarring to hear the admiral state such an iffy proposition quite so positively. "Well, sir, I wouldn't hold out much hope, but I do have an idea of which sites Azeri's adult daughter wanted to investigate around the time of her father's death, which was a few years ago now."

"And where were those sites?" asked the admiral.

"Southern Africa, sir."

"Well, you and Catharine are going there together," said the admiral. He leaned into David apologetically. "Professor, I've been ordered to forswear your company for the time being."

"*My* company?" said David. "Why?"

"Because, as far as the Commander-in-Chief is concerned," said the admiral, "you're mad, bad, and dangerous to know. He's ordered me back to Washington."

To David, the prospect of searching remote locations in southern Africa without the sage guidance of the admiral was truly daunting. While Catharine, as a U.S. Navy lieutenant commander, would no doubt be of substantial aid, David couldn't help feeling like Frodo in *Lord of the Rings*, one small person being sent nearly alone into wild and hostile country on the off-chance he might accomplish a task so profound it could turn the tide of battle. And at least Frodo knew the Cracks of Doom awaited. David, on the other hand, would be searching for someone who might not even be there.

"*I'm* dangerous to know?" David exclaimed. "*Me?* It's *you* they're after." But after a moment's thought, real doubt crept into his mind. "It *is* you, isn't it?"

"No," said the admiral, shaking his head. "True, they're keeping an eye on me, but for the moment they're keeping their distance. *You,* on the other hand, are a high-value target and they want to talk to you … in the worst way."

David was still incredulous.

The admiral placed his hands on his hips and continued in a tone of exasperation. "Think about it. The only thing they took from the plane was *your* article. They sent two thugs to track *you* to that little clothier's shop. When you evaded them, they sent an *aircraft* to abduct *you* off the street in broad daylight in the middle of Paris, notwithstanding that you were being guarded by men with automatic weapons. And, when they lost track of you again, they thought it important enough to *reacquire* you by enlisting your friend Shawn and tracing his call through *your* phone to *Catharine's* phone, and then to invade the freaking American Embassy. *Starting to see a pattern develop?*"

David stood on the deck, thunderstruck.

The admiral put his hand on David's shoulder. "Look, Dave—May I call you Dave?" David nodded absentmindedly. "Maybe you know as little about Azeri as you think you do, but you have to consider the possibility that you know more than you think. In any event, *those* bastards think you know a *lot* more, and if they get their hands on you, they won't stop until you've remembered and told them every damned thing you know. So here's the story." He beckoned toward Catharine and lowered his voice. "Catharine, you listen carefully, too. Until further notice, you're Mister and Missus Roger and Eve Thornhill of New York, New York. There's a hatch at the base of this little pleasure craft leading to a mini-submersible—"

"A—a *submarine?*" asked David.

Now it was William's turn to put a hand on David's shoulder. "Don't worry, prof. It's a little tourist sub, much smaller than the drug cartels use. It's got windows and everything. We won't be goin' deep. The river's too shallow to allow it."

David looked at William as though he were mad. "We're going all the way to the coast of southern Africa in a *tourist* sub?"

"No," said William. "That would be foolhardy. This little craft is only good in the river, and it's powered by a monster set of Tesla batteries. It's not even seaworthy enough to cross the Channel. Besides, I've got to be up in Clyde in a week for the last leg of the Perisher course, so you'll have to change vessels at least once."

"Should be twice," confirmed the admiral. "I'll have a smuggler's sub pick you up at Le Havre and take you to Cornwall. The sub that ends up taking you all the way to southern Africa will be a big nuclear job, maybe even an American boomer. Depends who's heading that way. But you'll be traveling only by submarine. I don't want them tracking you. As far as those bastards are concerned, you've disappeared from the face of the planet. You'll have no radio, wireless, phone, Internet, telegraph … no electronic communications whatever. No credit cards. If you need to contact me *en route*, you're gonna need a carrier pigeon. The big sub will have a radio. It absolutely needs one for its own purposes, but there'll be no mention of *either* of you on it. Those cigar bastards are so far advanced, I don't even trust U.S. encryption any more, which is the best in the world. Once you reach your African port, you'll be given cash and you can pick up some burner phones. What I need to know right now is your disembarkation port in Africa. Where do you need to be dropped off to start your search?"

David's head was spinning. "Can I look at a map? First I have to locate the ancient sites on a map and then figure out the modern names of those locations and the nearest ports."

"Fair enough," said the admiral. "William, do you have land maps of Africa in the submersible?"

William shook his head apologetically. "No, admiral. If I'd known they'd be needed—"

The admiral said, "None of us knew."

David pointed to a storefront across the street. "There's a pretty big bookstore over there," he said. "I'd bet *they* have maps."

The admiral brightened up. "William, would you go and pick up some map books on Africa, including history and geography?"

"Could you get Azeri's books, as well?" asked David.

Catharine shook her head. "They'll be in French."

The admiral agreed with her. "Besides that, there'd be an electronic record revealing that those books were bought at that location. Forget that. Just get the Africa books. In English, if they've got any." William ran off in the direction of the bookstore.

The admiral pressed his finger into David's chest. "When you get to

England, you'll need to tell Captain Bellinger your destination, and that I told him he's to keep it secret, except to tell me, the sub captain, and the chief navigator."

"What about David's new suits?" asked Catharine. "I haven't paid Petit for them, and they'll be ready tomorrow morning."

David was shocked that she would ask a question so banal under these circumstances, but he admired how thorough and down-to-earth she was. Always thinking of everything.

The admiral nodded reluctantly. "I haven't even been to the hotel yet. When I go there tonight, I'll pick up David's stuff. I'll have it forwarded to you when I learn your destination port. Somebody experienced from the intelligence services will meet you there, so be on the lookout." He looked to Catharine. "Will that be satisfactory, lieutenant commander?"

"Quite, sir," she replied. "Thank you, sir."

"Is that it?" asked the admiral. "Because I really have to take Harry in for treatment. Burns can get infected quickly."

"One more thing, sir," said David, "if I may. Can you tell us what's happening with this … invasion … or whatever it is? I haven't seen a television set since first thing this morning."

"All I can tell you is there's UFO activity being reported everywhere, though governments are doing their best to suppress that information—keep it off the airwaves. As for the aliens, they have more than one type of craft. In addition to the cigars, they have at least two more, namely, flying saucers and pyramid-shaped craft, which has led to speculation that there's more than one type of alien, and they may be working together or at cross-purposes.

"Right now, our primary concern is that saucers are massing around the nuclear silos of every nuclear-armed nation on Earth. And if that doesn't scare the crap out of you—well, it oughta. Godspeed."

CHAPTER 8

MOORED TO THE surface craft was the smallest, most futuristic submarine in the world. Virtually every surface was composed of plexiglass, fiberglass, or some other reinforced composite. It was barely large enough to hold four passengers with minimal baggage.

It took only a few minutes for the three of them to board and batten the top hatch.

"Sit *here*," Catharine told David, tapping her hand on the only seat next to William's. She went to the space aft of the front seats to remove her makeup, change out of her business suit, and don some spare crewman's clothing consisting of white tennis shoes, beige slacks, and a flattering (though outsized) navy blue turtleneck. When she was done, she tapped David on the shoulder and pointed her thumb aft. "Crew travels back there," she said with a wink. "I'll assist the captain. Meanwhile, read your maps. Some are even in English."

David assented wearily, surrendered his seat to Catharine, and plopped down on one of the two cots, where he changed into a set of crewman's clothing that fit surprisingly well.

"Prepare to dive," said William, pressing a button that played a pleasantly soft recording of an ahooga horn.

With a hiss, the sub submerged. As it escaped the shadow of the surface craft, the cabin was momentarily flooded with sunlight penetrating the water above.

"Dive complete!" announced William a moment later, as he leveled off the sub. "Four meters under the keel. Ahead, touring speed." He checked the sonar again to ensure there were no craft nearby, then pressed another button. "Ahead, cruising speed."

David had heard little noise from street traffic before their mini-sub left the surface. What little he'd heard then was completely gone now, replaced by the lazy, muted sound of water lapping against the hull. He cracked open the map book (which mercifully *was* in English) and noticed, after only a few minutes, that the daylight in the cabin had already begun to fade and would soon be entirely replaced by the soft bluish glow of the cabin lights.

As they cruised down the Seine, David searched the book and found a map of Zimbabwe, a country that took its name from its most dramatic ruins, those of the Great Zimbabwe near Lake Mutirikwi, a series of intricate stoneworks with a large central enclosure.

If David's recollection was accurate, Azeri's daughter had wished to search the ancient gold mines west of that site for any remaining evidence of an Anunnaki presence. He sighed, dismayed by the feeling that they were on a hopeless chase. Though in theory Azeri's daughter Miriam could be there still (or again), the probabilities were stacked against it. His understanding of her intentions was nearly ten years old, and people move on with their lives.

Even if they found Azeri's daughter, what was the likelihood she'd have her father's notes? They might have been burned or lost in a move. What troubled David most was that the NSA had been unable to locate Azeri's heirs—the very NSA that has access to every electronic record in the world. Credit cards, if nothing else, should have made quick work of finding Azeri's heirs. *Could they be living off the grid? Could they all be dead by now?*

Theories attributing construction of the Great Zimbabwe to non-Africans had—with some justification—long been denounced as racist inventions of the minority white government of Rhodesia, which was Zimbabwe's colonial name.

Indeed, as Azeri had observed, the stonework of the ruins bore none of the hallmarks of Anunnaki architecture. For one thing, underlying the ruins of the Great Zimbabwe were no megaliths, the primary unit of construction being rather a brick-sized stone. But Azeri had also observed that—though the culture that built the Great Zimbabwe was most likely African—it had not sprung up whole, as the Sumerian culture seemed to have done millennia before.

To Azeri, the Great Zimbabwe seemed a recently constructed waystation lying between the ancient gold mines about forty miles to the west and the international trading hub of Rapta, reputed to occupy one of several islands in the Indian Ocean to the east of present-day Mozambique. (*Recent* being a relative term, especially in archaeology, Azeri used it in this instance to mean that the Great Zimbabwe had been built only *after* the birth of Jesus.)

From the maps, David concluded that the great port nearest the ancient gold mines was located at Beira, on the eastern coast of

Mozambique. The port of Maputo, though likewise in Mozambique, was hundreds of miles to the south.

Their choice of port would probably be dictated by several considerations, the first being the port's relative depth, which needed to be sufficient for a close approach by a sizable nuclear submarine. The second consideration would be which port was served by the higher-functioning airport, as it was unlikely the admiral would await the results of a two-way overland trek covering some eight hundred miles. Finally, they would no doubt wish to avoid any port that was crime-ridden or politically hostile to Americans.

To mark his page, David placed a fresh facial tissue against the binding, closed the book, and placed it on the nightstand. He turned to lie on his back and gaze through the window over his bunk.

A watery kaleidoscope occupied his entire field of view. He watched for a few minutes as daylight faded. The sub's console emitted a pleasant rhythmic beep confirming the craft's safe distance from the riverbed. He began to feel sleepy, and the hushed conversation between William and Catharine only made him drowsier.

⇒∘⊂✦⊃∘⇐

IN THE UNDERWATER quiet, William and Catharine chatted in subdued tones.

Catharine pointed to William's dog-eared book with *Perisher* in the title. "I take it you're seeking to qualify to captain a *nuclear* sub?"

"Aye," said William with a grin. "I sure hope I make it. It's *up or out,* y'know. If you fail to qualify, you're barred from the Silent Service for life."

"I'm aware," said Catharine. "Never seemed fair to me."

"How would you know about the up-or-out rule, I wonder?"

Catharine removed a keychain from her pocket and showed William her golden dolphins. "Been there. Done that."

William's eyebrows shot up as he glanced at the dolphins. "How far did you get, may I ask?"

"All the way through," she said smugly.

"No joke!" he said, nodding his head respectfully.

She put the keychain back in her pocket. "But I'm qualified in diesel-electric only."

"A Yank?" he said. "With all the nukes you lot have, why would that be of use to you?"

"As you might have detected," she said, "I'm not *all* Yank. London-born am I. But, more to the point, I've always been involved in intelligence work," she explained. "It's hard to see how I'd ever be called on to pilot a nuke. But diesel-electric? That's what every little country uses. And … it tends to be what the bad guys use, too."

"'Nuff said," said William with a wink. "No tellin' what you might be called on to do in one of those." He pointed his chin toward the console. "I'll warrant you could handle this baby just fine. Hell, in the daytime you can even see where you're goin'!"

Catharine took a closer look at the console. "Well, nothing's where I'd expect it to be … and you have no crew. But I suppose I could get the hang of it."

Behind them, David snorted loudly in his sleep, making Catharine and William smile and suppress a laugh.

William ventured, "You seem to admire that bloke. Am I right?"

"Well …" she said with a shrug.

"Sorry, lieutenant commander," he said abashedly. "Didn't mean to pry."

She smiled. "Is it that obvious?"

"I like to think I can detect a bit o' romantic interest," he replied. "Been a while for *me*, though."

⇒∘⊂⟱⊃∘⇐

AGAINST HIS WILL and better judgment, David closed his eyes and fell asleep.

He's sitting alone at a table on the veranda of a posh seaside café in the Port of Beira, a hot, fluky breeze wafting in off the Indian Ocean, though he has the nagging feeling someone's supposed to be here with him. Someone's missing. But, in his hand is a dry Sapphire Gibson on the rocks with three onions, just the way he likes it. It's hard to get too worked up about something amiss while enjoying a Gibson, which he's always found to be strong consolation.

The beads of perspiration on his forehead are a small price to pay for the serenity he feels at this moment, entirely undaunted by the prospect of flying to Lake Mutirikwi tomorrow morning in a little Cessna Denali.

Instantly, it's next morning. There's bright sunshine, and he's seated next to a non-descript pilot, overflying a lush section of Zimbabwe. Though the plane could easily carry more, David's the lone passenger, due to the secrecy of his mission.

The engines drone on, and the breathtaking landscape slips effortlessly under them. Up ahead, more beautiful than he could ever imagine, lies a vast lake in primeval condition, its waters untouched, clean and clear. He wonders how near he is to the source of the Nile, which he's learned is somewhere in the vicinity. An airstrip comes into view on the horizon. Although it's barely long enough to land the Cessna safely, the tarmac looks well maintained.

The scene shifts again. He's alone, standing atop a hill overlooking the pristine lake, feeling lucky to be here, certain there's nowhere else on Earth so untroubled by the soiled hand of civilization.

A beautiful woman with long brown hair parted in the center, dressed in a shiny blue sari and shod in sandals, elegantly climbs a winding trail toward him. When she draws near him at the top of the hill, he nearly stops breathing as he recognizes her as his loved-and-lost. His heart aches for her again.

Somehow, he knows it can't really be Sharon, as—for the first time in any dream he's had since her passing—he knows she's dead and assumes he's dreaming. But still, he's willing to play along ... to enjoy her company, her love, just one more time. Just this once.

⟶∘⟨⟋⟍⟍⟍∘⟵

WILLIAM CHANGED THE subject. "You only *suppose* you could drive this boat?" he asked Catharine. "See anything unfamiliar to you?"

She observed the complex display on the console. "Not really. There are one or two things I *don't* see, but I expect those functions are automated on this model ... or unnecessary."

"*What* don't you see?"

She considered the question. "Well, for one thing, I don't see an ELF receiver."

ELF is an acronym for *Extremely Low Frequency*, a laboriously slow method of communication that requires enormous power, but can reach submarines even at extreme operating depths. The heft of the equipment needed to transmit an ELF signal precludes its being carried aboard a submarine, but any sub can receive and, with the right codes, decipher such a transmission. Because it can take several minutes to transmit a single alphanumeric character, ELF is usually reserved for the purpose of ordering a sub to periscope depth so that a more efficient method of communication can be established.

William snickered. "Funny you should mention it. I've had an ELF receiver installed on her … just because I could, even though we can't go deep enough to need it. This craft is really just a backup transport for extracting general officers from the embassy at need. Although it's been used before—for convenience—I don't think it's ever *needed* to be used until today."

On the console, suddenly a silent red warning light flashed. It said *ELF*.

"Neat trick," she said. "How'd you trigger the idiot light?"

A look of dread crossed his face.

"I didn't," he muttered.

"*Hmph*," said Catharine. "Speak of the devil and she shall appear."

Another indicator lit up with a warning and a deciphered message: *CAUTION UNVERIFIED: All boats to periscope depth.*

SUDDENLY, AN INTRUDER materializes between David and Sharon. Out of nowhere appears the woman who's melded into Sharon's form in his recent dreams. But now, while the two women are standing a little apart, the stark differences between them make David wonder how he could ever have been duped into thinking them one and the same.

As WILLIAM SWITCHED off the ELF translator, another light flashed on, signaling incoming digital communications.

"What new devilry is this?" he muttered, switching on the display of incoming messages. The console immediately filled with incoming data. "Wow! It's a torrent!"

"Is that encrypted?" asked Catharine.

The message was so lengthy, and the letters and numbers rifled past so quickly, it resembled a data dump. "If it's encoded, it's overwhelmed our little computer's capacity to decipher." William scratched his head. "It could be directed to any sub. It's not necessarily for *us*." He scratched his head as he watched the letters and numbers fly by, and said hesitantly, "It looks like … *audiovisual* signal. But, even for that, it's highly complex."

Behind them, David whimpered loudly in his sleep like a puppy suffering a nightmare.

William and Catharine exchanged an apprehensive glance, as it occurred to them simultaneously that the message might be for David *personally*—that someone might be trying to pick his brain.

⟶○❦○⟵

THOUGH THE INTRUDER is also dark and beautiful, she's dressed like a wanton, her swollen breasts more pronounced than ever before, their milky tops swelling out of a very ... calculated decolletage. Her gown is red, and slit all the way up the front, exposing—not a mere leg—but the cleft of her womanhood. She steps athwart Sharon's path, her hand raised like a policeman's calling a halt to progress.

Much to his amazement, Sharon stops and curtsies respectfully to the other woman, which makes David's blood boil.

The two women are close enough for him to overhear their voices. While Sharon's humble words escape his hearing entirely, he can catch the occasional word from the other woman, who has a stronger voice, and is clearly accustomed to command.

Sharon raises her hand to point to David.

But the wanton slaps her hand away, and says, "No! Your time with him is through. When will you understand? You are a dead thing." She points back the way Sharon climbed the hill. "Return to my sister's service at once," the wanton pronounces and, to David's amazement, Sharon curtsies to her again, turns, and meekly descends the way she came.

David mournfully watches her disappear from view. His heart follows her until she's well out of sight.

"You truly loved her, didn't you, son of Yussif?" asks the woman in red, who has somehow instantly covered the distance between them and now stands right next to him, a most sympathetic expression on her face.

⟶○❦○⟵

"WAIT!" SAID WILLIAM. "I've seen a signal like this before. You know what it is?"

"I'm all ears," replied Catharine.

"It's a ... VR signal. Virtual Reality."

Behind them, David shouted, nearly startling them out of their seats. *"My father's name was Jacob!"* he protested loudly.

"Look!" said William, pointing to the visual data flying across the screen. "His voice was just *transmitted!* Jesus, we're *broadcasting* his responses." He looked at Catharine, bewildered. "But who's *listening?*"

Catharine turned around and glanced at David, who was tossing and turning in his bunk as though wrestling with angels.

"Shut down the radio now!" she commanded.

"MY FATHER'S NAME was Jacob!" protests David.

"So was Yussif's," says the woman in red. "And you resemble Yussif very much."

"Who is Yussif?"

"He was a progenitor of yours, but, alas, he passed ... long ago. Like you, he was a dreamer," she says, stroking David's hair. "He interpreted dreams for Pharaoh." She smiles seductively. "Will you interpret my dreams?"

David was disinclined to discuss anything with this woman. While by rights he should have shoved her hand away, as she had poor Sharon's, he couldn't bring himself to do it. She was just so ... desirable.

And so powerful.

"THE RADIO IS still on!" said Catharine with her teeth clenched.

"It *can't* be, lieutenant commander. You see this switch?" asked William. "It's in the *off* position."

"Well, the data's still flying across the screen," she said. "The switch has obviously been overridden! Isn't there a circuit breaker?"

William shook his head. "Never *needed* one, ma'am. There's not going to be a serious electrical spike in this setting. The radio runs off its own battery."

"Where's the battery?" she demanded.

To William's amazement, she drew her sidearm.

"*No!*" said William in alarm. "No firearms in this little bucket o' bolts, ma'am," he said, eyes agog. "May I remind the lieutenant commander that we're submerged in a craft with skin only a little thicker than that of a handheld hair dryer? We *can't* shoot out the battery. I have to turn a few screws to get at it, and I'll do it as fast as I can." He put his hand over the gun and encouraged her to put it away. "I understand you're trying to save the professor, ma'am, but if you discharge that sidearm, the mission will fail, and he'll die. And so will you and I."

She put the gun back in her pocket. "Well, we've got to do *something!*"

William exhaled. "It'll take me no more than two minutes to reach the battery and pull it out." He pointed to a circular sonar screen. "See up there? About three hundred meters ahead … on the right?"

"Looks like a hole in the riverbank," she said.

"It's a submerged cavity," he said, searching for a better word, "… a … a *grotto.* It's big enough for us to hide inside. Not sure we can surface in there, but that's not important at the moment. Maybe their signal won't reach us in there, and I'll have time to pull out the flippin' battery."

"We already know their signals can pierce solid lead," she said. "But maybe the granite of the riverbed will shield us. Get us in there, and pull out the damned battery!"

⟶•◦❧◦•⟵

"WHY DON'T YOU make love with me?" implores the wanton with a comely, but phony, smile. "It would be good for your future."

From the back of his mind, David can hear the voice of the Orthodox Jew. Don't make love to her. To whom? The girl of your dreams.

Is this whom he meant by the girl of my dreams? Girl of my nightmares is more like it.

"Tell me more about this Yussif," he says, playing for time. "Is he an ancestor of mine?"

She looks at him askance. "Yes, but who is that person who told you not to make love to me?"

Since she can evidently see whatever David's imagining, he resolves to suppress the name and likeness of the man he met at the hotel. That's who she wants to know about. She couldn't care less about the British Jew. She wants to know what brazen soul has dared set his face against her inexorable will. She's just asking about the Jew to find a way around David's resistance.

"That little man with the funny sideburns," she says. "Who is he?"

He's relieved that, thus far, she seems to have seen only Yakov.

The image and name of the good doctor try to surface in his mind (or is she dredging them up?), but he won't allow her to see his face or hear his name. "That man's name was Yakov. Why do you wish to know?"

She regards him suspiciously. "I wish to know who told Yakov to tell you not to make love to me." Fury grows in her eyes. Though he does not wish to cross her, he'll have no choice if pressed, as it appears that the good doctor might be an adversary of this wanton goddess—and so a prospective friend to David.

Though David cannot help but envision the hotel dining room where he met the old man, in his mind he superimposes a cartoon character's face over the good doctor's. Yogi Bear's, in fact.

Apparently, she's seeing his image of old Yogi. "What is that?" she demands, smoldering. "Show me who warned you against me, damn it!"

As he glares at her, half expecting to die, her image first grows faint, then sputters in and out of existence like a hologram running out of power.

And then all at once, as though by merciful magic ... she's gone.

⟶◦⟪⟫◦⟵

WHEN DAVID OPENED his eyes, the cabin was pitch dark, save for the light of an upturned trouble light on the floor that illuminated the underside of the console. William lay on his back next to the light with his hands extended upward, tugging on something that evidently didn't wish to be moved.

Catharine sat beside David on the bunk. "How are you faring?" she asked softly.

He shook the cobwebs from his mind. "I ... I had a helluva dream."

"Yeah," she said, "we know."

"Where *are* we?" asked David.

"In an underwater grotto on the Seine," she said, and looked up apprehensively. "We have only two meters clearance above and below, and we're completely cut off from the outside world. Brilliant move, no?"

"Why would we want that?" asked David.

"So you don't get any more special little dreams tonight," she replied.

"What do you mean?"

"Your dream," said Catharine. "It was computer-assisted. They started sending a complex signal to your brain through the sub's radio link. William says it resembled a *virtual reality* signal. We were afraid it would kill you, or at least give away our position. At my request, William shut down all signals. That means we have no radio, no radar, no sonar. No signals at all. We've still got ventilation and heat," she said, trying to paint a better face on their predicament, "but that's about it."

David looked up at her, bewildered. "So, you saw my dream?"

"Hardly. The signals were much too fast to read, let alone interpret," she said. "We did hear you protest in your sleep a few times."

"What did I say?"

"Well, one time you insisted that your father's name was *Jacob*, as though someone had told you it was no such thing. Then it sounded as though you were being pressed to tell your inquisitor someone's name. But you refused. At that point, if you don't mind my saying so, you seemed more than a little frightened."

He nodded.

"Were you?" she asked.

He considered how to respond. "Terrified," he said.

She put her hand on his, and stroked it comfortingly.

He looked at her hand and said, "Aren't you afraid they'll zap me out of here, and your hand will come with me?"

"Nope. It's all part of my grand scheme," she replied with a wink. "If they take you, they take me, too."

David's heart welled up with gratitude. Here was a true companion, such as he'd expected never again to meet in this life.

David glanced down at William, who was shifting positions under the console but showed no immediate intention of emerging from his workspace.

Safe from prying eyes, David drew Catharine close in the dark and kissed her long on the lips. She responded with equal ardor. In a moment David could feel her tears fall on his face.

She sat up straight again.

"Care to talk about it?" he asked, with sympathy for her obvious sadness.

Catharine wiped her eyes with a tissue and shook her head. "No," she said, "I want you to tell me your dream. It was about a woman, wasn't it?"

"How could you tell?" asked David.

"Women know these things," she said evasively. "At first you seemed to pine for someone. Who was that?"

"Let me tell you the whole thing, and all your questions will be answered." He sighed. "I'll skip the irrelevancies and tell you the part with the women."

"*Women?*" she said with surprise. "There was more than one?"

"I was all alone on a mountaintop overlooking the lake in Zimbabwe where we're going. A woman in a blue sari was walking up a trail toward me. When she got close enough for me to see her face, I realized she was—"

"Sharon," said Catharine, completing his thought.

"Yes, young lady," he said in a fatherly voice, "but I doubt you'll be able to guess much else. Shall I continue with my tale or simply tuck you in right now?"

She leaned into him, and whispered saucily, "Either would be fine."

Just when he thought he'd never feel okay again, he suddenly felt okay. "Well, I can only do the *one* right now, so listen patiently: When Sharon was nearly eye-to-eye with me, *she* showed up."

"The evil queen?" suggested Catharine.

"That's a more accurate description than you might imagine," he said. "The evil queen was dressed very strumpet-like. Her boobs were jutting out the top of her dress and her skirt was slit up the front."

"You mean the side," she suggested, "to show some leg."

"I mean up the front," he corrected. "Use your imagination."

She inhaled suddenly. "That's shameless," she remarked.

"Well, don't blame me. I didn't make her up. In fact, I don't think I made *any* of this up. Anyway, she held up her hand and forbade Sharon to come to me and upbraided her, 'When will you learn that you're a *dead* thing? Go and serve my sister.'" He gulped involuntarily.

"How did it make you feel," asked Catharine, "to hear the wicked queen tell Sharon she was a dead thing?"

David took a moment to compose himself. "I wanted to kill her with my own two hands."

"Understandable," said Catharine indulgently. "How did Sharon react?"

"She seemed to take it in stride," replied David. "She obeyed the wicked queen and went back down the mountain."

"Is that how Sharon would have reacted in life?" asked Catharine.

"Are you kidding? Sharon would have eaten her alive."

"Then that was *not* Sharon," Catharine assured him. "It was a figment of the queen's imagination designed to show *you* how powerful she is."

David nodded and continued his story. "Then the image of Yakov came to mind, the Orthodox Jew who rescued us from the tailor's shop, and that's when I realized that she could *see* his image in my mind. Then, I remembered what Yakov told me: 'Don't make love to the girl of your dreams.'"

"Wait," said Catharine suspiciously, "I thought the girl of your dreams was Peggy Sue from Garfield High."

"There never was a Peggy Sue," he replied impatiently, "and I didn't attend Garfield High, wherever that may be. But it hadn't occurred to me that anyone might call the wicked queen the *girl of my dreams*."

"Hadn't occurred to you? But she's been in your dreams before," said Catharine, "hasn't she? How many of your dreams has she appeared in?"

He tried to recall. "Well, it's hard to say, because at first she appeared to me in the guise of Sharon." He shivered to think he could have mistaken this sorceress for his beloved wife. "I suppose my first dream with the wicked queen was the one I had on the admiral's plane to Joint Base Andrews. You woke me up from that dream."

"So—" Catharine began.

"Wait," he said. "No, maybe it was the dream I'd had earlier that morning, just before I got the call from Shawn in Jerusalem."

Catharine rubbed her chin sagely. "So, she already had her eye on you before any of this started. Smart cookie."

"She said I reminded her of my ancestor *Yussif,* who interpreted Pharaoh's dreams," said David. "She asked me if I would do that for *her*."

"Yussif interpreted Pharaoh's dreams?" she said. "Did she mean Joseph of the Bible?"

David nodded and shrugged at the same time.

"So, you're descended from Joseph of the Bible?" Catharine regarded him skeptically. "How *old* must this wicked queen be to know such things?"

"Old enough to have lived in pre-Judaic times as the Queen of Heaven."

"You mean, she's—?"

He nodded. "A *goddess*. One of the Anunnaki Pantheon of Twelve."

"Does she have a name?"

"Many."

Catharine looked at him impatiently.

"Her given name was Irninni. When she became Anu's consort, she was renamed *Inanna,* meaning *beloved of Anu,* which was how she was known in Sumeria. Later on, in the heyday of ancient Egypt, she was known as *Ishtar*. In Greece, she was *Aphrodite*; in Rome *Venus*." It suddenly occurred to him that the minisub had remained stationary for quite a while. "How long are we planning to stay here?" he asked.

At first Catharine seemed shell-shocked. "Wow!" she muttered to herself. "That was *one girl?* She must have had quite the publicist." She turned to David. "We're waiting to make sure they haven't found us. Figure a half hour. If nothing's happened by then, we'll power up and resume progress toward Le Havre."

"How can we be sure they haven't found us?" asked David.

Before Catharine could reply, there was a seismic thud far away. A few seconds later, their minisub shuddered, and the lapping of water against the hull intensified.

"Is that *them?*" David asked in a whisper.

At last William emerged from underneath the console and picked up the trouble light. "I had to clip the wire right away, but I finally got the blasted battery out."

There was another thud, this one much closer.

William held a finger up to his lips. "*Sssshhhh!* Probably *them*," he said and flicked off the trouble light, which had been the only light in the cabin.

They sat still and silent in the blackness for a good five minutes. Then there was another seismic thud that sounded quite loud and might have originated right outside the grotto. The minisub jerked backward suddenly.

William clenched his teeth and whispered, "That does it. I'm going to turn the screws just enough to maintain steerage, because if we smack into the side we're goners."

They know we're here, thought David in alarm. But on a rational level he knew it was more likely that their adversaries were just proceeding methodically down the Seine with little hope of reacquiring their quarry, and were likely to pass by none the wiser.

A loud hum began to approach, reminiscent of the one emitted by the flying cigar when it came upon David and Catharine's escort in the streets of Paris. To make things even more terrifying, the blackness of the cabin yielded to a bright white glow that seemed to originate in the water just outside the grotto.

David struggled to envision the craft hunting them down, but his imagination failed him. *Please don't let them see us,* he prayed. *Nobody's in here. Just pass by. Go by. Please, go away.*

The hum faded, seeming to move down the Seine. After a few more seismic thumps, each a bit further off than the last, silence prevailed.

Catharine ventured a whisper.

"I think they have trouble seeing through stone."

It wasn't much of a boon, David had to admit, but it was the first chink they'd found in their adversary's armor.

CHAPTER 9

The following afternoon, Admiral Simmons stood in a foyer in the West Wing of the White House, waiting to be fetched by the President's secretary and admitted to the Oval Office.

He stared out a window and mulled over an encoded message he'd received just an hour earlier—on *paper* of all things—disguised as a mundane message from his wife about an upcoming dinner party. Once deciphered, the message conveyed that the lieutenant commander and the professor had safely reached the sub base at Le Havre and were being transferred to a seaworthy British submarine for transit to Cornwall naval base.

While the message so far was reassuring, the admiral was baffled by a cryptic three-word message that the sender (probably the lieutenant commander) had insisted be sent to him at once: *Rock crushes paper.*

He put himself in the shoes of the one who sent the message, a practice he often used to aid in understanding. Catharine knew that—especially now—any message could fall into the wrong hands and be deciphered, so it would need to be framed in a manner enigmatic to the unauthorized viewer. As Catharine was no fool, she knew that the *more* important the message, the *more* enigmatic it must be to the unauthorized viewer. But ideally it should be as clear as possible to the intended recipient. As this message seemed cryptic even to the admiral, Catharine likely regarded it as highly important.

Rock crushes paper. He scratched his head. All that the message brought to mind was the childhood method of drawing lots: *Rock, Paper, Scissors.* But if that was the source of the expression, then the message got the rules *backward*; Paper covers rock. Rock crushes *scissors.*

He half-wished that he still smoked cigars so he had something to do with his hands. He felt as though he'd been passed by, not by the President, but by events. The world was under immediate threat, but just what *kind* of threat, no one knew, and no one seemed able to find out. He had no answers. He didn't even know the right questions. He couldn't even figure out the meaning of this blasted message.

But he *did* know that those bastards in the spaceships were massing in orbit around the Earth and interfering in human affairs in ways no one had ever anticipated. There was a tap on his shoulder.

"Admiral?" said Holly. The admiral forced a smile for her benefit. She was a sweet person, one who seemed to feel the anxiety of everyone waiting to see her boss. "Follow me," she said and turned toward the Oval Office with a clipboard under her arm.

Before opening the door to the Oval Office, she turned to him gravely. "I'm sure I don't have to tell you, admiral. He's had a miserable few days. All he's been getting is bad news. Try to cheer him up. Get him to have a drink, if you can. That single-malt Scotch you sent him is his favorite, but he's vowed not to drink it unless he can share it with you. It's in the bottom drawer of that old-style filing cabinet he keeps in there."

The admiral nodded wistfully.

Holly winked in return, and pointed to her own broad smile as *his* cue to enter smiling. For the second time in as many minutes, he forced a smile of his own. Holly opened the door and allowed him into the Oval Office.

The President rose from the *Resolute* desk and extended his hand. "Bob, y'old salt!" said the President. "What's the scuttlebutt?"

"Well, not much going on with the grandkids, Mister President—"

"Please, admiral," said the President confidentially, "if you're Bob, I'm *Jim*. I've got few enough real friends. Take a seat."

The admiral prepared to sit. "In that case … Jim … how's about a drink?"

The President nodded agreeably, as though he'd been awaiting the suggestion. "Let me ask Holly where—"

"It's in the bottom drawer of your filing cabinet."

The President smiled—for the first time today, by the look of it. "I see Holly has you primed."

The admiral shrugged. "What can I say? She's the best at what she does."

The President grabbed the bottle, two glasses from a tea tray, and placed them all on the coffee table before the admiral. "Please, Bob, do the honors, but take it easy. We've got some serious *hombres* to conference in."

The admiral poured an honest shot for each of them, handed the President a glass, and raised his own in a toast. "To *us*—getting the

United States of America *safely out* of present circumstances."

The President raised his glass and mulled over its contents before drinking. "I'm not sure there's enough of this stuff in the world to make me believe we're gonna do that."

They each took a sip and sighed.

"Well," said the admiral, "who're the *hombres* we're taking on this afternoon?"

"The big boys at North American Aerospace Defense," said the President. "But that's not for another few minutes. Besides, my predecessor told me it's always a good thing to keep generals waiting. Keeps them in their place." The President leaned into the admiral. "What's going on with your golden boy?"

It took the admiral a moment to realize whom he meant. "You mean the professor?"

The President nodded.

"He's in transit," said the admiral, silently mouthing the word *submarine* while making a diving motion with his hand.

"*Jesus,* Bob. If we have to whisper in here, we got problems."

The admiral shrugged and took another sip. "We got problems."

"What else do you hear?" asked the President.

The admiral picked up the bottle and waved it toward the President. "Want another belt first?" His jocular question had the opposite of its intended effect.

The President became glum again. "Why? What's happened?"

"Well," said the admiral, "they seem to have established a demilitarized zone having a ten-mile radius around the platform in Jerusalem, and another one around the Temple of Jupiter in Baalbek."

"They've *landed?*"

The admiral shook his head. "The perimeter is apparently unguarded. But weapons won't discharge inside the circle."

"Weapons … like *artillery?*"

The admiral shook his head. "*No* weapons seem to discharge in there. It was first brought to our attention after an IDF drill sergeant set up for rifle training. When he did an opening demonstration, he took aim and pulled the trigger, but all he got was a click. So he reloaded, pulled the trigger, and got the same result. Then he switched rifles and *still* got only a click. At this point, he was sure he was the butt of an elaborate joke, so he was fit to be tied. After extracting a couple hundred pushups from the recruits, he had *them* load and fire."

"Anything?" asked the President.

The admiral shook his head. "Silence. No discharge. The instructor canceled the exercise and dispersed the platoon. Thank heavens this was IDF. Those Israelis have got some brains. The drill instructor collected up the unspent rounds and tried them again at an officer's range about fifteen miles away."

"And?" said the President, taking a sip.

"The rounds fired. The DI brought it to the attention of the brass, and they tried firing exercises at five locations at varying distances from the platform. They quickly concluded that the no-fire radius was ten miles."

"So, any of our forces penetrating the zone would be relegated to sharp sticks." The President looked into his glass. "How the hell can anyone cause a chemical reaction to fizzle like that?"

"Unknown as yet, Jim. I've asked IDF to check a whole range of weapons inside the perimeter, except the really *big* stuff like nukes and fuel-air bombs. Awaiting results." He picked up the bottle. "Another?"

The President rubbed his eyes and shook his head. "Thanks, Bob, but I've been having trouble sleeping, and the doc says booze'll just make it worse. Let's call those generals. What do you say?"

The admiral nodded and knocked back the rest of his round.

"Holly," said the President pushing an intercom button, "could you get me NORAD?"

"They're on the line waiting for you, Mister President," she said. "Shall I patch them in?"

"Please," he said. "Put 'em on the squawkbox."

"Afternoon, Mister President," said the voice of an older man. "General Baltazar here. I've taken the liberty of getting the heads of each of the three zones in on the call. Shall I dismiss them until needed?"

"No, general," said the President. "They might as well stay on the line. I have Bob Simmons here with me."

The general chirped up. "*Admiral*, how're you? It's been a while."

"Much too long, general," said the admiral. "What have you got for us this afternoon?"

"Well, gentlemen," said the general, "I'm afraid I don't have encouraging news. Which component of the nuclear triad shall we begin with?"

"Your call, general," said the President.

"Let's start with our nuclear-armed bomber aircraft. The planes are operating fine. The readiness of the nuke warheads on the aircraft is monitored continuously by sensors connected to reinforced computers onboard. All aircraft now show that the missiles are fully functional, but the nuke triggers in the warheads are … inoperative."

The admiral watched helplessly as the President slunk further down in his chair.

The general continued. "Undersea, our boomers are operating fine, but their missiles also show triggers inoperative."

The admiral furrowed his brow. "Are the boomers still on routine patrol?"

"That's what the Navy tells us, admiral," said the general.

"Pointless," muttered the admiral.

"In a sense, putting boomers with inoperable triggers on routine patrol *is* pointless," said the general. "However, we have to bear in mind that we're being watched by numerous adversaries, not just the … aliens. If we were to take the boomers off patrol, it would be the first time since the 1960s and it *would* be noticed. Sooner or later, word would get around."

"Sooner or later?" said the President.

"Well, Mister President, in the past couple days the intelligence community has grown nervous that their radio messages are being intercepted and deciphered by … you-know-who. As a consequence, I'm a little embarrassed to admit that even *U.S.* signals intelligence has begun moving from point to point on *paper*. It's expensive and ridiculously slow, but it's pretty much foolproof."

Signals intelligence moving around on paper, thought the admiral. *Rock crushes paper. Was Catharine telling me that the aliens' signals can be blocked by ... stone?*

The general resumed. "As for the nuclear silos, Mister President, our ground communications ops have confirmed that the orbiting spacecraft are continuously sending down as many as four independent waves. At least three are electromagnetic. The fourth is complex. It appears to travel at the speed of sound, so it's at least partly sound waves, but our geeks tell us there's more than sound waves in the signal, and they haven't been able to get a handle on it."

"What's the purpose of these four waves?" asked the President.

"The purpose of at least one—probably two—appears to be disabling our nukes. For that purpose the rays *work,* unfortunately."

"General, Bob here. Have you been able to figure out *how* they disable nukes?"

"We can't tell precisely what process they're using—appears to be far ahead of our state of the art. We *can* tell what effect the rays seem to have, though. Good news first, if you can call it that: None of the waves appears to interfere with ignition or navigation on any of our submarines, aircraft, or missiles. So, they're not causing a rocketry or guidance problem."

"*Not yet,*" said the President.

"Quite right, Mister President," said the general. "We don't know the capabilities of any technology they haven't deployed. But, back to what we *do* know: The aliens' rays do two things. First, they disable our nuclear triggering mechanisms, so we can't commence atomic fission. We figure that problem might be surmountable if we can redesign the mechanism. But … there's worse."

"There always *is,*" said the President resignedly.

"We tested the fissile material. As you know, the uranium isotope we use to sustain fission is generally U-235."

"Yes," said the President.

"Well, we found significant quantities of *U-238* in the warheads, which won't sustain—in fact, *dampen*—the fissile reaction."

The admiral was confused. "You mean, they changed the isotope of the fissile material without physically removing it from the warhead?"

"Correct."

"Neat trick," said the President despondently. "So, they can add neutrons to the uranium atoms *remotely?*"

"So it appears, Mister President."

The President's face reddened. "Well, how the *hell* can they do that?"

"We're not sure, sir, but we expect it's their rays."

The President clenched up like a man expecting a blow to the face. "General," he said, "have the arsenals of the *other* nuclear powers been similarly affected?"

"They wouldn't tell us, of course, sir, but satellite surveillance shows they're in a blind panic. Their activities are consistent with having no effective nukes. They're pissing their pants, sir."

"So are *we*, general," said the President contemplatively. "So are we. Do you have anything to add to this news?"

"Not at present, sir. We're still trying to figure out how to fix the damage."

The President nodded. "And if a rogue nation solves this little engineering problem before the United States does, then that would give them a window to attack us with nukes without fear of retaliation in kind, and we'd be well and truly screwed. Wouldn't we?"

"Correct, sir."

The admiral asked, "Are there any warheads that have *not* been affected by their sabotage?"

"We're far from finished in our testing, admiral, but so far ... nothing."

The President looked at the phone darkly. "Well, fix this problem, general. I will not have the United States vulnerable to nuclear attack or blackmail on my goddam watch. *Do you understand?* Get some of those Ivy League physicists on your payroll to earn their freaking pay and *fix this!*"

"Night and day, sir. We're on it night and day."

Since it sounded like the call was winding down, the admiral figured the time was now or never to introduce his adjutant's apparent suggestion. "May I pose just one more question to the general, Mister President?"

The President nodded. "Shoot."

"General," said the admiral, "how did your people detect these rays in the first place?"

"Well, admiral, they have some pretty delicate sensors—"

"Could you assemble these sensors in some remote location? Fit 'em all in, say, a milk crate, so you could cap the crate with different materials, one after the other, to see what, if anything, blocks the rays?"

There was a momentary silence. "Please hold a sec, admiral. I've gotta check with a technician."

A minute later the general came back on the line. "Mister President. Admiral. The tech says he can do it, and especially likes the admiral's idea of doing it with all the sensors together at a remote location. There'll be less need to repeat each test, and it'll be less likely to draw unwelcome attention. He says the admiral is welcome to join his crew any time."

There was general laughter on the line, and the admiral smiled. "Tell your tech two things for me, general. First, tell him I'm old enough to know when I'm gettin' smoke blown up my keister." This was met with howls of laughter. "On a serious note, tell him that I've personally seen the aliens' scanning ray pierce straight through several inches of solid lead, then travel down four stories of a steel-frame building, and *continue to scan.* Now, I'm not telling him he'd be wasting his time trying out lead or other metallic shielding, but first he ought to try different kinds of rocks and stone, both crystalline and non-crystalline. And please tell him not to share the results with anyone but the people on this phone call."

"Rocks and stones, admiral. Got it."

"Thank you, general," said the President.

"Thank you, sir, and you, admiral."

The President hung up and handed the admiral his empty glass.

"One more drink won't kill us, Bob."

The admiral poured a short round and handed it to the President. "Jim, I notice you made no mention of the possibility that the *aliens themselves* could nuke us."

The President shrugged. "You think that's what they have in mind?"

The admiral shook his head. "It can't be their primary intention; otherwise, we'd already be toast. I'm not saying they won't change their minds but, till now, every time they've encountered an Earth vehicle trying to force them to land, they've disabled its weapons and shut down its engine. Although an engine shutdown is obviously deadly to anything that flies, it's a far cry from a direct attack on a population."

"Tell that to the families of the dead crewmen," said the President.

The admiral sighed. "Unfortunate losses, Jim, but nowhere near the scale we'd suffer during an attack."

The President took a hearty swig.

"So what do the aliens *want?*"

The admiral just shrugged and took a swig of his own.

⟶ ∘ ⌾⟋⟍⌾ ∘ ⟵

DAVID AND CATHARINE sat alone with their duffel bags in a small room at the Cornwall naval base awaiting orders to board U.S.S. *Columbia* (SSBN-826), a state-of-the-art nuclear-powered "boomer" submarine armed with a dozen Trident II nuclear-tipped intercontinental ballistic missiles and a full complement of heavyweight torpedoes.

The two watched a wide-screen television above the transom tuned to CNN, its audio set just above the threshold of audibility. It seemed to David an awful waste of resources to be using a *boomer* to transport two people around the southern tip of Africa. But he supposed the sub had likely been headed in that direction anyway.

A young man barged in. It was William, who'd piloted them to Le Havre and then switched them to a larger sub and escorted them safely to their present location. Now wearing civilian clothing, William was smiling from ear to ear.

"*Aha!*" he said jauntily, looking them up and down. "I see *Columbia* will have all the dead weight it needs. That's reassuring."

David nervously nodded in greeting, but Catharine rose and swaggered over to William.

"Headed to Scotland, limey?" she asked.

"Sure am, yank," he replied. "You know me, always livin' life in the Faslane."

She scowled. "That's an awful pun, sailor. Looking forward to getting the Perisher over with?"

His smile disappeared momentarily. "Rather lookin' forward to kickin' ass and takin' names, lieutenant commander."

"That's the spirit, William. I've observed your seamanship closely and have every confidence you'll make a fine submarine commander. Best of luck to you!"

Her sincerity knocked the swagger out of him for a moment, and he straightened up with real pride. "That's a great vote o' confidence, ma'am, and heartening comin' from you. Any final tips for me?"

"Well, I'm sworn to secrecy about the course, as you know," she said, then glanced about and beckoned him closer. In a lowered voice, she said, "Do you know the most common grounds for a senior officer to lose immediate command of his submarine?"

William gave it some serious thought and nodded. "Shiphandling errors."

She nodded approvingly. "What aspect of command have you been studying hardest for the past few months?"

He shrugged. "Tactics, I suppose."

"So, you've got tactics in the *front* of your mind," she said, touching his forehead with the palm of her left hand. "Right?"

He nodded.

She smiled knowingly. "So, what's in the *back* of your mind?"

He looked at her, confused.

She said to him intently, "Well, if you don't recall what you just said, permit me to remind you. You've put *shiphandling* in the back of your mind. That's a mistake. Remember, they're testing your situational awareness. Don't let the difficulty of the course distract you. Keep *shiphandling* in the front of your mind," she said, palm to his forehead again. "Put the safety of your vessel first, last, and always."

He looked at her as though she'd quoted from the Holy Bible and he wanted as much of a sermon as he could get. From her expression, she knew it.

"If you can't walk," she continued, "you can't dance. If you can't talk, you can't sing. If you can't handle the ship, you can't *fight* the ship, which is your only reason for command." She sighed in resignation. "And, as you know, while there may be such a thing as a damaged *surface* vessel …" She stopped, inviting him to finish her thought.

He nodded with conviction. "There's no such thing as a damaged submarine. There's only a *dead* submarine." He looked at her with conviction. "Aye, ma'am. *Shiphandling* is the order of the day—and *every* day. Thanks, lieutenant commander." He thrust his hand out to her.

"You showing me your *hand*, sailor?" She ignored it and smacked him hard on the shoulder with her open hand. "Come back and show me your *certificate*. Now, go kick ass and take names."

William picked up his bag and paused for a second, saluted, and turned on his heel. He marched out as with a purpose.

Catharine returned to her seat and could feel David's eyes boring into her. She looked his way.

"*What?*" she said.

"You're a fine leader, Catharine."

She smirked.

"No, really," he said with admiration. "You doubled his confidence and commitment to success."

She looked at him saucily. "Do you find that attractive?"

"That? Attractive *about you?*" He scoffed. "I've added it to my growing list."

He glanced up at the television, which was showing some footage taken in the desert, possibly with an aging smartphone. The image was jostling; evidently, the cameraman was riding a camel. On the sound-track, a man (probably the cameraman) was speaking what sounded like Egyptian Arabic. As yet, no English subtitles had been added, so the footage was probably quite recent.

For a long moment, the camera seemed to dwell on the horizon, with nothing coming into focus. When the cameraman shifted his angle slightly, the focus came to rest on the Great Pyramid. But it looked as though someone had taken a giant axe to it and cleanly chopped off the top.

"More from your bad guys?" asked Catharine.

"Anunnaki?" said David, as he searched for the television's remote. "That'd be my guess. The top piece of a pyramid, which was often removable from the main structure, is called a *pyramidion*. Historically, if it were composed of a single stone, it would have all sorts of carvings on it, and be called a *ben-ben* stone. Many of them were removed over the years; some are in museums to this day."

"But why would they cut off the top of the Great Pyramid?" she asked.

"Good question," he said, raising the volume with the remote. "I have a theory, of course, but a lawyer always has a theory."

Unsurprisingly, the newsreader was speaking with a British accent. "The Great Pyramid had not been scaled since a Danish photographer and his assistant climbed it one night and filmed themselves engaged in a sex act. Cairo authorities have denied that either that photographer or anyone else has ever been authorized to climb the pyramid or remove any portion of that priceless relic of mankind's remote past."

The picture cut away to a harried, Arabic-speaking official being interviewed at the base of the pyramid. There were English subtitles: "All Egypt is outraged by this act of vandalism. When the perpetrators are apprehended, they will be severely punished."

A reporter interrupted with a question. "Is there any sign of the removed material?"

"None," came the answer.

"Is it possible that the material slid down the face of the pyramid and now rests at its base?"

"No," said the official, allowing his irritation to show. "Official archaeologists have searched the whole area. There is no sign that this damage was done by nature."

David turned the sound down to its original level.

"This official's awfully worked up," he remarked.

Catharine nodded. "Let's face it, he's got a right to be."

David turned to her with a smirk. "Even if the material's been removed by the same ones who put it there in the first place?"

A young seaman walked in.

"Good evening, I'm here from the U.S.S. *Columbia*. All aboard that's goin' aboard." He winked at Catharine.

Catharine rose, a bit irritated by the seaman's breeziness. "I'm Lieutenant Commander Weldon, United States Navy."

The seaman opened his eyes wide. "Sorry, lieutenant commander. I didn't realize either of you were navy. They just said you were passengers." He reached for their duffel bags, but Catharine waved him off. "We'll carry our own," she said. When the seaman raised his eyebrows, she muttered, "Classified material." She pointed to David. "This is Professor Schubert."

"Yes, ma'am. This gentleman has been assigned to special quarters. Captain says he's to sleep in the closest thing we've got to a Faraday cage, whatever that is. Well, we don't have one of those onboard, but we've got a spare torpedo room with lots of metal shelves and other paraphernalia, so it should serve well enough. We call it the *bomb shop*."

"Oh, how pleasant," said David sardonically. "I'll be sleeping soundly among high explosives."

The seaman laughed. "In that, you'll be no worse off than the rest of us, sir. This whole vessel's full of hydrogen bombs. You'll get used to it. Besides, you'll be the only one aboard to have a room of his own."

"Are there women's quarters onboard?" asked Catharine.

"No, ma'am. But the executive officer's volunteered to give you his stateroom. The shower and latrine room are all you'll have to share, and that's with the captain, who's a true gentleman, or so I'm told."

"Please convey my compliments and sincere thanks to the XO, seaman, but I'll be sharing the bomb shop with the professor." This got another raised eyebrow. "He's in my care, and we're Special Ops on this voyage."

"Very well, ma'am," said the seaman with newfound respect. "Please follow me aboard. When a passenger boards, it's customary to ask the top enlisted man for permission to breathe his air and eat his food."

Catharine pulled out her keychain and showed him her golden dolphins.

The seaman snapped to attention. "Please follow me below. We'll get you all set up in poopy suits."

⟶○⟨⟨⟨⟩○⟵

IN A FEW minutes, the seaman led them to the bomb shop that would serve as their lodgings. When he opened the hatch, a vague smell of petroleum escaped, but the room was vacant and clean. It was lined with heavy shelves holding what appeared to be spare or damaged torpedo casings. A small shop floor occupied the center of the room with two sturdy polymer tables bolted to the floor.

Bolted to one wall was a double-decker bunk, where Catharine and David dropped their duffel bags on the floor.

"Captain's wise," remarked Catharine. "This *is* a damned Faraday cage."

The seaman pointed to a shelf stocked with towels. "Towels are over there. Over here's the latrine and shower," he said, rapping on a metal door. "There's a small medicine chest on the wall with a mirror for shavin' or … whatever." It was obvious he'd narrowly stopped himself from saying *or makeup*. "You two are lucky. This is as close as you get to private quarters on a submarine." He turned to Catharine. "Lieutenant commander, the executive officer asked me to send his compliments and invite you to share meals with the officers."

Catharine nodded. "Please extend my compliments to the XO, but I won't be leaving the professor for long enough to share a meal. If the XO has room for both of us, however, we'd be pleased to take him up on his offer."

The seaman shuffled, staring at his feet. "Ma'am, you have top-secret clearance. Does the professor here?"

Catharine shook her head. "No. But he had high enough clearance to travel with Admiral Simmons and barely escape with his life from a cockup at the U.S. Embassy in Paris. He's also met … one of those … things."

"*Things,* ma'am?"

She pointed straight up. "Those things coming from outer space."

"He's actually *met* one?" asked the seaman in amazement.

"One of them has repeatedly come to him in his dreams. They seem to think he's pretty important."

"In dreams?" said the seaman skeptically.

Catharine looked to David to reply.

"*Repeatedly,* seaman," said David. "Why do you think they put me in this Faraday cage? To block complex radio transmissions."

"What do they look like?" asked the seaman ingenuously.

"They look like … us, a bit taller. Or rather, *we* look like *them,* but a bit shorter."

The seaman nodded, obviously not fully understanding. "Be that as it may, lieutenant commander—and I will immediately inform the XO of that—it may not be high enough clearance for the professor to attend officer's mess if there's to be a briefing."

"I understand," said Catharine. "If we can't join the officer's mess, please let the XO know that I'm available for private discussion, eighteen seven."

David wondered why she didn't say *twenty-four* seven, but held his tongue.

"Very well," said the seaman, preparing to leave. "Is there anything I can get you from the cook for the time being?"

Catharine gave it some thought. "Please bring me a big roll of aluminum foil, if he can spare it. We may need it to make some hats."

The seaman looked at her strangely, nodded, and stepped off.

David pointed to the bunks. "Top or bottom?" he asked.

"I like to be on top," she said.

Of course, being a man, he heard that as a sexual remark. When he looked at her, to his amazement her face showed that she meant it to be taken precisely that way. He felt his face flush. "I meant, which bunk?"

She smiled wryly. "What *else* would you have meant?" she said, and tossed her duffel bag on the top bunk.

CHAPTER 10

THE BOOMER CAST off and proceeded apace toward the open sea. Catharine was summoned by the captain, leaving David alone in the deserted bomb shop.

Resigned to an indefinite bit of solitude, David stretched out on his bunk with the intention of napping, but sleep would not come. Instead, all sorts of nagging questions kept popping into his head.

He quickly shoved aside speculation about the possibility that humanity was about to be destroyed, as that left nothing to contemplate but sheer horror.

In contemplating the other possibilities, what troubled him most was that he simply could not envision a world where the return of the Anunnaki would leave human civilization intact. *Would humanity be disarmed? Subjugated? Enslaved?* (None of these possibilities seemed outlandish, as the human species had originally been fashioned to serve as gold-mining slaves.) *Would humanity be restricted to geographic areas deemed inhospitable by the new occupiers? Would the Anunnaki put an end to human life unless humans were to mend their ways? What if there were widespread disobedience to Anunnaki rule?*

A knock on the door dispelled the worst of these thoughts.

Catharine stuck her head in and smiled.

"Are you decent?" she asked.

"No," he said, "but I *am* fully clothed."

"Pity," she said, entering.

"*Which* is a pity?"

She ignored the question. Too silly for her, he imagined.

"The sub'll be diving in a minute," she replied, "so get ready for some noise."

She left the door open and started unpacking her duffel bag.

"Captain wants you to brief him in eight hours," she said matter-of-factly, "so let's get some sleep."

He looked at her askance. "How much does the captain 'need to know' in order to drop us off at a designated deep-water port?"

"Captains want to know everything," she said blithely.

"Well, that's not going to happen."

She stopped unpacking. "*What's* not going to happen?"

"I can't brief anybody on this," he protested. "I don't know any-thing—just *guessing* a lot of stuff. I'd just as soon not endanger this vessel and all its occupants by saying something unfounded that turns out to be dead wrong."

"And if you're right?"

He looked at her skeptically. "Then it's probably the end of the world as we know it. Does the captain really need to hear that? It's not prescriptive; it's just depressing." He cocked his head. "What does he *already* know?"

She nodded. "Before we came aboard, he already knew that the nu-clear triggers on his warheads don't work. He'd also learned that the Anunnaki have disabled all our weapons in proximity to them, right down to guns that won't fire."

"They can disable our guns? Including small weapons like rifles and pistols?"

"So it appears."

He shook his head in amazement. "Well, that's hardly reason for me to babble on about the return of the ancient gods."

She placed her hands on her hips. "And while I was in the captain's stateroom, he received orders from the admiral, some of which were directed to you and me."

"From *our* admiral?" asked David.

She nodded.

"I thought he was retired," said David.

"He is," she replied. "Technically, the orders came from the Presi-dent of the United States. He was there with the admiral."

"No kidding?" asked David skeptically.

"None," she replied.

"What were the admiral's orders?"

She shrugged. "Do *you* really need to know?" She waited a moment for her point to sink in before resuming. "The admiral ordered the captain to take apart one of the warheads to see if it's still fissionable."

"They're taking apart a nuclear warhead *on this submarine?*" asked David, astonished.

"Look on the bright side. If they mess up, we won't have to worry about getting murdered in Mozambique … or zapped in Zimbabwe."

"I see what you mean," said David. "Well, since you were in touch with the admiral, why didn't you ask for leave for me to brief the captain?"

She smiled. "I did, and he gave you leave." She pulled a torn paper from her breast pocket and dropped it on David's chest.

He picked it up and unfolded it. It said: *Smoked paprika.* That was all. Nothing else.

"Pardon my impertinence, lieutenant commander," said David drily, "but this is an otherwise blank piece of paper that says *smoked paprika.* Somehow, I feel the need for a bit more before I risk a firing squad by blabbing to the captain."

She shrugged. "Well, that's all you're gonna get for now."

"What the hell does it even *mean?*" he demanded. "Do you have a code book that says—"

She rolled her eyes. "It means 'permission granted.'"

"In what code?"

"The informal code the admiral and I have been using for the past five years. I pose as his wife preparing a dinner party, and ask him to bring home something that I used up. He guesses what I want. If he guesses something green, like oregano, it means *no.* If it's something red, it means *yes.* Paprika is red."

"Didn't the admiral order us not to use the radio?"

She shook her head. "No. He said we can't use the radio *ourselves* or be mentioned on it."

He waved the paper at her. "What'd you ask him, that he answered in such a *spicy* way?"

"Whether the captain could speak freely with our wine steward."

"So, now I'm a wine steward?" asked David indignantly.

"He knew what I was asking."

"How can you be sure?"

"Because he guessed something red," she shot back.

Although he wasn't quite satisfied, he could see she felt certain. "Other than the captain, do the officers and crew know about the disabled nukes?"

She shook her head.

"Just as well," he said. "Learning that wouldn't do much for their *esprit de corps.* And what I'm going to tell the captain would be far more dispiriting for them to hear."

She nodded in agreement. "Incidentally, you never told me why you suspect the Anunnaki stole the top off the Great Pyramid."

He nodded. "When you imagine the top of the Great Pyramid disappearing, what's the shape of the thing that disappeared?"

"A little pyramid," she said. "A *pyramidion*, I guess, is what you called it."

"And what shape would be most stable for something replacing the cap that disappeared?"

"A little pyramid of the same size as the one removed, I guess."

"Specifically, a pyramid having four sides like the Great Pyramid, and the same angle of incline as the Great Pyramid. Remember the three shapes of the alien craft that our forces have spotted thus far?"

She nodded. "Cigar-shaped, flying saucer-shaped, and—"

"And pyramid-shaped," he said, finishing her thought. "Want to bet they're four-sided with the same incline as the Great Pyramid?"

"So … one of those pyramid spaceships is going to land there?"

He nodded somberly. "Probably the one with the most important Anunnaki on board."

"The *big cheese*," she said.

"And when it lands there," he said, "we'll probably learn who's in charge on Nibiru, which will largely determine the fate of humanity."

A klaxon sounded and a voice came on the intercom.

"Diving sequence commenced!"

⋙◦⋘

THE BOOMER HAD reached cruising depth at last, which was deep indeed. The few lights that remained on in David and Catharine's makeshift dormitory were mercifully dimmed, the silence interrupted only intermittently by an eerie groaning or popping of the hull.

The only other sound in the room was soft; it emanated from the upper bunk, where the playback device that Catharine bought at the base commissary endlessly repeated its small complement of rock/jazz fusion.

Six hours passed during which David slept dreamlessly.

With the umpteenth return of the song *Tomorrow's Girls*—a darkly humorous tune from the 1990s about an invasion of girls from outer space—the volume seemed to rise spontaneously.

They're mixing with the population/ A virus wearing pumps and pearls.

Though the music video had been quite old when David learned of it, it nonetheless became a favorite in his youth. Its humor somehow escaped him now, however, perhaps because there *was* a woman from outer space who really *was* invading his mind.

The mattress above him creaked, and he opened his eyes.

Catharine's pretty, upside-down face peered at him from the upper bunk with an enigmatic smile and a blonde ponytail that hung down next to her face. In that posture, she was just too adorable to be taken seriously. David felt a weight lift from his chest and he laughed quietly, momentarily transported from a desperate mission to a suburban slumber party complete with music and a *very* desirable woman.

"Want some company?" she asked.

"Only if it's you."

With surprising arm strength, Catharine let herself down from the upper bunk and swung into his, creeping under the blanket next to him and placing her head on his shoulder. Like David, she was wearing a white coverall, so the effect was less than erotic. Though he wanted her nonetheless, for the time being he resolved to be satisfied with the chasteness of the new arrangement. Besides, it would be simpler.

Something inside told him to remain passive and let her snuggle up to him, to treat her like a kid sister who'd just suffered a breakup and needed a big brother to comfort her. But he just couldn't do it. She was too beautiful, too admirable, too … near. And she wasn't his sister.

Against his better judgment, he gently stroked her cheek.

She moved in and kissed him ardently.

He was relieved to be lying down, because hers was the kind of kiss that made him weak in the knees. He could feel a desire for life well up in his chest until he thought it would burst. It was a feeling he hadn't had in … well, a long time.

He kissed her right back, perhaps even more ardently, but when at last he opened his eyes, tears were running down her cheeks.

"I guess I'm not much of a kisser," he said apologetically.

She snorted a chesty laugh that sprayed his face.

Ignoring his own face, he wiped hers with a tissue and kissed her on the cheek.

"So," he said after a decent interval, "you know plenty of my story, yet I know nothing of yours."

She scoffed. "I have no story. At best, I have an *almost* story."

"Well," he said gently, "I'm *almost* ready to hear it. . . whatever you care to share of it, anyway." When she seemed reluctant to open up her feelings, he added, "To begin with, did he have a name?"

"*Trevor*," she said, as though remembering something from another lifetime. "I was at university in Oxford. My dad was serving as His

Majesty's Chief Coastguard. *Lord* Trevor was in Coast Guard training, and Dad thought he would be just a *perfect* match for his lovely girl."

"Your dad was Chief Coastguard of the U.K.?"

She nodded.

"Pardon me for asking, but which of your parents was Jewish?"

"Why do you ask?"

"Well," he said, "I know things have changed over the past few decades, but it seems unusual for a Jew to be put in such a sought-after position."

She nodded. "My mother's Jewish. You know, those good Anglican boys can't resist women of the Tribe."

He smirked. "Well, they seem to have done so for an awfully long time."

"Her Majesty Queen Elizabeth let it be known that no such prejudice was acceptable any longer, and it vanished, seemingly overnight."

"And did Lord Trevor turn out to be the pillar of virtue your father had hoped for?"

She sighed. "So he seemed … for a few weeks … until I found him with another girl, and dumped him." She sighed again. "See what I mean about my having only an *almost* story?"

"I'm sorry" was all David could think to say.

"Don't be. It was painful, but that's when I decided to become an American. No lords and ladies in America. I applied to the Naval Academy at Annapolis and did surprisingly well."

"Evidently," he said.

She turned and lay on her back to stare at the bottom of her own bunk. "Isn't this where you're supposed to risk all by touching me inappropriately and trying to remove my clothing?"

He looked at her with chagrin. "Sorry. With no time to pack, I seem to have left home without my copy of *The Lout's Handbook*."

She laughed again. "I would never think you a lout." She dug an elbow into the mattress and turned toward him, resting her head on her fist. "You sound as though you'd rather have a tête-à-tête than fool around with me. Should I be insulted?"

"Quite the contrary," he assured her. "It means I'd rather start a long-term relationship with you than risk blowing my chances at the start."

"Well," she said, evidently impressed, "that's not something a girl hears every day." She looked at him skeptically. "You're not …?"

He opened his eyes wide, the picture of innocence. "Not *what?*"

"Don't make this harder than it has to be," she said.

"I'm not *gay*, if that's what you're getting at," he said. "I'm a widower, which could be *worse* from your viewpoint."

"Why?" asked Catharine. "Are you still in love with her?"

He sighed. "I'll always love her memory, I suppose. But, no, I've reached the point where there's room in my heart for someone … like you."

She smiled. "You mean, someone … *living?*"

He smiled back at her. "For your information, it's been years since I found any woman as attractive as I do you."

"Then why aren't you making mad love to me?" She turned to him suspiciously. "Is there someone else?"

"Someone else?" he echoed. "No one in my sights," he said, "but I find myself in the sights of one very powerful woman."

She returned to lying on her back. "I might have known."

"You *do* know. I'm talking about the one they call Inanna, Ishtar, Aphrodite, Venus."

"Oh, so now the alien *is* the girl of your dreams?" she scoffed.

"Hardly," said David thoughtfully. "To tell the truth, she scares the daylights out of me. Her … *history* … with men has been well known for millennia."

"You mean there are ancient tablets about it?" asked Catharine incredulously.

David nodded. "About two thousand years before the birth of Jesus, Gilgamesh was a great king of the Sumerian city of Uruk. He was tyrannical, but extraordinarily strong and brave. He also believed himself to be *more* than a demigod, that is, more than one-half Anunnaki, and so was vexed when his mother told him he would not enjoy the Anunnaki's seemingly infinite life span."

"I've heard that story. It's about the Great Flood, right?"

"Not exactly, although after Gilgamesh and his friend go to the ends of the Earth to accomplish things that no ordinary mortals could have done, he asks the advice of Ziusudra (whom we call Noah), who'd been given extraordinarily long life by Enlil when the Flood subsided."

"How did Ziusudra advise Gilgamesh?"

"To paraphrase, he told him, 'Go home and enjoy your life as it is, because the Anunnaki have decided not to confer their extraordinary life span on you.' So, the two travelers headed back to Uruk with Gilgamesh resigned to his mortality. Just before they reached the city, however, Gilgamesh was accosted by Inanna—"

"The girl of your dreams," suggested Catharine.

"The woman who's *commandeered* my dreams," he corrected, and continued the tale. "She offered herself to Gilgamesh to be his wife. But Gilgamesh knew that Inanna had a habit of marrying extraordinary men and shoving them toward greatness. Sometimes it worked—for a while. Sometimes it didn't. And when it didn't, her husband would generally end up condemned to a life of pain, exiled, or dead."

Catharine furrowed her brow. "Did Gilgamesh accept her proposal of marriage?"

"Hardly. He insulted her directly by reciting the lousy endings of every one of her former men; husbands and lovers alike."

She clucked her tongue. "That's not the way to a woman's heart. What did Inanna do?"

"She shrieked at the insult and would not be satisfied with killing Gilgamesh outright or laying some ordinary trap for him. Instead, she went to her great-grandfather and former lover Anu, Lord of the planet Nibiru and father to Enlil and Enki, and demanded that he set the Bull of Heaven on Gilgamesh—the Bull of Heaven being the model for the Constellation Taurus. Anu tried to calm her down, but she insisted. So he set the Bull of Heaven on Gilgamesh. It chased and fought Gilgamesh and his friend all the way back to Uruk. By the time they could no longer run, Gilgamesh's friend had identified the Bull's weakness, and he helped Gilgamesh to kill it."

Catharine's mouth hung open. "This was four thousand years ago?"

David nodded somberly.

Catharine showed some sympathy. "Poor you! And she doesn't seem the type to mellow with age."

"You're such a comfort," he said sarcastically.

The gentle hum of the engines suddenly spiked, and the sub accelerated.

Catharine pondered a moment, then asked, "Do you expect you'll end up with her?"

David shook his head emphatically. "Not if I can help it. But I have a feeling it's not going to be entirely up to me."

Outside the room, someone hurriedly descended the stairs and knocked urgently on the door.

Through the door came the voice of the seaman who'd escorted them onto the sub. "Lieutenant commander? Professor? May I come in?"

David shot out of the bunk and plopped onto a nearby chair. Catharine rose and opened the door. "Come," she said, gesturing him in.

The seaman was out of breath and seemed a little alarmed, but spoke quietly. "Ma'am, Captain's about to call general quarters and he wants you and the professor on the bridge before he gives the order. Please accompany me at once."

Catharine replied, "The captain is a considerate gentleman. If we're not there before general quarters, we'll be run over in the hallway." She turned to David and beckoned him sternly with a crooked finger. "Showtime, professor. Come quick."

David followed the seaman and Catharine as they raced up the stairs. "What the devil is *general quarters?*" he whispered.

Without pausing, she turned and said, "Battle stations."

<hr />

As soon as they turned the corner to the bridge, the captain spotted them and turned to his executive officer. "XO, bring the ship to general quarters. Maintain course, depth, and speed … for now."

A klaxon sounded, followed by a series of orders on the public address system. David could hear the formerly quiet halls behind them thunder with the sound of running men.

Catharine approached the captain, followed by David, who was feeling more than a bit sheepish. "How can we help, captain?" she asked.

"Professor," said the captain, pointing to a circular sweep display, "what are those incoming blips?"

David nodded respectfully to the captain and stepped up to get a closer look. There were a half-dozen different shapes, each a different color.

"Am I looking at radar or sonar, captain?" asked David.

"Radar. Those targets are above the ocean's surface and dropping fast."

"What's their range?" asked David.

"At their present course and speed, they should splash down no more than two miles away."

David nodded. "May I assume these colors and shapes were arbitrarily assigned by your radarman and bear no relation to the actual shapes of the vehicles?"

"You may," said the captain.

David took a step back and shook his head. "It would help a great deal if I could see a video, sir. Based on this display, I can't—"

The XO overheard the conversation and grabbed a phone. "Comms, Bridge. This is the XO. Has that Photo-SLOT buoy broken the surface yet?"

"Bridge, Comms," came the reply on a nearby loudspeaker. "In ten seconds, XO … five. Breaking surface now, sir."

"Comms, Bridge. Give us a visual close-up of those bogeys as soon as you can."

"Bridge, Comms. They're dropping fast, sir, but I think our buoy'll give us a good tracking shot."

In another moment, the XO drew David's attention to a large video screen, where the image of three falling objects appeared, too distant to make out.

David said, "Can we get closer?"

The XO picked up the phone again. "Comms, Bridge. Maximum magnification, please."

In what seemed to David like a modern miracle, the shot moved in so close that one of the objects nearly filled the screen. There was some blurring and distortion around the perimeter, but the geometric shape was clear enough. He turned to check if Catharine was seeing the same thing. She nodded and pointed her chin toward the captain, as though to say, *Tell him.*

"It's *them*, sir," said David dismally.

"Them?" asked the captain.

David nodded. "The ones who've been … tinkering with our … equipment." He was reluctant to say more with so many unauthorized ears about.

"How can you tell?" asked the captain.

"The shape, sir. It's a pyramidion. Unless the captain knows of another world power employing vehicles of that shape, we can be fairly confident it's … one of *theirs*."

"Can you tell me who's aboard the … pyramidion?"

David was surprised to see how readily the captain adopted his word.

"I can only speculate, sir," said David. Then something occurred to him. "Unless—do we know the total number of pyramidions in this formation?"

"Twelve," said the captain.

David exhaled loudly. "Then I expect that each vehicle is occupied by one of their top twelve, sir. That's the number in their pantheon. Of course, I expect that they didn't bring their king, so one of the pyramidions probably contains someone else."

The XO suggested, "We could send a Harpoon missile, sir."

The captain sighed. "I salute your enthusiasm, XO, but they've made no outwardly aggressive move. Unless they do so, our orders are to stand down and stand by."

The video screen now showed the pyramidion splashing into the water and disappearing below the surface with no evident damage.

The XO picked up a phone. "TMA, Bridge. This is the XO. Have you picked up the submerged targets that just splashed?"

"Bridge, TMA. We're tracking them, XO. Shall we designate Hostiles 1 through 12, sir?"

"So designate, TMA. What are they doing now that they're underwater?"

"Dropping like a rock, sir. Straight down. They're already at seven hundred meters. We're seeing them through one thermal layer already. If they go through another, we'll probably lose track entirely. They're very quiet, sir."

"Any sign they've opened a hatch or made any aggressive move?" asked the XO.

"None, sir. They haven't shown the least sign they're aware of us."

"Cheeky," remarked the XO, turning to the captain. "Orders for depth, course, and speed, captain?"

"Maintain depth and speed. Maintain quiet. Adopt a racetrack pattern, at least until I've done interviewing our new friends. Stand down from general quarters, but if you see those things do anything unexpected, buzz me at once."

The captain ushered David and Catharine into his stateroom and closed the door.

⇒∘C═══⟆∘⇐

AFTER TWENTY MINUTES' conversation, the captain sat shellshocked at his desk.

"They *created* us?" he asked incredulously.

David nodded patiently. "As gold-mining slaves, sir."

"From scratch?"

"No, sir. They started with the DNA of a hominid, probably Cro-Magnon, and mixed it."

"With whose DNA?"

"Their *own*, sir," said David.

"So ... they're part of *us*?"

"That's one way to look at it."

"Then, why is their technology so far ahead of ours?"

"Happenstance. The speculation is that, for some unknown reason, they started evolving much earlier than we," said David. "Of course, it's also possible that their planet was seeded by an even older form of life."

"The mind boggles," observed the captain.

"What's important for our purposes right now is that their planet was embroiled in great wars long before they came to Earth. They were as technologically advanced as we are now four thousand years ago."

The captain kneaded his brow. "They've had four thousand years to improve that technology. No wonder we can't touch them." He shook his head mournfully. "Good God! A four-thousand-year head start."

"And it's also no wonder they're not impeded by our military capabilities," said David. "It appears they can neutralize us whenever and wherever they wish."

The captain shook his head and asked. "So, what do they want?"

David shrugged. "Right now, they want us to worry about them."

"Well, if it's *worry* they want, they're doing a damned good job of it. Do not let a word of this get out to my officers or crew. They'll be crushed." He looked at Catharine. "Admiral Simmons suggested that your safe arrival at Beira may be necessary to any hope of defeating these … intruders. Was his understanding accurate?"

As hopeless as Catharine felt, she couldn't live with herself if she left the captain without a thin thread of hope. "It's not our *only* hope, sir, but it may put us in a position to find an answer to the question you just asked, namely, *What do they want? Or, put another way, Why are they here?"

The captain nodded contemplatively and added, *"And how the devil can we be rid of them?* Let me know if I can outfit you with anything that might help you in your task. *Anything."*

"Thank you, captain," said Catharine.

"Meanwhile," said the captain, "have *you* any questions?"

Catharine and David began to speak at once. As soon as David realized Catharine was talking, he let her finish.

"How long do you expect we'll be holding a racetrack pattern?" she asked.

"Till we receive orders to proceed," said the captain. "Even though we're at depth, the SLOT buoy allows us to communicate with command. Professor, had *you* a question?"

"I'm curious to know the point we've reached in our journey," said David.

The captain nodded as though he was expecting the question. "At the moment, we're several hundred miles due west of Sierra Leone. If we're soon released from our stay-put order, sometime tomorrow we should arrive at the same latitude as your destination, except we'll be on the *western* side of the African continent. Command is giving consideration to having us drop you two off at Walvis Bay in Namibia. That's on the west coast."

"Begging the captain's pardon," said Catharine. "That's about four hundred miles west of the airport at Windhoek, is it not?"

The captain nodded. "That's about right."

"But sir," she replied, "Windhoek is still *two thousand miles* from our ultimate destination in Zimbabwe. How would we get there?"

The captain shrugged. "Those logistics are out of my ken, lieutenant commander. Based on long experience, however, I'd warrant that if U.S. Naval Intelligence can get you there from Beira, then they can get you there just as well from Walvis Bay. The need may never arise. But if this ship is re-purposed to the Atlantic, we'll have no choice."

There was a buzz on the captain's intercom. He reached backward in his chair and threw a switch. A voice came on the intercom. "Captain, it's the XO. Command says we'll be holding at this location for at least another hour."

The captain scratched his head thoughtfully, pressed the Talk button and said, "Send the senior engineer to the bomb room with the package. Hold." The captain released the Talk button and asked Catharine, "Is that where you're quartered?"

"Aye, captain."

There was a twinkle in the captain's eye as he pressed the Talk button again. "Tell the engineer to send over two extra radiation suits first." He released the button and rested his arms on his blotter. "You two had better get back down there and suit up."

⟶∘⟨⟩∘⟵

WHEN CATHARINE AND David returned to the bomb room, they found a folded radiation suit on each of their bunks. Each suit had a green badge on the chest that would change colors if the radiation level rose. Though the navy had much more sophisticated radiation dosimeters, they needed to be read by a remote computer. For hands-on workers, it was more important to know the moment a hazard appeared, so the area could be evacuated at once.

Catharine assisted David in donning his suit, a cumbersome affair that made him feel a bit suffocated. Nonetheless, he returned the favor and fastened some clasps at the rear of Catharine's suit.

A moment later, there entered a similarly suited nuclear engineer carrying what looked like a full toolbox in his left hand. Accompanying him was a videographer brought along to memorialize the occasion.

The engineer stopped a moment and slickly introduced himself from behind his mask, reaching for David's hand. "Lieutenant commander?"

David shook the engineer's hand and smiled. "I'm Professor Schubert." He tilted his head toward Catharine. "*That's* the lieutenant commander."

With no hesitation or chagrin, the engineer shifted his hand to Catharine. "Welcome aboard, lieutenant commander." He did nothing to hide his annoyance that someone had presented him with two people to choose from, obviously causing a mistake for which he would accept no responsibility.

"I'm Paul Flanagan, Senior Nuclear Engineer," he said through a mouth full of whitened teeth. "I take it you folks are staying on for the … operation?"

"We are," replied Catharine. David nodded apprehensively.

There was a knock at the door. The videographer opened it, and two men entered carrying a lead box between them about the width of a coffin and half the length, emblazoned with brightly colored stickers warning that its contents posed a serious radioactivity hazard.

Flanagan silently pointed to one of the worktables bolted to the floor. The men left the box on the table and swiftly departed.

"Before we get started," said Flanagan, "are there any questions?"

David spoke up sheepishly. "*Er*, yes, one or two. You're going to open up a warhead here?"

Flanagan regarded him with thinly veiled derision. "That's why I'm here, professor."

"When you open it, will an alarm sound or something?"

"No," he began, but then equivocated. "Well … *you* won't hear anything, but when the inner casing is opened, the device transmits an encoded radio signal—strong enough to be picked up at NORAD at the Mountain in Colorado, informing them of the nature of the breach and the device's global position."

"What's the GPS data for?" asked David.

"If NORAD determines that unauthorized personnel have opened a warhead, they can quickly turn the offender and his workshop into a giant crater."

"Can the transmission be disabled?" asked David.

"No," said Flanagan, "but NORAD is expecting our signal, so they won't attack us."

"If NORAD can hear it," said David, "then I expect anybody closer can hear it as well."

Flanagan was unperturbed. "They'd have to know which frequency to expect it on, as well as how to decipher the message. You might be comforted to know there are a dozen failsafe devices hardwired into the warhead casing. Unfortunately, we have to disable all of them in order to open it up."

"Heartwarming," said David.

Flanagan laughed. "You can take comfort in knowing that the risk of serious radiation exposure is extremely low."

Catharine cleared her throat. "And the risk of unwanted … fission?"

Flanagan smiled broadly at Catharine in a suggestive way that made David want to punch his lights out. David could see that Catharine's reaction was similar.

"Well," said the engineer, "avoiding *that* is my most important job. Fortunately, your chances of survival are no worse than the captain's."

"Meaning that the whole ship would be vaporized," said Catharine.

Flanagan nodded, then cocked his head with theatrical assurance. "With proper handling," he said, "the possibility of that is extremely low. I'll show you when we open 'er up."

The engineer opened the shielded box using a combination he'd committed to memory. As the lock released, he shot Catharine another smile, which set her teeth on edge. He removed the device from the box and gingerly set it down on the table.

"Looks like you've done this before," said Catharine.

"Several times, ma'am. Now, if it's all the same to you, captain's waiting for the results, so we'll begin." He turned to the cameraman. "You can turn that on now."

"Been filming since the package arrived," said the cameraman.

Flanagan grabbed a chair, slid it over to the table with the device on it, sat down, and smiled for the camera.

Catharine looked to David. Even through his filmy mask, he could see her roll her eyes. Still, she was too curious to stand aside while the warhead casing was opened, so she sidled up to the engineer, leaving a defensive distance between them.

Flanagan put down the toolbox he'd been carrying and flipped it open. Apparently, it contained a mobile two-piece radiation detector he referred to as a Geiger counter. He flipped it on; it showed low residual radiation levels.

"It always amazes me," said Flanagan, "how clean of radiation this room is." He picked up a screwdriver and opened the outer casing, being careful to follow protocol, which he also evidently knew by heart. A few minutes later, he'd disabled all the failsafe mechanisms and was ready to open the inner casing.

"Professor," said Flanagan, "if you'd care to see what the guts of this thing look like, now's the time. Just don't *touch* anything."

David could see that Flanagan was perspiring heavily under his suit and could only imagine how much more *he'd* be perspiring in charge of a delicate operation that could destroy the sub and cause an international uproar.

Using a fine machine-tooled screwdriver with a file handle to give the user the best possible grip, Flanagan unscrewed the four screws holding the inner casing in place.

David felt a jolt up his spine as he realized that, in a moment, he was going to be looking close up … at an *atomic bomb* substantially more powerful than the two used to end the Second World War.

"Here goes nothin'," said Flanagan as he lifted the plate off the warhead and placed it on the table next to the device. Inside were more fine wires and circuits than David could count.

On either side of a shielded unit at the center were identical metallic hemispheres.

Flanagan turned to Catharine and David, who were practically touching each other. "Well, that's it, kids. The only way fission could possibly happen, even assuming the isotope hasn't degraded, is if *that*"—he pointed to one of the metal hemispheres—"gets hammered into *that*"—he pointed to the other one. "Now, let's see how much radioactivity we've got here," he said and picked up the six-inch barrel-shaped sensor of the Geiger counter.

But before he could get a measurement, a loud klaxon came over the PA.

"General quarters!" said the XO's excited voice. "*This is not a drill!* Bridge to Captain, Bridge to Captain. One of the craft that splashed down is coming straight for us. Fast!"

In a moment, the sub's speed seemed to double and its movement through the water became audible.

"We're cavitating," said Flanagan. "This target must be coming on *fast!*" He looked down in dismay at the dismantled warhead and almost shrieked in frustration. "Of all the freakin' *luck!*"

David looked at Flanagan, eyes wide. "It's no coincidence, Mister Flanagan. *We caused it!*" he said. "They heard the device's transmission and it's bringing them to us."

When David looked at the device once again, he couldn't believe his eyes. "*What the hell is going on?*" he shouted.

The metal hemispheres had come loose from their casing and were now *levitated* two feet above their former positions inside the warhead.

Flanagan turned to the device, and his eyes went wide as saucers. "My God!" he said. "If those two things come together, we're all *goners!* I've got to put them back, but if I touch them, I'm dead."

To David's amazement, Catharine tried to do just what Flanagan said would kill anyone who tried. In a desperate effort to save the sub, she reached up for the hemispheres, which evaded her grasp by slipping up another two feet and hovering there.

To his credit, Flanagan pushed Catharine's arms away, and reached up to grab the hemispheres himself. As though they could see him coming, they slipped up yet another two feet. Then they began slowly revolving around a point equidistant between them, with their flat sides toward each other.

David shook his head in disbelief. "They're moving at precisely the same speed, so one never approaches the other. It's almost like someone is playing a *joke* on us."

"A *joke?*" shrieked Flanagan. "If those things come together, we'll all die! Who'd find that amusing?"

Only one of the gods would, thought David, and he hoped he was right about which one.

The hemispheres revolved faster and faster around their imaginary axis until they were moving so fast they became a blur, no longer recognizable as individual objects. Instead they resembled a small whirlwind that began to glow an oceanic green.

"Video, are you getting this?"

"Getting it all, engineer," came the nervous reply.

Suddenly, the lights in the room shut off, bringing the green whirlwind into sharp relief.

Flanagan shook off the hypnotic effect. "I have to get the captain down here," he muttered, and began toward the phone.

"Don't do it!" commanded David.

Flanagan looked at him as though he'd lost his mind. "What do you mean?"

"Captain's on the bridge preparing to fight off an intruder," shouted David. "He won't come, and you'll be court-martialed for distracting him."

"*Distracting* him?" said Flanagan incredulously. "If these things come together just *once*, it'll be the end of the ship."

"But look at them!" said David. "They're *not* touching. And they're not *going* to touch."

"How do you—" Flanagan looked at David suspiciously. "*Do you know who's doing this?*"

Another luminous form gradually took shape in the hovering whirlwind above them and glowed like neon. It was a message without words—a beautifully formed, familiar symbol: Hermes' staff. A *caduceus*, but this one was a luminous pink and it was animated. Two green snakes writhed around the pole as though very much alive.

The fearsome sound of men in a panic came through the open door.

A bell struck several times and the XO's voice came over the public address system. "PREPARE FOR COLLISION! Hang onto something, men!"

If David hadn't felt transported to another world by the lightshow in the room, he'd have been terrified by the whirring sound penetrating the hull—the sound of another vessel rapidly approaching. As the intruder came nearer still, a deep rumble arose outside the sub, began its rapid crescendo, reaching a thundering peak, and then …

It was gone.

"He's passed us," said David in the eerie silence. "Just another game of chicken."

As the sound faded, whatever spell had kept the two metallic hemispheres in their death dance now *flung* them to opposite sides of the room. Catharine and Flanagan froze, anticipating an instant death.

Flanagan ran to the phone once again.

"Don't do it!" shouted David again.

"Captain *must* be told!" said Flanagan. "It's his ship!"

"Not yet," said David.

Flanagan ran to David and grabbed him by the shoulders.

"You didn't answer me before," he said accusatorily. "*Do you know who did this?*"

"I think I do," said David. "But the only way to be sure is for you to tell me whether those hemispheres are comprised of U-235. I expect they're not."

"Well, how the devil would *you* know that?" demanded Flanagan, shaking David by the shoulders.

David shook his head but remained calm. "Mister Flanagan," he demanded, "what color is my badge?"

Flanagan released David from his grasp and took a step back to get a good look at the badge. His face was a study in conflicting emotions. "It's … *green*." He looked at Catharine's badge. *Green.* He looked at his own. *Green.*

David nodded. "If those hemispheres were composed of U-235, would my badge be green?"

"No," Flanagan replied, and shook his head in wonderment. "But your badge wouldn't be green even if they were made of U-*238!* We'd already have suffered a wicked dose." He approached one of the hemispheres lying in a corner. "The metal is *yellow!*" he said incredulously. Grabbing the Geiger counter, he thrust the barrel a mere six inches from the hemisphere, turned to David and said, "It's—It's no more radioactive than the hull of this ship. What the hell *is* it?"

In a move that made even David gasp, Flanagan touched the hemisphere with his gloved hand. "It's cool," he said and *picked it up*. Placing it carefully on the table, he studied it closely.

"This appears to be … *gold!*" said Flanagan in wonderment.

Catharine laughed with relief.

David shook his head. "Don't you see?" he said to Catharine. "He's perfected the alchemist's art of elemental transmutation—and *remotely*, no less." He turned to Flanagan. "I now know who did this, but I can tell only the captain."

Flanagan, who by now had confirmed that the other hemisphere was composed of the same substance, placed it on the opposite table, as though it would be unsafe to keep the hemispheres together, even in their apparently innocuous new form.

"I thought I was about to meet my Maker," Flanagan said softly.

David smirked. "You *did*."

CHAPTER 11

AT SUNSET ON the plains of southern Zimbabwe, the horizon was festooned with bands of bright reds and blues. While Miriam Azeri serenely tracked the sun's slow recession behind a distant hill, her small campfire burned nearby, safely contained within a circular firebreak.

An attractive blonde, Miriam had earnestly continued her father's research, but to do that she'd needed to spend long periods in far-flung, sparsely populated locations, which had put a damper on her strong desire to find an admirable young man to settle down with. Since turning forty some months earlier, she'd been seriously considering accepting a professorship at one of the universities that had invited her in the past.

Gazing at the setting sun, she knew that the nocturnal fauna would soon emerge, including the big cats, and that it would be unwise to remain outside her tent much longer. Still, this seemed the perfect setting for a nightcap, which would be much more pleasant in the open air than in a stuffy tent. As she rose to fetch the bottle of absinthe she'd brought along for a serene occasion such as this, her nine-year-old helper Taurayi suddenly appeared at her side and broke the spell.

A member of the local Ndebele tribe, Taurayi was known to run like the wind. Mere walking seemed anathema to him. Most days, he seemed to be everywhere at once, depending on the whims of his nimble mind and young limbs.

"Madam Azeri," said Taurayi, excitedly pointing east, "now is coming your friend, Doctor Iskender."

Miriam turned to him. "I appreciate the announcement, Taurayi. Have you eaten supper yet? The sun will be down quite soon."

He gave her a toothy grin. "I ate fruit all day, Madam Azeri. I have a full belly now. If I eat more, I will pass gas all night."

She frowned. "That's more than I needed to know, young man. Please go to your tent. And promise me you will not wander far and wide this evening, as you have of late. This place is full of dangerous night beasts, and it would be most bothersome if I had to tell your parents you'd been trampled by a black rhino."

He laughed. "The black rhino goes to sleep when the sun goes down, Madam Azeri. I promise that I will not be trampled by one tonight," he replied through his big smile. "And I will not let a lion eat me."

She shrugged with uncertainty. "Lions are known to be quite rude," she reminded him. "They rarely ask your permission before devouring you."

From the grassy plain to the east, the aging Doctor Iskender hobbled toward them on his cane, wearing his customary brightly-colored, loose-fitting shirt and khaki pants. On his head sat a Panama hat with a purple hatband, the bright colors contrasting with his dark complexion.

"Taurayi," said Miriam, "please bring a chair for the good doctor." When there was no response, she turned toward the place where Taurayi formerly stood, only to find he'd already set out a folding chair next to hers and disappeared.

The good doctor waved to her. "Miriam," he hailed, shouting ahead as an older person will sometimes do when wishing to make his impending arrival known before he can reach his destination.

She waved back.

"Good evening, my fine lady," he said, arriving a bit out of breath. "How have your gold mining explorations gone this week?"

She remarked to herself that the old fellow's accent still recalled something of his years at Cambridge, though he'd lived in his native Ethiopia for the past thirty years.

"Daniel Iskender," she said sternly, "why have you come so late? You know I value your advice, but my two assistants just drove the Jeep into town and won't return till morning."

"That's quite satisfactory," said Daniel. "I can easily walk back to my hut."

"Not before dark, Daniel," she replied. "You're thinking of yourself thirty years ago, perhaps."

He plopped down on the seat next to hers. "I've already eaten a full meal. If need be—" he smacked his hands on the chair's arms "—I can sleep in this chair."

She looked at him skeptically. "Don't be ridiculous," she said. "You can sleep in the pup tent next to mine. There's a box of supplies in there. We'll just move it into the big tent to make room."

He smiled. "You know how to solve *every* difficulty, Miriam. Truly, you know *everything*."

She replied with a smirk. "Hardly. I keep you around because I *don't* know the many languages you do. You come in handy when I discover something interesting, which unfortunately I did not this week."

He bowed in his chair. "It is my pleasure to assist in any way I can."

"Have you heard from the university?"

His eyebrows rose. "You mean, Addis Ababa?"

"From which *other* university are you expecting a call?"

He dug the point of his cane into the ground by his feet and rested his chin on his hand. "To tell the truth, at this point I'm not expecting a call from *any* university—even Addis Ababa."

She was surprised. "Even after all your years as an instructor there?"

He nodded wistfully. "*Because* of all my years of instruction. It's *nature*, Miriam. The old must make room for the young—even though so many of the young know … so little."

"I know just the thing to fix such an attitude," she said, and went to her tent to fetch the bottle of absinthe and two clear-plastic glasses. She handed him an empty glass and filled it halfway, then did the same with her own glass, recorking the bottle and resting it on the ground beside her chair.

As she resumed her seat, the last of the sun disappeared behind the hill, and the sky was growing dark. It was her favorite time of day, because at night the sky was so full of stars and wonder. Still, in light of the local fauna, she deftly removed her revolver from her pocket, checked to ensure the safety was engaged, and placed it on her lap.

She offered Daniel a smile and raised her glass in a toast.

"To good old friends," she said.

"To good old friends," he echoed, and tapped her glass with his own. "But I don't think your forty years counts as old, with all due respect."

Miriam scoffed. "You don't have to be old to be an old *friend*."

He nodded in agreement, and each of them savored a sip, lost in thought.

They added a bit of wood to the fire, and sat in comfortable silence until it was full dark.

"It's times like this," she said, "that I pity everyone in the world who doesn't see the sky this way, unobstructed by ceilings and clouds, undiluted by city lights. It makes one realize how vast the universe is, and makes our own problems seem quite small by comparison." She glanced toward Daniel. "You know which celestial phenomenon I love to see most while sitting under this canopy of stars?"

"Well," said Daniel, "I can only guess it's the same thing *I* love most."

"What's that?" she asked.

"Shooting stars," he said. "That's what reminds us that we're not separate from the universe, but rather an integral part of it." He was right, of course.

The quietly competitive pair sat back and looked up, each hoping to be first to spot a shooting star.

But something very bright far off in the distance caught their attention at the same moment. It was easily the brightest object in the sky—brighter even than the gibbous moon. Whatever it was seemed to be dropping rapidly toward the horizon behind a nearby hill but, because of the lack of perspective, it was impossible to tell its size or distance.

Then the light disappeared behind the hill, and the old friends braced for the seismic rumbling of a meteoric impact that never came. Or perhaps it *did* come, but only after they both dropped off to sleep a moment later—at the same instant.

⟶∘⊂⟿∘⊂⟶

MIRIAM STIRRED FROM her restful slumber only to find she'd never left her chair. She opened her eyes and found it was full dark. If it weren't for the glow from the remaining embers of her little campfire, she would have been unable to see that Daniel had drifted off in his chair right next to her.

Wait. Wasn't the wood still *aflame* when she drifted off? How much time had passed? She looked up at the sky. The constellations had shifted considerably since she fell asleep, and some had dropped below the horizon.

Remembering her revolver, she felt for it in her lap. It was gone. In a panic, she reached down next to her chair and realized it had fallen to the ground. *How careless*, she thought, though she was relieved to find the safety still engaged.

She could make out the bare outline of the absinthe bottle, too, which had evidently been knocked over by the tumbling handgun. Once again she was relieved; the bottle remained securely corked and nothing had spilled.

So, no harm done.

Except we're sitting in chairs in the dark on the Zimbabwean plain without even the shelter of a tent. And our fire's about done. She was about to rise, awaken Daniel, and prepare to retire for the night. But she had an eerie feeling of being watched.

She gripped the revolver, flipped off the safety, and listened for any threatening sounds, such as movement in the brush. There was a brief rustling to her right. It sounded perhaps thirty feet away, but distance is hard to judge with no visual cues. She waited.

And there it was again. A momentary rustling. But now it was a bit closer. Or did it just *seem* closer, since she'd focused on it now?

Pssst!

It was a sound of very obviously human origin, but that didn't mean it was friendly. She obstinately refused to answer.

There came a whisper from the brush only a few feet away. "Madam Azeri. It's me, Taurayi."

This was irritating. "What are you doing out and about in the middle of the night?" she said.

"I saw the light in the sky," whispered Taurayi. "I went to see. But I fell asleep. Just like you and the good doctor."

Oh, that's right! We saw a light in the sky, and that was the last thing I knew before I woke up just now.

"Taurayi, why are you whispering?" she asked.

There was a brief hiatus in the conversation, during which Miriam had the feeling that a quiet conference was going on about how to reply to her.

"Because I do not wish to wake the good doctor," said the boy.

She shook her head at the boy's uncharacteristic reticence and tossed a few sticks of wood on the fire, raising both the light and heat at the campsite.

"Oh, hokum! Show yourself," she quietly demanded.

There was another gap in the conversation.

"Who is there with you, Taurayi?" she said. "I sense that there's someone with you."

"He is … my new friend," said the boy hesitantly.

"Then introduce him to me," she said wearily.

"I would, madam. Only he is very … ugly."

"Nonsense," she said—loudly enough to stir Daniel, who puffed and snorted himself awake.

"What happened?" asked Daniel. "We were talking, and then … that's the last thing I remember."

"Welcome to the party, Daniel," she said. "Taurayi is hiding in the bushes over there with a new friend who's quite shy."

"Oh?" said Daniel, turning to speak to the place where Miriam just pointed. "Tell him to show his face."

"Taurayi says his friend is too ugly to show us," she said.

Daniel considered this new information. "Taurayi?" he said.

"Yes, good doctor?" replied Taurayi.

"Is your friend a *leper?*"

"No, good doctor."

"Has his face been eaten by lions?"

"No, good doctor."

"Well, Taurayi," said Daniel, "Madam Azeri and I have both spoken with lepers and men whose faces had been torn apart by lions, so I don't think we'll be too shocked by your friend's appearance. Bring him into the clearing or Madam Azeri will be quite cross with you."

There was a rustling in the place where Taurayi was speaking from.

"My friend has something to ask of Madam Azeri," said Taurayi. "He asks Madam Azeri to put down her gun."

Daniel turned to Miriam with eyebrows raised. "Are you sporting a *gun*, Miriam?"

Miriam nodded to Daniel, but spoke to Taurayi. "I won't put the gun down, Taurayi, but I'll engage the safety, so that the gun won't fire by accident." She raised the revolver so it could easily be seen by the firelight and conspicuously engaged the safety. "That's it. Now come out, or you can both return to wherever you came from."

There was another pause. Then Taurayi said, "Okay, we are both coming out now. Please don't shoot us."

Taurayi shyly emerged from the brush into the firelight holding the hand of ... something ghastly, the likes of which Miriam had never seen.

"Good lord!" said Daniel, lurching backward hard enough to knock over his chair and tumble backwards to the ground. He righted his chair, resumed his seat, and said, "What *is* that?"

Miriam, who'd leapt to her feet at the sight of Taurayi's friend, stood frozen with fear. Remembering her promise, she kept the revolver pointed at the ground and rubbed her eyes to get a better look at Taurayi's new *friend*.

Its general form was that of a tall biped ... vaguely hominid. Its smooth skin had the appearance of a leathery amphibious hide. In the firelight, its color seemed a dull jade, suggesting the possibility that it was wearing a protective layer over its true skin. Its face was long, perhaps one-fifth its entire height. It had large eyes that looked like polished obsidian, a shiny black with no whites or irises to provide definition. At the base of its throat protruded what looked like two symmetrical goiters that wobbled whenever it turned its head, jiggling in a way that vaguely reminded Miriam of breasts, but they had no nipples or other clues as to their function. Only secondarily did it occur to her that these might be a breathing apparatus or aid to respiration.

Covering its torso was a frock-like garment of unfamiliar cloth, purplish in hue, that shimmered in the firelight as it wafted in the light breeze.

Miriam bowed respectfully at the waist, never taking her eyes off Taurayi's friend. "What is your name, friend?"

The thing looked to Taurayi, evidently seeking advice or assistance. Taurayi placed a hand next to his own mouth, and opened and closed it to simulate talking. "*Talk*, friend. Make a sound."

What followed was stranger than what preceded it. To Miriam its voice sounded as though an animal with the vocal structure of a lizard was straining to speak a human language. If it *was* a human language, Miriam didn't recognize it. And it had a muffled quality, as though it were being spoken into a mask and reproduced by a tinny little loudspeaker.

At the end of nearly every phrase came the sound of an epiglottis closing, followed by a vocalized noise sounding something like *glick*.

Taurayi's new friend put its hand to its chest and said what sounded like *Hanee Dagon*, but the initial breath may have been just an exhalation. The accent was clearly placed on the second and third syllables: *ha-NEE DA-gon. Glick.*

Miriam looked to Doctor Iskender and shrugged.

Iskender's face bore a curious expression. He said one word to the thing.

"Again," he said.

When it didn't reply immediately, he made a rolling motion with his index finger and said, "Shanah. *Hanee—*"

"*Dagon*," said the thing, completing the phrase. "*Hanee Dagon. Glick,*" it repeated.

Hesitating a moment, Daniel turned to Miriam. "He seems to be speaking a *Semitic* language. If that's what it is, perhaps I can communicate with him."

Miriam gaped back at him. "Say something to him."

Daniel floundered a moment as though he was about to take a wild shot in the dark, one *so* wild that his colleagues, were they present, would think he'd taken leave of his senses. He braced himself and addressed the thing, putting his hand to his own chest.

"*Anee Daniel,*" he said.

The thing nodded and said, "*Atah Daniel*." Taking a cue from Miriam's earlier show of respect, the thing bowed at the neck and said, "*Sagam. Glick*."

Daniel's mouth hung agape and he laughed.

"What?" said Miriam. "What's funny?"

"I think our friend here is speaking *Hittite*," said Daniel, "an early progenitor of both Hebrew and Arabic last spoken, oh, about … four thousand years ago. I *think* he just said—" Daniel's expression was somewhere between chagrin and embarrassment. "I think," he began again, "he just said *shalom*."

"So," said Miriam, "effectively, he said *I come in peace?*"

Daniel nodded. "Sounds a bit hackneyed for an alien, but that appears to be his meaning. He also seems to understand nodding one's head as meaning *yes* and shaking it as meaning *no*. That likely means that his ancestors either *learned* their language here on Earth or—"

Miriam nodded sagely. "Or they *taught* it to us. Could he be … *Anunnaki?*"

"*Lo!*" said Dagon excitedly, putting his hand on his chest and shaking his head. "*Lo Anunnaki. Glick.*" He hunched over, and a scaly ruff emerged around his head making him look rather fierce, like a giant frill-necked lizard on two legs.

Miriam dropped her pistol to the ground and prepared to run—and would have done so, had not Daniel calmly demanded her attention.

"Stay, Miriam! I think Dagon has just demonstrated how he feels about the … people you mentioned."

Dagon nodded.

"You see?" said Daniel. "His hostile display was meant to show how he feels about *them* … not about us. It may even have been involuntary on his part."

Dagon nodded again.

"Taurayi," said Daniel, "fetch your friend a chair. We would very much like to speak with him at length."

Dagon pointed to Miriam. "*Atah Azeri? Glick.*"

Miriam looked to Daniel, who said, "He wants to know if your name is *Azeri*."

"How should I reply?" she asked.

"Try saying *ken*."

She turned to Dagon and assembled a phrase from what little she'd learned. "*Ken, Anee Azeri.*"

Dagon bowed with evident satisfaction.

DAVID AND CATHARINE sat nervously at the desk in the captain's stateroom next to Engineer Flanagan. Across from them all sat a disgruntled captain who'd just watched the recording of the incident of the open warhead.

The captain ejected the shiny silver DVD from his computer and handed it back to the engineer. "Flanagan," he said, "there are so many violations of navy regulations on this recording, I could have you court-martialed and in the slammer at the drop of a hat." He shook his head dourly.

"But—" began the engineer. It took only one glare from the captain to shut him up.

"I'm not done," said the captain. "Relax. I have no intention of doing so—at the very least because no engineer could have anticipated that hemispheres of fissionable material would self-levitate and begin revolving around an imaginary point at accelerating speed, maintaining precisely one hundred eighty degrees of arc between them." He looked in sequence at Catharine and Flanagan. "And I laud the courage displayed by both the lieutenant commander and my engineer in attempting to recapture the hemispheres and secure them back in their safe positions. They can each be credited with a magnificent display of naval preparedness and self-sacrifice. Flanagan, did you bring along your Geiger counter and the decommissioned hemispheres?"

"I did, sir."

"Put 'em on the desk," said the captain.

"On the captain's desk?" asked Flanagan uncertainly.

The captain nodded.

The engineer said, "But, sir, what if they're radioactive again?"

"Engineer," said the captain derisively, "it's a little late to think of that *now*, isn't it? You've been working closely on them for an hour."

"Yes, captain," said Flanagan as he placed the Geiger counter and the two golden hemispheres side-by-side on the desk.

"Besides," said the captain, "do you know whether it's even possible for someone to reconvert them remotely into fissionable material?"

"No idea, captain, as I don't know how they were rendered innocuous in the first place."

"Exactly. Now, show me the residual radioactivity of the two hemispheres."

The engineer switched on the Geiger counter and moved the barrel-shaped sensor deliberately across both hemispheres. The needle never budged.

"My God," said the captain, "the radioactivity level is *ambient*. Have you tested their elemental properties, engineer?"

"Yes, sir," said Flanagan. "We submerged the hemispheres in a salt-water bath to determine their volume, then put 'em on a counterweight laboratory scale. They have precisely the weight of an equivalent volume of pure gold. They appear to be gold."

"But couldn't that conclusion be inaccurate if they contain air pockets or alloys?" asked the captain. "At least theoretically there could be some other metal in there ... or a salt, or even trapped gas."

The engineer shook his head. "Can't be, sir, because they also have the *conductive* properties of gold, both for heat and electrical current. And, when we took them out of the salt bath, we detected no sign of oxidation. Of course," he conceded, "there *are* a few noble metals that would also show no oxidation after such a brief submersion."

"Did you try the acid test?" asked the captain.

"Yes, captain. We bring only a few drops of nitric acid aboard because it becomes explosive under a variety of circumstances, but the little we have is reserved for testing purposes like this."

"And?"

"No reaction, sir. The metal did not react at all."

The captain ran his fingers through his hair. "Well, I'll be damned. You know what you've got there, engineer?"

The engineer smiled and nodded. "Yes, sir. I've got a few pounds of solid gold belonging to the United States Navy."

"Yes, you do," said the captain. "But, unfortunately, Uranium-235 costs a helluva lot more per pound than gold, so Uncle Sam is out a *lot* of money." The captain dialed open the combination lock on his wall safe and flipped open the door. "Chuck 'em in here, Mister Flanagan, and resume your regular duties. I'll let you know if I have more questions."

Flanagan did as he was told.

The captain firmly shut the safe door and spun the dial.

Flanagan dawdled briefly before going. "Sir, if the same thing has happened to the other warheads aboard—"

"Let *me* worry about the rest of the arsenal, Mister Flanagan. Meanwhile, my order to keep mum about what happened in the bomb shop remains in effect." The captain leaned over his desk and presented Flanagan with a warface. "And if you violate that order, you won't get a court-martial. You'll be summarily flushed out a torpedo tube at depth."

He sat back, self-satisfied. "I'll just tell 'em you wanted to feed the fish."

The engineer stood up straight. "Yes, captain. I read you loud and clear," he said, and closed the door behind him.

"Not a bad kid," muttered the captain. "A little full of himself, though." He turned to David. "Okay, professor. You think you know who did this?"

"Yes, captain. I believe it was *Ea*, also known as *Enki*. He's one of the two half-brothers originally put in charge of the Earth."

"Was Enki the military one, or the engineering genius?"

"The engineering genius, captain. The one who fashioned *us* out of early hominids."

"Why do you think this … alchemy was performed by Enki?"

"Enki was the one put in charge of mining gold on Earth in order to save the atmosphere on his home planet of Nibiru. He first tried to mine gold from the waters of the Persian Gulf. When that failed, he was responsible for exploring for, and mining, gold in what we now call Zimbabwe, and down into South Africa. So, Enki's kind of synonymous with gold. There's even an ancient stone sculpture of him in a museum where his right hand and forearm have been fashioned of solid gold."

"Any other basis to believe this was Enki's doing?"

"Yes. He was always sought out by the other gods to develop anything requiring extensive (and intensive) knowledge of medicine, science, or engineering. He was the one who created mankind to mine for gold. He raised the land at the mouth of the Nile River, by far the greatest earthmoving feat of the ancient world. By the way, 'Egypt' means *land that has been raised*. But there are two things even more unmistakable. The lesser of the two is the game of *chicken* he played with this ship while simultaneously turning uranium to gold and conducting the terrifying light show captured in the video you just saw. Most convincing of all is the ephemeral image created by the golden hemispheres. It lasted only a moment. Did you catch it? In green and pink?"

"I saw *something*. Wasn't it the symbol of medicine?" asked the captain.

"Not exactly. The symbol of medicine is the Rod of Aesculapius, which bears only a single serpent. The double-serpented *caduceus*, on the other hand, was the symbol of Enki in Sumeria, well more than five thousand years ago. Eventually, Enki handed down his preeminence in the practice of medicine—and its symbol—to his son, Ningishzidda (known in Egypt as Thoth), whom the Greeks called Hermes and the

Romans Mercury. And if you observe the symbol carefully, you'll detect a resemblance to the double-helix of DNA. If you want to see a good example of Enki's handiwork with DNA, take a close look at yourself or me. Or, for a truly *excellent* example, you might refer to the lieutenant commander."

Catharine shoved David with a laugh.

The captain blushed. "It doesn't get any better than that. Alright, then, what does that tell us about the Anunnaki right now?"

"A few things. First, unless Enki's been replaced by a descendant, he's still alive and right now he's here on Earth. As he's the one who fashioned mankind and saved us from the Great Flood, presumably he would disfavor our destruction. That distinguishes him starkly from his half-brother Enlil, who not only couldn't have cared less if our species perished in the Flood, but was rather looking forward to it."

The captain nodded equivocally. "Well, that's something. But it doesn't tell me anything about their weaknesses, which is what the admiral really needs to know." He folded his hands and leaned forward over his blotter. "Can you infiltrate their ranks, professor?"

"I?" said David. "I don't see how."

"Didn't you say that Inanna was courting you in dreams?"

David nodded. "She's been mercifully unable to reach me in the bomb shop, which is pretty much a Faraday cage submerged under a quarter-mile of seawater, but prior to that, *yes*, she was haunting my dreams."

"Perhaps you should take her up on her offer."

"Inanna is *Enlil's* granddaughter, captain. If Enlil has died or simply didn't care to make the trip to Earth, Inanna would be Enki's chief *opponent*."

The captain shrugged. "While infiltrating a friendly faction can provide good intelligence, it's really the adversarial faction we *need* to infiltrate."

Catharine spoke up. "We're still unsure of their intentions, captain. And to infiltrate the enemy's ranks is a lot to ask of an untrained civilian."

The captain sighed. "I'm not sure we have the luxury of distinguishing scrupulously between service members and civilians. We may *all* have to do our part."

David said, "I'd really prefer it if someone else could undertake that project, captain, as I fear it won't end well. But if no one else can do it, I suppose I'll have no choice."

David and Catharine rose and awaited dismissal. But the captain seemed loath to dismiss them, as though he was equivocating about something.

"Sit down a minute," he said at last. "I want to show you something."

He pulled up an image on his laptop. "This was sent to me by our Target/Motion Analysis people a couple of minutes ago; we call them TMA. It's a barebones reconstruction of that pyramidion playing chicken with this submarine. The display is a simple line-drawing based on data collected from the ship's underwater listening devices and sensors, as well as data picked up from the SLOT-buoy we sent up to the surface before all hell broke loose."

Frozen on the screen was the opening frame of an animation consisting of line drawings of the submarine and the pyramidion-shaped intruder. Judging by the scale marker, the vessels would start this demonstration about three hundred meters apart.

The captain scratched his head. "This animation is nothing fancy, just a crudely animated line drawing of the last few seconds before the collision."

Catharine cocked her head. "Doesn't the captain mean *near-collision*?"

The captain smirked. "You tell *me*, lieutenant commander," he said and clicked the button to begin the animated sequence. "The animation is greatly slowed down so you can see what's happening."

The pyramidion moved up toward the sub, closely passed it on the viewer's side, and continued its upward motion with no damage to either vessel. Since the animation lasted only ten seconds or so, the captain ran it three times in rapid sequence.

"What do you think?" he asked.

Catharine said, "I think they passed within a few meters of the sub. Thank God you didn't jink, or we'd all be on the bottom."

The captain nodded indulgently. "That's what *I* thought ... at first. But, with the extremely fast sensors all over the exterior of this ship and the miracle of fast computers, our TMA guys added a module that lets me rotate the animation. Shall we watch it from a theoretical camera, say, three hundred meters in front of the sub?"

The opening frame appeared on the screen again, just as it had the first time, but when the captain turned the mouse on his computer, the drawing turned with it. So now it looked as though the sub was coming straight at the viewer and the pyramidion was moving away from the viewer on course for a head-on collision with the sub. Once again, the drawing showed the pyramidion just below the sub on a slight upward trajectory.

The captain clicked the button to play the animation. The pyramidion came up and passed right *through* the sub and out the top with no damage to either vessel. The captain clicked the start button twice more, and it showed the same thing.

"What do you think now?" asked the captain.

"Wait," said Catharine with a confused expression. "*What?*"

"What did you see?" asked the captain.

At last she dragged her gaze off the animation and looked the captain in the eye. "I see what looks like a collision." She scoffed. "Oh, that's got to be an artifact of the technology."

The captain shook his head. "When I saw this animation, I reamed out the TSA specialist who sent it. His boss got on the horn and swore to its accuracy. That goddam pyramid passed right through the bottom of this submarine and out the top." He leaned in. "Now what the hell kind of technology is *that?*"

Catharine tried to shake the cobwebs out of her brain. "Looks like magic."

"To say the least," said the captain.

There was silence for a few seconds as they tried to wrap their minds around the phenomenon.

"*Magic?*" David muttered. "We're members of a cargo cult." When the others looked at him, he asked, "You know the phenomenon of the *cargo cult?*"

"Refresh my recollection," said the captain.

"In the South Pacific during the Second World War, some native islanders observed naval and aerial battles between the Americans and the Japanese. When the battles ended and the combatants left, enormous numbers of artifacts were left behind. Because the locals didn't under-stand what they were or how to use them, they regarded them as magical relics. To this day, they ritually re-enact the rudiments of the battles in the hope that their demonstrations of devotion will persuade the gods to return and bring more wonders."

"So, we're the cargo cultists for these Anunnaki types?" asked the captain.

David shrugged with chagrin. "Until a couple thousand years ago, we even referred to them as ... gods."

Catharine said, "But the difference between us and the islanders is we want 'em to go the hell away."

MIRIAM SENT TAURAYI to sleep on the floor of her tent while she and Daniel Iskender spoke with the alien under the starry sky.

In addition to posing questions of his own, Daniel acted as translator between Miriam and Dagon.

"Ask him how he knew I was named *Azeri*," began Miriam.

Daniel reframed the question into something like Hebrew. After a moment's thought, the alien replied in his reptilian speech and ended with a final *glick*. Daniel translated for Miriam.

"For some months, we have been listening to messages among the Anunnaki. They speculated that Abraham Azeri, before he died, had learned the Anunnaki's reason for returning to Earth. The Anunnaki fear that such reason will be discovered. They worry that Abraham Azeri might have told others the secret before he died."

"Well," said Miriam with a sigh, "he didn't tell *me*."

As translated by Daniel, Dagon said, "The Anunnaki messages disclosed that they do not know what happened to Abraham's private writings when he died. Azeri, do you know?"

Miriam declined to respond. "Tell me why Dagon wishes to know this."

"First," translated Daniel, "Dagon is the name of my planet and my people. My personal name would be too difficult for you to pronounce, but you may call me *Brosa*. I will tell you why the Dagon wish to know."

After much verbal stumbling between Daniel and Brosa, Daniel translated at length.

"Long ago, at a time you would think of as the beginning, a star in Dagon's system exploded. The explosion cast Planet Nibiru out into space between the stars at very great speed. Dagon expected that all people on Nibiru either died in the explosion or would soon freeze to death, but this was not so. The planet kept the air around it, and the heat from inside the planet was sufficient to sustain life in the coldness of space.

"The Dagon sent adventurers to orbit the planet from time to time, to see if the people yet lived. They did, and remained peaceful for a long time. After a time, they began to fight with each other: north against south. Then they invented terrible weapons and used them against each other. The Dagon expected that, over time, Nibiru would become a threat to Dagon and to every planet they could reach, so we continued to track them. After many years, the long fighting between the ruling families on

Nibiru resulted in a single king over the whole planet. His name was Anu. His descendants are therefore Anunnaki.

"The Dagon calculated that Nibiru was heading to the star around which Earth revolves. We foresaw that Nibiru would be pulled in and captured by your gas giants and your sun, but that there would be many problems. Nibiru would be moving in the direction *opposite* all the other planets, creating a serious risk of collision. Eventually, there *was* a terrible collision in which some of the moons of Nibiru smashed a planet in two. One half of the planet was smashed into many small pieces, which became an asteroid belt. The remaining half of the destroyed planet was hurled into an orbit much closer to the sun. The new planet— Earth, on which we now sit—kept a very large moon that once revolved around the destroyed planet. Eventually, much water and oxygen formed on and around Earth, and life developed here.

"Over many years, the Anunnaki learned how to fly, first in their atmosphere, and then in space. They passed very close to Earth from time to time, and eventually learned how to land here. Predicting the timing and precise direction of Nibiru's new orbit required very complex mathematics, because Nibiru's orbit changes depending upon which planets it encounters in its orbit around the sun.

"The Anunnaki first came to Earth about a half-million Earth years ago. After some time, they made your species and tried to control you, but you bred too fast and eventually, by sheer numbers, you escaped their control. The Anunnaki foolishly used their terrible weapons against each other on Earth at one time, killing many humans and Anunnaki also, and realized they were not well suited to thrive here. So, the latest time they passed Earth, they returned to their home planet. "For some reason we do not know, they now intend to return to Earth in preparation for their coming pass.

"The Dagon have landed on Earth before now. We have studied your kind and found that you are descended from a native species that mixed with the Anunnaki. You are like the Anunnaki in some ways, but not all. You are violent by nature, as they are, but you breed much more quickly. Your planet is now so full of you that you strangle yourself. The only thing that saves you is that you have short lives."

[Here, Daniel interrupted the narrative and spoke in his own voice. "*Strangle* is my word, Miriam. It's as close as I could come to Brosa's meaning."]

"When we learned that the Anunnaki would return to Earth before Nibiru's next pass, we landed several times in a place called Mali, on this continent, and spoke with the people there. One of them told us that he had just returned from Zimbabwe, where he worked for the daughter of Abraham Azeri exploring the Anunnaki's ancient gold mines. At first, we thought he was a fool, but the Dagon sent Brosa here to find you, and now I find that the man spoke truth.

"We contacted the Anunnaki and warned them not to land on Earth without first speaking with us. We have—

[Here Brosa broke off for a time formulating what he would say.]

"We have one very important technology that they do not have, and so they respect us—up to a point. We are hopeful that they will not land on Earth soon. We wish to help humanity defend itself from the Anunnaki. Without Dagon's help, you will be at the mercy of Anunnaki. You cannot defeat them at your present state of technology. So, Azeri, can you help us find out the reason for the Anunnaki's return?"

Miriam sat amazed to hear that everything her father learned in interpreting the Sumerian, Hittite, and Babylonian writing was true. *Oh, Father,* she thought, *I wish you had lived to see this day.*

She rose and bowed to Brosa. "Please, my friend Brosa, allow me to discuss this with Professor Iskender before giving you my answer."

When this was translated for the Dagon, she took Daniel by the arm and walked a few paces away. "I don't have the knowledge he is seeking, but I do have some of my father's notes that he was working on at the time of his passing."

"Where are they kept?" asked Daniel.

She peeked at the alien to make sure he couldn't overhear or record her, and whispered in Daniel's ear. "In a safe-deposit box associated with a numbered bank account … in London."

"I'm concerned," said Daniel. "This fellow seems honest enough, but what if the Dagon are in league with the Anunnaki? Alternatively, the Dagon could even be more formidable adversaries to humankind than the Anunnaki would be. After all, the Anunnaki are our ancestors." He was silent for a moment. "Whatever the truth of the matter, however, if the Dagon are looking for these papers, then they're not the *only* ones. The Anunnaki will be looking for them, too."

Miriam nodded. "One of my cousins posted me a letter saying that the American intelligence agencies are looking for them also. No one has told them where I am."

Daniel pondered for a few minutes, then said, "I think we have to go and fetch the papers, if for no reason other than to have something to trade with whoever ultimately grabs power. And if we find that the knowledge contained in the papers could tilt the balance of power in favor of humankind, your path will be clear."

After their short discussion, they returned to Brosa. Miriam bowed again. "Brosa, I have some papers that belonged to my father, but they are not here in Zimbabwe. They are very far from here."

When Daniel translated her remark to Brosa, the alien nodded his head thoughtfully.

"How far are the papers from here?" asked Brosa.

"Only *I* personally can retrieve them," replied Miriam, "and it will take some days for me to arrive at the place where they are being held."

"Will you share the information with Brosa when you find them?" asked Brosa.

"Yes," said Miriam, "unless I find that turning over the information to you will cause harm to humankind."

"I give you my word that humankind will be better off if the Dagon learn what is in the papers," said Brosa, "but I respect your reservation. So, will you fetch the papers?"

"I will begin the journey tomorrow morning."

"I could fly you there tonight, if you like," offered Brosa.

"Thank you for your kind offer," she said, "but I must find certain papers that I need in order to be admitted to the place of their keeping, and those papers are not here, either. I prefer to travel as my kind customarily does."

Brosa nodded soberly. "Very well, but be forewarned," he said, "the Anunnaki are seeking you with every means at their disposal. If they find you, they will do anything to get these papers from you."

Miriam's mind reeled at the thought. "How will I contact you when I have them?" she asked. "Shall we meet here?"

Brosa shook his head. "No. If the Anunnaki learn you have the papers, they will be there waiting for you. We will be watching them. It is only by the grace of our joint Creator that I found you first. If you find the papers and escape the Anunnaki, bring them to the Dagon people in Mali. That is what they call themselves. They will know how to signal the Dagon. They have done so before."

"Very well," said Miriam. "Do you wish my young friend to assist you back to your craft?"

Brosa did something Miriam would have thought impossible. He … smiled. It was not a pretty sight, resembling more rictus than merriment. Still, it showed that Brosa harbored some fondness for Taurayi.

"No," he said. "Let Taurayi sleep. I can find my way, and if I am attacked by a beast, I have strong weapons to keep it away."

With that, Brosa bowed finally, and disappeared into the brush the way he came.

Once he disappeared, Daniel turned to Miriam. "Do you wish me to accompany you, Miriam? It would do my heart good."

"If you think I'm letting you out of my sight, Daniel, then you've lost your mind," she said. "Let's get a little sleep now, if we can. In the morning, we'll head straight to Beira."

⟶∘⟶⟋⟍∘⟵

DAVID FOUND LIVING on a boomer disorienting.

A nuclear-armed submarine is ever alive with activity. Its crew is divided into three equal parts, with one-third of the crew on a six-hour watch at any time. The sub doesn't conform to a twenty-four-hour day; its day is *eighteen* hours long, to conform with the six-hour shifts. Fortunately, a boomer rarely surfaces, so, for the most part, the concepts of day and night are irrelevant. True, when the crew goes on leave, it will experience a colossal case of *jet lag*, but such breaks are rare, while work aboard the sub is relentless.

It struck David as strange that the crew wasn't simply divided into *four* parts, instead of three, so the ship could conform to the same twenty-four-hour day experienced by the rest of the world. But he guessed that *one-fourth* of the crew might be insufficient to operate the vessel. He was sure that, even if he served some function onboard, he'd never be able to synch his clock with the ship's.

Continuous quiet was hard to come by, as was undisturbed sleep. Their makeshift dorm was adjacent to the on-duty torpedo room, which remained as vigilant as the rest of the sub. There was always something heavy and metallic, it seemed, that required lifting, moving, and putting down.

Catharine had taken to sleeping fully clothed in David's bunk with her head on his shoulder. Men being what they are, a couple of times each night David had to fight himself to keep his hands from wandering, and chase away his increasingly wild erotic dreams. In a sense, it was a relief to anticipate that, in less than two days' time, they'd arrive at Beira by night to be offloaded in a rubber craft by Navy SEALS. Presumably, Catharine wouldn't be chastely sleeping with him every night after that. What a future with her would look like was unclear.

David prayed that the admiral would have someone there to see to their itinerary … and give them some *money*, as he was carrying only the cash that was in his pocket on the morning he was spirited out of his classroom by the FBI, less a few dollars spent at the navy base commissary in the U.K. He had a couple of credit cards, but had been ordered not to use them. He wondered how he was supposed to get a hotel room, since every respectable hotel demands a credit card that can be charged if the guest leaves without paying in full.

He had a recurring nightmare that his dreams of Inanna would resume as soon as he spent a night on the surface. The irony of having a dream about a dream did not escape him, but that was the world he occupied now. The ocean's deep had come to seem protective, and it would be hard to be without it. It occurred to him that, although Inanna appeared at will in his dreams, it was he who chose the setting. He'd make sure to find a setting she'd find repugnant. Perhaps that would make her go away.

Perhaps.

CHAPTER 12

DAVID HAD BEEN wrong about how they would be dropped off at the port. He'd thought the boomer would surface and they'd be taken to the dock by rubber boat. But that's because he was unaware that the sub harbored a four-seat electric submersible that could be launched at periscope depth. He was right about one thing, though. The craft would be piloted by Navy SEALS.

Wearing sailing clothes and pastel cotton sweaters stylish enough to fit in at a posh hotel, David and Catharine climbed into the submersible's rear seats and the hatch was shut behind them. On each of their laps lay a light backpack containing everything that had been in their possession when they left Paris, which wasn't much.

The two SEALS in the front seats pressed a few buttons, and in a minute the compartment housing the minisub was flooded and the submersible dropped out of the mother sub and began gliding independently through the water. Although there were only four people in the minisub and they were close enough to whisper to one another, the driver made an announcement over the PA.

"Good evening, folks. Welcome aboard the SS Pipsqueak. We'll be flying at 30,000 feet. The weather report calls for clear skies all the way to Orlando. Flying time should be about one hour. Please buckle up, and be sure to tip your flight attendant, who'll be coming along for beverage orders once she's sobered up."

While the humor was corny, neither Catharine nor David could hold back their laughter at the idea of someone coming by to take drink orders, as the spare room in the compartment was barely large enough to accommodate a deck of cards.

After they'd been en route a few minutes, David recalled his dream of Beira last week, where he'd felt so terribly alone, as though someone was missing. Fortunately here he was, nearly arrived at port, in the company of the most competent, beautiful companion he could ever hope for. He subtly moved his hand and placed it on hers affectionately, and she turned to him with an enigmatic smile. Having been unattached for a few years, he paid little heed to her reticence and leaned in to kiss her.

Though she reciprocated politely, her coolness was unmistakable. He drew back and looked at her face. She'd already turned to face front, and her chin was up and lips pursed. Her struggle to contain her negative feelings was obvious.

Rough weather ahead, flashed the sign in David's head. Knowing full well that he was approaching troubled waters, he ran his finger along the top of her hand to get her attention. Then, as every woman he'd ever met would have done, she went and said something.

"Oh, so *now* you're feeling amorous?" she said, glaring at him.

He looked at the tops of the SEALS' heads sticking up over the backs of their seats. They couldn't have been more than three feet away. While they were no doubt accustomed to ignoring passengers' personal banter, David really wished to avoid any unpleasantness in such cramped quarters. He turned to her.

"I'm just very grateful to have you here with me," said David sincerely. "This whole trip would have been an ordeal without you. I feel … *protected* having you here."

"*Protected?*" she said, as though he'd insulted her. "So … what? I'm your *mommy* now? We shared a room for *five nights.*" She snorted derisively. "I might as *well* have been your mommy."

David could see the SEALS' heads turn to glance at each other.

"We discussed this onboard, Catharine, didn't we?" He touched her hand again. "I can see you're upset. Let's continue this later." But he could see her emotions surfacing and despaired of any cooperation.

"Why not discuss it *now?*" she demanded, then saw him glance at the SEALS. "Because of *those* guys? They're *Navy SEALS* for heaven's sake! I guarantee they're strong enough to overhear a little honest discussion. They're tough. They beat up *sharks* for a living."

The tops of the SEALS' heads bobbed up and down with silent laughter. Catharine noticed it and said to them, "So, what are you two … on *his* side now? Did I say something *funny? Don't SEALS beat up sharks?*"

The measured reply (obviously fashioned bearing in mind that this particular woman was a lieutenant commander) came from the more senior SEAL sitting in the passenger's seat.

"*At need*, ma'am," he said, nodding emphatically.

David rolled his eyes. These guys would have given her the "right" answer if she'd demanded confirmation that minnows eat whales.

She turned back to David. "See?" she said. "They're *tough*."

David heard the senior SEAL mutter to the driver. "Does this thing go any faster?"

The driver shook his head. "Pedal's to the metal, boss."

David sighed. "Catharine, I told you. I find you irresistible."

"*Hah!* Well, somehow you managed to resist. Do you have any idea how *insulting* that is?"

He glared at her. "You *know* I can't discuss my reasons now. Do you really think it's fair to air this out *here?*" It particularly bugged him that these two macho types were now thinking he'd disappointed a beautiful woman in the sack. Looking for anything to change the subject, he said, "You know what's puzzling *me* now?"

"What?" she said, as though she couldn't care less.

"Well, we don't know anyone in port, do we?"

She didn't reply. Just glared at him.

He continued nonetheless. "I've only been to Beira a couple of times myself."

She looked at him skeptically. "You've been to Mozambique … *twice?*"

"No, I was joking," he said, but she didn't seem amused. "And we don't know whom we're meeting, do we?"

"No," she confirmed, now mildly interested.

"So, the only way we'll be known is by our *names*, right?"

She wasn't following.

"So," he shrugged, "what are our names?"

"What do you mean?"

"The admiral told us not to use our real names—for obvious reasons." She looked puzzled. "So what did he say our names were?"

"You don't remember?" she asked.

"No," he said. "Do *you?*"

She sat back, and David was relieved not to be the object of her scrutiny for a moment.

She looked out the porthole at nothing. The water was pitch dark. "Do *I* have to remember everything?" she said. "Naturally, I thought *you* would remember that."

Against his better judgment—which seemed to have taken an untimely leave of absence—he said, "Why would *I* remember that especially? I thought you knew *everything!* Why don't you check your codebook? Oh, *that's* right! You don't have a codebook. You have a *spice rack!*" He put his index finger to his cheek as though contemplating a difficult puzzle. "*Let's see, is cardamom purple or yellow?*"

"It's *beige*, you idiot," she muttered.

"Oh, so you've broken the code! Wonderful!" he said, turning on her. "So then*, what's my name?*"

"You can't remember your own name, and that's *my* fault?" she said.

He becalmed himself and tried to remember the names the admiral assigned to them. "I remember that the names were based on characters in an old Hitchcock movie."

"Oh, *that* you can remember?" she spat out.

The senior SEAL turned around, glowering, and stared them both down. "If you kids can't keep a civil tongue in your head," he said, "we'll turn this thing right around, and you can cool down a couple days in the *brig.*"

Catharine and David quietly pouted, refusing to look at each other.

"That's better," said the SEAL.

"Thornhill," muttered David.

"*What?*" said the SEAL with a threatening look in his eye.

"That's our name," said David calmly. "I just remembered. It's Thornhill. Mister and Missus Roger Thornhill of New York City."

"Do I have a first name?" she asked calmly.

"Eve," replied David. "By the way, you don't happen to speak Portuguese, do you?"

She looked at him askance. "Not a word."

And they spent the rest of the trip in silence.

⟿∘⟾∘⟵

IT WAS JUST after dark in Beira when the submersible surfaced and quietly pulled up to the end of a dock several hundred feet long. The top hatch opened and the passengers stood up.

It's a good thing the SEALS were there, as one of them narrowly stopped David from falling into the water, which would have posed a major problem, since he had no extra clothing but for an unmarked U.S. Navy windbreaker.

Once the two passengers stood safely on the dock with their backpacks, the sub turned about and motored toward the open water. David and Catharine shouted their thanks to the SEALS, who waved back and shouted, "Hope you two work things out."

As arriving by submarine had been deemed likely to draw unwanted attention, David and Catharine had been instructed not to dally long enough to watch the minisub submerge.

David took Catharine's hand and turned away from the ocean. Together, they paused a moment to savor the warm, fresh air, which presented such a stark contrast to the stale atmosphere in the boomer.

Both felt a sense of relief at having gotten this far, as well as a sense of optimism—regardless that they had no idea where they'd spend the night. For David's part, he wondered if the submarine odors of cooking grease, cigarette smoke, and petroleum lubricant would ever wash off his hair and body.

A brightly lit hotel, seven stories high, stood just inland of the dock. Standing in the driveway was a young black man built like a professional football player, wearing what vaguely resembled a driver's uniform. Catching sight of the new arrivals, he waved and began jogging toward them. "Mister Thornhill," he shouted as he came into hailing distance.

"That's me," said David, reaching out his hand. The man reached them a bit breathless, despite his youth, and shook David's hand.

"Mister Thornhill," said the fellow (with no accent David could detect), "welcome to Mozambique! My name is Franklin. I'm the concierge on duty at the hotel. Your uncle left me a message that you would be arriving with Missus Thornhill by sea just after sunset. He sent your clothing up to your room on the top floor, but before going up there, I think you'll wish to pick up a package he left for you in the hotel safe."

"Thank you, Franklin," said David. "I was informed that everyone speaks Portuguese in Mozambique. Yet, you speak English beautifully."

"Thank you very much, Mister Thornhill. Your English is excellent, as well."

David was unaccustomed to being told how well he spoke his native language. "Where are you from, Franklin?"

"Parsippany, New Jersey, sir. Where are you and your wife from?"

"New York, New York," said David with a smile. "No wonder your English comes so naturally."

Franklin leaned into David. "Your uncle and mine are one and the same," he said quietly.

David smiled. "And a fine old fellow he is, too." He turned to Catharine. "Darling, what do you say we take Franklin's advice and pick up the items from the hotel safe first?"

"I think that would be an excellent idea, sweetheart," she replied, then muttered under her breath, "Dinner will be so much more pleasant if we can pay for it."

⤐∘◦⟨⟨⟨⟩⟩⟩◦∘⤏

UNCLE SAM HAD left a manila envelope in the safe for Roger Thornhill. It's a good thing David didn't need to prove his identity, because he couldn't have done it.

Franklin invited David and Catharine to use a side room to examine the envelope's contents privately before checking in. In the envelope, David was pleased to find well-worn (albeit forged) identification papers for both himself and Catharine under their Thornhill names. He wondered in passing how Naval Intelligence had gotten hold of recent snapshots of him for the passport and a New York State driver's license.

Roger's passport showed recent stamps for the United Kingdom, France, Italy, Egypt, and (of all places) Mali. Eve's showed the same stamps with the same dates, so evidently they'd been traveling together for the past two months. David only wished he was well-heeled enough to have spent the past two months seeing the sights with Catharine. Looking further into the envelope, he came up with a hefty wad of American money in varied denominations, plus major credit cards with the same account numbers for Roger and Eve.

David handed Catharine her identification papers and half the cash, but wagged an admonishing finger at her before handing her Eve's credit cards. "Now, I'm going to trust you with these credit cards, Eve, but I assume you'll use them prudently."

She grabbed them from his hand with her lips pursed, but David could see a twinkle of humor light up her face. "Oh, Roger," she said, "I'll be careful with them, because I know you'll have to write checks to cover everything once we get home."

He kissed her again, but this time she was far more responsive.

"I can't wait," she said, "to see which of my clothes made it to our room."

"Let's check in, and we'll go and find out."

As David signed the guest register, he glanced at a television turned to CNN. While the soundtrack was in Portuguese and he couldn't understand the words, at least there were no videos of pyramids or flying saucers. He wondered what could have caused the Anunnakis' delay in landing, and hoped beyond reason that they'd decided not to land at all.

After watching him sign the register, Franklin said, "Supper is served until ten, but formal wear is a must, I'm afraid. Please call the desk and let us know when you wish to be seated."

WHEN THEY GOT to their room, they found it to be a whole suite, complete with two large bathrooms and two king-size beds.

David was delighted to find in his closet all the beautiful suits he'd ordered at *Petit et Fils* in Paris. There was also a classic tuxedo from the clothier that he'd never even tried on, together with all the trimmings: a pale blue tux shirt, black satin bowtie, old-fashioned cummerbund, and both cufflinks and studs with emerald chips. He knew without looking that the shoe tree would be holding at least one pair of black patent-leather shoes of a quality he never would have sprung for on a professor's pay.

"I'll have to try one of these on," he muttered. "I never made it to the second fitting at Petit's."

"Go right for the tux," she advised. "I'm dying to see you in it. Besides, then we can go to dinner. I'm starved."

He smiled. "Boomer food didn't do it for you, huh?"

She squinched up her face with disapproval, which only made her more adorable, then went to her own closet and began looking through the dresses and suits hanging there.

David almost laughed aloud at the way she'd examine each item dispassionately, then forcefully shove it aside like a dry cleaner.

She chose a classic low-cut, wine-colored floral A-Line gown to match the classic style of his tux, and tossed it on the bed. She reached into a drawer, pulled out a bra and panties, and took them into her bathroom, leaving the door ajar. Her shower came on.

David listened to her splashing for a moment, imagining her in the shower, then retreated to his own bathroom (which was well equipped with shaving equipment of every kind) and used an electric shaver.

Before jumping into the shower, he took a moment to admire the stonework, and relish how much better this would be than the submarine showers he'd gotten accustomed to in the past few days.

Everyone who steps onto a submarine is instructed that his shower will consist of stepping into the stall, wetting his body for no more than thirty seconds, turning the water off, lathering up, then turning the water back on and rinsing off for no more than one minute—*and you're done, seaman.* It has to be that way, of course, because every drop of water must be recycled for reuse in cooking, drinking, flushing toilets, and for every other imaginable purpose.

With naval austerity behind him, tonight he indulged in the incalculable luxury of rinsing off for an extra few minutes. When he was done, he was surprised to realize that he no longer exuded *eau de boomer*. Not even a little bit. He stepped out of the shower, put on a hotel bathrobe, and returned to the bedroom where he found that Catharine had already taken her gown into her spacious bathroom.

David, sitting on the edge of one of the beds, began the fussy process of putting on a tux, quietly muttering the customary profanities while he inserted the studs, buttoned the shirt, donned the cufflinks, and tied and straightened the bowtie. When he was done, he heaved a sigh of relief, stood up, and turned around.

There stood Catharine, fully dressed and made up, with a small white purse in the crook of one arm and a white sweater with mother-of-pearl buttons draped over the other. She was so beautiful it took his breath away. She looked like Grace Kelly in Hollywood's most glamorous days.

"Do you like it?" she asked, and did a turn for him. Her face and body were gorgeous from every angle.

David was speechless. Emotions returned to him that he hadn't felt since years before. Tears came to his eyes.

Catharine could see he was smitten, and raised her chin with the satisfaction of knowing that she'd *finally* gotten the appreciation she deserved.

She tossed the purse and sweater onto the bed and came over to him, gently wiped the tears from his eyes, and kissed him.

He was pleased that his knees held firm and that he still had enough of his old maleness to place his hand behind her head, bend her backward over his left arm, and kiss her the way a man kisses a woman he loves. It was only *then* that he realized he loved her.

He'd always known that life could be like that, that sometimes you have to watch yourself doing something before you realize how right it is.

Collecting his wits enough to find the words, he said huskily, "*You* are the only goddess I want."

And they made love.

AN HOUR LATER, Catharine and David had showered together and were getting dressed again. David picked up the phone and was put through to Franklin.

"Franklin, sorry for the delay. I see it's nearly nine, but could you accommodate us in about fifteen minutes?"

"I'm sorry, Mister Thornhill, but the main dining room is full. I'd offer you our spacious private dining room, but a white lady from Zimbabwe just booked it for her and a black male friend."

David was confused. "I don't know what kind of jerk you take me for, Franklin, but I'm obviously a completely different *kind* of jerk. Why would I care about their races?"

Franklin laughed softly. "I don't think you're a jerk at all, Mister Thornhill, but there are still people in Mozambique who are repelled by the mixing of races. I expect the lady requested a private dining room to avoid such people. I doubt she and her friend are … *involved* anyway, as they accepted rooms in different parts of the hotel. They're in a rush and will be on their way in the morning."

"You said the private dining room was spacious, Franklin. Could you ask the lady kindly whether she would object to sharing the room with two broad-minded New Yorkers?"

"There she is. She just stepped off the elevator. If you'll wait a moment, I'll ask her."

Annoying telephone music came on the earpiece, but David waited as patiently as he could. In a minute, Franklin came back on.

"The lady said she wouldn't mind sharing the dining room, but asked to have your table set up on the far end, as she and her companion will be discussing private matters."

"Excellent!" said David. "We'll leave them undisturbed. What's her name?"

"Let me check the register," said Franklin. "She's Patricia Smith. I don't know her companion's name, as *she* booked both rooms."

David cupped his hand over the room phone so Catharine wouldn't hear. "Please put a dozen roses at our table," he said, "and another dozen at Ms. Smith's table. Put them both on my tab."

"I'll do so at once, Mister Thornhill," said Franklin. "That's quite lavish of you, but I'm sure your uncle will deem it money well spent."

"Oh, Franklin," David said tongue-in-cheek, "why must everything come down to money with you Americans? We'll be down there in ten."

Franklin laughed quietly. "Very well, sir."

"One last thing, Franklin. Could you get us a few burner phones?"

"How many?"

"A half-dozen should suffice, I think," said David.

"They'll arrive while you're still at dinner," said Franklin. "I'll personally drop them off in your room."

CHAPTER 13

"THIS WAY, SIR," said the *maître d'hôtel*.

David extended his left elbow and walked into the dark-paneled private dining room with Catharine on his arm. A window that occupied a whole wall provided every seat with an exquisite view of the moon and stars reflecting off the Indian Ocean.

At one end of the room was David and Catharine's table, which could easily have accommodated six.

At an equally roomy table at the opposite end, a pretty blonde with long legs, presumably Ms. Smith, was seated with her escort, a mature African fellow.

David was pleased to see that a dozen roses had been placed there, just as he'd ordered, and he instinctively smiled at the lady, who looked up as they entered. He knew at once that he'd seen her face before, whether in person or likeness, and forced himself to look away and take his seat across from Catharine.

"You recognize her," declared Catharine. "Pretty. Who is she? Peggy Sue from Garfield High?"

David shook his head. "I can't remember *who* she is, and it's driving me crazy. Something tells me that I knew her when she was quite young."

The sommelier came over and offered David the wine list, but he waved it away and ordered champagne. "Veuve Clicquot, Cave Privée Rose. Do you have … Vintage 1990?"

The sommelier's eyebrows went up. "I'll have to check, sir." He sidled up to David before going off, and whispered, "If we have it, sir, a bottle would be eight hundred fifty dollars American."

"That's fine," said David.

A very surprised sommelier went to check.

Catharine smiled. "You know, someone at the office *will* check our expenses. You could end up with a bill."

David shook his head. "First, I'd gladly spend twice that out of my own pocket to celebrate my first real night with you. Second, do you know what my billable rate is? Let's just say it will easily cover the cost of a bottle of good champagne."

She giggled. "Do you plan on sending a legal bill to the office?"

"Only if they give me a hard time. If worse comes to worst"—he put the back of his wrist to his forehead as though portraying grief in a silent movie—"I'll *work* an hour."

Her eyes grew wide. "Heaven forbid it should come to *that!*"

The older black gentleman supping with Ms. Smith appeared at David's elbow, and said in a pleasing basso voice, "Mister Thornhill, Ms. Jones has asked me to thank you very much for your gallantry in sending over the beautiful roses." The voice was vaguely familiar.

David looked up into the man's kindly eyes, and identified him right away, though he was a good fifteen years older than at their previous meeting. This was … Doctor Daniel Iskender, an Ethiopian linguist who'd addressed a convocation of the Assyriology Center at the university. David had conversed with him at the ensuing cocktail party.

"How are you, Doctor Iskender?" said David, rising with his hand extended. "Incidentally, the lady is registered under the name *Smith*, not Jones. Could it be that *neither* of those is her real name?" He smiled.

Iskender's eyes went wide at his mistake, and he tried to beg out gracefully. "Pardon me, sir. I think you've mistaken me for someone else."

Now David remembered who the *lady* was. She was Miriam Azeri, oldest daughter of Abraham Azeri—the very person they'd rounded the Cape to find. If he mentally subtracted fifteen years from her face and form, she was the spit and image of the young woman depicted in a black-and-white author's photo on the back of one of Azeri's later books. Indeed, he'd seen her once in person.

Evidently, there would be no need to travel halfway across Africa to find her; however, to succeed in their quest, they still needed to gain her confidence at this chance meeting.

"The lady is Miriam Azeri, is she not?" asked David.

Catharine's eyebrows shot up and, against her will, she looked directly at the woman.

"Sir," said Iskender with chagrin. "You have me on the hip. We are here under false names."

David remembered David Mamet's ironic definition of a confidence game as one where the con man gives his confidence to the mark in order to get the mark's confidence in return. He decided to put it into practice.

"I have no advantage over you, sir," said David, "although I salute your Shakespearean referent in the matter. You see, this lovely lady and I are likewise here under false names."

Catharine rolled her eyes, no doubt because he'd blown their cover within two hours of their arrival.

"Is that so?" said Iskender.

"Yes, it is. If I may suggest, sir: Why don't you tell the lady that *I* recognized *her* as soon as I walked in?"

Iskender regarded him with a skeptical frown. "But, wouldn't that be false?"

David shook his head. "Not really," he said. "I recognized her on sight, and was running through all her possible identities even before you came over to our table." He pointed to Catharine. "Isn't that true, dear?"

"It's true, Doctor Iskender," she said. "You have my word."

Iskender glanced toward his own table, where Miriam seemed concerned about his extended absence. He turned to David. "I shall do so," he confirmed, and returned to his table.

The sommelier returned with the bottle and exhibited it to David.

"*Monsieur le Sommelier*," said David without taking his eyes off Iskender, "please wait a few moments. There may be an adjustment in our seating, and we may require more of your kind service."

The sommelier bowed his head with a gratified smile, and backed away.

David glanced over at Catharine, who was openly impressed at David's *savoir faire*. He nodded humbly.

Iskender returned and said, "Ms. Smith has placed me in an awkward position. She is embarrassed to say that she does not remember you. May I tell her your name?"

David smiled. "I can do better than that. You can tell the lady that, when she was in college, she visited the New York apartment I shared with my wife. You may also tell her that I spoke with her father on the phone for many hours before he passed, may he rest in peace. I'm a great admirer of his work. If you and the lady promise not to call me—or refer to me—by my true name, I'll tell you."

Iskender nodded thoughtfully. "I assume you will do the same for us? Forswear divulging real names, I mean?"

"Certainly," said David.

"In that case, I accept your offer. Who are you?"

"I'm Law Professor David Schubert, a good friend of Fareed Sinar of the Assyriology Center in New York, and a member of the law faculty at the same university."

Iskender nodded vigorously. "Oh, that's right. You and I met after my speech." He slapped his forehead.

"So we did," replied David. "Please tell Ms. Smith who I am, and ask her if she and her companion would care to join us for dinner. Our table is certainly large enough."

Iskender bowed and returned to the lady. After a moment's conversation, she looked over at David. "*Now* I remember him!" she said. Then, speaking in a voice loud enough to be heard across the room, she said to David, "Father used to talk about you all the *time!*"

David thanked heaven there was no one of importance in the room to overhear her, and cautioned her by putting his index finger to his lips.

Iskender gently admonished Miriam for her outburst. She rose abashedly from her chair and approached David with Iskender in tow.

David rose to greet her. In a whisper, he said, "Hello, Miriam. I'm very sorry for the loss of your father. And also that I haven't seen you these many years."

Miriam had finally taken the hint that it was necessary to speak in hushed tones. "I thought I recognized you when you came in." She glanced at Catharine and stopped cold. "Oh, I'm sorry," said Miriam. "Your wife was so lovely. Have you … divorced?"

David shook his head sadly. "Sharon died a few years ago, of cancer, but I've soldiered on." He indicated Catharine. "*This* lovely young lady is a business associate." He whispered. "Catharine, this is Miriam Azeri, the daughter of Abraham Azeri, the great Sumerologist."

"David speaks of your father all the time," Catharine said graciously. "Won't you and the good doctor join us for dinner?"

Miriam glanced at Daniel, who nodded vigorously.

"That would be lovely," replied Miriam. "Tell me, what brings you two to Mozambique?"

Catharine deferred to David. "To be completely frank, Miriam, we came to find *you*. Tomorrow, we were going to find a flight to the ancient Anunnaki mines in Zimbabwe." He turned away for a moment. "Sommelier! *Two* bottles of the Veuve Clicquot, please. And two more glasses."

The sommelier smiled, bowed profoundly, and snapped his fingers at his assistant, who picked up the roses from the other table and brought them over to David's.

"You came looking for me?" asked Miriam incredulously. "What ever for?"

"Because … they're coming back," said David. "Haven't you been listening to the news? The Al-Aqsa Mosque and the Temple of Jupiter have disappeared and been magically reassembled elsewhere overnight. Then, saucers and other craft appeared in orbit around the Earth. Then the top of the Great Pyramid disappeared. Does any of this sound familiar?"

Miriam was incredulous.

David was shocked that anyone could be so out of touch. "Where have you *been* for the past few weeks, Miriam?"

She sighed. "In a land five thousand years before Christ, I suppose," she replied as though in a trance. "Daniel and I were at those very Zimbabwean mines you mentioned, and it never once occurred to me to check on current events."

"Well," said David, "now you know why *we're* here. What brought *you* to Beira?"

The sommelier opened the first bottle and poured champagne for each of them. He placed the bottle in a wine bucket next to David and stepped away.

David raised his glass. "To the memory of the greatest Sumerologist who ever lived," he said softly. "He was a man. When comes such another?"

"To Abraham," said Daniel quietly.

They all clinked glasses, sipped, and put them down.

Miriam sipped her champagne moodily. "You asked what brought us to Beira," said Miriam. "We'll tell you, if you tell us something first."

"Tit for tat?" said David. "I so enjoy it. What do you wish to know?"

"*Why* were you looking for me, really … I mean, just now?"

David took a healthy sip. "Your father *may* have compiled notes on something extremely important before he died," said David. "Catharine and I are searching for such notes. We need to make sure that, if they exist, they don't fall into the wrong hands."

"But what was Father researching at that time?" asked Miriam.

"I've thought about little else for weeks," said David, "and I can't recall him telling me anything new that he'd found Earth-shaking. Do you have the papers he was working on just before he passed away?"

"You're not the only ones looking for them," said Miriam.

"I'm aware of that. There's the Anunnaki, too."

"*And* the U.S. Government," she said.

David looked at Catharine. "To be frank, that's who sent *us*," said David.

Catharine looked at him impatiently, as though he'd stupidly revealed more than he needed to. Perhaps she was right. But he knew he had to be forthcoming before Miriam would feel impelled to reciprocate.

"And there's someone *else* looking for Father's papers," said Miriam, "someone Daniel and I met … the night before last."

Now it was Iskender's turn to roll his eyes. David took that to mean he was getting somewhere.

"Whom did you meet?" asked Catharine, who'd been fairly quiet until now.

Miriam looked to Iskender to reply. He cleared his throat. "We were on the plains of Zimbabwe the other night, when Taurayi, Miriam's young helper, came to us hand-in-hand with someone from … another world." When no one laughed, Daniel was surprised but encouraged. "He said his people are called *Dagon*. They come from a planet in the same star system as Nibiru, and tracked that planet from the time it was forcefully expelled by a massive stellar explosion. The Dagon are aware of the collision that occurred eons later between Nibiru's moons and a large planet that was split in two, whose halves became the asteroid belt and Earth."

"How could the Dagon know that?" asked David. "It would have occurred *billions* of years ago."

Daniel shrugged. "Possibly the same way the Anunnaki found out. Perhaps they tested to see if isotopes on the two planets match, or perhaps the tale of the planetary collision was recorded in a series of tablets like the Sumerians' *Enuma Elish*. There may have been Anunnaki who witnessed it and recorded the event. In any event, the Dagon representative said that they've asked the Anunnaki not to land on Earth, and have apparently managed to delay their landing until now. The Dagon do not know why the Anunnaki wish to land here, but they suspect, as you do, that Abraham Azeri had somehow learned why the Anunnaki would choose to return. The Dagon also wish to know why, and we'd like to tell them."

Miriam took another sip of champagne. "Daniel and I are on our way to fetch my father's remaining papers."

"Where are they kept?" asked David.

"In a numbered safe-deposit box in London—*Westminster*, really," she replied. "We're on our way there before first light."

"Mind if we meet up with you there?" asked David.

"Do we have your word that you will not attempt to take the papers away from us?" asked Miriam.

David looked to Catharine, who curtly nodded.

"You have our word," he confirmed. "We just need to know what the Anunnaki want out of their impending visit, which might give us some assurance of how long they intend to stay."

"We've made reservations at the Marriott Grosvenor on Hyde Park," said Miriam. "Once we arrive, I'll have to make arrangements locally to retrieve the papers."

"The U.S. Embassy is just across the Thames in Vauxhall," offered Catharine. "Once you retrieve the papers, you might wish to open them there."

"We'll think about it," said Miriam. "At least we'll have little jet lag, as London and Beira are in adjacent time zones."

"Great!" said David. "Now let's order. I'm starved. And it's all on Uncle Sam."

Catharine frowned. "You're enjoying this expense account entirely too much."

David did his best to look defensive. "Look how much time and money we saved not having to search for Miriam all over Zimbabwe," said David. "We may *never* have found her, and it would have cost a large fortune and possibly wasted *months*. I think we've saved an amount well in excess of the price of a seafood dinner for four! Even *with* good champagne." He raised his hand.

"Waiter!"

⇒○◖○◗○⇐

IT WAS FOUR in the morning Beira time when the U.S.S. *Columbia* came to periscope depth in the Mozambique Channel just west of Madagascar. By prearrangement, Phil Castro, Captain of the *Columbia*, sat at the desk in his stateroom awaiting a heavily encrypted phone call from retired Admiral Simmons.

"Captain, Comms. You've got an incoming phone call from the brass in London. They're two hours earlier. Should I put it through to your stateroom?"

"Go ahead, Comms."

The phone buzzed and the captain picked up.

"Is that Bob?" he said with unfelt vigor.

A dejected voice came on the line. "A piece of him. Received your latest report, Phil. I'm not sure whether to laugh or cry. These bastards can hand us anything they want, and we've just got to eat it. Every sub in the navy is experiencing the same weapons failure. I'm having some of them continue to check, but every one that's been checked so far has been a dud. And I don't even want to discuss the experience of the other two legs of the triad."

"Is any shielding showing promise?"

"Almost nothing. We've got some mineral deposits that seem to have some effect at high densities. Problem is, at usable thickness they'd be too damned heavy to transport by air—or even sea."

"What about the guys in the dirt?"

"Marginal, but we're trying everything we can think of."

"By the way," said Castro, "your package was delivered in good condition. SEALS say they were bickering like a married couple when they got dropped off."

That failed to get a laugh.

Instead, Admiral Simmons sighed. "I'm sure that'd be a fun discussion in other circumstances, Phil, but right now I feel like I haven't slept in a year. Thanks for dropping off the package. Keep your guys sharp. As soon as we've got a practical fix, you're first to know."

"I know it, Bob. Get some shuteye."

"Out."

⟶∘⟶

IN ORBIT THIRTY miles above the surface of the Earth, the conversation between the admiral and the captain was overheard and recorded. It was deciphered by computer fourteen minutes later, and required an additional hour to be read and understood. A plot was mapped out showing the location of all deepwater ports within eight hours' travel time of the boomer's present position.

Then *she* was notified.

⟶∘⟶

BY FOUR-THIRTY IN the morning, Miriam and Daniel were seated in an airliner about to take off for Tel Aviv on their way to London. As the plane taxied toward the runway, its transponder switched on, which set off a buzzer in Brosa's chamber. He happened to be awake. He threw a switch and watched the takeoff. After a few uneventful minutes, he turned off the video and went to sleep.

The computer would keep track of the flight.

DAVID AND CATHARINE had had their fill of food and champagne, and stumbled back to their room by eleven. Just inside the door, David had found the small satchel containing the burner phones he'd requested. He'd brought the satchel to the granite bench in his bathroom and placed it next to the clothing he'd laid out for the next day.

Catharine had intended to draw a laugh by putting a tin-foil hat on each of their heads before retiring, but in the heat of the moment she forgot. They made torrid love until half past midnight, and fell asleep at one in the morning in a satiated tangle of naked arms and legs.

David's dreams consisted of the usual hodge-podge of mangled early memories and overly intense feelings over some ill-defined, ever-changing dilemma. After several hours, he awoke momentarily to Catharine's scent and, when he slept again, his dreams turned adolescent, which meant … women.

He was sitting in dark sunglasses in the morning at the bar outside the hotel, looking out at an ocean bathed in sunlight. The chaise longue next to him showed no sign of being occupied by anyone. He could have sworn he was with a woman at the hotel, but there was no one with him now.

He felt a familiar knock inside his head. By now he recognized what it signified: His dream was about to be invaded by her.

Remembering that he had the power to choose the setting of his encounter with Inanna, he imagined himself in the grocery section of the Walmart in Ithaca, New York, wearing sunglasses and a pair of bright pink Bermuda shorts with a garish floral shirt. Quickly, he surrounded himself with people in the most outlandish shopping outfits he could remember seeing on the Internet, fat bosoms tucked under waistbands, fat men dressed in cheap fairy costumes five sizes too small.

He turned to his right and there she was. Inanna. And she was not happy.

"What kind of place is this that you bring me to?" she demanded.

"This is an indoor market of the present day."

She gazed about at the people and their bizarre forms of dress. "This market is for … crazy people?"

"No," he replied without any hint of humor. "They are ordinary people."

"But they show their—how do you say?"

"Their buttcracks? Only a few of them."

"And some dress as though they believe they are characters in a play."

"Yes, some do," said David. "Some are drunk or stoned on other substances. Some are ... crazy, as you say."

She viewed him skeptically. "They are permitted to walk around this way?"

"As long as they don't hurt anyone else, yes."

"Why?"

"My Queen," said David respectfully before he could stop himself, "most are harmless. Besides, there are eight billion of us. We can't control eight billion. How many of you are there? Fifteen hundred, like the last time?"

"We can control these people," she said emphatically.

"No, you can't. You can only kill them."

"Are you prepared to be in my service?" she asked.

"I'm loyal to these people. If you tell me why you have returned to Earth, and if you can assure me that you mean them no harm, I will seriously consider it."

"Does the slave demand assurance from the queen?" she asked haughtily.

"I'm no one's slave," said David. "I'm a free man and I carve for myself. You can't control me."

"There are ways to control people without killing them," she replied darkly.

"Not this many people. And not me."

She regarded him coldly, as though her patience was exhausted.

"We shall soon see if there is no way to control you, son of Joseph."

He awoke, and she was gone.

Catharine was sitting beside him on the edge of the bed. Day was breaking.

"That was her, wasn't it?" she asked.

He nodded.

"I thought so," said Catharine. "You tightened up like a knot. What does she want?"

"She wants me in her service. I still have no idea why. I also have no idea why they've come back here or what their intentions are with respect to ... us—human beings."

"Are you going to work for her?"

He reached for Catharine. "I don't even want to *think* about her. I'm thinking about you."

"You're sweet," she said, her eyes darting about. "But she may have found us, so I want to get out of here."

There was a sudden pounding on the door. Catharine put on a robe, and her Glock appeared in her right hand.

Full of surprises, thought David, and grabbed his bathrobe. "Let me answer it."

She nodded reluctantly.

The pounding resumed.

David went to the door and quickly swung it open. "What do you think you—" David had to rub his eyes before he could feel confident who this was. "Doctor ... *Zia?*"

CHAPTER 14

DOCTOR ZIA STOOD outside the door. "I'm sorry for making such a dreadful commotion," he said, "but this is most urgent." He peered inside. "May I come in?"

David glanced at Catharine.

She nodded and said, "Only *him*."

"I assure you, I'm alone," said Doctor Zia. "My driver Enkidu is waiting in the car downstairs."

David couldn't help but notice as Zia entered that he was wearing a slightly lighter-weight version of the same dark suit he'd been wearing in Paris.

Zia eyed Catharine warily. "Professor," he said, "can I speak with you … alone?"

Catharine replied. "Whatever you can say to him, you can say to me."

Doctor Zia shrugged, and asked David. "Does this young woman know about … Anunnaki?"

Catharine answered. "I've heard about little else for the past two weeks," she said. "Are you armed?"

"No," he said. "I carry no weapons. *Defensive* items sometimes, but no weapons. Umm … might I ask you to lower *your* weapon?"

Catharine cautiously put her pistol in the pocket of her robe.

David regarded Zia with some irritation. "What's so urgent that you had to pound on our door before sunrise?"

Zia looked around as though there might be enemies everywhere. "*She* knows you're here. In an hour, this place will be overrun with Igigi and if you're *still* here, they'll take you."

"And Catharine?" asked David. "Will they take *her*?"

Zia shook his head. "Very unlikely. And if they do, they're unlikely to keep her long."

"What would they do with her?" asked David.

"Well, they'd probably release her eventually," said Zia. "They consider repugnant the deliberate killing of sentient beings."

"Oh, *do* they?" asked David skeptically.

Zia laughed quietly. "If you doubt that, you might check your copy of the Ten Commandments."

David's head spun with possibilities. *Did the Anunnaki craft the Ten Commandments? Are the Anunnaki bound by them?*

"As for the lady," Zia continued, "I suppose they might imprison her for some time, but only to stop her from revealing secrets."

David realized that this conversation would need to continue for some time. "We have only an hour?" asked David.

"We have barely that long to vacate these premises," said Doctor Zia, "and I urge you not to push your luck. However, we can continue this conversation in my car. The roof is shielded from her tracking rays. I beg you to put on your clothes and come with me. I assure you I am *not* in Inanna's service. My driver will take you anywhere you wish to go and I can give you a device that will mask your whereabouts so that she'll have enormous difficulty reacquiring you."

David looked to Catharine. "I like the sound of that."

Catharine let David's remark pass, and addressed Zia. "You have such a device?"

Zia drew something the size of a cigarette case out of his pocket. It had a mineral surface of roughly polished stone, and what looked like two pushbuttons: one red, the other black. "I'll give it to you if you come with me. It will work for only one of your days in total, but you can choose when to turn it on and off. Used judiciously, it should get you quite far from here."

David looked to Catharine, who nodded and disappeared into the bathroom to take a submarine shower and dress. David waited with Zia.

"She's truly lovely," said the old man wearily. "Blonde hair and blue eyes ... or at least eyes that aren't brown. By her coloring, she could be Enki's own daughter."

David regarded him apprehensively. "She's not, *is* she?"

Zia laughed aloud and took a moment to becalm himself. "No. Pardon me, professor, but I haven't had a good laugh since the possibility of returning to Earth began being debated in earnest some time ago."

Catharine reappeared in a summer dress, looking as feminine as could be, except for the pistol in her waistband. She sat across from Zia while David washed and dressed, and not a word passed between them until he returned and Zia rose to lead them out.

"I hate to mention something so trivial," said Catharine, "but can we forward our wardrobes? It took a lot to get them here."

Zia checked his watch and shook his head. "I'm afraid we haven't time. Even if you were to ask your friend Franklin to forward your clothing and he were capable of removing it before they arrive (which is itself doubtful), they'd realize it's missing and tear the hotel apart to find it, and that would enable them to track *you*."

Catharine rose, looking disappointed. "That's what I thought. Come on," she said. "Let's get out of here."

⟶∘⟨⟨⟩∘⟵

IN THE DRIVEWAY outside the hotel waited a black stretch limousine and a staunch-looking driver dressed in the traditional dark suit and a black felt mariner's cap.

"Good morning, Enkidu," said Doctor Zia.

"Good morning, Doctor Zia," came the reply.

The driver opened the door for Catharine first, waited for her to settle in her preferred place in the horseshoe-shaped passenger's cabin, then walked the men to the opposite side of the car and opened a door for them.

"Where *to*, sir?" asked the driver.

Zia looked to David to express a preference.

David shrugged. "Maputo?" he guessed.

Zia contemplated a moment. "No," he muttered. "She'll have every port in east Africa covered. First thing is to get us off the coast." As the driver stepped into his seat and locked the doors, Zia said to him, "Enkidu, please take well-traveled roads west toward the interior. And give us the smallest tracking profile possible for at least an hour."

David admired the unusually smooth ride, even over what looked like bumpy stretches of road. After a controlled departure, the car soon reached smooth blacktop and sped off.

"Now tell me this," said David. "Who *are* you?"

The old fellow smiled. "I told you the truth. I'm Doctor Zia."

"On your business card is the Staff of Hermes, the Greek version of Enki's son Ningishzidda. Do you work for him?"

"No. It's the Staff of *Enki*. I am in Enki's service. He merely *lent* it to Ningishzidda."

"So, as I suspected," said David, "Enki still lives. Bless his name." David regarded Zia warily. "Are you … *human?*"

Zia looked at the ceiling, as though David had posed a complex question. "Yes, I suppose I *am*," said Zia, "as you understand that term. But I have some Anunnaki traits, too."

"How *old* are you?" asked David.

Zia sighed long, as though he wasn't quite sure how to calculate his age. "I've been around a very, *very* long time by your standards."

"Is Zia your family name?"

"No. When I was born, we had no need of family names. My birth name was Ziusudra."

David sat up aghast.

"Who's Ziusudra?" asked Catharine. "Should I *know* who he is?"

David turned to her slowly, as he was about to say something that would sound like madness. "Doctor Zia is … *Noah*."

It took a moment for Catharine to realize whom he meant.

"You mean, from Noah's *Ark?*" she asked incredulously.

Doctor Zia turned to her. "At your service," he said, clearly expecting to be disbelieved.

"According to Abe Azeri," said David, "that would make you more than thirteen thousand years old."

Doctor Zia smiled wanly. "And Enki is much older than *I*."

David regarded the old man with wonder. "The hotelier, Jacques de la Fontaine, said that generations of your ancestors had stayed at the family's hotel. He said that his grandfather knew your grandfather, his father your father—"

Doctor Zia laughed softly and shook his head. "They all knew *me*, not my ancestors."

"So you knew them *all?*"

Zia smiled fondly. "All of them. Fine people. Professional and trustworthy (but for one, who always seemed to be holding something back). We should have more like them in this world."

David studied his face. "That scar on your head—"

Zia nodded. "I got it on the Ark. When the first wave came—properly called a *tsunami*, since it wasn't truly tidal—the vessel capsized, but then immediately righted itself. Everyone *else* instinctively grabbed onto something and escaped injury. But because I was walking, I didn't feel it coming."

"The *Ark?*" said Catharine, evidently stuck a few mental steps behind.

"Well," Zia conceded, "it wasn't like the one described in the Bible. It was a very large version of a circular boat that Enki had already developed for use in the river. With the approach of the Flood, Enki came up with ways to make his riverboat design both impervious to water and capable of righting itself."

"And you had aboard two of every land animal?" asked Catharine skeptically.

Doctor Zia shook his head. "No, we had the *essence* of every land animal, and were able to regenerate nearly every species once we landed. A few didn't make it."

"*Essence,* meaning …?"

"Sperm and egg, mostly. But for species capable of producing food for those aboard, we brought live animals, to be sure."

"How come you've lived so long?" she asked.

Doctor Zia grew quite serious. "When the rains ended and the Ark came to rest on the peaks of Mount Ararat—and the waters receded below the twin mountaintops—we disembarked and conducted a fiery animal sacrifice to the Anunnaki. (Mortals such as we were forbidden to eat animals at that time.) The Anunnaki saw what we had done and landed close by. They left their craft and came over to us. They were a truly wretched lot, having eaten only canned rations as they watched us from orbit for an entire year.

"They devoured our offerings. Their bodies, unlike ours, are de-signed to consume animal flesh. On this occasion, they craved it terribly, and ate ravenously. Once they'd eaten their fill, Enlil admitted to his half-brother Enki that he'd been wrong to insist that mankind be allowed to perish in the Flood. To make partial amends with Enki, Enlil then took my wife and me by the hand and led us back into the Ark, where he placed a finger upon each of our foreheads and granted us the immortali-ty of the Anunnaki."

"Is your wife still alive, then?" asked Catharine.

Doctor Zia became morose and shook his head. "My wife, whose memory is a blessing to me and all mankind, lived a very long and full life—indeed, many times longer than the natural life of a human being. But she was killed centuries ago in a volcanic explosion on Nibiru that claimed thousands of lives. Long life does not confer protection from accidents, intentional acts, or some few diseases."

"And you work for *Enki* now?" said David.

Zia nodded. "Enki fashioned us from apes. He loved us and never wished us to perish. In fairness, Inanna herself was terribly upset about the near-elimination of mankind, regardless that she descended from Enlil."

"But so many people *did* perish in the Flood!" said Catharine.

"That's true," said Zia, "but the Anunnaki didn't *cause* the Flood. Some time before Nibiru's approach, those lower-level Anunnaki whose job it was to remain ever in orbit around Earth (or at a base on the sixth planet) could see that, with the coming end of the Ice Age, the ice that covered nearly an entire continent would plunge into the sea upon Nibiru's next approach, raising water levels drastically throughout the world. Nearly every human—at least in our part of the world—would have perished *regardless* of anything the Anunnaki did or didn't do."

Doctor Zia checked his watch. "The Igigi have certainly reached your hotel room by now." He leaned forward and opened the partition between the passenger cabin and the driver. "Enkidu, please switch on the stealth generator and head toward … Windhoek. Treetop level."

"Windhoek?" asked Catharine. "It'll take us all day and night to get there, and that's assuming that nothing's blocking the roa—*Whoa!*"

The limo soared into the air over the road.

David felt his gorge rise as he struggled to dispel the conviction that they'd fallen off a cliff. Wide-eyed, he and Catharine instinctively clasped each other's hands and grabbed the straps by their seats.

The car leveled off and headed due west over the woods.

"It's all right," said Zia reassuringly. "It's all right. I'm sorry. I completely forgot that your cars don't fly."

David gaped out the window. The limo had leveled off at an altitude roughly a hundred feet above the treetops.

"But this—this vehicle has no wings!" David exclaimed, still shocked out of his wits.

Zia laughed softly. "That's very astute. It has no wings. It doesn't fly by means of Bernoulli's Principle, but rather by straddling the uneven striations of the electromagnetic field generated by large massive bodies, such as the Earth. It's the same way the megaliths were excavated, moved, and emplaced in erecting massive structures thousands of years ago."

"This vehicle makes no use *whatever* of the airfoil?" asked David as he watched the treetops rapidly passing beneath the limo.

"No," said Doctor Zia, "but why is that so amazing? Your *rockets* don't require airfoils."

"But they require massive continuous inputs of energy."

"So does this vehicle. In fact, that's why I asked Enkidu to wait before turning on the stealth generator. It draws a great deal of power. That's also why the battery in your handheld version can work for no longer than a day. This vehicle is far more stable than an airfoil. It doesn't require motion to remain aloft. Permit me to demonstrate. Enkidu," he said, "stop the car."

The vehicle slowed down and in a moment, they sat stationary above a single point on the ground. A gust of wind came and rocked the vehicle gently. A bird flew by. David's head was spinning. "Please, doctor. Let's resume our way."

"Of course," said Zia. "Enkidu, you heard the gentleman."

The vehicle began moving again and quickly regained its former speed. Doctor Zia closed the driver's partition.

"How fast will this vehicle travel … up here?" asked Catharine.

"It can reach five hundred kilometers per hour in a pinch. Over long distances, we generally keep it down to three hundred sixty. Let's see: It's about two thousand three hundred kilometers to Windhoek, so figure seven hours. No refueling is necessary."

"Or possible," David reminded him.

Doctor Zia smiled. "Just so."

"Doesn't your driver become fatigued?" asked Catharine.

Zia leaned close to them and whispered. "No, he's a … synthetic person."

"Does he not know that?" asked Catharine.

"He knows," Zia assured her, "but there's no reason to throw it in his face."

"Snowflake robots," she said, rolling her eyes. "What'll they think of next?"

David said, "I've noticed you call him Enkidu. Wasn't that the name of Gilgamesh's friend, the one who helped slay the Bull of Heaven?"

Zia was so impressed, he bowed his head. "This fellow is an updated version of that … Enkidu model. You must remember that Enki created the whole field of robotics just to assist Bilgames."

"Who's Bilgames?" asked Catharine.

David replied for Zia. "That's the Sumerian pronunciation of Gilgamesh." He turned to Zia. "Doctor Zia, you appear very prominently in the tale of Gilgamesh. Was he a real person?"

"He *was*, professor, king of an important city, but not someone you'd have cared to meet. He was barbaric in many ways—indeed, the most determined brute I've ever met. When I had no choice but to tell him that the Anunnaki would not grant him immortality, I sincerely thought he would crush me with his bare hands. To this day, I think the only reason he didn't was that it would have lost him any chance of further support from Enki."

For whatever lingering mistrust David might have of Doctor Zia, he was enthralled to be in the presence of history, to be one of only a handful of people who'd ever had the opportunity to ask Ziusudra about Gilgamesh. Glancing out the window, he spotted a famous place.

"Look there, doctor!" said David. "It's Lake Mutirikwi and Great Zimbabwe. Is it true that Enki lived in Great Zimbabwe to oversee the gold mines?"

Doctor Zia looked down. "You mean, that large ring of stone? No, that wasn't there at that time. Besides, Enki would never choose to live so far from the water. His favored place to reside was always on an isolated island in a placid lake, such as *that* lake. Although it wasn't called Mutirikwi at the time, I can't recall what the Anunnaki called it. You might be interested to know that we're passing directly over the birthplace of *the adam* and his wife."

Catharine said, "You mean this is the Garden of Eden?"

At first Zia seemed confused by the question, but then realized the source of the confusion. "Oh, I see why you're asking. You were taught that the first man and woman were brought into being in Eden." He shook his head. "They weren't. Enki and his half-sister Ninharsag created them right here, after much trial and error. No, Eden is in Mesopotamia, in present-day Iraq, and the Garden of Eden to which Adam and Eve were transported, and from which they were ultimately expelled by Enlil when Enki gave them the ability to have children, is now mostly submerged under the Red Sea."

Catharine gazed out the windows in wonderment. But eventually the *practical* Catharine returned and she decided to pose the question that had been on her mind since Zia showed up.

"Doctor Zia, thank you for helping us to escape the clutches of Inanna. Can you tell us what *you* want from us?"

After thinking for a moment, Zia said, "No, I truly cannot. I suppose what I would *like* is as much of an alliance between us as circumstance will allow. Let me explain my own feelings on this earthly visitation by the Anunnaki.

"I must thank Enlil for the long life he bestowed upon my wife and me.

"I must thank *Enki* for just about everything else: the existence of humanity which, for all its many flaws, I believe to be a species worth saving. I must also thank Enki for the lives of myself and my family, who would have died but for his intercession. I would willingly die for him and, for all I know, someday I shall."

He shifted in his seat before completing his thought.

"On the other hand, my first allegiance is to my family, and I'm fortunate to have a very large one. Every person on Earth is a descendant of mine and my wife's, and of one of my three sons. Unless the people of this planet thrive and continue to seek their destiny, I am nothing; I would be alone. And all that I have striven for in my whole long life would count for nought. I would not stand by and watch anyone—even Enki—sacrifice my family for any reason, no matter how justifiable."

Catharine said, "Does Enki know this?"

Doctor Zia smiled wryly. "There is precious little Enki doesn't know about the universe. And there's *nothing* he doesn't know about *me*. I've long ceased to hide my feelings from him. I think that's why he trusts me and occasionally looks to me for guidance.

"Your next question would be: *Why did I help you escape the clutches of Inanna?* As David knows her history, he knows that she is well-meaning but ambitious. She loves men more than reason. And she is clever. Not clever like Enki. No, the best English word for Inanna is *devious*. Though she means well and feels with a true heart, she can be ruthless to those who stand in her way.

"I, for one, don't care for her, and she knows it. Perhaps as a consequence, she *loathes* me. She often has me tracked, and her people are everywhere. If the Anunnaki are to return to Earth and remain for any considerable time, I would not have her in charge of this planet, and I would not have her ascendant. If, in some small measure, I can stand in her way, I intend to. Consider yourselves beneficiaries of my ... personality quirks."

David nodded and, to Catharine's amazement, began nodding *off*.

She reached over to wake him, but Zia stopped her short with a frown. "Let him sleep. She can't trouble his dreams in here."

With that assurance, Catharine cradled David and fell asleep herself.

⟶∘⟨⟩∘⟵

IT WAS NEAR mid-afternoon and they were approaching Windhoek when Doctor Zia awakened them.

"I presume you two wish to be dropped off at Hosea Kutako, as that's Windhoek's international airport. It's east of the city, so we can drop you off someplace where you won't become entangled with the traffic or need to hire a cab."

"That would be most courteous of you, doctor," said David, wiping the sleep from his eyes.

"I'm afraid I can't supply you with clothing," said Zia with disappointment. "Indeed, I wouldn't know how to dress you, as I have no idea where you're going. But I *can* give you American money to buy some clothes."

"That won't be necessary," said Catharine. "I grabbed our money and travel papers before we left the hotel."

"Excellent!" said Zia. "I think it would make you a bit less conspicuous if you were carrying some luggage. Enkidu has a couple of extra valises in his compartment. We can give you those."

David felt very fortunate indeed to have made Zia's acquaintance. "That would be most helpful."

Zia smiled fondly. "Meantime, here's the handheld cloaking device. If you wish to go *off the grid*, as people say nowadays, just push the black button. It won't make you disappear in person, but it will temporarily wipe you off Inanna's electronic search grid. Be careful to use it only when she doesn't know where you are, for once she has you in her sights, you're unlikely to escape—even with aid of the device. Remember also that it won't work for more than twenty-four hours in total. After that, the power source will become quite unreliable, so you won't know for certain whether you're shielded."

"That's ingenious," said David. "Who invented it?"

Zia laughed to himself. "Enki, of course. He made it so I could avoid detection by Inanna whenever it suits me."

"He made it for *you?*" asked Catharine.

Zia nodded.

David shook his head. "We can't deprive you of it, then," he said and tendered it back to Zia.

"It's a spare," Zia assured them. "I have mine right here." He removed it from the pocket of his jacket and showed it to them. "I almost forgot; it has one other function."

"What's that?" asked Catharine.

"If you press the red button three times in rapid succession, then, as it shuts off, it will transmit your coordinates to *my* device and also … to Enki. Its purpose is to assure rescue."

Zia opened the partition, gave instructions to Enkidu, and turned back to David and Catharine. "We'll be landing in-motion on a two-lane road a few miles east of the airport and drive you right to the terminal. Before we let you out, there's something I want to say to you, David, as I know you're being sought by Inanna."

David and Catharine nodded, dread etched on both their faces.

"If either of you is ever taken before Inanna or any other Great Anunnaki, if you treat them with deference and patience they will more than likely treat you humanely."

"How much deference should we show them?" asked David.

Zia contemplated the question. "Pretend it's four hundred years ago, and you're appearing before a King or Queen of England. That should do it. Remember, on Earth they've always been treated as gods, and on Nibiru they're global royalty."

Catharine, near tears, clutched David's shoulder, as though afraid they would be coming for him at any moment.

"David, I don't want you *going* with her!" she exclaimed, and turned to Doctor Zia. "Doctor, please bring this vehicle down on the main road at Omitara. I know someone there who can help us."

Zia nodded, opened the partition and asked Enkidu, "Do you know where Omitara is?"

"Yes, sir," came the reply. "It's about two minutes from here. Oh, but sir …"

"Yes?"

"There's nothing there," said Enkidu. "It's on the plains, with a couple of mountains in the distance. The only buildings are a railway station and a couple of tin-roof dwellings."

Catharine leaned forward and spoke loudly enough for the driver to hear. "There's also a watering hole, isn't there? A makeshift tavern?"

"It doesn't even have a name," said Enkidu, and took his eyes off the instrument panel just long enough for a quick glance at Catharine's face. "You're serious," he observed.

"Yes," she replied.

Enkidu shrugged. "Many of the men there are known to carry modified Kalashnikovs. I have some weapons in the trunk if you wish, madam."

Zia's eyebrows shot up. "Madam, what business have you at a place like that?"

Catharine smirked in embarrassment. "I know the owner. He's an American expatriate."

"Doctor Zia," said Enkidu, "we're coming up on it in one minute. Do you wish me to discharge the passengers at this place?"

Doctor Zia shook his head emphatically, but looked to David to break the tie.

David turned to Catharine. "Do we need more weapons at this

place?"

She shook her head without hesitation. "They'd do us no good."

David rolled his eyes at her less-than-assuring response.

Yet, against his better judgment, he nodded to Zia.

CHAPTER 15

In Omitara, Doctor Zia's limo discharged two of its passengers before a ramshackle wood hut with a rusted tin roof. The exterior had been sloppily painted in primary colors that had obviously faded long ago. Swaying gently in each window, hung by its neck, was a model skeleton in a black sombrero. A crudely lettered sign was nailed to the front door:

Bienvenidos, amigos mexicanos, a El Paso.

David studied the sign's message before carrying their bags to the entrance. Eyeing Catharine skeptically, he said, "You're sure this guy is good with directions?"

She folded her arms and shrugged. "In the *service*, he was."

As there was no *Closed* sign and the door was unlocked, Catharine swung it open. A bell on the inside of the door jangled to announce their entrance. Despite the bell, the three men inside were all asleep.

The decor was *fiesta*, circa 1942. Two snoring men sat opposite each other with their heads on the table between them and their arms sprawled out in front of them. A bottle of cheap whiskey lay uncorked on the table, and next to each man lay an empty shot glass and a well-worn AK-47.

Behind the bar, a man wearing an apron sat asleep on a stool, sprawled across the bar in much the same posture as his customers. An empty whiskey bottle of the same brand lay on the bar by his hand, leaving little doubt who'd finished it.

"Man," said David, "I've never seen a place so rough that the *bartender* passes out drunk. What the devil are we *doing* here?"

The bartender snorted and, spying prospective customers, sat up and struggled to focus his eyes on them. "Can I get you folks something?" he mumbled.

"I'd like some *huevos rancheros*, please," said David, which seemed humorous, as they were in Africa and there was no sign of a grill.

Catharine frowned at him and turned to the bartender.

"Is Gary here?"

"Umm … *Gary?*" asked the bartender, checking his watch.

"Yes, you know," said Catharine, "the *owner?*"

The bartender arched an eyebrow. "I know who Gary is, ma'am. He should be here any minute. He's doing maintenance on one of the aircraft."

Behind them came the sound of a jeep rolling up and a couple of men walking toward the entrance door. Catharine took a step away from the door, discreetly drew her Glock, and snapped off the safety.

The torpid patrons were evidently not too drunk to be brought back to the edge of consciousness for, at that sound, they both sat up smartly, drew their weapons off the table and aimed them at Catharine. The bartender drew his, too.

Surprised, Catharine dangled her pistol at arm's length by the trigger guard and snapped the safety back on, as though providing instruction in gun safety.

The two newcomers walked in, oblivious to the events leading up to present circumstances. The one who entered first, clearly the elder and stronger of the two, was six feet three inches tall, noticeably fit, with black hair and salt-and-pepper sideburns. The younger fellow was about the same height, but gangly, and lacking the prominent shoulders and chest of his companion.

The one with the grizzled sideburns immediately spotted the guns all around, took one look at Catharine's chagrined expression, and laughed aloud.

Barely moving, Catharine shook her head. "You always *did* have a strange sense of humor, Gary."

"Okay," said Gary in an authentic West Texas drawl, "everybody just go back to the way you were. This lady's an old friend of mine from the service, not some gun-wieldin' moll."

The three whose guns were trained on Catharine were slow to put their weapons down. Noticing their reluctance, Gary added:

"And she's *not* a cop."

As though he'd uttered some magical incantation, the guns instantly disappeared from view—except Catharine's, which still dangled from her fingers. With a smile, Gary plucked Catharine's gun like a ripe fruit and put the stock in her hand. "I trust you'll be on best behavior, Catharine. You here on business or pleasure?"

"You know me, Gary," said Catharine as she put the gun in her waistband. "All business, all the time."

Gary sized up David and extended his hand. "Sorry for not introducin' myself earlier, chief."

David shook his hand. "Pleased to meet ya, Gary," he said pleasantly. "Any friend of Catharine's is a friend of mine."

Gary turned to the barkeep. "A Jack Daniels for me and the kid here." He looked to Catharine and David. "You two drinkin'?"

Catharine smiled and put on a bit of a drawl. "I'll take a Coca Cola, if ya got it, and thank ya kindly."

Gary raised an inquiring eyebrow at David.

"None for me, thanks," said David. "I make it a practice not to drink so soon after pissin' myself."

That tickled Gary's funnybone, and he laughed aloud.

The barkeep pressed a button that put on some old country music, and turned it up just enough to provide some privacy for any business the boss might wish to conduct.

One of the two fellows at the table took out a deck of cards and started dealing.

Gary led David, Catharine, and the *kid* to an isolated table and the drinks came out right away. As they sat down, Gary introduced the kid by one name: *Gonçalves*. Since the kid didn't say a word, it was unclear what language he spoke.

"Okay, princess," said Gary as he sipped his drink, "since you're all bidness, what brings you here? I got a feelin' y'all need a lift."

"Ya got that right off the bat," said Catharine.

"How fur ya goin'?"

Catharine sipped her Coke. "Only about … seven thousand miles," she said.

That got a raised eyebrow from the otherwise cool Gary. "Well, I just filled up the Jeep, but I think that's a little outside her range. I mean, she's got at least another twenty thousand miles left in 'er, but it'd take an awful long time for her to cover seven thousand miles." He shrugged. "And then she'd have to come all the way back, so that's *twice* seven thousand." He took another sip and leaned into Catharine. "I take it you're here about *flyin'*."

"You know I am," she said.

"I don't know if I can help ya," he said with concern. "Gonçalves n' me're headin' out on a long haul tonight."

Catharine looked at him and shook her head disapprovingly. "Contraband?"

Gary smiled. "I don't know why you'd suggest such a thing, ma'am. You know I've always had a good head on m'shoulders."

"Oh? Is that why you have a sign out front welcoming all your Mexican friends to El Paso?"

He feigned disapproval. "What's the matter? Y'all got somethin' against Mexicans?"

"Not at all," replied Catharine. "I just can't imagine that too many Mexicans have seen that sign. And it's a little strange that you're welcoming them to *El Paso*."

"Why's that?" asked Gary.

"Because El Paso's in west Texas and, in case you haven't noticed, we're in *Namibia*." She sipped her Coke. "Strikes me that's more than a few miles off."

Gary laughed. David was quietly getting jealous of the easy way Catharine had lapsed into nonsense talk with this tall Texan.

"Look," said Gary, "I'd like to help you, and we *are* light goin' out. But even so, I'm not sure we can carry your load. Whatcha transportin'?"

Catharine said, "Two passengers with personal luggage. Just the professor and me."

Gary sat back in his chair with an incredulous expression. "Why don't ya just get two seats outta Windhoek on British Airways? Hell, you could travel *first class* and beat the hell out of what *I'd* cost ya."

"British Airways can't provide what you offer. *Anonymity*."

Gary was surprised. "You still in the service?"

Catharine nodded.

"What's your rank now?"

"Lieutenant commander."

Gary looked at her askew, as though he couldn't fathom why she wouldn't be flying in the service network. On the other hand, she could be trusted to know her own business, and *he* wasn't in the business of turning away willing customers.

"Where do you need to go?"

"Heathrow."

"Well, hell, I'm headin' up to Marseille Provence Airport tonight. Long haul, but I could accommodate ya. In fact, I could drop you off first. I'd *like* to show up at Heathrow with respectable citizens. Last time I flew up in there, I had a couple Mexicans with me. Only reason they didn't have prison records was they hadn't been caught yet. The authorities were pretty sure I was smugglin'." He looked at her suspiciously. "*You're* not on the lam, are ya?"

She smirked. "Nope. Gubmint bidness." She glanced around. "But I hasten to add that it's got nothin' to do with law enforcement."

"No?" said Gary. "Well, what's it got to do with?"

"Can't say," she replied.

"Not lookin' fer chapter and verse, kid. But, gimme a hint or we're not takin' ya."

She was reluctant to say anything.

"Wait a minute," said Gary, leaning in to avoid being overheard. "This got anything to do with them … flyin' cigars they keep showin' on the TV?"

Instead of replying, Catharine pointed with her chin toward Gonçalves.

Gary took the hint and said to Gonçalves, "Gimme two minutes with this blonde bombshell, wouldja kid?"

The kid nodded, got up from his chair and went to the bar to chat with the barkeep.

"Well?" asked Gary.

Catharine looked at the floor, then back up at Gary with an intensity David had rarely seen on her face. In the slightest and quickest gesture David had ever seen, and with no change of expression whatever, she nodded her head. It was so fast, it was like the two of them were cheating at cards on a heavily armed high roller.

Gary sat back in amazement. "Well, I'll be goddamned. So that stuff's fer real." He sighed. "Okay, but here's the deal. It'll cost you thirty grand plus the cost of fuel from Marseille to Heathrow and back."

"Do I look like I was born yesterday?" she asked. "Why so much in fuel? You're savin' a takeoff and landing at Marseille."

Gary shook his head cynically. "End of the frickin' world, but ya *still* got time to dicker. Okay, I'll give ya credit for the cost of fuel for *one* takeoff and landing."

"Okay," she said, "but *twenty* grand." When he glowered at her, she smiled back and said pertly, *"Friends and family?"*

He laughed, then looked at her skeptically. "Okay, but I want a real good look at that luggage, 'cause it might get a real close look at Heathrow."

"Oh, I forgot," she added as though it were a mere afterthought, "I can only give you ten now. The rest is going to have to wait a couple weeks. I have to get it from Naval Intelligence."

"And if they pull that *fleet is out* excuse?"

"I'll have Daddy write me a check, and you can send me your wire transfer information. You'll be paid. Guaranteed."

Gary rubbed his chin. "I'll give you the bank info for a corporate cutout in Netherlands Antilles. Can't afford to have the Federal Reserve lookin' into muh bidness."

Catharine pointed to the bags sitting next to the table.

"Feast your eyes."

"Not here," said Gary, beckoning Gonçalves over, then pointing to the bags. "Give these the once over, kid. We'll be at the hangar in a couple minutes."

⟶∘⟪✦⟫∘⟵

THE HANGAR WAS much larger than David expected, as was the plane, a cargo Boeing 737 of a type used not long before by the online retailer Amazon. Painted pure white, it was sleek and impressive.

"Well, kids," said Gary, "here she is. Waddya think?"

David let out a long descending whistle. "Isn't this kind of … big … to fly two people to the U.K.?"

Gary nodded. "It would be," he said, "but that's not why we're takin' her out tonight. We'll be real light all the way to Heathrow. Cargo duty starts in Marseille and we'll be hoppin' all over the E.U. before comin' home."

"You're coming home empty?" asked Catharine.

"No," said Gary, "we'll be carryin' a few things, but mostly for the gubmint." He smiled toothily. "We find that good relations with our host country is of prime importance to our continued success." He looked toward the shop at the back of the hangar. "Where is that kid?" He walked past the tail in an effort to catch sight of his assistant.

Catharine leaned in to David, and spoke like a commercial announcer completing the commercial that Gary began. "And we find that bribing government officials also keeps us out of prison!"

"Oh, there he is," Gary called out, "wavin' like a flag. I'll be back in a few. Meanwhile, help yourself to coffee and donuts over there in the corner."

⟶∘⟪✦⟫∘⟵

DAVID AND CATHARINE helped themselves to cups of coffee, but hadn't even finished them before Gary returned with a concerned expression.

"Come with me, kids. Got somethin' to show ya."

They walked past the plane and through a wide door into a mechanical shop stocked with carefully stacked spare parts. Their bags were sitting on a luggage scale crowded by other electronic measuring instruments.

David said, "Something tells me, the kid's been doing more with the bags than weighing them."

Gary nodded. "We found a few surprises, chief. First, I assume you know you're carrying a bunch of burner phones."

David nodded.

Gary produced the jamming device that Doctor Zia had handed David a few hours earlier. "You kids also knew about this, didn't ya?"

Catharine spoke up. "Yes, it was given to us by the fellow who dropped us off. When it's on, it stops a particular hostile from tracking us."

"That's what we figured. And it's operating right now."

Catharine nodded. "We turned it on just before we entered the *El Paso*."

"Wait here," said Gary, and walked to the other side of the hangar where he put the jamming device down on a spare table.

"There's another surprise," he said as he returned. "There's a transmitter sewn into one o' your bags, and it's transmittin' like a sumbitch right now."

Catharine and David exchanged a fearful glance. The possibilities spun through their minds.

"You mind if the kid ruins a seam so's he can remove the transmitter from your bag?" asked Gary.

"Go right ahead," replied Catharine, half in shock.

Gary nodded to Gonçalves, who took a Bowie knife from his utility belt and made a careful incision in an inner seam of the bag. He hung the knife back on his belt and fished under the cloth with two fingers. In a moment, he pulled out what looked like a cigarette case of roughly polished stone much like that of Doctor Zia's jamming device.

"I'll be damned," muttered David.

Gary smiled. "If you like that, chief, you're gonna *love* this." He took the transmitter to a frequency detector with a dial. "I'll mark the frequency it's transmittin' on." He put an erasable mark on the crystal. "Single frequency," said Gary with a shrug. "Nothin' fancy."

Gary told Gonçalves to carry the transmitter to the place across the hangar where he'd earlier placed the jammer, to leave the transmitter there and return with the jammer.

"Sure thing, boss." Those were the first words they'd heard the kid speak. He spoke in Portuguese-inflected English, much as you might hear anywhere in the USA. He did precisely as he was told.

Gary took the jammer. "Watch this," he said, and placed it up against the frequency detector. The dial went to the very place he'd marked to show the transmitter's operating frequency. "*Voila!*"

"Oh, shit," muttered David.

"What?" said Catharine. "What does it mean?"

"Chief," said Gary, "would you do the honors of explaining this to the lieutenant commander … and me?"

David ran his fingers distractedly through his hair. "Don't you see?" he said, primarily to Catharine. "The only reason we haven't been tracked by the *dreamgirl* is that these two devices are physically so close together. This transmitter has been trying to tell her all along where the bag is located, but first Zia's jammer and now *our* jammer has been jamming its outgoing signal."

Catharine seemed confused. "But why would Zia bug us, and then hand us a way to block the bug's signal?"

"He almost certainly wouldn't," said David. "He didn't bug our bag. It's not our bag; it's *his*." Catharine was clearly confused. "*She* bugged *his* bag! That was her way of keeping tabs on him. She didn't know he'd be lending his bags to us. Gary, can you switch off the transmitter?"

Gary shook his head. "No switch." He shrugged. "I suppose we *could* smash the battery."

"*Don't do that here!*" said David. "The goddam thing could be a mini-*reactor* for all we know. Who knows what kind of damage it could do if it's breached?" His head was spinning. "On the other hand, the jammer *does* have an *off* switch and won't last more than another twenty-two hours of operation. If we switch the jammer off—or if it just gets physically separated from the transmitter—then she'll learn *immediately* where the bag is located. As soon as she realizes it's not where *Zia's* located, she'll know the bag is with *us* and send someone to scoop us up."

Gary shrugged. "Look, I don't know who this *dreamgirl* is, but it would take time for her to get someone here, wouldn't it?"

Catharine replied. "Not if they're already in orbit. Depending on how far away they are, they could get here in a matter of minutes."

Gary's eyes went wide. "In orbit?" he said. "*In orbit around the frickin' Earth? Is that* what you mean?"

Catharine nodded.

David started pacing. "We can't smash the transmitter. And we can't take it with us because, if we do, then as soon as the jammer fails, she'll have us in her sights. If we leave it *here*—"

"No way in *hell* are we leavin' it here!" said Gary. "'Cuz then as soon as we fly outta here with the jammer, this place'll be crawlin' with all her little henchmen. No way."

David nodded. "And she'd also know that Catharine and I had recently been here. From that point, she'd just have to check for aircraft that left this vicinity in the previous hour or so. Geez, she could intercept us in midflight."

Gary looked as though he'd seen a ghost. "She can *do* that?"

"Afraid so," said Catharine. "It's already been done to the *admiral.* We were in the plane with him."

Neither David nor Catharine dared tell Gary that the aliens could shut down aircraft engines. He'd never fly them out after learning that.

"That transmitter is the hot potato," said David. "Gary, could you get one of your guys here to tie the transmitter to a big rock or something, drive it as fast and far from here as he can and throw it in a pit? Meanwhile, we fly the hell out of here as quietly as we can. Have you filed a flight plan?"

"Nuh-uh," said Gary. "I *could* fly out snake-shit low. No transponder. No radio. No lights. Only one problem."

"What's that?" asked Catharine.

"Well, each of those measures would maximize the possibility of collision with another aircraft, especially an equally reckless one."

David said, "You mean, like another smuggler?"

Gary nodded grimly. "On the bright side," he said, "if it's gonna be over with, it'll be quick. Let's get movin'."

⟶∘C⟋⟍⟍∘◠

ALTHOUGH HENDRICK HAD been asleep when the two strangers came into the *El Paso*, he'd known they'd be trouble as soon as the safety on the stranger's handgun clicked off. That had given him quite a start.

After the brief standoff ended and Hendrick had started playing five-card stud with Festus, he couldn't help but overhear bits and pieces of the boss's conversation with the lady. Very strange.

A little later, Gonçalves had shown Hendrick a transmitter found hidden in the lady's baggage and had encouraged Hendrick to take a close look at it. In one corner there was unusual red lettering that reminded him of Israeli writing that he'd seen years before on a visit to his wife's family in Ethiopia.

Gonçalves had entrusted the transmitter to Hendrick and instructed him to ensure its destruction someplace as far away from the hangar as could be reached in ten minutes' drive. As it was important to keep the transmitter in the general vicinity of the plane (for some reason no one would explain), Gonçalves had told him to choose a place of disposal somewhere near the plane's flight path. To Hendrick that meant only one place for the disposal: the pit where the Germans formerly dumped slag from a mine that ran dry when he was a boy. There was nothing out there now. Not even water. Just desert.

Hendrick duct-taped a full stick of dynamite to the transmitter, tucked the assembly between two throw pillows, taped the throw pillows together with only the fuse jutting out, and carefully placed the whole package on the Jeep's passenger seat. The pillows were there to keep the dynamite from being jostled during the upcoming race over rough terrain. He'd learned from years of experience that dynamite becomes increasingly unstable over time. And one never got two chances with dynamite.

The sun had receded behind the western mountains by the time Hendrick drove the Jeep around to the tarmac where the 737 was nearly done being fueled and serviced. Gonçalves, who was standing by the mobile staircase, spotted the Jeep and signaled Hendrick to await instructions. Gonçalves took the flip phone from his pocket and placed a call, most likely to the cockpit. After a moment's conversation, he gave Hendrick the *go* signal.

Once clear of the plane, the Jeep sped eastward down the runway. When it neared the end of the tarmac, Hendrick practically stood on the accelerator pedal, and the Jeep hopped onto the dry turf, scattering pebbles in every direction and leaving behind an outsized cloud of dust.

"Yee-haw!" shouted Hendrick—something he'd learned from the boss. Evidently that was something shouted at exciting moments in old El Paso.

⇢ ୦ c⇒ ୦ c⇐

As DAVID AND Catharine sat in the cockpit watching Gary run through preflight diagnostics and check off each step on his clipboard, behind them they could hear the exterior door being firmly shut and the mobile staircase being wheeled away.

Gonçalves came straight to the cockpit and pointed through the windshield at a Jeep hopping off the runway up ahead, leaving a cloud of dust and speeding off into the distance.

"Will you look at that, boss?" said Gonçalves. "That guy's gonna kill himself before he even reaches the pit."

Gary looked up for a split second to see the dust cloud left behind by the Jeep. "Whozat? Hendrick?"

"Yeah," said Gonçalves.

Gary shrugged. "Well … he's a good driver. He'll get it there." He looked up at Catharine "We should be outta here in ten minutes, just in time to see the sun behind us for a few minutes."

"Aren't we headed north?" asked David.

"Yeah, but we take off headin' east to stay clear of Windhoek's airports."

In a few minutes, David and Catharine took their seats in the passenger cabin and the plane began its progress down the runway. Gonçalves lodged the cockpit door open so everyone could talk, and took a seat across from David and Catharine.

"No copilot needed?" asked Catharine.

"Not for the moment," said the kid. "He likes to take the plane out by himself."

Catharine nodded. "Typical navy jockey."

Sooner than David expected, the plane was aloft and flying low.

In about a minute, he gazed out a window and could make out the Jeep's dissipating dust cloud on the horizon up ahead. Just beyond it was a manmade pit with a circular mouth about fifty feet across, too deep for David to see the bottom from this far away.

David squinted, and it became evident that Hendrick had already reached his destination, tossed his hot potato into the pit, and raced back to the Jeep. He'd just leapt into the Jeep and begun his return trip to the runway.

There was a bright, sudden flash down in the pit. The concussion sounded like a sharp crack.

"Well, that's that," said Gary, prematurely as it turned out.

Then came a second explosion, the likes of which David had never imagined.

The whole mouth of the pit vomited up intense orange flames two hundred feet into the air, like magma expelled from an exploding volcano. The concussion felt like the plane had been smacked by the hand of God. It was violent and impossibly *deep*. It rattled the bolts in the groaning airframe and shook the passengers hard enough to give them a bellyache.

The plane pitched forward.

"Holy Mother o' Christ!" exclaimed Gary. "I'm swervin' around this chimney." The plane tilted noticeably to the left, then allowed itself to be righted, barely avoiding contact with the grey cloud spreading out at their altitude. "Gonçalves, how many frickin' sticks of dynamite did Hendrick use?"

"He said *one*," answered the kid in a state of shock, his face pale and sweaty.

"The second explosion wasn't the dynamite," said David. "It was the *battery*."

"The *battery?*" said Gary. "What kinda battery? The battery o' the *gods?*"

David and Catharine exchanged a knowing look. Gary had no idea how close he'd come to the truth of it.

"Commander?" said Gary. "Would you do me the honor of stepping into the cockpit for a moment?"

Catharine came into the cockpit.

"What can I do for you, captain?"

"You can check me out on somethin'." Gary flipped a switch on the control panel, and video of an explosion appeared on one of the screens above the windshield. When the resulting cloud reached its most dramatic dimensions, he froze the frame. "Wuddya think?" he asked.

"About *that?*" she asked, pointing to the screen. "It looks like a one-kiloton fission explosion," she said. "Are you asking me to compare it to the explosion we just witnessed?"

He smirked without taking his eyes of the windshield. "That *is* the explosion we just witnessed. Thanks for your opinion, commander. I concur. On the way to your seat, would you send Gonçalves in here?"

A second later, the kid appeared. "Yes, sir?" he said.

"Did you check that transmitter for possible radioactive content?"

"Absolutely, Gary. It showed nothing."

"How about the jamming device?"

"Same. Nothing."

Gary nodded. "That's what I thought. Thanks, kid," he said. "Could you send in the professor?"

David entered, steadying himself against the cockpit walls. "Yes?"

"Chief," said Gary, "you still have that jammin' device on ya?"

"I do," said David.

Gary nodded his head. "Please … don't *drop* it."

David smirked. "I won't. Promise."

"Good deal, professor." When David didn't leave immediately, Gary said, "Somethin' on yer mind?"

"I'm concerned that my dreamgirl's goons saw that explosion and will soon realize that we passed through here." He shrugged. "Maybe they didn't see it. How long will it be lit up, do you suppose?"

Gary shook his head dejectedly. "It'll burn for a couple," he said.

"Couple what?"

"Couple *months*, prob'ly. Y'see, there's a slag heap at the bottom of that pit, mostly coal. Whatever wasn't burned in the explosion'll burn till it's used up."

"Perfect," said David dejectedly. "We're so screwed." Looking for a silver lining, he studied the freeze-frame of the explosion on the screen above the windshield. "Do you suppose it's possible that explosion just wasn't big enough to be seen from orbit?"

Gary glanced up at the screen. "Hate to tell ya this, chief, but with the right optical equipment, that explosion could be seen from the surface of *Mars*."

————————————

AND IT WAS.

CHAPTER 16

BY TEN THAT evening, the 737 was a white phantom hurtling across the black ocean off West Africa, unlit but for moonlight reflecting off the fuselage. Inside it was dark as well, except that the cockpit was gently bathed in the dim glow of the control panel.

Gary's voice came on the intercom. "Just turned on the outer lights and the transponder. We'll be landing briefly at both Lagos and Casablanca before flyin' on to London."

Catharine shouted her question through the open cockpit doorway. "Why both?"

"Because," came the amplified voice, "this is one of those old-fashioned planes that require refueling from time to time. Besides, our friends at Lagos sometimes have some unexpected cargo for us to take to Casablanca. Discreetly, of course."

"Of course," said Catharine.

A bit later, when David and Catharine began to yawn, Gonçalves dragged a thick queen-size mattress out of the cargo hold and dropped it on the floor of the passenger compartment. After buckling the mattress to the airframe, he showed them how to strap themselves onto it to avoid injury in case of turbulence.

David and Catharine agreed that, by Doctor Zia's reckoning, the battery in the cloaking device was good for another eighteen hours of operation. They hoped that turning it off now wouldn't allow Inanna to invade David's dreams tonight, but they weren't quite sure what made it possible for her to do that anyway; as it seemed to both of them that in the past Inanna had found him only when she pretty well knew where to look, they crossed their fingers and shut off the device.

THE DRONE OF the engines transported Catharine safely to dreamland. Only on landing and takeoff did she approach consciousness and check to make sure David was still sleeping soundly. He seemed to be.

After what felt like a long sleep, there was a nudge on her shoulder and she opened her eyes a slit. Gary was crouching next to her.

"We're an hour out of Heathrow—just in case you two want to get your papers together … and your story straight."

Catharine sniffed and unbuckled the restraint. "Who's flying the plane?"

"Well, let's see. It's either the professor or Gonçalves." He pointed to David, who was stirring from sleep. "And the professor's right there, so my guess would be Gonçalves. Just for futures, what do your papers say your names are?"

"Roger and Eve Thornhill of New York, New York," she said. "We don't have much of a back story. So, I guess he'll be a lawyer, I'll be a housewife, and we've been traveling together for the past couple months, seeing the sights of the world."

"Housewife's okay for you, though you're a bit too good-lookin' for it to be really plausible."

She rolled her eyes. "Smooth."

He laughed softly. "But, for the chief here, you should choose a different racket. New York has a publicly accessible database of every lawyer admitted to practice. If he ain't in there under that name, you've got a problem." He searched his mind for an alternative occupation. "I know. Make him a *private hedge fund* guy. Nobody knows what the hell they do, anyway. Hell, I'm not sure *I* do." He put out his hand. "Mind if I do a once-over on your papers?"

She sat up and handed both their passports to Gary, who studied the stamps showing where they'd been. "*Mali*, huh?" He took a close look at the detail work. "These are damned good," he said. "I don't know who did 'em for ya, but *I'd* offer him a job."

She took back the passports and said, "I'll be sure to tell Naval Intelligence."

"Another question," said Gary, "how'd it happen that you two steered clear of British Airways and wound up on my freighter?"

"Simple matter of timing," she said blithely. "We were in a hurry. Taking the next British Airways flight would have required us to wait a long time. As for you: I knew you from your years of flying in the service, and remembered that you were operating out of Windhoek."

"What was your hurry?"

"Well," she shrugged, "when David was a lawyer, I would have said he had an upcoming trial in the U.K., but now—?"

"So now," Gary suggested alternatively, "he's got a big real estate prospect and his contacts are leavin' London in a couple days. Wait here a second. I want to check something."

He disappeared into the cockpit and reappeared with an unfolded British Airways flight schedule. Spread out, it looked a lot bigger than the ones Catharine was familiar with. Must have been an *all-flights* schedule meant specifically for pilots.

"When did you check for a BA flight from Windhoek, Namibia to London, U.K.?"

"It was just before we showed up at El Paso, *Namibia,*" she replied drolly.

He smirked. "Okay, I see your point. *El Paso, Namibia* sounds wacked. Well, you arrived at the bar about three yesterday afternoon." He ran his finger down a column. "You're in luck. You'd have run into a forty-eight-hour wait. Hell, if you'd gone British Airways, you wouldn't even be in the *air* yet."

———⟶o⟨⟩o⟵———

THE 737 SAT on the tarmac at Heathrow with its engines off. A battery-powered golf cart pulled up, while stairs were wheeled to the passengers' door.

As the sun hadn't dropped below the horizon yet, Gary leaned over David and Catharine, peering out the window at the assigned Border Force officer, who hopped out of his vehicle and up the stairs.

"Good," said Gary. "I know this guy and I can handle him."

"What do you mean?" asked Catharine.

"Catharine," said David sternly, "let the man do his job."

Gary strode away and opened the door to greet the officer.

Catharine muttered, "I just don't want Gary bribing anyone on our account."

David rolled his eyes. "What do you care?" he whispered.

"Well, if I *know* what he's doing, I'll feel responsible."

"Precisely, dear," said David. "So, please take a bit of legal advice: The key is to *not* know what he's doing."

She scowled.

He leaned in to her. "May I point out that you and I are presenting the officer with forged papers? Is *that* okay?"

"My, but aren't we *snippy* when we wake up?" she said.

"I'm sorry," he said. "I'm just so sick and tired of running away from

Inanna. I'd like some free time to spend with my *real* dreamgirl. You."

She smiled at that.

When the agent came over to them, Catharine handed him their passports. "Good evening, officer," she said, sounding a bit more British than usual.

"Oh!" said the officer. "Do I detect a bit o' London in that voice?"

"You do, indeed," she said with a smile that, David observed, could have melted the polar ice cap.

"And you, suh?" said the officer to David.

"No, officer," said David. "I'm from one of the rebel colonies, specifically New York, but I plead the Treaty of Ghent."

"That's all right, suh," said the officer. "We don't impress Americans into His Majesty's navy no more; not since we discovered you lot were good for nothin' but ballast." He pointed with his thumb in Gary's direction. "How'd you two nice people get mixed up with this old smuggler?"

Catharine replied. "We needed to get here promptly from Windhoek, and British Airways didn't have a flight for a couple of days. And I knew Gary was former U.S. Navy flying out of Windhoek, so I figured he'd do fine."

The officer nodded credulously. "Sounds about right for BA," he said. "Wish I could say the same for your choice o' pilots, but I suppose he'll do in a pinch. Got any pets or plants with you?"

Catharine looked at David, and they both shook their heads.

David said, "We're carrying nothing but a change of clothes, officer. Our bags are right there," he said, pointing.

The officer glanced over his shoulder at the bags. "Those two little things?"

They nodded.

He shrugged and waved a bar code reader over their passports. There was no nasty little beep, so he'd obviously received approval. He handed them back to Catharine and said, "Welcome to the United Kingdom, Mister and Missus Thornhill. Enjoy your stay."

⇒○◅▰▻○⇐

To GET TO the hotel, they hailed one of those London taxis that could turn around on a dime. As they got in, the driver turned his head around for a look at his passengers.

"Marriott Grosvenor, please," said David.

The driver grinned like the cat who ate the cream, and turned to drive off.

"Did I say something stupid *already?*" asked David.

"No, suh," said the driver. "Just that, depending upon which room you've got, you'll have a front-row seat to the aerial show that's takin' place every night over Hyde Park."

David was annoyed. "Is it noisy?" he asked.

"No, suh," said the driver. "It's been described as *eerily quiet.*"

"What time of night does it finish?"

"Well, I wouldn't rightly know, suh, but I hear it's a little different every night." The driver looked backwards again to see if David was having him on, but was persuaded by David's evident perplexity, and returned his eyes to the road. "I suppose you've been shut up in planes and trains the past couple days, suh. Please pardon my jest. Didn't mean nothin' by it. There's apparently a couple of them spaceships what fly over the park every night."

David could feel the anger rise in his chest. He seethed in silence.

"Spaceships?" said Catharine. "What ever would a spaceship look like?"

"They say there's a few different kinds. I caught a glimpse o' one of 'em meself a couple nights ago. Looked like one of them cardboard cylinders inside a kitchen roll. But *big*, y'know?"

"The shape of a cigar?" she asked innocently.

"Yeah," he replied. "A cylinder like."

"How low do they fly?" asked Catharine.

The taxi swerved to avoid a speeding car that was passing to the right, honking its horn angrily. Their driver shook his fist out the window. "Blighter!" he shouted, then muttered, "They'll give a license to any muttonhead with a set o' keys, nowadays, I swear. Sorry, madam. What did you say?"

"How low to the ground was the … spaceship you saw?"

"That's a tough question, ma'am. I wish I could tell. It was dark outside. If I knew how big it was, I might could venture a guess how *near*." He gave it a bit more thought. "It was flyin' low enough for me to see its lights. If I had to guess, I s'pose it was flyin' about as low as the top of, oh, a thirty-story building. If that's how low it was flyin', then I'd hazard a guess it was the length of a ten-story buildin' … but layin' down like."

"That must have been frightening," said Catharine.

"That one wasn't too frightenin'," said the driver, "'cept, o' course, that it had no business bein' there. I hear tell there's one of 'em looks like a shiny metal ball."

Catharine looked to David skeptically and mouthed *metal ball*.

"Do the different spaceships come at the same time?" she asked.

"I'm sure I don't know, madam, but I suppose you'll get an earful from the concierge at the hotel if you want one. Even if they don't want to talk about it, they can't get away from it 'cause everybody's askin' all the time. Strangest thing about it is, you don't see nothin' in the newspapers about it, nothin' on the telly. It's like the government doesn't even know it's happenin'."

"The government *knows*," said David darkly. "That's *why* it's not in the papers or on TV."

The driver's eyes met David's in the rear-view mirror. "What do ya suppose it all means, suh?"

"We'll learn soon enough," said David. "Pretty soon they won't be able to keep it quiet and then they'll *have* to tell us."

The taxi pulled into the drive. The driver got out to hand them their paltry luggage, and David handed him a good tip.

"It's U.S. currency," said David. "I hope you don't mind, but it's all I've got."

"Not a problem, sir. It spends just fine. Worst that can happen, I'll change it at the bank. Thank you, sir. Hope you and the missus have a wonderful time." He winked. "Keep an eye out for the little green men."

⸺⊸∘⧘∘⊷⸺

WHEN THE CONCIERGE spotted David and Catharine, he emerged from his office and snapped his fingers for a bellman, who put their two bags on a big brass cart (making them look even smaller) and wheeled them into an alcove.

"Good evening," said the concierge. "Whom have I the pleasure of greeting?"

Catharine spoke up. "This is Roger and I'm Eve. Unfortunately, we've been in no position to make a reservation. I hope you have room for us."

"Is it just *monsieur* and *madame*, or are you part of a larger party?"

"There'll just be the two of us," she assured him.

"Then we most assuredly can accommodate you, madam."

"Actually," said David, "we were hoping to meet some people here, but we're not sure whether they've arrived."

"*Their* name, sir?"

"The lady is generally the one who makes reservations for that couple. Her name is … er, Smith."

"Come into my office and I'll check the computer." A minute later, he shook his head. "No, sir. We have no couple registered under the name Smith. In fact, no one is currently registered under that name at all, if you can imagine. Who'd have thought there'd be a large hotel in London without a single Smith occupying at least one room?"

"Perhaps they used the gentleman's name," said David. "An African fellow? I believe his name may be Jones."

Catharine shrugged. If Iskender could misstate Miriam's pseudonym as Jones once, he could just as likely do it twice.

"No," said the concierge. "No Jones, either. Were they supposed to meet you here?"

"Yes," said Catharine, "but we arrived by widely divergent routes, so we lost track of each other on the way."

The concierge searched his memory. "A white woman and an African fellow, did you say?"

"Yes," said Catharine.

"Wait a moment," he said, as though recalling something. "What's *your* surname, if I may ask?"

"Thornhill," Catharine said.

The concierge snapped his fingers. "Such a couple was here yesterday, only briefly. They left their bags with the bellman and had the morning buffet here—we have *quite* a lovely breakfast buffet—"

"You do indeed," said Catharine. "We've stayed here before and enjoyed the breakfast buffet greatly."

The concierge bowed his head in thanks, and said, "Our staff is quite dedicated, Missus Thornhill. I can assure you they do their *level* best."

"And *succeed*, I might observe," said Catharine, once more casting him her thousand-watt smile.

The concierge glanced at David (who glared back impatiently) and returned at once to the matter at hand. "Yes, about the lady and gentleman," said the concierge. "The lady received a phone call through the desk, which is unusual for someone who hasn't yet checked in, as you might imagine."

"A one-in-a-million shot," said Catharine. David threw her an impatient expression.

"But the lady took the call," said the concierge, "and seemed quite disturbed by it. She came to me apologetically, and told me that they would not be checking in at the hotel, after all. But before taking their bags, she foretold that the *Thornhills* would arrive in the coming days and left a note for you in a sealed envelope at the front desk. Shall I fetch it?"

"That would be *much* appreciated," said Catharine.

David interjected as the concierge rose, "But please don't open it. I expect it may be quite personal."

The concierge seemed almost affronted. "Why, I wouldn't *dream* of it, sir."

"I expected no less of you, sir," said David. "I just wanted to be clear. Thank you so much."

In a moment, the concierge returned with the note. David and Catharine thanked him courteously and left his office.

Catharine gravitated toward the main dining room, which was still set up for dinner. "If only there were a buffet now, we could read the note there—over coffee and oranges."

David took the note to the lobby, where they set themselves down on an upholstered couch. He opened the envelope crudely with his index finger, and drew out Miriam's note, which he quietly read to Catharine.

"*Dear Roger, We were about to check into the Grosvenor this morning, but before we could do so, I received a call from our new friend from the Zimbabwean plains. I do not know how he managed to get his hands on an ordinary telephone, but I have no doubt it was he. No one could imitate the sound of his voice. We two will be settling at a nearby hotel, but I see no reason for you to hesitate to check into the Grosvenor. I don't know if you've heard, but they have a lovely morning buffet.*"

David rolled his eyes in exasperation. "Why does every American arriving in England immediately become rapt by trivialities?"

"I suppose it's something in the air," said Catharine, tongue in cheek. "Thank heavens *you're* immune. Pray, continue reading."

David resumed. "*Once you check in, please call my mobile phone. The number's written below. It operates in the U.K. Yours, etc., M. Jones.*" He rolled his eyes again. "M. *Jones!* How's it possible she can't keep her own pseudonym straight?" He folded the note, stuffed it haphazardly into its ragged envelope, and handed it to Catharine. "So, shall we check into this hotel?" he asked.

"Why not?" she asked.

He was thoroughly exasperated by her casual reply. "Well, where to begin? For one thing, we lit up the starting line in our race up here with an explosion big enough to be seen from space. (Gary said it's still burning—just in case Inanna's goons missed it initially.) For another, our passports were just scanned at Heathrow under the same names we used to sign into the hotel in Beira where she *found* us and we narrowly escaped capture. As she sent her goons there, it's a pretty good bet they saw our false names in the registry. And now we're going to register under the *same* names at a hotel that's being haunted every night by UFOs." He threw his hands up. "What could go wrong?"

She arched her back primly and said with forbearance, "Shall we go somewhere else, Roger?"

"I suppose not," he said. An idea occurred to him. "But perhaps we could check in under another name."

"But our credit cards have those names on them."

"Even so," said David, "at least the registry and phone systems will list different names."

"Do you suppose an alien is going to march up to the front desk and ask for the Thornhills?"

"No, but they could send a human being to do it."

"Fine," said Catharine. "What names would you suggest?"

David searched his memory. "How about *Neil and Carol Armstrong?*"

"Why *those* names, especially?" she asked.

"First man on the moon, and his second wife."

"Was he widowered?"

"Divorced."

"What was his first wife's name?"

"Janet, I think."

"I'll be Janet. Janet Armstrong."

He looked at her askew. "Is that some kind of political statement?"

She smiled. "It's just that I'm the type who doesn't give up on a man. I may not be his first wife, but I'll be his last."

He smiled back. "I hope so. Don't you think it's about time to get in touch with your inner spice rack?"

It took a moment for her to realize he was suggesting she call the admiral. "I suppose I should, but I'm afraid that any contact has to be done in person."

"Where is our friend?"

"Likely here in London."

"At the embassy?"

She nodded. "That's part of the problem."

"Why?"

"You're not allowed to enter a U.S. embassy."

"Why not?"

"Orders of the Department of State. Evidently, the Secretary was not … pleased … with the condition of the embassy in Paris when we left it."

"That's ridiculous," he said. "I'm an American citizen. I can't be barred from a U.S. embassy in a foreign country."

"Can be. Have been. Sorry."

"Can't our retired friend overrule that?"

"We'll see. Let me make contact first."

"How?"

"I'll do a walk-in."

"But you'll be seen from above," he protested.

"I'll be a brunette by then," she said. "They'll never know."

David felt a pang in his gut that the aliens might abduct her or harm her in some way. "I can't let you put yourself in harm's way on my account."

She looked at him with raised eyebrow. "I beg your pardon? Who's the spy here, you or I?"

"You are, but I'm the object of this whole circus and I can't bear the thought of losing you."

She kissed him on the cheek. "Let's both pick up some fresh clothing at the gift shop."

"Okay. Then, let's sign in under our new names and go up to the room. I want to call Ms. Smith/Jones first, and find out whether she's gone to see the … bagatelle."

CHAPTER 17

"Thank you very much, Mister Armstrong," said the bellman on his way out. "Enjoy your stay at the Grosvenor."

Catharine sat on the edge of the bed, and David plopped down on a chair with his bag in his lap. He took out one of the burner phones they'd brought all the way from Beira and threw the power switch.

A red pilot light came on.

"We have power," he said.

He flipped it open and listened at the earpiece. There was a half-minute of clicking, and then—"We have dial tone." He handed the phone to Catharine, who took Miriam's note from her pocket.

"We have phone number," said Catharine, as though continuing the checklist begun by David. Then she stopped a moment. "What time is it?" she asked.

David pointed to the digital clock resting on the television that said it was a quarter to eight. "What does it matter?"

"Oh," she said, waving away her hesitation. "I expect they're done with supper by now."

"You have to be kidding me," said David. "We're being chased by aliens from outer space, and you're concerned about interrupting someone's supper? Hand me the phone."

"I will *not*," said Catharine, and imposed her decision by dialing and putting the phone to her ear. "Hello, Miriam? It's Eve. Yes, we're at the Grosvenor."

David couldn't hear Miriam's voice on the other end of the line, so he had no choice but to wait as Miriam droned on.

"No, dear, we haven't," said Catharine, forcing a word in edgewise.

Another long pause.

"No, dear. We arrived only a few minutes ago, so the breakfast buffet was not set up."

David rolled his eyes, and waved to get Catharine's attention. When he got it, he made a rolling motion with his index finger to try to move things along. Catharine nodded reassuringly.

"Well, I'd love to discuss the buffet further, Miriam," she said, "but we're in a bit of a fix at the moment. As you know, the Grosvenor overlooks Hyde Park, which has recently acquired a reputation for being visited at night by UFOs." *Pause.* "The taxi driver who brought us here from the airport." *Pause.* "No, he said nothing critical of Hyde Park." *Pause.* "Yes, I know how close it is to Kensington Palace. Listen, Miriam." *Pause.* "When are you planning to go to the box?" *Pause.*

Now even Catharine rolled her eyes. "Yes, the *safe-deposit* box," she said, followed by a long pause. Her eyes turned wide with interest. "He called you *again?*" *Pause.* "We don't mind at all. He may be a valuable ally. Um, where is he now?" *Pause.* "I understand, of course. Shall we come to your hotel now?" *Pause.* "Well, I don't know. Are there any quiet pubs in London? Churchill Arms? Give us a few minutes to wash up and we'll meet you and Daniel there. Say, half past nine? We look forward to it. See you there. *Ta.*"

David came over to the bed and sat next to her. She looked at him inquiringly, and he kissed her. When he came up for air, he said huskily, "I love to hear you say *we*, meaning you and me."

She threw her arms around his neck, smiled, and said "we," and he kissed her again … and again and again.

⇒∘⟨≋⟩∘⇐

AFTER SHOWERING, DAVID and Catharine put on some fresh clothes. As they were preparing to leave, David looked around suspiciously and said, "I know we're checked in already, but I want to take one bag with us."

"Why?" asked Catharine.

He looked at her uncertainly and said, "Because this room is going to be broken into while we're out."

"And you know that …. how?"

"The rational answer would be: Because the hotel ran a charge on the credit card as soon as we checked in and those interplanetary bastards have a trace on it. But the real answer is: I can just *feel* it."

"Well, what do we *have* that would be tragic to lose?" she asked.

"Let's take our papers, the burner phones, the cash, and the jammer. Also, I'm going to leave the phone number of this burner at the desk."

"You think they'll take our clothes?" she asked forlornly.

He shook his head. "No, they won't take them, but you won't want them after they've gone through them."

Catharine shrugged and pointed to one of the bags, only slightly larger than a gym bag. "You should be able to stuff it all in that one." She wilted. "Are you telling me we're going to lose our meager wardrobe *again?*"

He nodded.

"Then I'm taking two scarves and the new skirt and sweater I picked up downstairs. The rest they can keep. Take the bigger bag."

⟶∘◦⟾∘∘⟸◦∘⟵

THE CHURCHILL WAS a beautiful dark-paneled place at least two centuries old. That night the bar was abustle, but the dining room was not too busy for the four visitors to find a booth remote enough to hold a private conversation.

Catharine and David were famished. They hadn't eaten since the four sandwiches Gonçalves doled out to each of them on the plane. They were small and widely separated in time. Though they'd been surprisingly good in light of the setting, they'd hardly been enough to satiate anyone.

After ordering hearty pub fare, they handed the waitress their menus and got down to business.

"What time are you going to the bank tomorrow?" asked David.

"Actually," said Miriam, "it's not a bank. Rather, they operate a purpose-built vault. Their only business is safekeeping, and they observe every formality, believe me. Just today, I met with Father's former solicitor, who guaranteed my signature, and we have an appointment tomorrow morning at nine sharp."

"Do you remember the quantity of papers in the vault?"

"You know, I haven't seen them since a few weeks after Father passed away. How long ago is that, five years? As I recall, it was all contained in a single box of lightweight wood, perhaps a half-meter square and … thirty centimeters high."

"Loose papers?" asked David.

"A few were loose, but mostly they were arranged by subject matter into manila folders. And there was a binder there from some scientist at … Massachusetts Institute of Technology, I think. Perhaps five centimeters thick. Lots of repetitive drawings. I didn't read it. Too technical. And I was busy mourning Father."

Catharine looked around to ensure no one was listening. "Miriam, you said that Brosa called you again?"

"Oh, yes," said Miriam, "but I handed the phone immediately to

Doctor Iskender. They both speak that language."

Catharine and David looked to Iskender, who took a swig on his pint.

"He speaks a variant of Hittite," said Daniel, "which is a precursor to Hebrew. His voice is a little hard to make out sometimes, as though he has marbles at the back of his throat. In any event, he told us that we should expect company tomorrow once we leave the vault."

"Oh?" asked Catharine. "Is he sending an escort?"

Miriam shivered. "I shiver to imagine the chilly reception that would greet a dozen of those hideous creatures marching down the streets of Westminster."

"No," said Daniel, "by *company* he meant we'd be confronted by the Anunnaki and, although they'd likely stay clear of us until we fetch the papers, they would most certainly interfere with our bringing the papers to the government's offices. Brosa recommended a name for us to call in the government."

David was busy selecting the perfect chip when it occurred to him what Daniel had said. "I beg your pardon? Brosa told you whom to call in *which* government?"

Daniel was surprised by the question. "Why, the U.K. government, of course."

"And you called such person?"

"Yes," replied Daniel.

"And he or she took you seriously?" asked Catharine.

"Very much so. I spoke to a Colonel Singh and explained the whole situation about Miriam's father and the alien invaders. I told him that you two would be coming with us."

"You *told* him about us?" asked Catharine. "What names did you give him?"

"Well, this was a government agent. I had to trust him. We gave him your real names: David Schubert and Catharine," said Daniel.

Miriam placated Catharine with a light touch on the cuff. "I'm sorry, dear. Daniel couldn't recall your last name, nor could I."

"I don't think I mentioned it," said Catharine, and turned back to Daniel. "Did you tell him to contact the U.S. authorities?"

Daniel shook his head as though the thought never entered his mind. "No. He assured me that we'll have a fighting escort as soon as we leave the vault."

Catharine regarded Daniel skeptically. "Which escort? MI-5? MI-6?"

Daniel shook his head. "SAS, he said."

"The Scandinavian airline?" asked David.

Catharine frowned at him. "Special Air Service. They're the toughest hand-to-hand combat troops in the world. The British version of our SEALS."

David replied. "Do *they* beat up sharks, too? *Ow!*" Catharine had kicked him under the table.

Catharine looked uneasy. "I'm not confident that this colonel was taking them seriously. He may just have been humoring them."

Daniel was surprised. "The colonel seemed to have heard your name, David."

David turned to Catharine. "You think they talked to … our guy?"

Catharine shrugged. "I don't know where else he could have heard your name."

They'd just finished eating when the unfamiliar buzz of the burner phone went off in David's breast pocket. He immediately locked eyes with Catharine, and held his index finger up to Miriam and Daniel. He took the phone from his pocket, flipped it open, and put it to his ear.

"Hello?" he said with some trepidation.

There was a long silence on David's end throughout which a man on the other end of the line was speaking excitedly.

David's eyes met Catharine's and he nodded gravely.

"Mr. Richards," said David at last, "I quite understand what happened. Fortunately, we left no valuables in the room so there's no serious harm done." *Pause.* "No, unfortunately that sort of thing can happen anywhere in the world, regardless of tight security." *Pause.* "We have nothing but the highest regard for the hotel, and we'll be sure to stay there again. But could I ask you for a favor? It would be very helpful to us if you could sign us out of the room immediately and leave our bags in storage. We'll find another place to stay, just in case the intruders plan on returning."

At the word *intruders*, Miriam gasped and Daniel patted her hand to comfort her and quiet her down.

"I very much appreciate your reversing the room charges," said David. *Pause.* "Thank you so much for the invitation, Mister Richards, but I doubt we'll be able to take advantage of the morning buffet on this trip." There was a pause, during which David looked heavenward imploringly. "Yes, it *is* lovely. No doubt about it. Thank you, Mister Richards." He hung up.

"What happened?" asked Miriam.

David put the phone back in his pocket. "Our room was broken into. Nothing appears to have been stolen."

Iskender looked askance at David. "I must admire your composure, professor. I would be considerably more upset than you are at such news."

David nodded pensively. "Perhaps that's because you haven't been dogged by these creatures for the past couple of weeks over a distance of—" he performed a mental calculation "—about thirty thousand miles. Catharine and I have come to expect this kind of intrusiveness. The worst part of it is that we now have no room for the night, and we can no longer use our credit cards to secure another."

Miriam chimed in helpfully. "Daniel and I have separate rooms. Each has a foldout bed in a common area. If you'd like, David, you could stay with Daniel, and Catharine with me."

When David and Catharine didn't leap on the suggestion, Iskender laughed quietly and said, "Miriam, perhaps I could stay on the foldout bed in your suite, and David and Catharine could have my suite to themselves." He turned to Catharine apologetically. "Please pardon me if I'm being presumptuous."

Catharine waved away his apology. "No problem, Daniel. I'm under orders not to let *this* one out of my sight." She pointed her chin at David. "Thank you for your kind offer. We accept."

"Well," said Miriam, "now that that's settled, I'd like to retire for the evening."

Catharine yawned. "I think I would, too. Let's share a taxi."

Daniel gave his room keycard to David.

An idea bubbled up in David's head. "If you don't mind, Daniel, perhaps you and I could stay here for one more pint."

"Certainly," said Daniel curiously.

⸺⸺⸺⸺◦◦∞◦◦⸺⸺⸺⸺

DAVID WOULDN'T HAVE slept at all that night, but making love with Catharine was like a heavenly liquor that eased his mind and body for hours, and he'd slept like a baby.

He awoke to the sound of a running shower. The first thing he realized was that by opening one eye he could watch Catharine shower, his vision hindered only slightly by a mottled glass shower door. His imagination was unimpaired.

The second thing he realized was that this would probably be the last day of his life, and that he would survive it only if all his conjectures turned out to be accurate, his allies staunch and true, and his own performance stellar. He well knew that the odds against that combination were daunting.

The clock said it was half-past six. The daylight seeping through the crack in the draperies showed that morning would be uncommonly sunny for an autumn day in Westminster.

"What time did you get in last night?" asked Catharine. She was already out of the shower, toweling her hair dry. "I struggled to stay awake for you."

"We were less than an hour behind you," he replied. "When I came in, you were out like a light, snoring like a buzzsaw. I would have been annoyed if you hadn't been so receptive to my advances."

She winked at him. "As Shakespeare said, 'Women are light at midnight.'"

"Well," he mumbled, tossing the blanket off himself, "time to prepare the corpse."

"That's the spirit, Cassandra," she said, grabbing the hair dryer.

"And, like Cassandra's prophecies," he said, "mine are true but disbelieved."

Catharine's flippant response to that bit of literacy was to switch on the hair dryer, which whined loudly enough to chase David from his bed into the shower.

In a half hour, they met Miriam and Daniel at the hotel's lobby buffet, which was clearly designed for those in a rush. They each had coffee and a scone.

As they left, David wondered if he'd ever see the inside of another hotel.

CHAPTER 18

THE FOUR OF them shared a taxi to an old street-level building with a single sign outside it lettered in Old English writing, *Westminster Safekeeping*.

David was last to emerge from the cab. Glancing at the sky, his stomach turned as he spotted something hovering a few thousand feet above the Thames about a half mile away: a cigar-shaped spacecraft.

In the opposite direction, at roughly the same altitude and distance away, was a stationary silver ball so reflective that it seemed not to be fully *there*. It seemed rather a diaphanous moon in the daytime sky, defined only hazily against a field of azure.

"Let's get below ground," said Miriam. "I don't like being watched."

"Neither do I," muttered David.

The four of them entered Westminster Safekeeping. As Miriam had foreseen, it was a few steps down to the waiting room, which was a formal place where customers were separated from employees by a massive vault door with an impressive combination lock.

Next to the door was a cashier's cage such as one might see in an ancient bank, framed in granite under a well-polished brass sign saying *Cashier*. It all seemed designed to make any customer without a cage of equal heft and a sign identifying him as *Customer* feel a little under-dressed. In any event, they were the only customers in the place so early in the morning, and they'd barely had time to sit when a young male clerk appeared in the cage.

"Ms. Azeri?" he said, his eyes taking in each of the four faces.

Miriam stepped up to the cage and set out her papers. The young clerk examined them carefully, paying especial heed to the gold seals on each paper, as well as the signatures and dates.

"Very well," said the clerk with a smile. "These are clearly the originals of copies we've already received by email from your solicitor's offices." He looked past Miriam to the three strangers she'd arrived with. "Which of these fine people will be accompanying you into the vault?"

"All of them," said Miriam. "They're all experts."

"Are any of them citizens of a country other than the United Kingdom?"

"All of them."

"Ah, I see," said the young clerk. "I'll need to see and copy each of their passports."

"Oh, dear," said Miriam, putting her hand to her cheek. "I don't know whether they—" She turned around to see each of them holding up a passport. Turning back to the clerk, she asked, "Which would you like to see first?"

"The older gentleman first," said the clerk, "if I may." Daniel stepped up to the cashier's window and awaited the clerk's inevitable comparison between the passport photo and his face. The clerk then inked manual notes on a file folder and returned the passport to its owner, then did the same with Catharine and David.

The vault door was slowly opened from the opposite side by a substantial older fellow in a grey uniform with a keychain hanging from his belt. He let them in and led them down a succession of hallways to a locked room, where he searched through the keys on his belt and opened the door. Only after they'd all entered did he follow them in and lock the door behind.

The room was lined with finely crafted, numbered brass drawers, each having its own keyhole and combination lock. At the center of the room stood a dark wooden table, quite ordinary-looking but for its advanced age. Around the table stood six chairs, only four of which matched the table. The other two, having evidently originated with a newer set, were stained a brighter color.

The officer located Miriam's drawer, inserted the key, and manipulated the dial on the combination lock, carefully concealing his movements from any prying eyes. Once that was done, the lock opened with a light thud, and the officer tugged the handle, causing the heavy drawer to glide open over well-lubricated ball bearings. One could smell the graphite lubricant as the drawer reached its limit.

The officer placed his left arm under the drawer, removed it from its slot, and placed it down on the table. The contents were covered by a piece of black vinyl, which he rolled back and out of the way. Inside was a single wooden box. The officer turned to Miriam and bowed formally.

"When shall I return, madam?" he asked.

"I imagine we should be done in an hour," she replied. "Why don't you give us a knock then?"

"As you wish," he said, bowed again, walked out, and locked the door from the outside.

David was surprised to find that they were actually locked *in.* "Reminds me of the old tale by Edgar Allan Poe," he muttered, which was answered by the other three saying in near-unison, *The Cask of Amontillado.*

"Yes, that one," he said, a bit deflated.

Miriam removed numerous manila folders from the box and sat down to examine them.

The binder that she'd referred to earlier had been shoved into a corner of the box, as having no particular importance.

"Miriam," he said, indicating the binder, "would you mind if I examined that first?"

"Not at all," she replied. "In fact, I could use some help. Daniel, Catharine, if you've a mind to, leaf through a few of these yourselves. Just keep everything on the desk so we can all examine them. The folders in the box are in no particular order. I tossed them in haphazardly as soon as Father passed away—in light of what the FBI did with Nikolai Tesla's papers on his death."

"What did they do with those?" asked Catharine.

As Miriam was already engrossed in reading, David replied. "They took all of Tesla's files into federal custody. Many of them have never seen the light of day since."

Catharine seemed dismayed by that information, but she was game to pitch in and took a few files to read through.

David picked up the binder and took a seat at the opposite end of the table on one of the mismatched blond chairs.

Just as Miriam had recalled, the binder's worn cover identified it as in some way related to the Massachusetts Institute of Technology, but no particular respect had been paid to the school's name during the binder's long life, as stickers had obviously been applied over it and roughly removed many times, leaving the lettering barely legible.

The binder itself was utilitarian and shopworn, and the impression made on David was that it had been utilized on many different projects long before being put to its current use. Nothing on the cover identified its current contents, nor its current owner, nor the person who'd made the many diagrams and equations appearing on the papers inside.

With some trepidation, he opened the cover.

Inside, the first page was divided by a horizontal line dividing the top and bottom into fields of roughly equal size.

The top half of the page was divided in half by a vertical line. In the left half were written four lines, each a statement of equivalence, as each began with a different letter followed by an *equals* sign. The top line began with N=, the next with U=, the next S=, and the last J=. After the *equals* sign on each line appeared three numbers separated by spaces alone, with no operator showing how the first number was to affect the second, nor the second the third, and so on.

The right half of the top section was filled with equations with which David was entirely unfamiliar.

The lower half of the page consisted of a pencil sketch depicting three spheres of different size; one large, the second somewhat smaller, and the third smallest of all. No artistic embellishment had been provided to aid the uninitiated in identifying what each sphere was intended to represent (if indeed the drawing was representational at all), except that each sphere bore two arrows, one showing the direction of its motion, and the other apparently its direction of spin. To the unaided eye, the spheres might have represented anything from subatomic particles to spaldeens to … planets.

The second page was laid out much the same as the first. But the top half of the second page assigned different values to N, U, S, and J. Although the drawing on the bottom showed the same three spheres, there were subtle differences between this drawing and that on the preceding page. While in both cases there was some distance between the spheres, the gaps between them on the second page differed from those depicted on the first page.

David leafed through the next few pages, which followed the same pattern. On each page, the values assigned to N, U, S, and J differed.

So, what was he looking at? Why were there always *four* assigned values but only *three* depicted spheres? What did each value represent, if not one of the spheres? He shook his head in the realization that he'd surely be unable to make any sense of that discrepancy without far more knowledge than could be gleaned in this isolated room.

But one thing seemed clear. Each page showed a different case of a similar phenomenon. As he understood the drawings, when N, U, S, and J had different values assigned at the top of each page, the spheres on the bottom of that page would end up in a different configuration.

Any understanding of the pertinent mathematics so far exceeded David's grasp that it embarrassed him, making him feel like a three-year-old. So, he proceeded as a three-year-old would under such circumstances and focused on the drawings alone. As he turned each page, the configuration of the spheres was always a little different from the preceding cases, but there was always *some* space between the spheres.

When he reached the next-to-last page, he found himself too un-nerved to turn to the last page. His hands had become like icicles, and he'd begun sweating at the back of his neck. He glanced up only to realize that his three companions were watching him, rapt. He could barely imagine what he looked like, as full of dread as he was.

He forced himself against every impulse to turn the page.

And there it was at the bottom of the last page.

There was *no space at all* between the largest sphere and the small-est. On the largest sphere, the draftsman had scrawled ragged lines radiating from its point of contact with the smallest sphere, crudely representing stress fractures. The smallest sphere was depicted as breaking apart.

And David knew:

The largest sphere was Nibiru.

The intermediate sphere was Earth.

The smallest sphere was Earth's moon, which would smash into Nibiru's equator, destroying all life on that planet—and quite possibly the planet itself.

The lettered variables must stand for the gas giants that are the most massive planets in the solar system: Neptune, Uranus, Saturn, and Jupiter, listed in the sequence in which they would be encountered by a body such as Nibiru entering the solar system from its outermost reaches. The values assigned to them probably represented their assumed locations at the points of Nibiru's closest approach.

Assuming Nibiru were to encounter those four planets at the loca-tions assigned on the last page of the binder, there would be no more life on Nibiru, Earth would have no moon (and no tides), and the survival of life on Earth would be anything but certain.

There could be little doubt that *this* is what the Anunnaki didn't want anyone to find out, for what it suggested was that they were coming to Earth *to stay*—because in a few years they might have nowhere else to go.

But what David found most horrifying was that, at the point of colli-sion, Nibiru would be less than a quarter-million miles from Earth, suggesting that the slightest deviation from the values assigned on the last page could mean the destruction of Earth itself, whether as collateral damage from the collision between Nibiru and the moon ... or by direct collision between Nibiru and *Earth*.

David stood up and addressed the others as though he'd convened them for the purpose. "The unattributed work in this binder appears to address numerous variations in the extent to which Nibiru's approach past the outer planets will affect the closeness of its next approach to Earth. It suggests that there is … a *possibility* … that, on Nibiru's next passage by the Earth, it will collide catastrophically with Earth's moon."

For half a minute, the room was as quiet as though a bomb had just gone off. No one spoke, nor shifted in his chair, nor breathed more than necessary. Only Catharine showed any sign of life at all, as she nervously fingered a cellophane tape dispenser on the table.

At last, Miriam spoke up, though her voice was a bit choked. "Is there a person's name on the cover of that binder?"

David picked it up again and looked in all the obvious places. "I don't see one."

Miriam picked up a paper from one of the folders she was examining and read out a name. "Sage Chappell?"

He picked up the book again, looking for the name. Finding none, he peeled back the remaining piece of a sticker on the binding, and peered closely at the place he'd uncovered. "It seems to say H-A-P-P-E-L-L. The rest of the name appears to have been peeled off with the sticker. Why? What have you got?"

"It's a letter to Father from Doctor Chappell, who taught at MIT at the time. It's dated about two months before Father's passing. It's not long; I'll read it to you and skip the opening pleasantries."

Enclosed are my summary transcriptions of the most likely alternatives. You must bear several things in mind, however. First, we have no accurate value for the mass of Nibiru. (The Anunnaki surely know such value, however.) In fact, we know shockingly little about Nibiru or its behavior other than that its orbital motion is retrograde to that of all the other planets, and that its orbit is at some variance from the ecliptic plane.

As we know the distance of neither Nibiru's apogee nor its perigee from any fixed point such as the sun, we can neither project its arc of approach nor deduce its velocity with any accuracy.

The Anunnaki postulated a "rule of thumb" to the effect that a single revolution of Nibiru (known as a "Sar") takes three thousand six hundred Earth Years, but you've acknowledged that the best empirical evidence we have of the current number of Earth Years in a Sar, based upon Nibiru's latest approach, was in fact approximately 3,100, so that its latest approach to Earth took place several centuries prior to the time predicted by the rule of thumb. In all the alternative scenarios set out in the binder, we have applied the assumption that the precise number of years in Nibiru's present orbit will be the same as in its latest orbit.

Based upon that assumption, in the enclosed binder we've calculated the twenty-four likeliest possibilities for the position of the four gas giants that could be massive enough to cause a material redirection of Nibiru's orbit. And here is another built-in imprecision: We've had to ignore factors (other than the passage of Nibiru) that could alter the orbit of those four planets before Nibiru passes them. For example, on those rare occasions when Jupiter closely approaches Saturn, there would likely be a resultant alteration in both their orbits. At this date, however, we just haven't scrutinized such phenomena with sufficient precision to form a judgment on the question. After all, those planets are dead, gassy rocks. There's no one living there to care what minor perturbations might occur in their orbits or periodicity, and we humans have no current plans to go there.

Finally, we don't know how many moons Nibiru still has, if any. We're taught by the Sumerian "Enuma Elish" tablets that one or more of Nibiru's moons was shaken loose or destroyed in the cataclysm that destroyed Planet Tiamat, whose remains formed both Earth and the asteroid belt. But how many moons does Nibiru have now? We know not.

In addition, as you may remember from early studies of planetary motion, even Sir Isaac Newton had no luck in developing a formula to determine the trajectory of a body subject to the pull of more than one other massive body. So, for example, if Neptune is where one of our models expects it to be, but Uranus is unexpectedly nearby, Nibiru could end up on a trajectory wildly at variance from our predictive model.

Of course, as the chaoticians will remind you at every turn, God has never issued an edict requiring the outcome of every complex system to be determinable in accordance with an elegant linear equation.

To conclude, as there are so many unknowns in this analysis and so many variables, it would be foolhardy to apply a numerical probability to any one outcome. And I strongly advise you as your friend: Beware the siren song of our twenty-fourth postulate. To quote the Bard, That way madness lies!

Remember above all things that no planet, however large, occupies more than a tiny fraction of the space it passes through in a single orbit.

Several of my students had a jolly time working on your puzzle. Alas, however, every good thing must meet its end, and their enjoyment of your puzzle must give way to the demands of their upcoming exami-

nations.

In any event, Sally and I very much look forward to sharing the winter holidays with you and Miriam, if you and she can make it.

Yours in space and time, Sage Chappell.

"CHEER UP, DAVID," said Miriam. "After all, what has changed since Chappell's letter? What have we learned that would make his twenty-fourth postulate any more likely than he thought?"

"That's true," said Daniel. "Chappell's letter is relatively recent. I'm no physicist, but we probably know little more now than we did when he wrote it. We *still* don't know Nibiru's mass, nor its velocity, nor its arc of approach."

None of this was raising David's spirits. "Perhaps *we* still don't know any of those things," said David, "but as Chappell off-handedly suggested, the Anunnaki know *all* of those things, and they've decided to return to Earth, which at least suggests the possibility that *they're* concerned about a possible collision."

He started to pace. "And they've had hundreds of thousands—perhaps *millions*—of years to determine their own planet's mass and velocity, its orbital periodicity, and its arc of approach. And they have experience re-entering the inner solar system many thousands of times. They don't need to conjecture about perturbations in their own orbit caused by close approaches to massive planets. They've experienced them. They've *measured* and *recorded* them."

"But the Anunnakis' mere presence here doesn't *prove* anything," said Miriam.

Catharine stood up. "Alone, it's not proof, although it is grounds for concern. But we have more than the Anunnakis' mere presence. We know they've been actively trying to track down Abraham Azeri's papers for many months … and they've dogged David's heels for thirty thousand miles or more. That seems to mean they fear the release of information contained in his final papers."

"I wonder where Doctor Chappell is," said Daniel. "We should try to contact him. He may be in danger."

Catharine nodded. "The grad students who worked on the project may be at risk, as well."

David said, "In the papers reviewed up to now, has anyone found anything equally Earth-shaking? Please pardon the expression."

The response by all three was a glum shake of the head.

David nodded. "Then let's collect these papers and get them to the authorities right away."

"What about the spaceships hovering over the neighborhood?" asked Miriam. "Colonel Singh and his men had better be out there."

Iskender said, "He'll be there. The question is who *else* will be there."

Miriam rose and said bravely, "David is right. The sooner we turn over these papers to the authorities, the better. Besides, even if the Anunnaki were to confiscate these records, *we* still know the secret and I assume Doctor Chappell's postulates can be recreated by physicists of equal learning."

"The only way for them to stop the secret from getting out now is to kill us all," said David, "and that doesn't seem to be their way."

Catharine looked worried. "They *could* take us all captive, I suppose."

"Let's not frighten ourselves into inaction," said David. "Miriam, would you care to call the officer?"

There were papers strewn everywhere, which they quickly tossed into the wooden box. Miriam placed the lid on it and handed it to Daniel, then pulled the black coverlet over the safe-deposit box.

She picked up the phone on the wall and told the operator she was ready to leave. In a moment, the officer returned.

"Has everything been found in satisfactory order, madam?" he asked in his formal way.

"Exactly as it should have been," replied Miriam. "You may return the box to its slot."

The officer was prepared for a much heavier box for, as soon as he lifted it, his eyebrows shot up. "If the box is empty, madam, you should tell the clerk on your way out, as there's a substantial discount for any period when there's nothing in the box."

Daniel's curiosity got the best of him. "Why would one keep a box if there's nothing in it?"

The officer said, "I'm sure I don't know, sir, but some families retain their boxes for many generations." He winked at Daniel, as though he'd intimated enough for Daniel to figure it out for himself. And evidently he had, as Daniel smiled abashedly.

Catharine retracted the black coverlet, fingered through the papers in the wooden box, and said, "Miriam, there are some items here of purely personal interest. Your father's passport. A few gold coins, some of which look quite old. Oh, and look! Here's an album of photographs of you and your father together, taken when you were quite young. Considering … what may happen when we leave this place, wouldn't you feel better leaving them here for safekeeping?"

Miriam nodded. "Yes, you're right, Catharine. I can always empty the box at a later time." She took the items that Catharine had mentioned, plus a few more, and placed them loose in the safe-deposit box.

The officer slid the box back onto its runners and rolled it gently into its slot. He turned to the door and, as he opened it with his key, the floor shook seismically. Seeing the startled reactions, the officer said, "It's all right, folks. Just the Underground passing beneath us. *Whew!* Nervous lot."

David, for his part, wondered how he'd managed to remain standing through the rumbling of the underground train, when every fiber of his being was telling him to run for his life. He forced a smile as the officer led the party back to the waiting room.

The clerk bowed to Miriam as she passed. "Will madam care to retain the box?" asked the clerk.

"Yes, please."

"Very well," said the clerk as he made a notation on the outside of a folder, applied the date, and handed the pen to Miriam.

She initialed the inscription and the officer let them out through the heavy vault door. Daniel was first to set foot on the stairs.

Before they began mounting the stairs, David said, "Daniel, would it be all right for Catharine and me to take the lead?"

Daniel removed his foot from the first step and gestured with his chin for them to go ahead of him.

David stepped ahead of him and turned around to address his companions. "If there's a problem, I urge you to take Catharine's advice, as she's the only one of us whose training isn't purely academic."

As David tugged open the door to the sidewalk, his heart sank, for the moment of truth had at last arrived.

CHAPTER 19

As David stepped out the door of Westminster Safekeeping and up the stairs to the street, he was flanked by two uniformed British soldiers each of whom grabbed him by a shoulder.

"Are you Professor David Schubert?" demanded the more senior.

David nodded nervously.

"Then you'll need to come with us, sir."

"*Hold it,* you two!" Catharine shouted in their faces as she emerged from the doorway. "This gentleman is property of the United States Navy, entrusted to my care. I'm Lieutenant Commander Catharine Weldon." She flashed her Navy ID at them, then took out her keychain and showed them the dolphins.

The ranking soldier said, "This is the United Kingdom, ma'am."

"I'm *aware*, young man," she said sternly. "We're allies with a special relationship, right?"

The two Brits exchanged a glance. "The professor needs to come with us. Please follow us smartly, ma'am," said the ranking soldier, pointing toward the sky with his chin. "If you'll open your eyes wide, you'll see this is an impending combat situation, so we'll thank you for your prompt cooperation."

The soldiers muscled David across the street and pulled him under an awning where they were awaited by a short, swarthy superior officer.

The officer watched as Catharine followed his men. "Lieutenant Commander Weldon, I presume?"

She nodded curtly. "Colonel Singh, I presume?"

"Correct, ma'am," said Singh. He raised his hand and beckoned another pair of soldiers standing with Miriam and Daniel under the Westminster Safekeeping awning across the street. Daniel had been jostled and was struggling to hold onto the box.

Miriam smiled at Colonel Singh. "Colonel, if it's all the same to His Majesty's forces, we'd like to go now."

"Well," said the colonel, "I can understand how you feel, but there are aliens nearby who've declared their intention to abduct the professor and you, and take you into space against your will. Wouldn't you prefer His Majesty's protection?"

"Certainly," she said, "but where *are* these aliens?"

Colonel Singh pointed up at the sky about a block away, where a flying cigar had descended to a few hundred feet from the ground. All at once, lights began to flash at the bottom of the craft and two sliding doors on the bottom opened wide.

A moment later a deep horn blasted and a box-shaped landing craft began a steady, deliberate descent with no visible means of remaining aloft. The landing craft was dark grey like its mother ship, and vaguely resembled the amphibious craft used to storm the beaches at Normandy, except that this flying version had a sealed lid.

"There's a green park with no perimeter fence over there, sir," one of the soldiers said to Colonel Singh. "It's large enough to accommodate that craft. I expect that's where they intend to land."

The colonel ordered the four noncombatants' military accompaniment to release their charges and rejoin the fighting force.

Singh turned to Catharine. "Have your people remain immediately behind us," he said. "If those aliens want you, they'll have to get past us, and we'll make it a bloody day for them."

The colonel strode to the middle of his unit. "We'll advance to the end of that block and turn left to face the enemy," he shouted. "Remember, boys, you should expect that your firearms *will not work*. His Majesty's rules of engagement are that we're not to start a fight with this lot unless violently provoked. It'll likely be blades against blades, and you've had plenty of training in that. *Fix bayonets!*"

"Fix bayonets?" muttered Catharine, shaking her head. "That's an order not much heard since the First World War." She looked at David. "It's a new day."

"More like a very *old* day," he replied. "Chamber a round in your pistol, take the safety *off*, and hand it to me."

Catharine looked at him as though he'd gone mad. "You heard the man. It won't work."

He smiled at her. "Let Daniel and *me* worry about that."

She hesitated a moment, then relented. "I know I'm going to regret this," she said as she deftly smacked in a fresh clip, flicked off the safety, and handed it to David. "Just forget where you got it."

"Got what?" asked David with a wink.

Reaching the corner, the whole unit turned left and waited in the middle of the road while their four charges remained in the rear.

Meanwhile, the sidewalks were lined with excited people taking photos and movies on their smart phones. Numerous flashes went off every second.

In the park beyond the end of the block ahead, the landing craft settled on the lawn and stood still.

"Come on out, you bastards," muttered a soldier a few feet from David.

All at once, the front panel on the landing craft dropped forward, providing the forces inside with a down ramp. An officer stepped out and moved quickly out of view.

Behind him were the foot soldiers of the Anunnaki, each rank consisting of eighteen troops arrayed in uniforms resembling those of Etruscan warriors. Each carried a straight sword and a shiny metal shield.

On a shouted command (in a language sounding something like Hebrew), the first rank tramped heavily down the ramp, moved forward twenty counted steps, and stopped in formation about three hundred yards in front of the SAS unit.

"Blimey, those bleeders are tall," said a nearby SAS man, "gotta be close to *two meters*."

They were indeed tall, remarked David; *seven feet* tall, broad, and muscular. The next rank marched out and stopped one pace behind the front rank. And so the procedure continued until there were eighteen ranks of warriors in the park. Not only were there more than three hundred of them, which was at least five times the number of SAS men in the unit, but each soldier was far more massive than the biggest SAS man on hand.

Colonel Singh came back toward David.

"Are those even … *men?*" he asked. "I mean, they *look* like men, but the scale!"

"We men are made partly of … them," answered David, not expecting to be understood. "It's complicated."

"Well, all I can say is thank God they have no firearms, no archers, and no spears," said the colonel, "as we've none either. We have no shields, as they do, and that's quite bad." He stepped in front of his men. "This is going to be hand to hand, boys. Wet work. You know what's expected of you." He raised his right fist. "God save the king!"

"God save the king!" answered the unit with professional *esprit de corps*.

But these unexpected odds were undeniably terrifying. If allowed to continue, this was going to be a massacre.

On a shouted command, the Anunnaki began marching straight out of the park and onto the blacktop toward the SAS unit. David watched in horror until their front line halted no more than thirty yards from the British.

A superior Anunnaki officer stepped up to read a scroll aloud to the SAS men. Fortunately, he spoke in English.

"Citizens of Eridu! I am Shulgi of Nibiru. The gods come to you in peace, but know that among you are four sworn enemies of the gods. We will free two of them, but we come to take the remaining two to the Anunnaki for questioning or to provide service. If you will surrender them now, we will take them and leave in peace. The gods assure you that no harm will come to them. If they are detained by the gods, the prisoners will be treated as honored guests. During their detention, only their freedom to move about will be restricted, and only as far as necessary to prevent their escape or their commission of acts of violence." He rolled up the scroll and placed it under his arm. "Who among you speaks for the whole?"

Colonel Singh raised his hand and stood to the fore. "I am Singh of Southall. I speak for the whole. You have unlawfully invaded the territory of the King of England, whose family has ruled this land peacefully for nearly a thousand years. By what claim of right do you do this?"

Shulgi frowned down upon Colonel Singh. "We come not to usurp your king's territory. And we come not to answer questions, but to pose them."

Singh seemed surprised. "If you will not answer that question, then I shall ask another. What crime has been committed against the Anunnaki by the two whom you seek?"

"The gods will make all things clear to you in *due course!*" replied Shulgi with a sneer, spitting out the words with undisguised contempt.

David turned to Daniel, who was still encumbered with the wooden box of papers. "As soon as I raise my hand," whispered David, "give the signal."

Before Colonel Singh could continue the parley, David strode to the front of the SAS unit and bowed to the amazed colonel. "Pardon me, sir," he said, "but this rather appears to be some business of mine."

Singh regarded him doubtfully. "I hope you know what you're doing," he said, and warily took two steps back.

David turned to Shulgi. "I am David of Canarsie. Am I one of the two deemed to have transgressed against the Anunnaki?"

Shulgi looked down at this little earthling and nodded. "If you are who you say you are."

"How ironic!" shouted David. "I am who I say I am, but I doubt *you* are who you say you are." There was a silent tension until David resumed. "You are *not* gods."

Shulgi sneered again. "What do you know of us?" he said proudly. "You cannot remember us, for your lives are as brief as mayflies'. We lived here on Eridu for many Sars before your firstborn came into being. We *created* you."

David shook his head defiantly. "No. You *fashioned* us genetically, combining the material of an ape with that of your kind. *We* do such things now, fashioning sturdy strains of sheep, and grain that resists disease. Are *we* gods now, by *your* standard?" Now he adopted his own derisive posture. "You are not gods. You are not creators, but *creatures*, like us. Like us, you are born, you eat, you shit, and you die. These are not the traits of a god. God is One. God is Eternal."

Shulgi seemed confused. "You *still* worship the one who calls himself Yahweh?"

"Some of us do."

A deep-throated laugh emerged from deep in Shulgi's chest. "I come to teach you not theology, but obedience."

"And I come to teach you a virtue you sorely lack, namely, *humility*. You have tracked and chased me all over this planet for a fortnight. *Why?* I have committed no crime against the Anunnaki, and he *lies* who says I have. If you are truly a god, tell me why tormenting me in this way has been just."

"I need not justify my actions to you," said Shulgi.

David raised his hand. "If you're to live with humanity on Eridu, you'd best learn some humility."

Above them one of the spaceships fired a laser weapon into the sky. Though it made no sound, the flash was blinding. A moment later, the other spaceship fired one.

David deliberately ignored them, raised Catharine's pistol, and aimed it at Shulgi's head. "Perhaps your troops might learn humility from seeing the Great Shulgi's brains splattered all over the pavement!"

Shulgi looked at him defiantly.

"What do you think, Shulgi?" laughed David. "Shall we try it out?" He shrugged ostentatiously. "Of course, you won't be around to see the results."

"That weapon won't fire, mayfly," said Shulgi menacingly.

"No?" asked David smugly. He aimed the gun at the street and pulled the trigger.

And it *fired.* With a shockingly loud report.

At last he saw in Shulgi's eyes what he was going for. *Fear.* David was buoyant that he was now foisting his own fear on his tormentors.

Colonel Singh was sharp enough to deduce that his men's rifles would likewise fire. "Company," he shouted, "train all firearms on the general and await my command."

The whole SAS unit locked and loaded, and aimed its rifles at Shulgi's head. The Anunnaki troops looked on with dismay, awaiting instructions.

David took an exaggerated step toward Shulgi and paraded about nervously with his upraised pistol ever trained on Shulgi's head.

"WHO COMES NOW TO BREAK THE KING'S PEACE WITH FORCE AND ARMS?" he shrieked. "Retreat, you son of a bitch, or I'll blow your freaking brains out because you're just too *stupid* to live!"

If an expression were capable of killing, Shulgi's would have smitten his adversary. But even *his* expression could not kill. And David observed with great pleasure that Shulgi's expression was no longer one of contempt, but the apoplectic fury of a humiliated equal.

"I'll give you to a count of three and then we'll *all* fire," repeated David. "Now, turn your *losers* around and take off in your little toy spaceship over there, or I'll blow your frickin' brains out with pleasure. *ONE!"*

Red-faced, Shulgi turned and gave an order for orderly retreat. His well-drilled troops turned and jogged to the landing craft and boarded in orderly fashion. Once the last of his men had boarded, Shulgi turned and pointed at David, as though to say this is not over.

True to his upbringing, David gave him the finger. But not just a simple finger: The *big* finger that the Italian guys in his old neighborhood used to give, with two crossed arms and two extended middle fingers.

By this time, the square was quiet, but for the popping of flashbulbs and the clicking of a thousand cameras.

The crowd remained hushed as the shuttle lifted off and returned to the spaceship through the same hatch from which it had emerged. As the hatch banged audibly shut, the crowd roared its approval and erupted with obscenities.

David turned toward the place where his friends had stood and gave a thumbs-up. His other arm hung by his side with the pistol dangling loosely from his hand. A lucky photographer caught what would shortly become the most republished picture in the history of photography.

Several SAS men wandered up to David and slapped him on the back. Some of the British accents were a bit too thick for David to understand, but he distinctly heard one of them say, "Ya got bigger balls n' brains, yank. Good job!" Another retorted. "He's got a bigger mouth than balls *or* brains. Wish mine got results like that."

It occurred to David that he'd better ditch the pistol or it would be traced back to Catharine. But as he looked around for a sewer grate to toss it into, a big hand from behind him wrenched the pistol from his grasp.

He turned to find himself face-to-face with Agent Duffy of the FBI.

"What the hell are *you* doing here?" David demanded. *"Where's my phone?"*

"I'll answer your questions in reverse order," said the unflappable Agent Duffy. "Your phone's still in D.C. I didn't know you'd be here, or I woulda brought it together with the cake I woulda baked ya. And what I'm *doing* here is saving your ass from a charge of felony gun possession. Brits don't like yanks runnin' around the streets o' London with guns. Follow me to that limo back there. Your friends are all waitin' for ya."

David was reluctant to move.

Agent Duffy rolled his eyes. "C'mon kid. I'm tryin' to get ya into the embassy before the bobbies come and arrest you. If they get you before we reach the embassy, you're goin' to jail."

David nodded and followed him to the limo. Duffy opened the door and let David into the passenger cab. While David would have liked to identify everyone in the cab before getting in, Duffy made that impossible, pressing him hard to get in quickly, which he did. Just in time, too, because a large crowd of rowdy well-wishers had begun to gather only a few feet away and, once the crowd grew beyond a certain point, its remaining caution would surely dissipate and the limo would be blocked.

As Duffy got in the front seat on the passenger's side and ordered the driver to move off, a hand was extended to David belonging to ...

"Admiral Simmons!" said David. *"You're* a welcome sight."

To one side of the admiral sat Catharine and Daniel, who both beamed at David. To his other side sat Miriam Azeri, whose expression was a bit more reserved.

"Congratulations, David," said the admiral. "You took a few insane risks, and now you're an international hero—a modern-day Lindbergh."

As the admiral's voice sounded less than pleased, David looked to his face, which was pretty much the same.

"I saw no alternative," said David. "Did you see the size of those fighters?"

The admiral nodded. "They were huge. It would have been a rout."

David corrected him. "It would have been a *massacre*, and the Anunnaki would have flown out of here with the papers that Doctor Iskender just brought to *you*."

The admiral shrugged ambiguously.

David was becoming irritated. "So, retaining those papers is no longer a big deal? Not only do we have Abraham Azeri's last papers (thanks to Miriam's sound discretion in trusting Catharine and me), but the Anunnaki don't know what's in them."

The admiral drew himself up and posed a couple of questions to Catharine and David. "Why wasn't I informed that you'd found Miriam? Or that you'd made contact with a potential ally from outer space?"

David glared at the admiral. "Why do I feel like I'm being required to defend myself? I just risked my life and put a big notch on the belts of Uncle Sam and King William—all with no loss of life! For your information, admiral, the contact with a potential alien ally wasn't made by Catharine and me. It was made by Miriam and Doctor Iskender, who were gracious enough to share that information with us.

"*You want to know why you weren't notified that we'd found Miriam, admiral?* Because the night Catharine and I bumped into Miriam and Daniel in Beira (the same night, incidentally, that we left the boomer), we spent our time persuading Miriam and Daniel of our trustworthiness. That same night, my dreams were invaded by one of the Anunnaki *again*. Before dawn, Miriam and Doctor Iskender began their journey here, and Catharine and I narrowly escaped our room before it was invaded by Anunnaki soldiers looking to capture us.

"Then Catharine and I made our way across Africa to Windhoek, where we learned that British Airways wouldn't have a London-bound flight for another *two days*. So, we took our lives in our hands and hired a smuggler to fly us to Heathrow in a freight aircraft. We arrived in London *yesterday morning*. And to cap it all off, we were under orders of the well-respected Admiral Simmons (whom you may know) *not* to use radios or telephones under *any* circumstances, nor to allow our presence to be detected. Add to that: We had no idea where you were or what you were doing."

David leaned toward the admiral defiantly. "What *were* you doing, by the way?"

The admiral stiffened. "It's none of your damned business what I was doing. And I've told you not to talk to me that way. Now, you have a choice. Either zip your lip until we get somewhere we can talk privately, or you can spend a couple weeks in the brig."

"The brig?" said David skeptically. "I'm not even in the navy."

"Our brig doesn't impose a service requirement, counselor. Your choice."

David folded his arms and silently looked out the window at the rapidly passing scenery.

CHAPTER 20

INANNA GRACED THE throne room of her pyramidion in the garb of an ancient Egyptian queen prepared to attend to matters of state. In geosynchronous orbit, the throne room provided a beautifully framed view of the ever-changing Earth. She could have chosen any view she liked, but looking out into the blackness of space, for all its wonder, held little interest for her; there was no one to look at, and (which was far worse) no one to look at *her*.

Inanna's throne room was a memorial reconstruction of Nefertiti's as it had appeared while her husband yet lived. As no full reproductions had survived, in designing the room Inanna had had little choice but to rely upon her own memory of visits she'd made to Nefertiti during her life.

Anachronistic electronic devices incapable of being concealed behind the pyramidion's walls were housed to appear much as they would have in Nefertiti's day, lending the room a motif that would, on Earth, be called Art Deco.

Although Shulgi's shuttle was due to dock with Inanna's pyramidion, as yet he had not appeared. She checked her chronometer and found that he was late. But his tardiness was to be expected, as she knew what had delayed him, namely, his unit's retreat from the field before an inferior force in the City of Westminster.

She'd already watched the hologram of the incident several times, but welcomed the opportunity to watch it again before Shulgi's appearance. Seated on her throne, she clapped her hands twice and said, "Again."

The hologram was projected onto the area immediately before her throne, called the *well*. Visually, it was as though Shulgi's approach to Westminster was being played out in three-dimensional miniature, with the well's floor serving as street level.

The viewpoint of the opening sequence was panoramic. To Inanna's left, the landing craft emerged from underneath Shulgi's cylinder craft and made its way slowly down to the surface. Once it landed, its front gate was thrown open, and Shulgi and his men stepped out of it and moved to her right in the direction of the earthling soldiers, who didn't seem particularly well organized.

Even from the distant vantage point of the holographer, it was obvious that Shulgi had committed the blunder of arming his troops with swords and shields alone, overly confident in the continuous operation of the cylinder's disarming ray.

The viewpoint now switched to a place just a few feet behind Shulgi, so that the viewer was peering over Shulgi's shoulder at the dark little colonel. The usual manly insults were exchanged between them, until David appeared and replaced the colonel as the center of attention: *David,* the man of her dreams, descended of Joseph, Pharaoh's dream interpreter.

David seemed harried, and began to shout at Shulgi, who refused to be drawn in. There were flashes in the sky that lit up the frame a few times, but David ignored them. Then he did something so brilliant it made her giggle like a schoolgirl. He pulled out an old-fashioned pistol and fired it into the ground.

Shulgi, despite his feint at impassivity, was obviously *shocked* that the pistol had discharged. Somehow, this earthling David had deduced (perhaps he'd dreamt it?) that the cylinder's disarming ray consumed too much energy to be operated at the same time as its high-powered weapons. And he'd apparently enlisted the help of the Frog People to fire into the air, thus drawing fire from the cylinder. For the seven minutes it would take for the ray's power source to regenerate, the disarming ray was now disabled—and every firearm in the vicinity would operate properly: the earthling's no less than the Anunnakis'.

Except that the Anunnaki unit had *brought* no firearms. The little colonel, seeing David's pistol successfully discharge, ordered his men to aim their firearms at Shulgi.

Inanna clapped with delight.

So, with a single archaic pistol, David had managed to overpower Shulgi's entire unit and force its humiliating retreat from the field.

When the hologram finished its run, Inanna's chief maidservant Shiduri knocked at the door.

"Come," said Inanna from her reginal perch.

"Anu's Beloved," said Shiduri, invoking the ancient Sumerian form of address, "General Shulgi has docked here at Your Majesty's pyramidion. Shall I admit him to your presence?"

"Certainly," said Inanna. "Show him in as soon as his raiment is appropriate."

Shiduri bowed low. "It shall be done." She disappeared.

A minute later, Shulgi entered the well alone, all out of sorts. Although he'd removed his boots and made an effort to cover himself in appropriate robes, it was obvious that, underneath it all, he remained in battle dress. He dropped his gaze, entered the well before the throne, bowed low, and waited to be spoken to.

"Rise, general," said Inanna. "Have you brought me the earthlings?"

"I must beg Your Majesty's forgiveness," he said, "but as yet I have been unable to secure them."

"Oh?" she said, feigning surprise. "I was under the impression that you were going to"—she searched her memory for his precise words—"teach the slaves obedience."

"Has Your Majesty had an opportunity to view the hologram?" he asked.

"Of course," she said. "I've watched it several times. While I couldn't hear every word, it appeared to me that you were handled rather roughly by this … David person."

Shulgi's face reddened. "It was my mistake to assume that the earthlings would have the grace to surrender in light of their own helplessness."

"And what was your reason for taking the field with such minimal weaponry?" Inanna asked.

Shulgi squirmed, obviously finding this inquiry unbearable. "It has been the consensus of all the Anunnaki that we should avoid instilling feelings of fear or resentment in the earthlings whenever possible. As I said, Majesty, it was *my* mistake."

"Evidently," she replied, "it was a mistake to assume the earthlings were helpless."

Shulgi nodded. "That infidel whom Your Majesty just mentioned," he said as though it was beneath him to pronounce the earthling's name, "had the temerity to say he'd come to teach me humility."

"Well," said Inanna, "I suppose that, for some, the first step toward humility is *humiliation*." She turned to him sharply. "And he humiliated you, did he not?"

Shulgi chafed at the query. But he'd been asked a direct question by a goddess, and protocol required a straight answer. "He did, Majesty, but the upstart can't hide forever. I'll settle my score with him, and teach him both humility and manners."

"Imagine," said Inanna wistfully, "*Enki's* glee when he watched a company of *my* swordsman being chased from the field by one earthling brandishing an old-style pistol." She turned grave. "You'll *not* settle this score with the earthling, general. You will rather learn to live with him. In fact, you will contact the military leaders of his country on my behalf and demand he be delivered into my service."

Shulgi winced. "Your Majesty is not, I hope, contemplating a union with this ... earthling?"

"I bed whom I please," she said with a flash of anger, "and will thank you to remember your place."

Shulgi bowed low at her show of displeasure. "Pardon, Majesty. I mentioned it only because your choice affects all your subjects."

She raised her chin. "I am *ever* mindful of my subjects' welfare, general."

"Yes, Majesty," replied Shulgi. "After today's unpleasantness, however, I doubt the earthlings' military leaders will credit me as Your Majesty's dispassionate emissary for purposes of securing this earthling's delivery." He bowed. "They will suspect that I harbor toward him some ... ill will."

Inanna nodded. "And it will be your penance for today's debacle to prove them wrong. They're waiting to hear from you. You are dismissed."

Shulgi bowed low and took two steps back before turning. As he was about to reach the door, Inanna spoke again.

"Oh, and general?" she said, and waited for him to turn toward her. "Do not disappoint me again with respect to this earthling. He is your charge, and you will care for him as though he were your own son."

Shulgi swallowed his resentment, bowed again, and disappeared through the door.

⇒◦◯◦⇐

WHEN DAVID FIRST opened his eyes, he was surrounded by darkness. He had no idea where he was until he sat up and looked down, catching sight of the artificial light seeping under the door at the far side of the sleeping cubicle. Then he remembered where he was. He was at the U.S. Embassy in London, which he couldn't leave for fear of being inundated by adoring well-wishers—and possible Anunnaki abductors.

He switched on a lamp by his cot, checked his watch, and found it was early morning. So at least this day would not begin (as so many others lately had) before dawn or after dark, but rather like everyone else's—at the beginning of the day. Even without more, he found that thought somewhat encouraging.

He picked up a British tabloid that had been slipped under his door while he slept. The front page was dominated by a picture of him, smiling scornfully while giving Shulgi the full-body double finger. He shook his head at the headline above it: *Kid from Canarsie Saves World*. It should have said *Kid from Canarsie Saves Own Life*, but that probably wouldn't have sold as many newspapers or garnered so many clicks.

He opened to Page Three, where there was much more about him, mostly about his Brooklyn origins. There were also a few other photos: a grainy copy of his high school senior portrait, a photo of him with some buddies at an unspecified rock concert, and a recent portrait taken from the law school website.

He wondered how many errors he'd find in all this writing, but he just didn't feel up to reading it. He wondered also whether his relatives and old acquaintances were now being hounded by reporters for background (or dirt) on him. But the only thing that interested him right now was taking a shower, getting out of this embassy, going home, and growing his budding romance with Catharine.

He tossed the newspaper aside and opened a wide, steel grey locker containing a garment rack. Reaching up to the top shelf, he grabbed a towel and an unopened bar of soap and marched off to the mini-gym shower room he'd been shown last night.

As he showered, he recalled with gratitude the admiral's persistent attempts yesterday to persuade the Secretary of State to allow him into the embassy. The secretary had stubbornly declined—until receiving a phone call from his boss, the President. Once David was admitted to the embassy, Miriam and Daniel returned to their hotel rooms and said they'd meet him and Catharine for lunch today, giving him something to look forward to.

Back in his room, David dried his hair and put on the clothes they'd sent for, including a green cotton turtleneck sweater, a pair of black Levi's, and a pair of dark leather Timberland walking shoes. They'd also bought him a navy blue Land's End jacket and a scarf, but he left those in the locker and headed off to the commissary.

As soon as he stepped out the door of his cubicle, he was waylaid by the admiral's secretary, who grabbed him by the arm and assured him she'd bring him some scones and coffee. As they walked toward the conference room, David said: "I suppose it wouldn't matter if I said I'd like a real breakfast."

She smiled and said, "Right you are."

She opened the door to the conference room, where a half-dozen people—mostly in naval uniform—were seated around a conference table. At the head of the table sat Admiral Simmons. To the admiral's right was Agent Duffy; to his left sat Catharine, in uniform.

The facial expressions of those in the room were respectful (except for Duffy's smirk), but there was no levity in this congregation.

David closed the door behind him and took a seat. "Good morning, admiral. Lieutenant commander. Agent Duffy." He nodded to the others and said, "You're not going to hang me, are you?"

"No, David," said the admiral, "that's not on the table. But we have some important decisions to make regarding your immediate future."

David said, "How kind of you to consult with me. So, we're here to talk … *investments?*"

Duffy rolled his eyes.

The admiral shook his head and said matter-of-factly:

"She wants you."

As David had no idea whom the admiral meant, he automatically looked to Catharine (who was looking away) and immediately regretted doing so, as he realized that the cagey old man had been deliberately ambiguous to see if David thought of *Catharine* when there was talk of his being wanted. David could have kicked himself for having fallen right into the trap with a single involuntary glance in her direction.

The admiral arched an eyebrow at Catharine, which she skillfully ignored.

The admiral continued. "Queen Inanna has contacted us through General Shulgi. As you may recall, that's the name of the officer you humiliated and threatened to kill yesterday."

The comment rankled David. "*Queen* Inanna? Queen of *what?*"

The admiral took a sip of coffee from a paper cup. "That's another conversation, albeit an interesting one. She wants us to surrender you to her service." He awaited a reaction from David.

But David was disinclined to react, and waited impassively for more.

The admiral reluctantly added, "And we were wondering what you thought about that."

David kept his cool. "Is the Navy in the business of delivering U.S. citizens into *bondage* now?"

The young man in a U.S. Space Force uniform sitting next to David shook his head in amazement. "Professor, you *do* realize you're a superstar now? There's not a news station or a newspaper in the world that's not singing your praises as the salvation of humanity."

David looked at the young fellow, who wore a gold pin with the name *Callow* on it. "That and three bucks'll get me on the IRT. What's your point?"

Callow blushed. "You've got a shot at Aphrodite, man ... at *Venus.* The actual *goddess* of love! And you're going to turn her down?" He sat there agape.

Although it pained David to reveal his true feelings in such a cold setting, he needed to articulate how he felt. Refusing to look at Catharine, he replied. "I don't want a shot at a goddess. I want a shot at ... real love."

It took a moment to sink in, but when it did Catharine began sobbing loudly. And that was it; despite David's best intentions, the cat was out of the bag. David cast his eyes down at the conference table and would neither speak nor move.

"Gentlemen," said the admiral, "uh, I'm going to suspend this meeting for now."

Agent Duffy and the rest picked up their papers and briefcases and got up to leave. Catharine was inconsolable, her shoulders heaving.

The admiral said, "I will expect your customary confidentiality. I'll call you all when we're ready to reconvene."

The others filed out past David, and when Callow passed, he good-naturedly patted David's shoulder and whispered, "Good for you, prof."

David didn't react. He waited to be alone with the admiral and Catharine.

When the door closed and the three of them were left alone, the admiral folded his hands, obviously waiting for someone else to broach the unspoken subject.

David shook his head. "You might've just *asked,* admiral."

The admiral stirred. "I didn't ask, David, because I didn't want to know. That type of fraternization is a violation of Naval Intelligence regulations, and I didn't want to create problems for my adjutant. I still don't. But now that I *do* know, I'll have to keep it in mind as we proceed." He took a sip of coffee.

"Could I get some of that?" asked David, pointing to the admiral's mug. "Your secretary said she'd bring some coffee and scones."

As though on cue, the admiral's secretary showed up with eight cups of coffee and eight scones. "What happened to everyone?" she asked with surprise, then spotted Catharine's tears. "Oh, well. I'll just leave these here for anyone who wants one." She put everything down and couldn't leave quickly enough.

David grabbed a coffee. "I'm sorry I didn't answer you directly, admiral, but I have no interest in becoming the property of Inanna. I'm an American citizen. Although I'm willing to serve my country, I refuse to lay down my liberty to do it. As the man said, I'd rather die on my feet than live on my knees."

"Understandable, David. I got the distinct impression that General Shulgi *expected* that he'd be required to negotiate a fixed term for your service—"

"I'm not *entering* her service—"

"Just hear me out, David. I've been doing this job a long time, and I was once young like you and had *my* plans, as well."

David nodded, sipped his coffee, and broke off a bit of scone.

"How would you like to be America's ambassador to Queen Inanna?" asked the admiral.

"Perhaps just a consular officer?" suggested David. "An ambassadorship requires a presidential appointment and approval by the Senate."

"True," said the admiral, "but with all the favorable coverage you're getting, I can probably get that done in a few weeks."

This was still sounding crazy, but a little less so now. "So I'd be on the State Department payroll?"

The admiral nodded. "I'm not saying Inanna will agree to your appointment, but, yes, that's what I'm contemplating. And you'd have ambassadorial immunity and the protection of the United States."

David scoffed. "A United States that has no way of protecting me."

The admiral nodded bitterly. "At the moment."

"What happens to Shawn? *He's* State Department, too."

"We'll demand his return as part of the deal. We're still not really sure why he was detained in the first place, but we can make the demand."

David turned to Catharine. "Lieutenant commander, how do you feel about this?"

Her eyeliner was a little smudged, but she still looked heartbreakingly beautiful to David. "That depends," she said to him. "Are you *Trevor* or David?"

David smirked. "Do I seem an upper-class twit to you?" he asked in the manner of an upper-class twit.

"No," she said. "I just can't go on wondering whether *every* man isn't Trevor."

"I'm definitely *not* Trevor," he replied sincerely.

"Then," she said, "I suppose I'll have to negotiate Queen Inanna's acceptance of you as U.S. ambassador."

"*You'll* have to negotiate?"

The admiral said, "As long as I detect no conflict of interest."

David said, "Okay, but I need a guaranty of physical security, safe passage, and safe return. Also, no Shawn … no deal."

"I'll do my best," said Catharine.

David turned to the admiral. "There are a few more knotty issues, as well. For one thing, is Inanna universally recognized as Queen of Nibiru?"

The admiral shrugged. "What of it?"

"If she's not, then there's probably at least one other faction requiring an ambassador. It appears that Enki is still alive. If that wasn't Enki who confronted the boomer off southern Africa, then it was probably his son Ningishzidda. And there may be yet *more* factions."

"If those factions are united in interest as regards the United States," said the admiral, "we can just add them to your portfolio."

"Or …" said David, "I could be appointed ambassador to *all* the Anunnaki. Since I have no orbiting spacecraft, the U.S. could create an institute in an international city, say, Geneva, the way it did when it withdrew recognition of Taiwan as an independent country. Since I'd have no orbiting consulate, I could *ride circuit* at the invitation of the different factions."

That idea excited the admiral so much that he stood up and started pacing. "That could put you in the role of *intermediary* among their factions—giving us a lot of clout and enabling us to gather considerable intelligence."

Catharine said, "But at the moment we've received interest from only *one* of the factions, and she hasn't agreed to receive you as an ambassador. Sounds more like she wants you as a sex slave."

David and the admiral looked at one another and burst into laughter.

"Did I say something funny?" asked Catharine with some irritation.

David looked at her sympathetically. "She may be a sex maniac, Catharine, but I think you overrate my attractiveness."

"*I'll* say," said the admiral.

David thought a while and said, "Why not just hand it to her as a *fait accompli?* 'Professor Schubert has been appointed U.S. Ambassador to the Anunnaki, and would be pleased to pay his first call upon the exalted Queen Inanna if she would deign to receive him in such capacity. In any event, the Ambassador will be pleased to receive the duly appointed representatives of each of the Anunnaki families at his Geneva headquarters.'"

"Why not headquarter in Washington?" asked the admiral.

"It makes it too nationalist. The idea is to make it effectively *Earth's* ambassadorship. Let the *Anunnaki* be the divided ones. We earthlings will be effectively united, at least to begin with."

"*National* wouldn't be good enough for you?" asked the admiral.

David feigned taking offense and pointed to himself. "With *this* kind of sex appeal?"

Catharine said, "What if they don't care to have civil relations with us?"

"If they're going to stay here and they're not going to wipe us out," said David, "sooner or later they're going to *have* to talk to us."

The admiral nodded. "Remember, they don't know that we suspect their planet will soon be destroyed and that they'll have no place else to go. And we want to make sure *they* don't know that *we* know."

"That reminds me," said David, "have you been able to locate the physicist who drew those alternative diagrams of Nibiru's next pass by the Earth?"

The admiral became quite serious. "Sage Chappell?" he said with a sigh. "He wandered off campus up in Cambridge about three months ago. Hasn't been seen since. Let's take a break. I took the liberty of inviting Miriam and Daniel to meet you at a private dining room here at the embassy."

David registered surprise.

The admiral laughed at his reaction. "If you think the public will give you a moment's peace once you leave here, you're nuts. We'll reconvene here in two hours. No outsiders. Just you three civilians, Catharine, and me. There's somebody important waiting to speak with all of you."

⟶∘⟅⟆∘⟸

DESPITE THE COMMON criticism that English food tends toward the bland, David had always found the basic ingredients, especially produce, to be top quality. Fortunately, the embassy's chef was first class, as well, and the service absurdly attentive. David found himself the object of admiring stares from the female staff and, unless his eyes were playing tricks on him, he didn't see the same face twice. It seemed they were all demanding their chance to say they'd actually served lunch to the Kid from Canarsie.

Miriam tried a couple of times to order wine (and Catharine joined the chorus), but the staff was under strict orders to politely refuse. Nevertheless, when the time came for them to reconvene with the admiral, they were all well fed and in a good mood.

The admiral was awaiting them. He rose when they entered, and carefully showed Daniel to the seat nearest the squawk box.

"We have an appointment to speak with Brosa the Dagon," said the admiral. "Doctor Iskender, I'll ask you to do the necessary translation. To ensure we're all on the same page before we establish a voice connection: Our international intelligence personnel have worked alongside our Semitic Language experts for many hours to ensure that the Dagon are not allied or sharing information with the Anunnaki. The Dagon appear to be substantially more advanced than the Anunnaki technologically, although, according to Brosa, the technological gap is shrinking, which is of major concern to the Dagon. We've informed the Dagon that Abraham Azeri had asked a physicist whether there could be a collision between Nibiru and either Earth or its moon on its next pass, and that he was told there was a possibility, but that it could not be quantified without more data. Brosa is cleared to receive any information you four have about Anunnaki technological capabilities and actions taken by the Anunnaki in current preparations for landing on Earth."

"Does that include the outcome of Chappell's work?" asked David.

"It does," said the admiral. "Don't worry, if I think you're getting too far ahead of yourselves, I'll interrupt and put you right. Ready?"

The four nodded their assent.

The admiral pressed a button on the phone, and the line opened.

"Brosa, it's the admiral."

"Good afternoon, admiral," came Brosa's tinny amphibian voice. "We will continue in English for a time if that is … satisfaction. We have been listening to your commercial entertainment to learn some English. We will be back right after this message. *Glick.*"

David looked at Daniel and silently mouthed, "*Glick?*"

Daniel shrugged.

The admiral's eyebrows shot up. He said, "Please hold the line for a moment, Brosa. We need to speak among ourselves privately."

"Yes," replied Brosa. "We don't touch that dial. Stay tuned. *Glick.*"

The admiral pressed the hold button. "I don't know about you," he said, "but I'd feel a lot better if Daniel conversed with Brosa in Hittite, or whatever that language is. Any objections?"

The four shook their heads.

David said, "Why does he keep saying *glick?*"

The admiral directed that question to Daniel.

"If you'd seen them," said Daniel, "you'd know they look nothing like us. Although they stand on two legs, they appear to be amphibious, and they don't breathe or speak the way we do. They have some other organ that produces their voices, and it makes that *glick* sound when they finish a phrase. But you'll see as we speak: it will quickly become easy to ignore. I agree with you, admiral. Interpreting can be time-consuming, but I think we'll understand each other better if we speak in Hittite."

David quipped. "Rather than in *Madison Avenue.*"

For two hours, David recounted his harrowing experiences being pursued by the Anunnaki, having his dreams electronically invaded by Inanna, and every other encounter or incident he'd had with them. David also mentioned their chance meeting with Miriam and Daniel and their narrow escape from Beira.

Brosa seemed interested in the incident on the submarine where the Anunnaki remotely levitated the two hemispheres of (formerly) Uranium-235, spun them into a glowing caduceus, and transmuted them into gold.

But the incident that *really* riveted Brosa's attention was the Anunnaki pyramidion's appearing to travel through the same space as the submarine without damaging either vessel. Brosa asked numerous questions about the incident, most of which greatly exceeded David's knowledge, and interrupted the conversation several times to converse with one of the Dagon engineers.

After allowing the discussion to continue for a while, the admiral said, "Brosa, I think it would be a good idea for our engineers to speak directly with yours on this topic. Can you tell us why this incident is of particular interest to you?"

Brosa had a brief conversation with his engineer, then came back on. "I do not know whether David knows of my first discussion with Miriam and Daniel in Zimbabwe. But, at that time, I mentioned that the Anunnaki lack one very important capability that the Dagon have."

"Miriam informed us of that conversation," said David. "Thank you for your concern, Brosa."

"In that conversation," said Brosa, "we mentioned that the Dagon know how to do something that the Anunnaki cannot yet do."

"What is that?" asked the admiral.

"The Anunnaki cannot travel through a vacuum faster than a light wave."

The admiral was stunned. "Brosa, are you saying that you can travel faster than ... *light?*"

"In a way."

The admiral was chagrined. "Pardon me, Brosa, but we have believed for over a century that nothing can travel faster than light, that there is essentially a cosmic speed limit."

It took some back-and-forth for Daniel and Brosa to make themselves understood. Finally, Brosa provided an explanation he believed the humans could follow.

"The Anunnaki and you earthlings have a basic misunderstanding of the nature of space. Without becoming too technical, you think that space is continuous, preponderantly straight, and incapable of compression. This is wrong. Although there is a speed limit through space, space itself can be compressed and folded. So, to an outside observer located at a fixed point in space, the Dagon may *appear* to move faster than light.

"To comprehend this technology fully requires any scientific regime to learn four separate lessons about space/time. The reason the Dagon wish to know more about the pyramidion passing through the submarine is that it may indicate that the Anunnaki have learned the first of these lessons. This is very bad. So long as the Anunnaki remain interested in conquest of other worlds, this is dangerous to all, including the Dagon."

The admiral's brow creased, showing his age and weariness. "How dangerous is it for the Anunnaki to have learned this lesson?"

There was a long silence on Brosa's end of the line and a discussion between him and his engineer. At last he resumed the conversation.

"It is far more dangerous," said Brosa, "than the Anunnaki returning to Earth. More dangerous even than the Anunnaki *destroying* the Earth. It could affect the fate of the whole galaxy ... the whole universe. So ... it is quite dangerous indeed."

CHAPTER 21

TWO WEEKS LATER, negotiations between Catharine and General Shulgi were essentially complete. Catharine had had no occasion to speak directly with Inanna.

David was to be appointed by the President and confirmed by the Senate as U.S. Ambassador to the Anunnaki to serve at least three years, which was the time remaining in the current U.S. presidential term. There was no legally binding way to assure Shulgi that the ambassadorship would survive the present term, as every President is constitutionally empowered to hire and fire his own ambassadors. If the current President were not elected to a second term, his successor could fire David and, absent a constitutional amendment, there would be no way to stop that from happening.

In addition, David would be afforded all customary diplomatic immunities, and his safety (and safe return) would be guaranteed by Inanna.

The demands by Inanna to which Catharine had been instructed to agree were few, but curious. Inanna, in person and with a full entourage, would make a twilight landing on the vacant platform at Baalbek, which was evidently located in a sector that had been under her control thousands of years ago. By agreement, her landing would be well-lit, and televised and streamed contemporaneously around the world. At that time and place, Her Majesty would demonstrate her humane justice by publicly releasing Shawn from his present custody aboard her pyramidion.

She would ceremonially accept David as U.S. Ambassador to her court, and transport him to her pyramidion for two periods of six months (with two weeks between), during which he would be assured of private quarters and untrammeled communications with the Secretary of State, with Admiral Simmons and his staff, and with any Anunnaki requesting access to him.

Certain of Inanna's requests were quietly granted in keeping with the time-honored ambassadorial practice of conforming to the customs of the receiving court, at least to the extent such customs were not barred by the customs of the ambassador's home country.

David would be required to refrain from eating animal products in any form beginning two weeks prior to Inanna's landing on Earth and ending with David's embassage. In this respect Shulgi explained apologetically that earthlings had not been permitted to eat animal products prior to the Deluge, and that Enlil's permission to do so *after* the Deluge was granted for the perverse purpose of harming human health, thus limiting growth of their population.

David would also be required to engage in a ritual bath in preparation for accompanying Her Majesty.

In addition, throughout the embassage (including the evening of Her Majesty's landing at Baalbek), David's outer clothing, which would be supplied to him by Inanna's court, would consist of traditional Anunnaki court robes made of an ancient silk-cotton blend, and his footwear would consist of open-toed sandals. David demanded that he be permitted such underwear and warming underclothes as he chose. Shulgi conceded the point on condition that such undergarments would be worn for no more than one day without being submitted for laundering by Her Majesty's servants.

⟶∘⟨⟨⟩∘⟨

To avoid being recognized when he left the embassy, David grew a mustache and short beard, which seemed to turn the trick.

Four days before the night of Inanna's landing, David and Catharine checked into the Grosvenor again, this time with the intention of staying the whole night.

There was nearly as much weeping as lovemaking, but there was a great deal of both. Once they'd calmed down with the aid of a good *pinot noir*, they began discussing the whirlwind they'd undergone since meeting barely a month earlier.

David leaned against the headboard with his hands behind his head. "It did feel as though we'd won quite a victory when we finally had a chance to tell the American authorities all we'd learned about this whole Anunnaki business."

Catharine said, "But don't you feel just a little remiss?"

He cocked his head. "About what?"

"Well," she said, "we didn't tell them *everything*."

He smirked. "You mean about your nearly blowing a hole in William's minisub?"

She slapped his knee. "No, silly. I mean about ... two things, y'know."

He shook his head. "Well, apparently I *don't* know."

"We didn't tell them about the jamming device," she said.

"Come to think of it, where is it?"

She said shyly, "I squirreled it."

As he tried to recall the last time he'd seen the device, his eyes rested on her, simply because there was—indeed, *could be*—nothing more pleasing to look at.

"*What?*" she said, as though he'd been eyeing her accusatively.

"You squirreled it away?" said David.

She nodded.

"Where?" he asked. "There wasn't a free moment between our being grabbed up by the SAS men and your getting tossed into the admiral's limo."

"Correct," she said, plainly proud of having outsmarted him. "I squirreled it in Miriam's safe-deposit box."

Now he began to recall. "Oh, you mean all that business about her keeping the box even though there was nothing much left in there?" He recalled whatever he could about that moment. "As soon as she tossed her father's old passport and photos in the box, the officer put it back in the wall—which means you must have done it prior to that discussion."

"Correct," she said with a giggle.

"Well, are we going to play *Hot and Cold?* Or—wait a second. I saw you fidgeting with the cellophane tape. You must have taped it inside the safe-deposit box before that conversation even began."

"Yes, but *where* in the box?" she asked in playful challenge.

"Well," he said, "if I were as devious as you—and I'm *not*, of course—in fact I don't *know* anyone as devious as you—I would have taped it to the inside of the front panel that had the box number on the outside."

"Very good," she conceded. "Why there?"

"Because it was the place least likely to be seen by the officer when he put the box back on its gliders. Have I got it?"

"You certainly do," she said. "And for being such a good boy, you get a big kiss." She planted one on him and began getting amorous.

"Hold on, Ms. Bonnie Parker," he said, holding her at arm's length. "I suppose the device is reasonably safe there so long as no one dynamites his way in. But you said there were *two* things we didn't tell the authorities about. What was the other?"

"Doctor Zia," she said, as though it were obvious.

"*Doctor Zia?*" he asked incredulously. "We *must* have mentioned him. Didn't we? We *must* have," he said vainly trying to persuade himself. "I recounted the whole trip for them from the time we got off the boomer in Beira."

She shook her head. "You mentioned that Inanna invaded your dream, and that we escaped our hotel room and headed to Windhoek. But you never mentioned how we got there. No mention of Doctor Zia, nor Enkidu … nor a flying car."

"Well," he said, "you've been alone with the admiral several times after that. Didn't *you* mention Zia to him?"

"No," she said ingenuously. "I assumed you deliberately didn't mention Zia, so I didn't either."

"What about Miriam and Daniel?" asked David. "Did we mention Zia to *them?*"

Catharine shook her head. "Not a once."

"Now that you mention it," he said, "it *does* seem strange that I'd forget to mention crossing Africa in a flying car belonging to Noah of the Bible, although now that I think of it, my unconscious hesitation may have arisen out of the incredulity that the truth would have been met with. You know what's even stranger? No one ever *asked* how we got to Windhoek in a single day."

"I suppose they assumed we'd caught a flight."

He shrugged. "I suppose. You think it's possible Doctor Zia unconsciously discouraged us from mentioning him?"

She smiled. "You mean, he cast a spell on us? Perhaps with a dram from the River Lethe?"

"Ah, more Shakespeare!" he said. "My hat's off to the lovely lady. You win the prize. Now come here."

She put her hands on her hips. "When this Inanna tries to jump your bones, are you going to give in?"

"No," he said. "And I doubt she will, but if she does I've got my guard up. Something else you should understand about me: I was without female companionship for *three years*. In all that time, I never met a woman who could bring back the desire for life that a man needs in order to want a woman. I could do six months of celibacy standing on my head. You're the only one who's brought me back from the edge. Not only am I eternally grateful, but I *need* you. I love you. I don't want no other woman. So you better treat me right."

She wept again. "Well, I love you, too," she said, "as if you didn't know. And I'm counting on you to come back to me. Don't need no more Trevors."

"No Trevors," he assured her.

⸻ ⸎ ⸻

As INANNA HAD demanded, David stopped eating animal products.

Early in the morning of the day that would see Inanna land on the ancient platform at Baalbek, David showed up for a ritual bath at an establishment in northeastern Israel that had long been used for that purpose by local Jews. Although not every part of the ritual made sense to him, he dutifully followed every stricture and emerged with a feeling that could best be described as solemn.

After the bath, he donned his accustomed underclothes and covered them with the robes sent by Inanna. As he emerged into the sunlight, the robes, which had seemed pure white indoors, shimmered with many colors. He looked at his arid surroundings and couldn't help but wonder why so much importance had been placed on this land since humanity emerged from the apes.

Before him awaited a sleek black stretch limousine with two plain-clothes soldiers: one driving, and one behind him in the rear with two heavy-duty close-in firearms, namely, a Mini Uzi held on his lap and a sawed-off shotgun lodged between him and the car door.

David got into the passenger's rear seat and immediately noticed that the radio was off. The car sped off.

Although both soldiers were plainly tense, David attributed that to the persistent threat to any IDF member having the temerity to enter an Arab country.

For David's part, his tension arose out of knowing he was about to leave his home planet for several months, meeting people (and creatures) completely unfamiliar to him, all while trying to please his hostess without succumbing to her considerable wiles. Lost in woolgathering, David didn't notice that his seatmate was watching him until he caught him from the corner of his eye.

"You're the Kid from Canarsie?" the soldier asked with an Israeli accent. He reached into a pouch built into the door next to him and withdrew a newspaper that he displayed to David.

On the front page was a large photo of David humbly shaking hands with the King of England. The writing was in an alphabet entirely unknown to David.

David smirked. "That's me," he confirmed.

"Can you read the writing?" asked the soldier.

David shook his head. "No. It's some form of Arabic, isn't it?"

"Not exactly," said the soldier. "It's Farsi. Persian Farsi. It's published in Teheran. You know what it says?"

David shook his head. "No, what?"

"It says it's a disgrace that the Great Satan—that's the USA—is sending an emissary to meet with pagan gods, which is abomination. And it's made worse because these gods 'destroyed' the Al-Aqsa Mosque."

David nodded. "Does it blame the USA for moving the mosque?"

The soldier smiled broadly, revealing a broad space between his front teeth. "Of course," he said.

"Don't tell me," said David. "And it's even worse that America's emissary is a Jew, right?"

"Yes," said the soldier. "Let me translate this part for you. 'This proves that the Jewish religion is a kind of … idol worship, as Muslim scholars have been saying for many years.'"

"Naturally," says David. "*I* worship idols, don't *you?*"

The soldier smirked and held up his index finger. "But that is not the worst."

"What's the worst?"

"I'll translate," said the soldier, searching through the strange writing. "'As is well known, the Jews wish themselves to be gods, which is why they chase after immortality. We have learned that the pagan gods know the secret of living forever, and have agreed to share the secret with the Jews, but only if they agree to destroy all the Muslims.' That's really *something,* no?"

David nodded. "We are truly despicable. Does it say which people are worthy of living forever?"

"Of course," said the soldier, "the Muslim people."

David nodded thoughtfully. "Does it say whether the Yankees won yesterday?"

"Who?" asked the soldier. "Oh, the New York Yankees baseball? No."

"Give me that," said David.

The soldier handed him the newspaper. David opened his window and tossed the paper from the moving car out into the desert.

The soldier was surprised. "Why you did that?"

"Because the only reason for a newspaper to be published is to tell its readers the baseball scores. Any newspaper without baseball scores is unworthy of immortality."

The soldiers laughed. When the laughter died down, the driver said, "They're not bad people, the Muslims, you know?"

David nodded gravely. "I know. I would not be alive today if it weren't for a Muslim who exposed himself to hostile fire for my sake. He died saving me. His name was Ibrahim. God rest his soul."

"Amen," said the soldiers solemnly.

⟶oᑕ◯ᗌo⟵

AS DAVID'S LIMO drove on toward Baalbek, it became obvious that the site was surrounded by checkpoints at five-mile intervals. Each time they were stopped, the local guards would ask them to pop open the trunk, get out of the limo, and submit their weapons for inspection.

At every checkpoint, like clockwork, the guards would notice David's unusual garb, and one of them would announce to the others a guttural throat-clearing version of *Kid from Canarsie*, which usually sounded something like *Chid Charnassi* (which, to David's ear, suggested he was a goat from Parnassus). Each guard acted as though this was a moment he would share with his grandchildren someday. On a couple of occasions, the guards came over and shook David's hand, insisting that he and his escort pose for a *zelfi*, to which he kindly acceded.

But, at the last five-mile checkpoint, the atmosphere was thick. Fifty yards behind the guard station were two full-height flagpoles from which flew only two flags: those of the United States and the United Nations. The guards were far more serious than they had been at more distant checkpoints, and they were clearly not local policemen. In fact, none of them appeared to be Lebanese.

When the limo pulled up to the checkpoint, David and the soldiers were rousted from the car. When one of the guards spotted the Uzi and the shotgun, there was a fiery commotion that David feared might erupt into a gunfight.

While David's escort was being questioned in almost accusatory fashion, David was firmly ushered toward an open-air tent where serious-looking intelligence agents sat on folding chairs in the shade. As he neared the tent, he overheard his escort shouting, "What difference does it make if we have weapons? They won't work here anyway! You expect us to guard him with our fists?" The voices quickly faded as David stepped over to the seated intelligence officer who, David could now see, was overweight and chewing a big fat cigar.

The officer rose as David approached.

"Well, well, don't tell me," said the officer in an East Texas drawl. "You the Kid from Canarsie?"

David was getting a bit tired of that epithet by now, and he didn't like the officer's attitude. "I'm Professor David Schubert of New York."

"'Zat right?" said the officer, and picked up an English-language newspaper from atop a cooler by his chair. He held up the photo next to David's face, comparing the two. "Says here, you're from Canarsie."

"That's where I grew up, sir," said David impatiently.

The officer looked at him askance. "'Zere somethin' 'bout me you don't like, son?"

"No, sir," said David. "You're like a little bit of home away from home."

"Oh, yeah?" said the officer. "Howzat?"

"Well, sir," said David, "ya can't get this kind o' petty abuse just *anywhere*, can ya?"

The officer stuck the stogie back in his mouth and stuck his face inches from David's. "You think this is some kind of joke, son?"

David shook his head and once again began listening to smartass remarks spoken by his own voice, which only barely resembled his own. It seemed to him that he wasn't forming the words himself, but rather hearing them as a bystander. "You might want to take a couple of steps back, sir. I'm property of the U.S. Department of State, and I'm scheduled to leave this planet in a spaceship tonight. My arrival is awaited by an admiral, a Navy lieutenant commander, the President of the United States, and a goddess. Why are you detaining me? Just because you *can*?"

The officer, apparently realizing that he was throwing his weight around needlessly, took a step back and let go a chesty laugh. "*Touché*, son. Those two guys you showed up with. They're *IDF*?"

"Yes," said David.

"Well, they can't bring their guns in, but I'll let 'em have their Bowie knives. Hell, they fight just as well with those, anyway. But I've got a favor to ask you, and you can't say no."

"Sir?"

"There's gonna be a crowd of more than fifty thousand people at Baalbek, but only sixty people on the main platform and I'm giving you a pass that'll get you up there." He tapped David's chest with his index finger. "Just you. Nobody else. If those meatheads try to follow you up there, you send 'em packin'. Deal?"

"Deal."

"Okay, then." The officer removed a multicolored plastic badge from a sheet of them, signed it, and scanned the bar code. "Here ya go then," he said, handing it to David. "You represent us well up there, ya hear?"

"I hope and intend to, sir. You take care now."

CHAPTER 22

IT TOOK AN unexpectedly long time for David's limo to get through the crowds. By the time he left his escort and climbed up to the main platform, less than an hour remained before Inanna's landing.

The sun lay across the horizon, and the clear azure sky was softening to a dark blue. As all air traffic had been barred for a radius of three hundred miles around Baalbek, it was quiet, but for the murmur of the celebratory crowd and an occasional gust of the evening breeze.

As David approached the small American reviewing stand, four Secret Service agents emerged from the wings and came straight up to him.

"Can I help you, sir?" asked the senior agent.

"I'm a diplomat invited by Admiral Simmons and expected by the President."

One of the junior agents read David's identification badge and turned to the others. "Whoa! This is Professor Schubert."

The senior agent, who'd been busy fidgeting with his earpiece, turned and said, "Who?"

"The Kid from Canarsie, sir. That's why he's dressed this way. He's goin' up tonight."

"Oh!" said the senior agent. He turned to David. "Sorry I didn't recognize you, sir, but security's very tight up here on the big platform."

"I understand, agent," replied David.

The senior agent glanced back at the President and eyed David with concern. "Mind if we frisk you?"

"Not at all," said David.

The junior agent frisked him and said, "He's clean, sir."

"Sorry for the delay, professor," said the senior agent. "Please go right ahead and take the seat next to the lieutenant commander. You're a lucky fellow. Every guy who's come up those stairs has asked to sit next to her."

David smirked. "Well, they can all go to hell, 'cause she's taken. I've never met the President before. You think it would be okay for me to introduce myself to him first?"

The agent shrugged. "I think protocol requires it."

David went over and waited by the admiral, who was talking to the President.

"Mister President," said the admiral, spying David, "allow me to introduce Professor Schubert."

The President shook David's hand. "Professor," he said, "I don't have to tell you how *concerned* about you we all were while Inanna's people were tracking you down or how *proud* we were when you faced down her general at Westminster."

David beamed. "Thank you, Mister President, but for me it was just a matter of self-preservation. Whatever we managed to learn about the limitations of their disarming ray was serendipitous."

"How did you know they couldn't block *our* weapons when they fired their own?" asked the President.

David felt a sudden confusion on the question. "I don't know, sir."

"Well done, in any event," said the President. "Go ahead and take the seat next to the lieutenant commander. You've earned it."

David shook Catharine's hand before taking the seat next to her.

She smiled at him. "A handshake seems a little superfluous at this point, doesn't it?"

He winked in return. "I'll deal with whatever formalities I need to in order to sit next to the prettiest girl in the joint."

Now that David had taken his seat, at last he had a moment to observe the elaborate preparations made for Inanna's brief visit. At one end of the platform, a vast stage had been erected. Before the stage stood a single lectern with a microphone.

Although no lights had yet been turned on, the platform was surrounded by more lighting than would be seen at a major rock concert, and the stereo sound system culminated in two multistory towers of loudspeakers flanking the stage. High-definition television and motion picture cameras were everywhere, and there were four jumbotrons, one aimed in each cardinal direction.

Whatever Inanna had in mind for this event, it was going to be first class, which made sense in light of the expected television audience of four billion people. It was, after all, the first officially acknowledged landing of an alien on Planet Earth.

The last of the sun disappeared behind the western horizon and the first flyover took place high up in the sky. At the edge of visibility, five glowing craft, each emitting its own unique bright color, spun in a circle. As one, they silently moved west to east and disappeared over the horizon in no more than three seconds. The flying was impressive, but the ships disappeared so fast it seemed anticlimactic. A brief chorus of *oohs* and *aahs* arose from the crowd around the main platform followed by a smattering of applause.

In a split second, the same circling craft appeared at half the altitude, and stopped momentarily before moving in the opposite direction and disappearing from view just as quickly.

It took David a moment to realize what was so awe-inspiring about this display, beyond the crafts' unimaginable speed: Even in formation, the craft were absolutely silent. For a crowd accustomed to the sonic boom emitted by aircraft moving through the atmosphere at supersonic speed, the absence of any sound at all was stunning—and a little frightening.

A few seconds later, the same formation appeared a third time, but this time as if out of nowhere, and remained motionless directly above the platform at an altitude no greater than three hundred feet. Their shape was now obvious. They were flying saucers closely resembling the fictional ones seen in every science fiction movie ever made. The craft hung so low and motionless over the platform that David could make out each individual light source, as well as the surface texture of each spacecraft.

That the platform could be overtaken so stealthily was more than a little unnerving. The crowd was no longer delighted, but rather awestruck.

Not only were the craft motionless and silent; neither their stationary positioning nor their movement created so much as a breeze around the platform. Neither their mass nor their motion seemed to disturb—or even displace—the air around them.

It took only a few seconds for the crowd's level of discomfort to approach panic. But, just as pandemonium was about to break out, the jumbotrons and the sound system sprang magically to life.

On the jumbotrons, twenty dancers appeared—men and women in roughly equal numbers arrayed in scant clothing of an ancient Egyptian style—and began dancing athletically to the rhythmic music pouring out of the speakers. Everything had a Middle Eastern flavor, and the music seemed a combination of Arabic and Indian. However exotic, the production was so slick that it delighted the crowd.

The belly of the saucer suspended directly over the stage opened up, and a self-lit flat landing craft began a slow, controlled descent to the stage. Atop the landing craft, slowly coming into the crowd's view were the very dancers whose images flashed simultaneously across the jumbotrons.

It wasn't until the platform had come nearly to rest on the stage that the main platform's lighting system came on, and the physical size of the dancers became evident. To David, they appeared *on average* to be well over six feet tall. A few were shorter; more were taller.

The polished voice of a very American announcer rose above the tumult.

"Ladies and Gentlemen," it said, "welcome to the return of Queen Inanna of Nibiru, who once ruled this spot and as far as the eye can see."

All at once, the dancers struck stationary poses, and the elaborate music was replaced by the drone of a single deep note denoting tension.

"Nearly a half million years ago," said the announcer dramatically, "people from Planet Nibiru came to Earth. Descendants of King Anu of Nibiru, they called themselves *Anunnaki*.

"Here on Earth, they found abundant natural resources, as well as a highly intelligent creature who stood upright but lacked the gifts of articulate speech and the capacity for higher-level thought. An Anunnaki genetic engineer gave the creature these gifts by combining his genetic material with their own. Let's give a big round of applause for the resulting creature, the most successful creature on this planet: *YOU!*"

David noticed the glaring omission of Enki's name and that of his half-sister Ninharsag, who'd actually accomplished the arduous feat of genetic engineering. But when he gazed down on members of the crowd, he found they were *eating it up*, many not only cheering (for themselves) but jumping into the air and parading around in conga lines.

The announcer resumed. "The Anunnaki taught this newly transformed creature the spoken and written word, mathematics and astronomy, measurement and construction, farming and animal husbandry."

More cheers from below. The drone became ominously louder and deeper.

"Then one day, the Anunnaki learned that all life on Earth would be extinguished by a Great Flood. To ensure that their beloved humanity would not be wiped out, the Anunnaki taught one man how to build an Ark that would save himself and his family. While the Floodwaters raged, the Anunnaki orbited the Earth in their spacecraft, unable to stop the Flood but unwilling to abandon their finest creation.

"Among those Anunnaki was one goddess who deeply mourned the loss of her beloved human friends. For an entire year, she took her eyes off events on the Earth *only* when overcome by sleep. To her great relief, the Ark did its job and humanity was saved."

To increase the tension, the drone on the soundtrack was joined by the low thrum of tympanies.

"Let's give a big hand to that goddess who so loved her human friends that she vowed never to allow them to perish."

There was a crescendo of tympanies as a silent pyramidion descended from the night sky and landed majestically on the upper platform about thirty yards from the American reviewing stand.

Catharine leaned over to David and said, "Can you believe how *cheesy* this whole thing is?"

David would have burst into laughter, but reminded himself that he would be leaving on that very pyramidion in a few minutes.

"Ladies and Gentlemen," came the announcer's artificially excited voice, "I give you the Queen of the Anunnaki, the lover of all mankind, known throughout the ages in every corner of the globe as the goddess of love, under such familiar names as Ishtar, Aphrodite … and Venus.

"I give you … QUEEN INANNA!"

A hangar door rumbled open at the front of the pyramidion. Out of the doorway poured a blinding white light. Barely visible at its center was the silhouette of what appeared to be one person. As the light receded, the figure of an extraordinarily tall, shapely woman began to coalesce.

Catharine threw up her hands in exasperation. "I don't get it. Okay, she's pretty. But *this?* What's she got … three tits?" Fortunately, the din on the platform was too loud for her voice to carry to the admiral or the President.

David turned to her with irritation. "Catharine, I'll have to put up with these tremendous egos for months at a time. Would you please *stop?*"

She turned away in dismay.

Now the front-lighting was cranked up, illuminating Inanna so brightly that at first the crowd shielded its eyes. There she was in real life, the woman who'd been invading David's dreams for weeks on end, the archetype, the most beautiful woman in the solar system. And suddenly David realized that she was well over six feet tall. Larger than life, indeed.

She was dressed as a royal ancient Egyptian, her face made up in the style of the ancient bust of Nefertiti kept at the Neues Museum in Berlin. But, instead of Nefertiti's headdress, Inanna wore a gold-and-diamond tiara with her straight dark hair falling loose around her shoulders and down her back, woven with ribbons of what, to the naked eye, looked like pure gold. Her simple white dress clung perfectly to her impressive curves.

The crowd gasped, and applauded its heart out for several minutes. David shook his head in disbelief. They had *no idea* what this woman had done, or was capable of doing ... perhaps even *to them*. They just knew they loved her.

For now they had their very own goddess.

When the general tumult died down, David could hear masculine chants of *Ve-NUS ... Ve-NUS ... Ve-NUS*, and even a few cowboy whistles and catcalls.

But Inanna just soaked it all in like it was her reason for living. For a better look at her beatific smile, David glanced up at a jumbotron. Though, out of respect for Catharine, he tried to resist thinking about Inanna's beauty, he couldn't help but admit to himself that she probably was the most perfectly formed woman he (or possibly anyone else) had ever seen.

He forced such thoughts from his mind and stared down at his sandals, then forced himself to look over at Catharine, who was staring at him forlornly. He mouthed to her, "I love *you!*" But she was too dismayed to accept his assurance.

General Shulgi appeared out of nowhere and lent Inanna the crook of his arm to escort her to the microphone.

Inanna seemed immune from the usual insecurities of someone unaccustomed to using a microphone. She didn't make the usual mistakes, such as blowing on it, or snapping her fingers to see if it was turned on, or speaking nonsense syllables into it to see whether the volume level was appropriate. She seemed entirely comfortable with it, and equally confident in herself.

For the first time, David saw that there was a short ramp leading to the lectern, presumably so that a mere mortal could stand next to her without appearing much shorter than she.

She leaned into the mic. "Good evening," she said in a breathy Egyptian accent, and the place erupted. But, instead of allowing the crowd to indulge in another cheering session, she smiled and coyly waved her hands for quiet. "Come, come. We do not wish to waste anyone's time. We have many important dignitaries to greet and we ask that each august person whose name we mention stand and wave, so that we can show off our peaceful relationship to the whole Earth … and anyone else who may be watching."

Shulgi whispered in her ear. She nodded to him and spoke again.

"Before we proceed with that, however, please allow us to return a few people who have been in our care for some weeks, having stumbled upon something that we did not wish them to see. On the understanding that they will not tell what it was, we now release them to their respective governments."

While other captives were escorted to representatives of their governments, General Shulgi personally escorted Shawn to the President, who greeted Shawn with a slap on the back. The President directed Shawn to David, who hugged him tearfully.

"Welcome back, dude!" said David. "Let me introduce you to my close friend Catharine."

A melancholy Catharine smiled politely and shook Shawn's hand. "Welcome back," she said absently.

"Thanks," Shawn replied. It wasn't hard to see what he was thinking.

"What'd you miss most?" joked David. "Home cookin'?"

"You got an extra blonde for me, Dave?" asked Shawn. "That used to be our deal."

"Just so happens I do," said David. "Her name is Miriam. Catharine will introduce you to her."

"Been so long, I'm not sure where I'd take her."

"I've got a suggestion for you there, too. Try the breakfast buffet at the Grosvenor Hotel in London. Just don't tell her I suggested it."

A State Department officer politely ushered Shawn from the upper platform.

"As we were saying," said Inanna over the PA, "we would like to introduce our esteemed dignitaries. First and foremost, we thank the President of the United States of America for coming here this evening. Mister President?"

The President rose and waved to the adoring crowd, another indication that the crowd was dominated by Americans.

Inanna then introduced her host, the President of Lebanon, as well as the President of France, and the Secretary-General of the United Nations.

"Finally," said Inanna, "we wish to introduce His Majesty King William of the United Kingdom of Great Britain and Northern Ireland." King William stood up and got a rousing welcome, proof that there were quite a few Brits here, as well. The opening lines of *God Save the King* rang out.

Inanna becalmed the crowd once again. "We regret that we cannot stay longer on this visit," she said, "but we have appointments elsewhere very shortly. So, please allow us to formally welcome aboard our humble pyramidion the newly appointed United States ambassador, Professor David Schubert. Ambassador Schubert, would you come up here? We have something to present to you."

Shulgi escorted David to the ramp that would elevate him to Inanna's height. David mounted the ramp and stood eye-to-eye with Inanna, whose face was now as close to his as it had been in his dreams. He bowed humbly, and the crowd cheered.

Inanna looked upon him fondly. "Ambassador Schubert, we would like to present you with this gift."

She presented David with an ancient mantle and he held it up for all to see. Just for a moment, the mantle thrummed as though it were alive and seemed to shift around of its own accord.

"This is the mantle," she said, "that belonged to the Hebrew prophet Elijah and then to his disciple Elisha." David was stunned to find himself holding what was not only a relic of the great prophets of the Bible, but one to which magical powers had been attributed, not unlike those of Moses' staff.

Inanna took advantage of David's discomposure to kiss him deeply on the mouth. Although he'd anticipated such a possibility, he'd deemed it improbable. If she were to try to kiss him, he'd planned to simply bow his way out of it. But she'd anticipated his reaction and thrown him off guard.

Her kiss was like nothing he'd ever felt before. It was as though his brain had been injected with opium. With all his willpower, he drew away from her and bowed low. But it was too late. The whole crowd had seen him overcome by the goddess's kiss, and cheered him good-naturedly.

Inanna looked remarkably self-satisfied. "Now, if the ambassador will follow us to our humble pyramidion, we must part." She raised her hand and waved to the crowd. "Thank you all for coming. May we have many years of peaceful relations together."

As Shulgi escorted Inanna to the pyramidion, David lagged behind and glanced over at the American reviewing stand. His heart sank as he realized Catharine was already gone. Scanning the whole platform, he caught sight of the back of her head as she walked down the steps from the platform and promptly disappeared from view.

And she didn't look back. Evidently, she'd seen enough. Every fiber of his being wanted to catch up with her and explain, but he'd been impressed into the service of Uncle Sam, and now his duty lay elsewhere.

Could it be that his whole adventure with Catharine would come to nought, and fade into memory? No, he resolved. That would not be allowed to happen.

He hurried into the pyramidion behind Inanna and Shulgi and, as the hangar door closed behind him, he was crushed by the prospect that he'd just lost any hope of happiness in this life.

And now he'd begun a new life he never wanted.

THE END

Thank you for reading *Goddess from the Lost Planet*. If you enjoyed the book, please consider leaving a review on your favorite retailer. Reviews greatly help authors both with reaching new readers and improving our stories. I would love to read your thoughts.

Here's a special preview of the next book in this thrilling trilogy, *Maker from the Lost Planet*.

MAKER FROM THE LOST PLANET
CHAPTER 1

THE PYRAMIDION OF THE QUEEN OF HEAVEN,
HER MAJESTY INANNA, BELOVED OF ANU

THE MOMENT DAVID was safely inside Inanna's pyramidion and the hatch slid shut behind him, he could feel the spacecraft rising gently from the ancient platform at Baalbek like a well-balanced elevator in a brand-new building.

There'd been no strapping in of passengers, no rumbling of rockets, no erupting off the pad. To the contrary, after the clamorous farewell David had received outside on the platform, this compartment seemed the hushed entryway to an ancient temple deeply embedded in solid rock. The cool, moist air had a barely detectable odor of lime, and the lighting was comfortably low.

The walls were nothing like he'd expected. Though straight as wallboard, their surface was far from smooth, closely resembling the rough mineral finish on the handheld transmitter discovered in the luggage lent him by Doctor Zia, survivor of the Great Flood.

David wasn't surprised that Inanna and General Shulgi had disappeared around a corner the moment he set foot inside the spacecraft, but he *was* surprised that the small crowd entering behind him had dispersed just as quickly. He'd expected that some subordinate would be assigned to him, at least to get him to his quarters. Without such guidance, not only had he no idea where to go, but he was still holding in his hands the few things he'd brought aboard. In one hand he held a laptop and the portfolio containing his commission and, in the other, Elijah's mantle, which seemed to have become dormant since its self-willed bout of wriggling.

Somewhere nearby, General Shulgi shouted, "Well, then, who the devil fired it?"

In a moment, the general rounded the corner with a subordinate in tow, a Middle-Eastern-looking young man in a military skirt called a *shendyt*; he was a few inches taller than David—rather short for an Anunnaki.

The sight of David standing alone, still holding his things, stopped Shulgi in his tracks and appeared to drive from his mind whatever he'd been shouting about. "What are you doing here?" he asked David.

David shrugged. "Where should I be?"

"Do you mean to say *nobody's* shown you to your quarters?"

"Correct, general."

"I regret the lapse," said Shulgi, turning to his subordinate. "Must I do everything around here? What do you people do after I return to my own ship? *Nothing?*" Shulgi pointed to David. "The ambassador should have been installed in his quarters immediately."

David changed the subject. "General, I apologize for meddling in matters beyond my concern, but did I overhear you saying that a shot has been fired?"

Shulgi snorted. "Yes," he replied. "Someone on your planet has fired a missile at this spacecraft. We're maintaining safe distance for now. Do you have any idea who would fire on us?"

"No, sir," said David. "Indeed, there are few nations on Earth with missiles capable of reaching space. *Which* such nation would be foolhardy enough to fire on an Anunnaki craft without provocation is beyond me—indeed, it's almost beyond comprehension. Would you care to enlist the assistance of the United States in this matter?"

Shulgi's eyebrow rose in bemusement. "Would the United States be willing to provide assistance?"

"Absolutely, general," said David. "It's my country's intention to reach a peaceful accommodation with the Anunnaki."

Shulgi nodded skeptically. "Whether that's possible remains to be seen," he muttered, "but I shall bear it in mind." He turned to his subordinate. "Kassam, take the ambassador's things to his quarters."

David handed Kassam the laptop, portfolio, and mantle.

"Ambassador," said Shulgi, "if you will please accompany me to the conn."

David was stunned.

Shulgi noticed his befuddlement. "What's wrong?"

David shrugged. "I'm humbled by your trust in inviting me onto the bridge."

Shulgi smirked. "Who knows? Perhaps you can help identify the aggressor nation."

David bowed courteously. "I'll do my best, general."

"But I have one request."

David braced himself. "What's that?"

"Please don't repeat your threat to splatter my brains all over the pavement."

David gritted his teeth, abashed at the coarseness of his own recent outburst. "Very well," he said, "if the general promises not to call me *mayfly*."

The general nodded.

"You do realize," said David, "that I would never have said that if you hadn't tracked me to the ends of the Earth … and cornered me?"

"It wasn't *I* who did that," came the cryptic reply. The general turned on his heel and escorted David to the elevator. To David's surprise, the elevator greeted each of them by name and sought a reply before moving.

⊷ ∘ ⟆⟆⟆ ∘ ⊷

WHEN GENERAL SHULGI and David stepped off the elevator onto the dimly lit bridge, five or six other officers were already seated there on well-upholstered chairs designed to protect their occupants from considerable shock.

Moving images were everywhere, though none seemed to be projected onto a screen; in fact, there appeared to be no projectors and no screens at all. Images seemed rather to appear out of thin air—*in* thin air. In front of each officer was an image evidently dedicated to his or her function, small and mostly monochromatic; at the base of each such image was a constantly refreshing spreadsheet, above which appeared a curve or a polygon whose contours changed as it was replotted every few milliseconds to reflect new data pouring in.

There were several images at the front of the bridge, which were brighter, comparatively large, and colorful, evidently there to be seen by all.

Front and center was a large hologram of an oncoming missile. Although it appeared to be moving at a constant rate of speed, David couldn't be sure whether that reflected the actual state of affairs or, alternatively, the tracking mechanism had been programmed to keep the image steady.

"Is that the offending missile?" asked David quietly.

Shulgi nodded. "Can you tell me whose it is?"

David studied the image. Though at this distance it was difficult to be sure, there appeared to be some identifying marks on the nose cone. "What's its range?" he asked.

Shulgi consulted a monochromatic chart that suddenly floated before him. "About a thousand kilometers."

"Is it moving at a constant velocity?"

Shulgi consulted his floating chart once again. "Direction and speed are constant. It's moving at about twice the speed of our ship. It's difficult to see how it could accelerate much, as it was likely launched from the surface of the Earth and, given earthlings' limited technology, must have used nearly all of its fuel in escaping Earth's gravitational pull."

David wondered how much information he should be sharing with Shulgi. "True—unless it's a *multistage* missile. Is an orbital camera sending us this video?"

Shulgi nodded.

"Can you move it in for a closer look at the nosecone?" asked David. The irony did not escape him that mere weeks earlier he was asked by a U.S. submarine captain to identify certain spacecraft, one of which he now inhabited.

Shulgi spoke his order aloud, evidently to no one in particular. "Nosecone. Maximum magnification."

A hologram of the nosecone, which bore three repeats of an emblem that seemed familiar to David, filled the front of the bridge. David pointed at it. "If this is what it looks like, the repeated insignia represents the five tenets of the religion of Islam," said David. "The center vertical line represents a sword."

"Where do you know it from?" asked Shulgi.

"It resembles the emblem on the flag of Iran," said David, "but I hasten to add that it's not identical to the Iranian emblem." He looked at Shulgi thoughtfully. "We should bear in mind that this *could* be a false-flag provocation. Do we know where the missile was launched from?"

"None of our craft caught sight of the launch," said Shulgi, "but it's unlikely it was launched from the eastern hemisphere."

"Because of your disabling ray?"

Shulgi smiled. "Yes … which you managed to disable, however briefly."

David shook his head. "That was weeks ago. I doubt that such occasion had anything to do with the launch of this missile," said David. "Presumably, it was launched much more recently."

"Correct," said Shulgi, indicating the image on the screen. "This missile was launched within the past few hours. We learned of it while we were on the landing platform. That's one of the reasons we cut the ceremony short. Incidentally, what do you mean by a *multistage* missile?"

David was surprised by the question. "I take it the Anunnaki have not used such missiles for a long time. As you recognize, Earth's missiles are still powered by fossil fuels. Each stage of a multistage missile contains its own fuel. The first stage, known as the *booster*, feeds the big rockets at the bottom end of the missile. Its fuel is consumed in achieving and maintaining escape velocity. Once its fuel has been exhausted, in order to minimize subsequent fuel use and maximize the acceleration of later stages, the booster is jettisoned, decreasing the mass of the remaining vehicle. That's why I suggested that a multistage missile *can* accelerate once in orbit or in space."

"Is the one chasing us a multistage missile?" asked Shulgi with concern.

David shrugged. "I expect so, although you can see that the booster's still attached." He turned to Shulgi with concern. "The missile may be holding onto the booster to lull us into feeling safe. If that's their plan, they would jettison the booster only at the point when, realizing our peril, we would nonetheless be unable to escape impact." Assaying the possible intentions of those who launched the missile, he suddenly became alarmed. "Is Queen Inanna still aboard?" he asked.

Shulgi nodded anxiously.

David was exasperated. "Then why haven't you shot down the missile?"

"This pyramidion doesn't carry weapons of aggression," said Shulgi, clearly chagrined.

"Well," said David impatiently, "this would rather be a *defensive* use of weapons, don't you think?"

"Perhaps. But we're not *certain* of its intention."

David was mystified by the Anunnaki. Though he'd benefitted by their self-restraint, their code of ethics nonetheless escaped his grasp.

"Have you tried to establish communications with the missile?" he asked.

"Yes, but no one answers. We think it's unmanned."

"Well, if it's hostile, as we must presume it to be," said David, "how long till it's too close for us to escape impact?"

Shulgi thought for a moment. "I suppose it depends upon how quickly it accelerates once it jettisons the booster."

"General," said David excitedly, "you can't *wait* for it to drop its booster. If it's hostile, that may be too late for you to escape."

One of the seated officers spoke aloud. "General," he said, "we are receiving a request from the Dagon craft to establish communications."

"*Aaach.* The frog people," muttered Shulgi, rolling his eyes.

"General," said David, abashed, "if you're going to establish a video link with the Dagon, I don't think I should be seen on your bridge. I'm a *diplomatic* officer, after all."

"It will not be a problem, ambassador," said Shulgi quietly. "If a question arises, I'll make it clear that you're here solely to observe." Raising his voice, he said, "Permission granted to send and receive audiovisual with the Dagon. Put them on the front holograph."

A large hologram of a hideous green figure with a long face appeared before them. David wondered whether this was Brosa, the Dagon who'd helped him disable the Anunnaki's ray.

"General Shulgi," said the Dagon, "I am Captain Brack. It is good to see you again. *Glick.*"

Shulgi sighed loudly. "Brack, please make this short. We're being dogged by a missile."

Brack nodded. "We wished to let you know where the missile was launched from, General Shulgi, in case it helps you."

"Thank you, Brack. Was it launched from the vicinity of Baalbek?"

"No," said Brack. "It emerged from the Beaufort Sea in northern Canada at the moment your pyramidion first touched down on the platform."

"Thank you, Brack," said the general. "We'll get back to you." The green figure nodded politely. "End transmission."

The Dagon's image vanished, and was replaced by that of the incoming missile just as it violently jettisoned its booster, and the second-stage fuel ignited. In a moment, the second stage had blasted clear of the satellite's view.

"It's coming on fast," said David.

Shulgi hit a virtual button, sounding a loud shipwide alarm.

Can't wait to see what happens next? Get your copy of *Maker from the Lost Planet* here.

https://books2read.com/u/mvyr9e

ABOUT THE AUTHOR

Neal Roberts and his wife live happily on Long Island, New York. They have two grown children and a handful of grandchildren. Neal is a practicing attorney and adjunct law professor, and spends as much time as possible researching his next novel while enhancing his lawyer's pallor. When he's not writing contemporary sci-fi novels or practicing law, he can generally be found teaching in the field of intellectual property law. Connect with Neal at his website (authornealroberts.com) or on Facebook (Facebook.com/authornealroberts) and join his mailing list (bitly.com/FreeHistorical) to know when upcoming books release and to grab your free short.

ALSO BY NEAL ROBERTS

In the Den of the English Lion

A Second Daniel, In the Den of the English Lion, Book 1 (Historical Mystery): London 1558. An orphan from a far-off land is renamed "Noah Ames," and given every advantage the English Crown can bestow.

London 1592. Now an experienced barrister, Noah witnesses what appears to be a botched robbery outside the Rose Theater, a crime he soon suspects to be part of a plot against Queen Elizabeth herself. Steadfast in his loyalty to the Queen, Noah must use every bit of his knowledge and skill to lure her most disloyal subject onto the only battlefield where Noah has the advantage … a court of law – though in doing so he risks public exposure of his darkest secret, a secret so shocking that its revelation could cost him everything: the love of the only woman who can offer him happiness, his livelihood … even his life.

The Impress of Heaven, In the Den of the English Lion, Book 2 (Historical Mystery): LONDON 1600. When the Earl of Essex is removed from command and placed under arrest for reaching a forbidden truce with the Irish rebels, Serjeant Noah Ames reluctantly accepts a commission to investigate the earl's fitness for command, and the two are pitted against each other once again. Meanwhile, Noah's beautiful daughter, Lady Jessica, has sought to remarry into the nobility, but events have thus far frustrated her plans. One day, Noah attends a briefing where the Queen's new commander displays maps of English military positions in Ireland. Noah's suspicions are aroused when he sees that one map is missing a watermark appearing on all the others. When he informs his young barrister friend Jonathan of his concern, he inadvertently sets in motion events that throw Jonathan and Lady Jessica together on a journey across England into ever greater peril.

A Dragon in the Ashes, In the Den of the English Lion, Book 3 (Historical Mystery): LONDON 1600. When an attempt is made on Queen

Elizabeth's life, Serjeant Noah Ames races to her rescue, then sets out to identify the culprit among a band of foreigners who've newly arrived from the Continent to join with the seditious Lord Essex. In the course of his investigation, Noah uncloaks an unmitigated reign of evil that has resulted in the murders of kings, queens, and religious minorities ... and which now threatens Noah's life for reasons no one would ever suspect. Will Noah pay the ultimate price for forgetting that the past is never past?

All the Men as Mad as He, In the Den of the English Lion, Book 4 (Historical Mystery): LONDON 1600. Though Queen Elizabeth has ordered the Earl of Essex's release from confinement, she's thwarted his return to social and military grace by barring him from court for an indefinite term. Unsatisfied with this humiliation, the Queen considers whether to cut off his sole remaining income, as well. Noah Ames strongly advises against it on grounds that the Queen will thereby lose any remaining influence over Essex's conduct and also place him in desperate financial straits. When several seemingly unrelated men are found murdered, Noah begins to suspect that such murders reveal Essex's treasonous intention to return to court in bloody defiance of the Queen's order.

Shakespeare's Treason, In the Den of the English Lion, Book 5 (Historical Mystery): LONDON 1600. The Earls of Essex and South-ampton, imprisoned in the Tower of London pending their trial for high treason, incriminate Noah Ames's dear friend Sir Henry Neville. When the one man whose testimony can save Sir Henry suddenly vanishes, Noah must solve the mystery of his abduction and bring him back in time to save Sir Henry from a traitor's death.

From Heaven to Earth They Came

Goddess from the Lost Planet, From Heaven to Earth They Came, Book 1

Maker from the Lost Planet, From Heaven to Earth They Came, Book 2

Destroyer from the Lost Planet, From Heaven to Earth They Came, Book 3